The Chinese Silk

*To Peggy,
Still my favorite,
illustrator!*

Fran Marian

FRAN MARIAN

RED HILLS PRESS
TUCSON, ARIZONA

The Chinese Silk

Published by Red Hills Press
Tucson, AZ 85748

Cover Illustration by Terry Medaris

http://www.FranMarian.com

ISBN: 0-9787848-1-2

Printed in the United States of America

First Edition October 2008

To John, my life partner, who listened, and listened, and listened, and listened, until his eyes glazed over.

Acknowledgments

My high school yearbook says I hoped to be an interior designer. That never happened. Instead I've ridden—I'm still riding—a magic carpet of eclectic experiences into senior citizenship. Some day I'll crash, but not before I let the world know that a foundation of precious family supports me and a group of generous friends uplifts me. They know who they are, but I want to tell you about some of them.

Janet Bezdikian not only let me use her name but also shared stories about her Lebanese family. I've twisted and teased what I learned, however, with liberal imagination. Janet's knowledge of languages is sprinkled throughout my books. My writer-friend Carlene Jones is the gatekeeper of my literary wanderings as well as the computer genius who formatted both of my books. It was a lucky day when phenomenal artist Terry Medaris offered to design The Chinese Silk cover. I'm grateful, too, to Meg Files, creative writing talent at Tucson's Pima Community College. She inspires while delivering a kick in the butt with perfection. I've been blessed by their talents and kindness.

Finally, a word of thanks to book clubs for encouragement, feedback, and fun—you're the best.

1

The Black Sea Coast, Asia Minor
1074 AD

Before his sister-in-law handed him the quivering brown bundle that was his daughter, Çatal had forgotten how love felt. His wife's warm amber eyes turned feral yellow waiting months, then years, for a child. And when his best friend accused him of willfully withholding his manhood—a rumor his wife spread—Çatal sought the companionship of his quiet, obedient camel, Sütlü—her name because she was the color of tea with milk. He watched her feed, brushed her creamy fur, and fashioned the kilim bags that would hang from her dual humps when they traveled together. His camel would be ready at the first indication supplies were needed. More than a way to show his value, the travels were an escape from his wife's thorny tongue.

But now his miracle child, trembling with her effort to cry, lay curled in one large, calloused palm while, with the other hand, he dipped the edge of a soft cloth in a bowl of warmed spring water to wipe away the birth blood from his daughter's body. The pink glow of her dark skin and the intensity of her expression filled him with unfamiliar emotion, feelings long encased in armor forged by hurt. He wrapped her in a clean swatch of wool and held her against his barrel chest, swelling with the promise that he would fill her world with love, even give his life to shelter her from harm. When his sister-in-law took her to suckle at his wife's breast, he was surprised to sense a loss beyond emptiness. They named her Rachel.

From the beginning, something in her expression, something in the way she moved, set her apart. She was restless and sometimes cried until neighbors held their heads and gave wide berth to Çatal's hut. At times her legs and arms pounded against her pallet. His wife became hysterical when the settlement's oldest woman said she'd seen an evil eye hovering at their door. "The child fights because she feels its presence," the old crone said to anyone who'd listen.

Çatal's reaction was to raise his arms to the heavens and ask for God's help. "That old woman hasn't made sense for years. Why do you listen to her?" Although he didn't share it with his wife, Çatal believed his child was crying out for knowledge in the only way she could.

Catal began to see himself as a teacher, not for his daughter alone, but for all the children in his village. Isolated as they were by the fog-shrouded Black Sea and the towering mountains, how could they know about the strange and wonderful people beyond their borders, the fragrance and exquisite flavors of their spices, or the dazzling colors of their clothing?

When he spoke of these things, his relatives laughed at him. Such knowledge didn't feed their families. How would they manage if their children left to see the world around them? Çatal bowed under their criticism until a child asked a question. Then like one raindrop after another, his words would begin to flow until a waterfall of information and imagination gushed forth and children filled the ground at his feet.

It seemed to Çatal that Rachel discovered her legs faster than a lamb shifted from mother's milk to grass. Suddenly, she appeared among the others, eager for his stories. She would slip between the larger children to find a spot at his feet where she stared at his lips and searched his face. Çatal hoarded these images in his heart like precious coins he could spend at will.

"An evil spirit lives in your mouth, Çatal. Everyone sees it," his wife said. She planted her booted feet and rocked side to side like a snake about to strike. "I can't keep her in my sight with all I must do to keep this miserable hole of a house. You're destroying her. She has no friends. They keep their distance. Can't you see?"

Çatal dropped his head, not just to dodge her spit, but to avoid looking at the angry red blotches breaking on her cheeks. He did not see what she saw. Rachel had intuition beyond her years. She had found her own path to harmony. She shadowed her mother, helping as she was able, and she ingratiated herself with the other women. Time and time again, Çatal saw her avoid the village troublemakers—usually the cocky boys. If their words troubled her, he noticed how her hands dropped to her sides and her fingers pulled at her skirt.

"Baba, do the mountains keep the monsters from our village?" she said on one such occasion. She tucked her long handspun skirt under her thighs and sat on her hands.

"Monsters? Bah! I've been over the mountains with Sütlü. No monsters there, my dear one. Better you should stay away from the monsters who told you such lies," Çatal said.

She nodded, clenched her jaw and pursed her red lips.

Yet he knew the day would come when she would seek her own way and leave his heart beating in a hollow space. That day arrived sooner than he hoped. A family in an adjacent village had been quietly observing Rachel each time she accompanied her mother to buy vegetables. As custom dictated, the father spoke to Çatal about his son. "Seventeen, ready and able to begin his own family," the man said.

This came as no surprise. Çatal understood the necessity and agreed, reluctantly. But when Çatal met the boy, his imperfections seemed endless: Soft hands. Did the boy work? Muddy boots. Did he have no care for his appearance? Ill-fitting clothes. Was he hiding a weak body? But Rachel liked him from their first meeting and, at fifteen, they became betrothed. Soon after the announcement, Çatal told his wife he would go to the bazaar in Erzurum to complete Rachel's dowry.

Men who live at the mercy of nature know when there is something new in the air, and on the morning of his departure Çatal knew spring had arrived. He woke in the dark, lifted the fleece that covered his bed and tucked it against his wife's back. Standing, he pulled on his wool tunic and sheep-hide trousers, fastening them around his waist with a wide length of woven cloth. He bent to finger the dried grass mat that covered the dirt floor, found his cap and pulled it down over his ears. Outside, a bitter wind whistled through the wooden slats of Sütlü's three-sided pen. The bells hanging from her proud neck tinkled as he led her out into the open and rested his head against her neck, felt her pulse throb against his cheek, and as he always did, thanked God for his patient, precious Sütlü.

Fragrant eucalyptus trees and cone-shaped evergreens formed a canopy over his head, dwarfing everything Çatal and his extended family had created for subsistence. Wood and manure blocks were stacked high for heat and cooking. Nine stone buildings formed a circle around a sheep corral of shaggy tree branches. And, off to the side was the latest village project: a two-story building of wood and stone. Sweet smelling hay for the animals was stored in the lower level, while the women occupied the upper level for weaving and gossiping, and no male past puberty dared ascend the narrow stone staircase without permission.

Çatal watched as the sun's rays lit the topmost tree branches and crept downward, slowly bringing shape to his small stone hut. He filled his lungs with the piney air and set to his task. He loaded kilim—the rugs he would use for trade—one by one into bags and eased them onto the natural curves of Sütlü's back. Finally he checked the remaining sacks that held his food and water.

Sütlü turned to look at him with languid eyes the color of wet sand. She groaned as Çatal swung his short bandy leg over her back and coaxed her to her feet. He knew the groan was not annoyance, but exertion. His camel was sweet natured, just one reason why she outranked his wife in his affections. For a time Çatal hoped the advent of a daughter would bring back the woman he'd married, but it hadn't.

He turned Sütlü's head away from the hut and forced his thoughts onto the road ahead to trace the route to Erzurum in his mind. There in the bazaar he would find an item for Rachel's dowry or something special for her alone. It would show itself to him, perhaps a string of glass beads the color of her eyes, the bright green of sprouting grasses along the stream.

Suddenly the wind offered a final nudge and he gathered up the rope that dangled from his camel's harness. As he turned toward the road, he glanced back through the hut's window where just beyond he knew his wife was sleeping. The journey ahead might be a respite from the daily drudgery and his wife's scorn, but it pinched to know his absence would shorten the time he had to enjoy his daughter. With thoughts of Rachel, he tapped his chest for reassurance that her baby ring, a keepsake she'd entrusted to him on her twelfth birthday, was in a pocket atop his heart. When the time came, he would place it on the finger of her first born, he promised. Then, giving Sütlü a nudge, he turned her head toward the trail.

2

Philadelphia, 2007

"Why'd you call me Skipper? It's a baby's name and I hate it."

My son's voice hit the bedroom before he did. I jumped and the lid of my suitcase slammed.

"Anyway, Thomas is my real name. Maybe Tom, but I'm not sure yet," he said at the doorway. His chin stuck out like it always did when he was in one of his challenging moods. I used to think I'd get used to them, but I hadn't. In the five years since our marriage, Carlos had proved to be a buffer between my son and me. Still, asking for a new name was a jolt I never expected. Maybe I should have. He was twelve, five-feet-five and in the right light, sprouting fine hairs on his cheeks.

Carlos got up, ran his hands through his dark curls and, for the first time, lost the frown he'd been wearing since we entered the bedroom. He hated packing.

"I've wondered about that myself," Carlos said, waving Tom to a chair while he walked to the overstuffed bedroom lounge, grabbed a kilim pillow from the seat, and settled against the back with the grace of an athlete. "What's the story?"

"It wasn't my idea," I said, moving my suitcase to the side and sitting on the bed. "We were on the Chesapeake with Uncle Val and you grabbed the tiller of his sailboat. He called you 'Skipper' and it stuck." Couldn't he go one day without accusing me of something? I glanced at Carlos for his reaction, invariably less emotional than mine. *He's still figuring things out*, he'd said. His peaceful nature helped cool the heat.

"Well, son, you got used to calling me Dad. I suppose we can get used to Tom or Thomas, if that's what you want."

When I looked back at my son, it reinforced what I already knew: he'd accept Carlos' words over mine anytime.

"I'll pass the word to your uncles," I said.

Satisfied, he pounded down the stairs and we heard the door slam.

"Didn't see that coming, did you?" I said, moving to the foot of the lounge to sit down.

"No, but it's not a big surprise either. He's beginning to see himself differently, yes?"

Afraid not. He'd entered my life as a stranger and I still struggled to understand him. Within months of his birth, Jared, my first husband, took over his care. Fine with me. The Oriental rugs I bought and sold for my business excited me with their beauty and mystery, and they demanded nothing except the vacuum cleaner. Admittedly, there was a dark side to that decision: Jared's care included cruel discipline and, though I was unaware, my son blamed me for not protecting him. Sometimes his anger still erupted unexpectedly.

I was glad Carlos couldn't see how my mind had wandered from his question. "Well, okay, but he still likes being in charge. No change there. Bossy from the start."

"So I've been told. Lots of water under the boat since then."

Carlos glanced at the clock and rubbed his stomach.

"Yeah, I know—anything to avoid packing." I grabbed his hand and we walked down two flights to the first floor. The stairs spilled out into the foyer, and I stopped to lift a vase of slightly wilted yellow roses from the round Chippendale table that had been my mother's. Filling the vase with my favorite flowers every Friday had become a ritual for Carlos, and for the millionth time I registered the contrast between the two

men I'd married. Jared manipulated and humiliated. Carlos
supported and encouraged. So why did I still feel like I had a
hole in my heart I couldn't fill?

In the kitchen I discarded the flowers and reached into the
refrigerator for a small, plastic-wrapped chicken.

"Listen up, chicken," I said, holding it high, "you will be
cooked a la Elena and be delicious."

That brought a laugh from Carlos who pulled three lemons
from a basket, cut each in half and started squeezing; he knew
his Spanish mother's recipes. The chicken would marinate in
the juice with a little olive oil and fresh rosemary for about an
hour. Then we'd stuff the cavity with small onions and more
rosemary, surround it with oiled potatoes, and roast it.

Mealtime was a valued interlude, something Carlos and I
shared. In Turkey where Carlos grew up and still had his
business, he began cooking with his mother and sister at an
early age. Likewise, my Lebanese-American family meals
were almost sacred. An empty chair was cause for mourning. I
knew it, my brothers knew it, and my parents never let us
forget it.

Carlos and I bumped against each other often in our small
wallpapered kitchen—one of the major drawbacks of living in
a four-story brownstone home on Philadelphia's Historic
Registry. It had been remodeled numerous times, but always
under the scrutiny of the Committee for Preservation, whose
stuffed-shirt members nitpicked their way through the plans,
concentrating on preservation and ignoring practicality. As a
result, plumbing, cabinets and appliances were updated but the
cooking space was still limited. Carlos, rubbing his body
against mine, said the close quarters were what he liked best.

"I'll tell you what surprises me," I said, washing oil off my
hands at the sink.

"Huh?"

"Sorry. I'm changing the subject back to Skip—I mean,
Thomas. I know we don't have a perfect relationship, but it's
better because of you."

The Chinese Silk

9

He shook his head and leaned over the counter. "My pleasure. He's a great kid but I worry he'll always carry some scars."

"Kids are resilient, I've been told." I turned away from him and opened the refrigerator. The cold air seeped over my hands, arms, and face—a prelude to old memories. Jared locked him in closets, threatened to drop him into a basement drain to discipline him, and those were only the things I'd found out about from the Denbys, our close friends and neighbors. I, on the other hand, instructed him on strength and independence because those were the qualities that held me together. For Tom, it was a lethal combination. He bottled up his emotions and hated me for making him do it.

I glanced sideways and caught Carlos studying my face. He put down the asparagus he was getting ready to rinse, wrapped his arms around my waist, and nuzzled into my neck.

After an hour of practicing "Thomas" at dinner, I was relieved when he left to go to the library with Marty Denby. I poured fresh coffee into mugs, and Carlos and I walked through the den to the outside deck. The air held the moisture of an early morning drizzle and smelled of freshly turned earth. From the second-floor level, the trees were at their fullest, providing a sight and sound barrier from neighbors. I enjoyed the silence and Carlos' face until we'd drained our mugs. He gave my hand a squeeze and then reached over to pluck a piece of chicken from my collar.

"I predict that by the end of the week Thomas will have replaced Skipper altogether," he said.

"Do my best. Let's get the leftover chicken in the refrigerator."

When the last soiled plate went into the dishwasher, we went back to the task we'd left in the bedroom: packing for the summer in Ankara, Turkey. This time, in addition to buying rugs for my business, Carlos and I looked forward to two new activities: a visit from the Denbys and finding a house. I pulled out my jeans and a paint-splattered T-shirt and held them out.

"That looks like work," Carlos said.

"No woman likes the colors chosen by another woman."

He groaned.

In Ankara we'd been living in an apartment several floors below Carlos' mother Elena. Seeing her every day bonded our families together and when my brothers, Val and Philip, visited, we spent hours laughing together about our common heritage in the Middle East. But, as good as those times were, it was not the best for Thomas. He needed more activity, more interaction with some of the boys he'd met—a place where loud voices and heavy stomping didn't brand us as the family with the loud kid.

And there was another consideration. We had to face the fact that Elena's health was slipping. Within the last six months, she'd been having dizzy spells and her doctor had suggested that Tapis should monitor the medication Elena needed to take daily. Though willing, Carlos' sister had just married and moved into her own home with Mehmet. The time had come to discuss other arrangements with Elena, perhaps a small suite of her own in our home. She was ambivalent about the suggestion, protective of her independence on one hand, reluctant to be separated from her first grandson on the other.

Family needs were important to Carlos and me, but one of my own concerns was beginning to nag. Summers in Turkey had taken a toll on my Oriental rug gallery and brokering business. It wasn't that Ed Gallo, my gallery manager, wasn't effective and conscientious, but I'd conditioned clients to expect my personal attention. I was religious about visiting their galleries along the East Coast once or twice each year. Since my marriage to Carlos, Ed made most of the phone calls, and I used his input to decide what to bring back from Turkey to replenish my inventory. My neglect was beginning to show on the books.

I folded several blouses and set them in the nearest suitcase. "Can we talk about my gallery for a few minutes?"

"Gladly." He walked to the lounge that still held his body's shape and settled in. I had a sudden flashback of making love in the folds of that chair the night we returned from a short honeymoon months after our wedding. My face flushed and the smirk Carlos was wearing didn't help.

"No you don't. I need you to listen; it's a serious problem."

"If it's so serious, why am I just hearing about it?"

"Because, Mr. Chairman of the Board, sometimes I like to seek out my own solutions before opening it to the floor."

He dropped the smile and looked disappointed.

"Ed and I are concerned about the steady decline in profits over the past five years. According to the figures I looked at this week, they're down about fifteen percent."

"What does Ed say?"

"He's had calls from some of the galleries I supply, asking when I planned to meet with them. Not many calls, but that's the only negative he could come up with. I think he's right." I reminded him of my former routine of at least one personal visit each year.

"Maybe you should cut back. Your life has changed, why not your business? You've got additional responsibilities now, more people in your life. You shouldn't expect business as usual."

"Are you planning to cut back on *your* business because you have more people in *your* life?" I filled the awkward silence by folding a lightweight jacket.

"We've known from the beginning our businesses would present us with tough questions. We set the questions aside until we were ready to deal with them, remember? We weren't going to let anything stand in the way of our family."

"Right. But we've adjusted to our new life together. Maybe it's time," I said.

"But you said so yourself—your relationship with Thomas is improved. Why would you want to change things?"

"Tweak maybe."

"But a tweak that improves your business." He straightened his back against the cushion in a way I didn't like.

"Am I supposed to feel guilty because I want my business to be successful? And don't throw the problems I've had with Thomas in my face. I made mistakes but I provided for our security." I was super glued to the floor, repelled by the soft chair that invited me to sit next to him.

"Let me put it another way. We've grown closer to Thomas and he to us because we made each other a priority."

I walked to the dresser, gathered a handful of slippery undergarments and dropped them into the suitcase. My mind flashed to the gallery I'd created. I saw the white marble steps, highly polished brass handrail, carved oak door, and the gold letters inscribed on thick beveled glass: "The Chestnut Street Persian Gallery, Nora Reardon, proprietor." As always, those words sent a warm wave through my veins.

"Sounds like you doubt I can be a good wife *and* mother *and* business woman. As I see it, I used to be alone and now I have you to share my goals. Everything should be easier, not harder."

I gave in to the pale blue upholstered chair next to him and folded myself into its contours. The coolness of the fabric seeped into my bare arms and I closed my eyes. Almost instantly past arguments inside those same walls flooded my memory—years of Jared using his lawyer-trained mind to manipulate me for his own gains.

Carlos argued with me but in a different way. He gave me the space to change my mind without feeling I'd lost an argument. He was doing it now with his silence. I shifted my body to face him.

"Here's what I think: You and Thomas leave as planned and I'll follow in—well, no more than a week. I'm sure your mother, and maybe Tapis, would be willing to spend time with Thomas when you have to work." I moved to his lap, waiting for him to agree. "Well?"

"There's no question about their help."

The following morning we called Elena, using the speaker phone. Already overjoyed to be a grandmother at long last, she said our plan presented an opportunity she'd been hoping for. During our separation, she said she'd been putting together an album for her grandson. She wanted him to learn about his new family's heritage and to show him photographs, old letters and "skeletons," as she called them.

"I can tell you right now he'll want to hear about the skeletons first," I said.

Her enthusiasm raised my spirits and her strong voice eased concerns we had about her energy level. In fact Carlos was saying goodbye when she interrupted.

"Last week at a friend's home, my hostess—a strong supporter of the Ottoman Heritage Museum—showed me a new rug. It was from Uzbekistan and extraordinarily beautiful. I rarely hear either of you mention Uzbekistan. Maybe you are missing something, yes?"

"You may have something there," I said. "Should I tell Muharrem he has competition?"

"Ah, dear Muharrem," Elena said. "Did I tell you he calls me from time to time?"

"I didn't know, but it doesn't surprise me." Muharrem, my Turkish agent for many years, was a loyal friend. From him I learned that a Turk's friendship always included family and friends. Unfortunately, hatreds shared the same inclusion.

When our conversation ended, Carlos proceeded to call his sister. I braced myself. Unlike Elena, Tapis, although dutifully cordial, had never really warmed to me. She rarely called us in Philadelphia and when we were in Ankara she called Carlos at his office. I hadn't forgotten her critical tone when on our first meeting she made it clear how she felt about the role of women: *When I marry I will quit my job and dedicate myself to my home and husband.*

I expected her to balk at helping out with Thomas. But I was wrong. There was only a moment of hesitation before she assured us she would be willing to help in any way while I remained in Philadelphia.

"I have many friends with children," she said. "Thomas will be welcome in our home. Mehmet will take him to the office to learn how an investigator works here in Turkey. He has done so with many school children."

"Thank you, Tapis. Thomas would like that."

Tom was insatiable, even a bit manic about learning, and soon after I told him what Tapis proposed, I began to see library books on detectives and investigation processes in his bedroom. Carlos laughed when I told him and asked jokingly if he should warn Mehmet to be prepared for a grilling.

The morning before Tom and Carlos were to leave, Carlos turned on his side and stroked my face which was half buried in the pillow.

"This will be our first separation since the wedding," he said in my ear. He slipped his hand inside my satin sleep shirt and stroked the side of my breast. I moved closer, lifted my chin to kiss him and felt the sting of his beard's overnight growth. I welcomed it. I knew the emptiness I'd face once he left for Turkey and wanted to gather every possible sensory token.

"I'm going to miss you so much," I said.

"At night maybe, but I know you, when you're with your rugs, they'll be all you need."

"A distraction, yes, but not all I need." True, I believed the rugs possessed their own spirits. They reminded me of my childhood, those carefree, secure days before I lost my parents. First, my father's heart gave out from fear when he was summarily cut from the university's staff. Then, my mother committed suicide to be with him. I doubted even Carlos knew the extent to which I'd wrapped myself inside those rugs so I could show my brothers and everyone else how strong and independent I was.

"You're everything to me, Carlos. You're my ancient moth."

He pulled back to look at me. It took several moments for him to register what I'd said, but slowly his face reflected my meaning. Earlier in our relationship, when Carlos was showing me a rare rug with moth damage, I asked him why the moth track hadn't lowered the cost. *People don't buy an antique rug for its design and fibers, but for the life it has lived. The damage enhances its lure.*

He pulled me over him and I melted from head to toe against him. His voice rumbled in my ear.

"Let's do some damage."

At breakfast, tension was already beginning to gather across my shoulders. By the time we loaded suitcases in the car and headed for the road to the airport, I tried to focus on the excitement I always felt before visiting clients. This time, though, the thrill was tempered by the reality of returning to an empty house. Carlos' absence would leave a hole in my life. He had insinuated himself into everything and everyone—my brothers, my son, my gallery and brokering business, even our neighbors, the Denbys. When I told them our plans, Carolyn and Jack specifically said they'd miss his visits for coffee. I wasn't aware he dropped by for coffee at their house after his early morning walks. Those visits had a lot to do with the Denbys' decision to visit Turkey during the summer school break.

"I'll miss you. Will you email me?" I said, standing at the edge of the gate.

"You'll be busy and so will I," he said. His chin was working its way forward.

"I'm never that busy."

He puffed out his cheeks and blew. "Yeah, right."

"Knock it off. Carlos?"

"Hardly the time." He glanced at his watch and said they needed to get to the gate. I moved forward and hugged him. Thomas stepped away.

"I'll be anxious to hear how your client visits go," Carlos said.

"Yeah, good luck with that," Tom said.

Their dark curly heads bobbed together as they walked down the corridor side by side. Suddenly Thomas turned and shouted: "I want you to call me Tom." He turned back before I could respond. What was there to say anyway? Perhaps this was how the teen years were for all parents. *He's changing and so must we.* Is that what he'd say now? My stomach knotted.

3

By midmorning the next day, I turned off Interstate 95 and headed toward the Delaware River, where the two-lane road narrowed and required close attention. I rolled down the window and welcomed the slap of cold wind. The edginess I felt as I watched Carlos and Tom receding down the airport corridor was still with me.

It would be easy to fall into my old pattern of misreading my son, a natural consequence with someone who masked his feelings and allowed resentments to build up until something triggered an explosion. For too many years, we'd produced ragged, unresolved memories that snagged like a hangnail and hurt all over again no matter how much time or how many happy experiences piled on top.

Maybe it would be good for Tom to spend time alone with Carlos. Maybe he'd pick up some pointers from the close relationship Carlos had with his mother. With that positive thought, I turned my attention to the road, shifted gears, and let the BMW's smooth acceleration ease me back into the leather contours.

I pulled up next to Max Khatibi's shop in New Hope, Pennsylvania, after entering the village center with its winding brick walkways and manicured landscape. His store was smartly situated among antique furniture and exotic curios, whose goods spread across the paths to slow down the shoppers from Philadelphia, Jersey, and New York. Foot traffic was heavy, a good sign and probably the reason why my friend, standing under his garish red and gold striped awning, was smiling broadly.

I stepped out and paused under his prized ginko tree.

"Looks like it's happy here," I said, fingering a leathery green butterfly-shaped leaf.

"That makes two of us. Hello, Nora."

Max's shop was my first visit for two reasons: it was geographically closer than the others, and I'd known Max, a Saudi, since I was seventeen, working after school in Sam Bezdikian's Oriental rug gallery in New York. When I lost both of my parents at fourteen, Sam became a surrogate father. Max was his best friend.

He joined me and ran his hands over the gray tree trunk.

"There's a tree like this in China, 3500 years old," he said. "The Chinese say if you plant one of these on a special occasion, it brings good luck."

"Worked for you, huh?"

"Yeah," he said. He noticed my sniffing. "We're back-to-back with Nature's Bounty, a tea and spice shop. Very nice. Come on, I'll make you a cup."

Max led the way to the back of the shop through narrow aisles of stacked Oriental rugs, while I noted the waddle of poundage since our last meeting. He pointed to a foldable canvas chair and lit the Sterno beneath a green enameled kettle. A shrill whistle sounded almost immediately.

"Cherries," I said when he poured the ruby liquid into my cup. "Nice."

We sat quietly for several moments, sipping. Tranquility seemed to be a quality shared by most Oriental rug handlers. When I was just beginning in the business, I believed the trait was the result of bargaining, of slowing down to note every facial expression, movement of the shoulders, position of the feet, anything to gain an advantage. These things were important, but later I discerned something else. Every time I stepped into my own gallery, the harmony and balance of the patterns, the colors, even the brilliant ones, seeped into my spirit and whisked me away into peacefulness.

"How are your rugs selling, Max?"

"Unevenly. You know how it is. The public's like a bee, always after new nectar."

"How's that?" I set my cup down and moved forward in the chair.

"I can sell one good pile rug and make as much as several kilim, but quantity-wise I'd say the demand for kilim is greater and I don't think it's because they're less expensive."

"Okay, you're saying it's not about the money, so what is it?"

"Who knows? Maybe this."

He handed me an Architecture Today magazine and after flipping a few pages, I understood. Oriental flatweaves were featured everywhere—hanging on walls, covering hardwood floors, and encasing the pillows that were tossed on leather and fabric sofas.

"Maybe," I said, "that's why I've been seeing a number of new innovations in kilim making. They've gotten rid of the slits between design motifs and they've reintroduced embroidery on top of the weaving. Are you interested in broadening your kilim selections?"

"I'd be a fool not to. But first, tell me about your new family."

"Doing great."

"Skipper?" he said, looking crossways at me.

Because of Max's friendship with Sam, he was aware of my difficulties, and making light of them would only seem a breach of trust. I took a breath.

"Twelve...changing." I smiled, as much for him as for me. "He's just declared Skipper a baby's name and wants to be called Tom. How 'bout that?" Max nodded, reminding me of Sam—and Carlos for that matter—when he wanted the rest of the story. "He's sprouting whiskers." Another series of nods followed but I glanced around the room.

"How's Tom getting along with his new dad?"

"Good, really good. You'd think Carlos studied child psychology or something."

"Tom's got a problem?"

"No, no, nothing like that."

"Glad to hear it. And how are things with you?" He'd put his mug down long ago. Now he leaned back in his chair, made a tent of his long brown fingers, and clamped onto my eyes.

"I'm fine, I—"

"No, I mean with Tom."

"It's okay, maybe not as warm and fuzzy as I'd like but he's twelve. You know those teenage years."

"You should've brought them with you. Haven't seen them since your wedding."

"They're in Turkey for the summer."

He raised his eyebrows, put his hands on his knees, and got up. "Business before pleasure? Time moves faster as you get older, did you know that?"

By the end of my visit with Max, I had a large order for kilim, some small silk pile rugs, and two medium-sized antique wools. Together it was the largest order he'd placed in two years—confirmation that personal visits were vital to my business. I decided to evaluate when I completed the trip but, as I buckled my seat belt and consulted my itinerary, the prospect of getting back on the highway lost its appeal. The sky was darkening and a headache was working its way across the back of my head. I decided to choose a motel about an hour north and to schedule my next visit in New York City for the next day. I wanted to kick off my shoes and flop across a bed with no memories.

I spent a day and a half in Manhattan visiting two well-established galleries and saved late afternoon and dinner for old friends Esther and Sam Bezdikian.

I wasn't surprised to find Sam waiting for me in the lobby of his apartment building. He greeted me with a Lebanese song my father used to sing. His voice boomed uninhibited in the small marbled reception room.

"My darling, when will you stop looking like the high school girl who worked in my gallery? You are as tall and slim as you were then."

"Flatterer."

It saddened me to notice how much he'd aged. He leaned heavily on a cane and his back curled considerably. I could still hear him and my father, both from Lebanon, teasing Max about being from Saudi Arabia. *You Saudis are so rich, it makes you lazy.* Max had turned to me suddenly and asked me to tell them I believed Saudis to be far more handsome than any Lebanese I'd ever seen. I remembered stammering, unable to speak. They all laughed and hugged me until I got over the embarrassment. Their bond was as fierce as it was firm. There was nothing they wouldn't do for each other.

Sam and I walked to the small rickety elevator at the rear of the lobby. He bombarded me with questions as we ascended to the twentieth floor, where he and Esther lived in a large apartment with a roof terrace overlooking Manhattan.

In contrast to Sam, Esther appeared the same: smooth olive skin, hair like wind-swept snow, and a smile that conveyed love and acceptance. I recalled Carlos' reaction to her when they met. He was captivated, his eyes rarely straying from her as she moved about the room to make us comfortable. Now I watched her grasp the fluid drape of her skirt to sit on a deeply carved, high-backed chair with a crimson cushion.

"Now, Nora, you are happy. I can see it in your eyes," Sam said, bending slowly to sit and place his cane within reach. I took the moment to absorb the breathtaking turn-of-the-century Persian Khorossan covering the parquet floors.

"You must be slipping, this is the same rug you had four years ago," I said.

"It's Esther's fault. She's making me slow down against my will."

I gave Esther a knowing look as she sat passively; she'd learned long ago to handle Sam with silence. Maybe it was a Middle Eastern trait since Carlos used the same technique with me.

"Speaking of slowing down, I thought you'd make some changes now that you're married and spending half of each year in Turkey. I don't mind telling you, letting Thomas and Carlos leave without you is wrong. Your place is with your family."

He shook his finger at me and his neck reddened. I felt my face flush and was about to answer when Esther took my arm.

"Let's look at some menus and order dinner. There's a wonderful little café nearby. Unfortunately the delivery takes forever," she said. I walked with her, resisting the urge to look back at Sam.

In the kitchen I cradled her face in my hands and kissed her forehead. "I wonder if I will ever learn to avoid arguments like you do. My brothers, especially Val, agree with Sam, and when they lay on the guilt because of my career, I get angry and frustrated. I fight back every time, even though I know I can't change their minds."

"Then stop trying," she said, like it was the simplest thing in the world.

I nodded and hugged her. "Thank God Carlos supports my ambition."

We passed the remainder of the late afternoon and early evening like the old family friends we were, talking about Tom, his experiences in Turkey, his progress at school, and how my brothers were. I left their apartment with a promise never to allow so much time between visits.

With scant daylight remaining, I checked the map and felt a pull toward Long Island to visit another pair of friends. Maybe this trip was as much about catching up with people as it was about business.

In forty-five minutes I pulled into the driveway of Sallie and Bertrand VanBomme's charming bed and breakfast. They'd been my clients during the refurbishing of one of Long Island's beachfront manors, a three-story Queen Ann Victorian beauty, originally built by a British admiral in the 1800s. For the renovation, the VanBommes wanted Oriental carpets in every room.

Sallie was drawn to symmetrical, geometric designs, and though it took almost a year of research, Muharrem found a rich source of small and large Holbein patterned rugs in Turkey. She loved them.

Like so many others, her attraction lay in the stories behind the rugs. Renaissance portraiture painters Hans Holbein the Elder and his son Hans Holbein the Younger frequently draped or hung the Turkish rugs near their subjects to add color and interest. It didn't take long before Europeans were demanding "Holbein" rugs for their homes, and Turkish weavers were quick to respond.

When the VanBommes opened their bed and breakfast, they escorted guests to their rooms telling the stories as they described the rooms' features. By the time the remodeling and furnishing were complete, we were fast friends.

When Bertrand answered the door, he stepped back, mouth agape, and called to Sallie.

"What a great surprise. How long's it been? You'll stay, of course. I've got just the room for you overlooking the ocean, the perfect spot for a hard working woman to recharge her sales batteries. And," he said, leading the way up a flight of stairs, "you must come to our private quarters and have supper with us when you're ready."

"Oh, my, no. You didn't know I was coming. I'm lucky you have a room for me." I'd forgotten they dined in the European style: late.

Sallie came down the corridor like a high fashion model on a runway, taking long strides in high-heeled silver sandals, wearing a form-fitting red sundress that picked up the highlights in her shoulder length auburn hair. A black lace shawl flowing from one shoulder fell to her arm as she reached out to hug me. The scent of flowers filled our space, delicately sweet.

"I'd given up ever seeing you again. *C'est magnifique*," she said.

"She's joining us for supper," he said to Sallie and then turned to me again. "No argument, please. It'll be a simple meal, just what we'd be having if you hadn't surprised us with your visit."

I nodded, despite the lingering fullness in my stomach and, after Bertrand said he'd bring my suitcase to me, they closed the door behind them. My eyes took in the canopy bed, the white eyelet bed skirt and European Matelasse coverlet, and then to what felt like an old friend: a small pattern Holbein pile Oriental rug on the polished dark wood floor. I remembered this rug. The first time I saw it, I wanted to keep it for myself. Complex repeating geometric figures filled the muted red center field, surrounded by a Kufic border, a stylized version of the endless knot. I tore myself away and freshened up for what I hoped would be as Bertrand promised: a simple meal.

A short time later we were engaged in conversation over a feather-light gruyère soufflé and a crisp vegetable salad dressed with fresh tarragon and white wine vinaigrette.

"I wonder what you'd create for a truly auspicious occasion," I said, scooping up the last piece of salad. He smiled, picked up my wine glass, coupled it with his, and opened the door to the outside deck. We sat in silence enjoying the crash and sigh of ocean waves below.

Sallie broke the quiet. "You know we both loved living in Paris. It had everything—fashion, the Louvre, history. But here in Long Island we have accomplished our dream. Curious, isn't it?"

Her comment launched a recounting of how they'd met while working for a major French hotel chain in Saint Denis. Young and ambitious, Sallie dreamed of owning a salon of interior design, Bertrand to manage his own hotel. One day in a Paris newspaper they read about the Long Island property and a year later they'd hung a sign: *"Un Coin de Paris,"* a corner of Paris, an elegant bed and breakfast overlooking the ocean.

It was about this time of year when we met. I was visiting clients and needed a quiet place to stay overnight when I noticed the scaffolding on a building I'd often admired. I parked my car and introduced myself, thinking they might need my help with floor covering. In fact, they were looking for rugs, but Sallie made it clear she knew exactly what she wanted.

Muharrem made a contact in Turkey's Canakkale region, near the ruins of ancient Troy. The weavers in that region had the designs and colors she sought. Then, Sallie threw another challenge at me. She wanted a different style altogether in their private quarters, something that would contrast with the rest of the house. She asked me to find floral designs in apricot, green and yellow, specifically Persian. I silently ticked off my contacts in Turkey and couldn't recall seeing anything like she described. But I needn't have worried.

Muharrem scoured his network of weavers who'd been helpful in the past, but found the prices exorbitant. Finally he located a broker in Pakistan representing villagers who'd been producing Persian-type carpets for hundreds of years. These had muted colors and flowing floral patterns. Sallie was ecstatic.

"What I remember most about those days was your tenacity," I said.

The clinking of ice broke through the ocean's background music and I looked up to see Bertrand, a bottle of Pinot Noir tilted toward my glass. "My wife, the sharp-toothed terrier," he said smiling at her.

"Just a bit and then I must go to bed. Tomorrow I plan to drive to Hyannis to make a call in the early afternoon." He poured and contrary to my words I settled back again. "Ah, it's hard to leave this."

It wasn't just the wine. I was still feeling the mild censure I'd gotten from Max and Sam. Old fashioned ideas about women. I got enough of that from my brothers. The VanBommes understood me and it felt good.

"What's happening on the home front? You went through a rough time after Jared's death, as I recall," Bertrand said.

"Yeah, I did. Family's grown. My brother Val married Grace, the psychologist who helped me so much with Tom. Then there's Grace's mom—a dear. And, best of all, Carlos' family in Turkey. They're wonderful." I paused, absorbing the truth, and the rarity, of the words. "We spend the school year in Philly and summers in Ankara. Matter of fact, Carlos and Tom are there now. "

"Sounds idyllic," Sallie said.

I soaked in those words. No comments about my mothering. They knew what it took to be successful in business.

The breeze lifted my hair, tugging at the ends, encouraging me to rise. But comfort kept me in the lounge, full wineglass in my hand. I took a sip and looked up at the bright pinpoints of light in the black sky.

Bertrand's voice broke the stillness. "You deserve the happiness. I remember how hard you worked to develop your brokering and then open your own gallery. You should be proud of your accomplishments and the security you gave your son when he needed it."

"We kind of wondered if you were still in business," Sallie said.

My mouth opened to deny her words, but I fought the reaction. I hadn't contacted them for four years; why wouldn't they think I'd sold my gallery?

"Just adjusting. You should see my gallery on Chestnut Street. It's fabulous. Not just the contemporary stuff. Carlos helped me acquire a collection of rare antiques. That's how I met him, remember? I'm excited about it."

"Now, that's the Nora we know and love," Bertrand said.

Everything seemed frozen for a moment, soundless except for the whisper of the sand absorbing the receding sea. I drained my goblet and told Sallie and Bertrand they'd given me a perfect evening.

My feet hardly touched the rug as I walked to my room.

4

The bedcovers were bunched and twisted when I woke the next morning, a sure sign I'd been busy all night—in my dreams. Snippets of scenes flitted in and out of my memory but dissolved like mist under the scrutiny of sunshine. It didn't matter. I was ready for the day, fully charged, recommitted.

I threw back the silky sheet and the air filled with lilies of the valley. Someday I had to remember to ask Sallie and Bertrand how they managed that. I hooked my finger on the handle of my toiletry bag and walked to the oversized bathroom.

I stopped at the full-length mirror. Wasn't thirty-seven too young for gray hair? Carlos said silver was beautiful, an opinion no doubt shaped by his mother's beautiful hair. I missed him. *The harder you work, the faster the time will go.*

A footed tub dominated the center of the room, bracketed on one side by a rack of thick sage-colored towels and on the other by a long, carved mahogany table cluttered with scented oils, assorted body washes, and a royal blue washcloth. It was tempting, but the day I had planned didn't lend itself to a relaxing bath. I grabbed the cloth and sniffed a handmade soap, choosing the corner shower instead. I set the water temperature just above chill.

Five minutes later, swaddled in an oversized towel, I dialed Carlos. It would be just about time for him to be home from the office. As it rang it occurred to me that Tom might answer and

I'd have the chance to ask him how he'd been spending his time the last three days. But it was Carlos.

"How's my Turkish lover?"

"Missing you. Where are you?"

I ran down my itinerary since I left them, emphasizing Max's large order and sharing some tidbits from Sam and Esther. "This afternoon I'll be in upstate New York calling on a client whose orders have...actually no order at all last year," I recalled. "I'm expecting a challenge."

"Good! Approach him as you would a new client and convince him that your products are his pathway to success. Remind him of his profits with you as his broker. If you have to, offer him a discount on his first reorder—"

"You don't have to lecture me. And by the way, the owner is Deanna Sardis, and she's always been a challenge for me."

More than a challenge, actually, Deanna was my nemesis. Of all my clients, she had the keenest mind for business, enviable energy and persistence, and I hated she was two inches taller than me. At five foot seven plus three-inch heels, I was used to the high view. But what I found most exasperating was her knowledge of shifts in the rug business. More times than I cared to remember I'd called her with news I believed would impact her inventory, only to hear she was already aware. How could that be? She lived in Paradise, hardly the epicenter of world events. As far as I knew she'd never been to the Middle East. Maybe she had relationships with rug distributors in key cities, but I never asked.

"Then you are just what she needs," Carlos said.

Part of me wanted to laugh at his cockeyed optimism, but he was rarely wrong. A salesperson usually gets what she expects.

"You'll be the first to know. Now, tell me what you and Tom have been up to."

The ocean breezes were blowing the window curtains horizontal and making me shiver. I pulled the frame down, noting a line of white clouds at the horizon.

"Tom's with Tapis, has been since we got here. I talk to him every day. He's having a ball."

"Doing what?" I bit the inside of my cheek.

"Listen to this: Most kids just want to have fun, go places, you know, be entertained. But my sister says Tom wants to talk about family customs, Turkish superstitions, and he wants to help her cook. They're having a great time together."

"That's nice. By the way, did you notice he didn't want me to kiss him at the airport?"

"I did, but what teenaged boy wants to be kissed by his mother in public? You make too much of these things. Believe me he'll change his personality again and again until he decides who he is. Don't make a big deal out of it."

"Don't you think it's a big deal when he talks to me like that? Why didn't you say something?"

I waited for his response until I began to think he hadn't heard me.

"That won't work," he said softly.

"He listens to you."

"True."

"Is that all you have to say?"

"For now. Look, be patient."

"Patience isn't my strong point, but I'll try. When will he be with you so I can talk to him?"

"You have Tapis' number."

"That's okay." I asked again when Tom would be home and Carlos explained he expected him sometime early next week.

"Next week?"

Carlos said Mehmet and Tapis were taking him to visit friends in Kuşadasi. They'd rented a yacht for a day of sailing on the Aegean.

"He'll love that. How good of Tapis and Mehmet. Tell me, how's your work? Anything new?"

Carlos' rug business was well established. Family friends, made during his father's years as curator of Istanbul's prestigious Museum of Art, were scattered throughout the

Middle East and Europe. Unlike me, it was relatively easy for him to be away for months at a time. His large staff handled internal affairs—inventory, sales and distribution—and Carlos concerned himself with maintaining those contacts and staying current with changes in the industry. With phone calls and email, his work could be managed from any location.

"I've been invited to Istanbul to a private viewing of a rug carbon dated to 500 B.C. It's shrouded in speculation and mystery."

I'd been sitting on the edge of the bed, but the tone of his voice had changed. Although Carlos was a man completely immersed in the realities of business, he was enchanted by the unexplainable, the mysterious, the magic of Oriental rugs. It set fire to his imagination. I fluffed up the pillow behind me and lay back to let his voice carry me along.

"In 1950 a team of archeologists, working near the Mascit mountain pass, excavated a silk-pile rug. Because of human and animal bones discovered at the same time, they believe the rug was being transported along the Silk Road and met with some kind of tragedy.

"Researchers are hot on the trail of the rug's origins. They'll tie down the facts, but that won't discourage the storytellers. Already, there are some fantastic rumors swirling about," he said.

"Like what?"

"Well, some are saying the rug carries a *nimet*, a blessing."

"Hmmm. I can tell your ear's against the wall. How long before you buy this rug?"

"Ha! You think you can read my mind. Even if I were interested, it's not for sale. Its owners are showing it in museums around the world. I've been invited to see it, that's all."

I was intrigued by the rug, but my mind wouldn't let go of Tapis and Tom talking, laughing, cooking, and sharing. What did she think she was doing?

5

Until I opened my own gallery, The Scheherazad Collection in Paradise, New York, was my standard of excellence. Deanna Sardis not only managed a superb collection, but she'd found a rare setting. Wealthy immigrant European farmers in search of life in the New World founded Paradise in 1800. There, twenty-five miles south of Albany, they'd built substantial homes that were passed on to succeeding generations. Oriental rugs covered the floors of these opulent homes and were treasured by subsequent owners.

Deanna capitalized on the town's healthy economy and found a clever way to engage the people. She created a weeklong Festival of a Thousand and One Nights, a modern version of Tales of the Arabian Nights, and invited a few famous storytellers to entertain inside a huge tent illuminated by lanterns. She covered the ground inside the tent with Oriental rugs and kilim-covered cushions on which people were invited to sit. After the event, the rugs and cushions were sold at discounted prices. Thousands of people attended and hundreds of townspeople volunteered their time. Deanna was a marketing genius.

I parked under an umbrella of oak branches and sat for a few minutes to collect my thoughts. It was late morning and, from the number of cars parked nearby, I imagined Deanna would be busy. If that were true, it would provide time for me to look over her inventory, learn what kinds of rugs she was offering, maybe even who had provided them during the past few years.

A bell tinkled as I opened the door. A young man looked up and smiled. Customers were scattered around the room.

"I'll be with you in a moment," he said, making some notes on a tablet. He walked toward me, stopping to say a few words to each group. I used the time to look over the gallery. The stock looked diminished, but there could be a number of reasons for that—rugs in storage, inventory review, to name a couple.

The young man approached with long, brisk steps, already giving me full attention with his eyes. I made a snap judgment he was not the type to look at you while listening to a conversation elsewhere.

"Hello. I'm Nora Reardon. Is Deanna Sar—"

"Oh, yes, I recognize your name. Mother's in the back. I'll tell her you're here."

His thick blond hair bounced as he walked down a hall at the back of the store. Within minutes I heard Deanna's voice and her heels clicking on the hardwood floor.

"Long time no see. I heard you remarried," she said.

Her words got lost in the shock of seeing her. My memory was of a vibrant, confident businesswoman. That was not the woman standing before me. She was stooped and withered. Not even the brightly colored turban could lift her sallow complexion.

"Yes, five years ago. Forgive me for being so blunt, but what's wrong?"

"Three years of breast cancer, that's what," she said, leaning against a pile of rugs. "Brad's been taking over gradually, and I'm lucky to have him."

"Don't believe a word of it," Brad injected. "I'm only helping out until she's done with chemotherapy. It really saps her energy, but it's doing its job and she'll be fine. Mom, why don't you take Mrs. Reardon to the back and have some of the coffee I just made?"

Deanna nodded and led the way. Seeing her from the back was even more of a shock. Her shoulder blades protruded from her blouse and I saw her hairless scalp through the folds of fabric wound around her head. A lump rose in my throat. I felt guilty about the thoughts that had run through my head on the way to Paradise.

I helped her to a chair and watched her pour coffee into two white iridescent teacups.

"Now, bring me up to date." She laced her long fingers together. Her usually long manicured nails were clipped to her finger tips.

"I'm trying to make up for my absence by—"

"No, no, bring me up to date on your family. Business can wait. It's Ghazerian now, isn't it?" she said. Her eyes were sparkling with interest, like her son's. Either she'd changed or my observation wasn't as keen as I thought.

"Right. Five years ago I married Carlos Ghazerian, a man I met in Ankara on one of my buying trips. He's a distributor of antique and contemporary Oriental rugs. We're very happy."

She gave me a broad smile and lifted her teacup to toast, but the cup shook so violently she had to steady it with her other hand. "That's wonderful news, not only for you but for Skipper."

"It's Tom now, and, yes, Carlos has made a big difference in our lives." I set my teacup on a small table. "Deanna, I came here wanting to reclaim you as a client but— Look, I don't presume to draw any conclusions, but you've got another challenge right now and the gallery's got to be a secondary focus until you're cured."

"Not my choice, that's for sure, but the chemo's boss right now. I'm over my head, not just the medical bills but running the gallery. Thanks to Brad and a few of my friends, the gallery is manageable, but what really upsets me is that I may have to cancel the festival this year. Realistically, it requires more than I've got to give." She sipped her coffee and choked.

I reached over to take her cup while kernels of new thoughts popped in my head like corn exposed to heat. Was she talking about her energy, her inventory of rugs, or something else?

"That'd be a tragedy after all you've done to create something of international scope," I said.

Her head dropped, exposing again the rosy sheen of her skull. I chewed my lower lip, worried my comment had just added to her frustration. Tragedy? Did she see it that way? If she did, this was another Deanna—not the one I knew. The truth was her grit, her talent, and her knowledge were equal to mine and sometimes better. What would she say to me if our roles were reversed? As if my thoughts gave off a sudden power surge, our heads lifted together and we looked at each other.

"What I mean is...can we talk about what's involved? Maybe I can help," I said.

"That's kind of you, but I don't see how. It takes so many people—all kinds of volunteers, lots of resources. You've got your own business to run. You can't take on another one."

I set my cup down. Her eyes had come to life. It spurred me on.

"The volunteers. Can you count on their help again?"

"Sure. They all love the festival and look forward to it every year. But, that's not all. What are you thinking?" She frowned.

"I'm thinking you need to learn something I'm just beginning to understand."

She shifted and settled her back into the curve of the chair.

"I've worn my independence like plate of armor—my way to show I didn't need anybody. Trouble was my son has grown up imitating me and now I can't get close to him. I may never be able to change that." I swallowed several times before I could continue. "Carlos has taught me that it's not only okay to accept help, but it actually strengthens relationships. I'll confess my progress has been slow—two steps forward and one step backward usually—but there's truth in what he says and I'm trying.

"Let all of us help you."

She looked surprised. If she was shocked by the personal disclosure, she wasn't the only one.

"But it's more than bodies on the ground. The rugs, my inventory...they're..." She sighed, shook her head, and started to get up.

"Maybe that's where I can help. I haven't thought this through, obviously, but what if I supplied the rugs for the tent floor on consignment? I could bring them here a few days before the event and stay to handle the sales and other general details? Do you think someone in town could handle the publicity and secure the storytellers with your supervision?"

Emotions rippled across her face—shock, disbelief, and she stifled a sob."

"I'm not looking to take over here."

"No, no, I don't...it's just...What the heck! You're absolutely right. The festival *is* a community involvement. People from all over look forward to it. It'd be a shame to call it off."

She got up, walked to the door and called to her son. I heard his quick steps approach, and he appeared with a pinched expression and his tablet clutched to his chest.

"Are you okay?"

"Sit down and listen to this. It's the happiest news I've heard in a long time."

He set the tablet down, poured himself a cup of coffee and listened to what I introduced as "a sketchy plan." By the time I finished, we were all smiling and wiping away our tears. I left shortly afterward, promising to call from Turkey with firmer plans.

Two days later I turned the car south toward home. I'd gone as far as Massachusetts. It was three o'clock, but the thought of another night in any bed other than my own was out of the question. I was exhausted and exhilarated at the same time. It had been a strange six days. Green order sheets, listing sizes and types of rugs, fanned out on the seat beside me. Somehow their importance was diminished. If I were an Oriental rug, Deanna Sardis would be my center field. I was shaken by her situation and excited about the opportunity to make a difference for her.

My mind was racing and so was the car. It took heavy traffic around New York City to slow me down, and I didn't get home until ten. In my haste to talk to Carlos, I accidentally dialed our apartment instead of the office. The chances I'd find Carlos at home in the middle of the afternoon were slim, but his groggy voice answered.

"It's okay. Just taking a little nap. Tom and I were up until one o'clock last night talking about his trip on the Aegean. Evidently it was great fun."

Fun. Someday I'd like to have some of that with my son. "Put him on."

"He's still with Tapis."

"Didn't they have enough time together on the ship?" My comment met with silence. "Listen, I have something to tell you."

Deanna's plight and my willingness to help her with the festival poured out. "It's held during the last week of August."

Carlos was quiet when I finished explaining how the weeklong event worked. It was all new information and I imagined he was digesting the details.

"You'd love it, Carlos. It captures the mythology of the Middle East and provides a perfect setting for the rugs. People come from all over the States, even other countries."

"Did you say you would need to work with her before the event?"

I flushed, picturing the calendar and understanding what he was thinking. Tom started school after Labor Day, the first week of September.

"Yes, it's the week before Tom goes back to school and I've thought about that," I lied. "Look, there are lots of details to be worked out. I'll talk to you about it when I get to Ankara, okay?"

"And I'll talk to Tom."

"I really don't think Tom will mind if I'm in New York when he goes back to school. You know how independent he is, don't you?"

My back, stiff from sitting in the car, began to ache. I stood and stretched, surprised to find that my whole body hurt.

"What I think or what you think isn't the main issue here. When are you going to learn that Tom needs to know he comes first with us? If we want him to consider us when he schedules something that affects the family, we need to give him the same courtesy."

I reached into my purse for aspirin and walked to the bathroom for water.

"I've already told Deanna I would help her," I said, pushing aside the contents of the medicine cabinet until the familiar bottle appeared.

"And I am not saying you shouldn't. In fact, what you're proposing is very kind." He paused. "Actually, you know, I may have an idea. We'll talk about it when you get here and I'll talk to Tom too."

"What? Huh?" I ran the water into a glass, took a mouthful and swallowed two caplets, the maximum dosage.

"I want to think it through a bit first—you know, the way you like to do before you discuss your problems with me." I pictured the smirk on his face.

Despite the tease, his comment was also a jab. My lack of openness annoyed him. I knew it but it was a hard habit to break. Too many years of judge-and-jury sessions with Jared had made me reluctant to share.

"This much I will tell you," he continued. "An Islamic principle may be the perfect solution in this case."

"Islamic? You're kidding. That's a little off the wall for a Christian guy." I rubbed my neck, wishing the aspirin would hurry up and do its work.

"You don't know Muslims. I've lived among them all of my life and their principles have served them well for thousands of years. I've never found you to be narrow minded."

"Okay, I'll hold my opinion until I hear more."

After our conversation I went through the motions of unpacking, loading the washing machine, listing the calls on the answering machine—anything to pass the time mindlessly. Finally, I crawled into bed, pulled the comforter up to my chin and waited for sleep. It didn't come. Carlos' insinuation that I hadn't put Tom first in my plans had put a damper on my enthusiasm.

Yes, Tom was moving along to another grade, but that was something he always handled with confidence. Why would seventh grade be different? I dismissed Carlos' concern and my "little white lie." Everything had happened so fast I just hadn't had time to look at the calendar. Besides, the fib hadn't hurt anyone. At some point in the early morning hours, I drifted off.

Ed Gallo was bent over the accounting ledger in the gallery office when I arrived the next day.

"Hey, I didn't expect you for a few days. Did you cut your trip short?" he said, standing and tightening the already-perfect tie. I often wondered if Ed was "spit and polish" by nature or if he got in the habit while serving as an Air Force major during the Viet Nam conflict. Within a few weeks of hiring him, I let him take over the job I hated most. I'd never been sorry. He was meticulous and seemed to thrive on balancing the columns.

I set my purse and order book on the edge of the desk and sat—more accurately, plopped—into the only other chair in the room, gesturing to Ed to sit down as well.

"I covered everyone I had to and then decided to drive directly home from Massachusetts. It was worth the long drive to get home to my own bed."

The office looked more orderly than when I left, a sure sign Ed had worked his military discipline on the clutter. Even the cherry wood desk gleamed.

"Good business?" he said.

"Better than I hoped, actually. You were right about the reason for the slide in profits. I heard a few grumbles, but it doesn't appear I've lost anyone, so that's good.

"Ed, do you remember meeting Deanna Sardis at our opening?"

"Paradise, New York?"

"Good memory. Yeah. She's getting chemo treatment for breast cancer and it's been tough going. Her son Brad's helping out in the gallery, but the fabulous annual event she runs is more than she can handle."

"Oh, the Festival of a Thousand and One Nights, in the tent, with—"

"That's it. I told her we could help."

"Count me in," he said with a huge toothy smile. "Whatever I can do."

"Great. We'll talk more as things start to fall in place." I left him to finish up the bookwork, but not before I noticed him use both hands to wipe his eyes.

In the main gallery, the lighted alcove caught my attention. A Moroccan runner, with animals and geometric shapes on a sunny yellow field, had been removed. In its place was a fifteen-by-twelve-foot Teheran pictorial produced in North Persia in the early twentieth century, a magical piece. Tawny camels walked between small trees on a black background around a center field of palest blue. Three trees converged in the center. Their branches held birds, squirrels, fruits and nuts amid pale leaves. Narrow golden borders encircled the inner and outer fields like nimbuses.

Ed had changed the spotlight to a soft yellow and the effect was not only artistic, it was masterful in the way it gave an illusion of depth to the border. The forty-thousand-dollar price tag seemed right, although I knew I'd forever envy the owner, whoever it might be.

Back in the office, I commented on the switch.

"Hope you don't mind. I got a call from Mr. Wei to say he was interested in another acquisition. I checked our records and he has nothing like this, right?"

Antique Oriental rugs were filling my long-time Chinese client's retirement with renewed passion. He'd begun with a single flatweave when I first opened my gallery, followed almost yearly with purchases of greater and greater value.

"*If* we're his only supplier." I said, pausing to picture Mr. Wei's black eyes, black holes whose gravity absorbed everything while allowing nothing to escape. "I think we've earned his trust. But don't ever relax with him. He's wily and knowledgeable and he has a nose for duplicity and weakness.

"The Teheran's a great choice. Do you know when he's coming in? I'd like to be here," I said.

"Soon, I think. When are you leaving for Turkey?"

"Oh, right." His grin gave him away. He wanted Mr. Wei all to himself. "I've got a few more days before I leave for Turkey. I'll be back to be sure you have everything you need, okay?"

Ed and I spent several hours compiling the orders I'd brought, and by mid-afternoon I left the gallery for home. I felt drained, but as I drove along the expressway, I suddenly remembered I hadn't called my brothers, a ritual Val and Philip had imposed on me since our parents' deaths. Being exhausted wouldn't count as an excuse from their perspective. No matter what, they wanted to hear from me promptly whenever I returned from a trip. I'd feel the barbs for at least a week, if I forgot. Carlos didn't understand why this annoyed me. *My family shares information eagerly,* he'd said. But, then, he didn't have a Val in his family.

At home I dropped my purse in the hall, made myself comfortable on the sofa in the den, and picked up the phone. Philip answered and broke into a throaty laugh.

"We just finished talking to Carlos. Missed Tom again though. Seems he's growing up, getting very independent. That's good."

A far cry from how they reacted to my independence. "Yeah, I'm proud of him too.

How are Val and Grace?"

"Rattling around. I told them they were crazy to buy such an old house. They'll never be done fixing it."

Philip's idea of home was a recliner and a book. Perhaps because he'd lived with persnickety Val for so long, he wasn't aware of how much upkeep there was to home ownership. He told me he was thinking of finding a small apartment for himself, but Val and Grace wanted him with them. The house they'd purchased had five large bedrooms and currently only four were occupied: Val and Grace in one; Grace's daughter, Penelope, in another; and Grace's mother, Mrs. Bonseur, in the third.

I kicked off my shoes. "Val loves a project. The house sounds like a perfect outlet for his energy," I said.

"Just so. He found the perfect partner in Grace. She never runs out of ideas and I suspect they've more to do with keeping Val out of trouble than sprucing up the house."

"Let's just be grateful she's willing to bring her work home. Our brother needs an in-house psychologist.

"Philip, I'd like all of you to come over before I leave for Ankara. Will you call Val's family for me and set it up?"

"I take it you had a successful visit with clients."

"I did. But wait 'til you hear about what I'm doing with Deanna Sardis." I briefly described the yearly event in Paradise and told him about her illness.

"Why haven't we gone to this festival? When is it?" Philip asked.

"Last week in August, before the kids go back to school. Vacationers are still in the area and, in fact, people come from all over the world. I hope you can go, especially since Carlos and I will be involved."

"Just so. Sounds like fun. See you soon."

Ten minutes later, when my hands were coated with flour, the phone rang. I knocked the receiver off with my elbow and pushed the speaker button, leaving a white dusting behind. When I heard Val's voice, I braced myself for more than a messy cleanup.

"You hate it when we call you 'baby sister' but when are you going to grow up and take responsibility?"

"Nice of you to welcome me home, Val."

"I'm doing you a favor. I want to get this off my chest before we come over."

"Say what you have to say and get it over with."

"You've obviously forgotten how uptight kids get about middle school. I've never seen Penny so nervous. What about Tom?"

I picked up the phone. To hell with the flour. "Planning, Val. A little beforehand planning is all it will take to make this work. Have you talked to Grace? I want all of us to be there. It's going to be great. You won't want to miss it. Philip wants to be there."

"Philip doesn't have kids."

I pictured his petulant face on the other end of the line. Suddenly it was the face he wore when our parents died. We were kids clinging to each other, afraid. Philip accepted our situation and moved on, but Val had a breakdown and I broke away from our circle of dependence. God, was he still trying to pull me back? Would he never let it go? I wasn't his mother and he wasn't mine.

"Do me a favor. Talk to Grace."

He hung up without saying "goodbye." I rubbed the sweat off my face, momentarily forgetting about the flour. I dumped the bowl of ingredients in the trash and left the kitchen to take a bath. Val would never understand me and I'd lost the desire for freshly baked rolls.

6

On The Trail To Erzurum, Asia Minor

Once Çatal left his small village, only the woods and an occasional rabbit entertained him. He loved the soft padding of his camel's feet, moving together on one side and then the other, providing a rocking motion that soothed his mind and released his sad thoughts like birds launching from the branches overhead. He held conversations with Sütlü and received his answers by noting a flick of her ears, the turning of her head, and the occasional, but especially meaningful, snort. And before he spread his fleece to sleep on the first night, he hand fed her the dried dates and apples she preferred.

By midday of the second day he reached a crossroads where he was joined by other travelers. Muscles he'd held taught relaxed at the sight of them, assured he would not be alone when they reached the Mascit mountain pass, where the trail narrowed, boulders the size of his hut threatened from the ledges overhead, and a bottomless black gorge gaped alongside. He tapped Sütlü to quicken her stride and match the pace of the others.

A man seated on a donkey in front of him twisted around.

"A strange color, your camel. Has she been blessed?"

Çatal flushed at the man's ignorance: the superstition surrounding any animal or child born with white skin.

"Do not worry, my friend, she has blessed my travels for ten years."

Though the crease remained between the man's eyes, he nodded and faced forward. Çatal chuckled to himself. He knew the man would find another spot at the first opportunity.

Around the next wide turn a valley of sunflowers, where traditionally the men stopped to share a late evening meal together, came into view. There, if he was lucky, he'd encounter a familiar face or two. He enjoyed listening to the others' experiences along the ancient road that moved silk, spices, gold, ivory, and much more from China to Europe. Trees with low-reaching branches, chattering birds, and tall golden grasses stretched as far as Çatal could see. Dozens of fires surrounded by men dotted the meadow. The smell of their sizzling food made Çatal's mouth water. His group filed past, eager to find their own base.

At sunset a cold mist rose from the sodden ground like a ghostly wanderer and suffused the air with the moldy smell of leaves becoming earth. Çatal's weary band sat around the fire to relax and tell stories—his favorite time. But a recent battle at Manzikert, an area in the south that Çatal had never seen, seemed to dominate the conversation.

"The high and mighty Emperor Romanus IV is as soft as a lamb's underbelly," said a man with a nose like a squash. "Because of him, the Seljuk Muslims think they can take what is ours." Sharp words and raised fists spiked the fire's curtain of smoke.

"Perhaps you prefer *Gazie* justice. I'm sure they put their ears to your mouth as your head rolls by."

Tempers rose until Çatal put some distance between himself and the crowd. They were condensing around the fire and shouting about the abuses of the Gazies, an outlaw Muslim tribe who called themselves Warriors of the Faith. Çatal had heard about the emperor's conciliatory nature; it appealed to his own ideology. He circled around the combative men, not to better hear their arguments, but to observe their character. Many difficulties could arise as they traveled. They would need each other. He noted who became violent and lost their reason.

"Listen to me," said a richly dressed merchant, whom Çatal had observed dressing the wound of his servant earlier. "Did you hear how the Seljuk Sultan treated our emperor?" All eyes turned toward the merchant's commanding voice. "The Sultan placed his boot on the emperor's neck and forced him to kiss the ground." Angry shouting answered but he held his arm high. "But, then, the Sultan treated him with great kindness, offered him terms of peace, and invited him to dine."

The men grumbled together in their separate groups, but the merchant, either because they respected his position or because he'd given them new information, had cooled their tempers. They turned their attention to food and bedding for the night. Çatal likewise walked to a space between two saplings where Sütlü, earlier relieved of her heavy load, was working her lips around a branch. Çatal's stomach grumbled. He withdrew a handful of nuts, dried fruit, and cheese. Then he tossed his various packs together and covered them with a blanket. Searching the surrounding ground, he chose several rocks and weighted the sides against a rise in the wind.

But as he unrolled his fleece in a spot next to Sütlü, he did not feel the need to sleep. Instead, he leaned against the tree and turned away from the campfires to the impenetrable dark beneath a canopy of winking stars. Çatal's thoughts turned to Rachel and the children in his village.

It was Çatal's habit after such fireside sessions to commit the stories and his new experiences to memory. This time he decided to set aside the actions of a handful of violent warriors and to appreciate the good contributions of the Seljuk Muslims. The Seljuk-built caravanserai in Erzurum provided safety and comfort for all who traveled to the bazaar. He got up, tossed a rug across his shoulders against the chill, and slowly strolled, satisfying his hunger while observing the fifty or sixty men, their camels and donkeys.

Taking care not to disturb those already asleep, Çatal passed among them. The Silk Road leading to Erzurum's bazaar drew men from the lands between four surrounding seas: the Marmara, the Aegean, the Mediterranean, and the Black. This crossroad for trade never failed to provide new material for his imagination. Some men carried fearsome weapons, perhaps because they came from border areas and were subjected to incursions. Those with feathered turbans of rich fabric had shops in the cities. He turned his head in time to see moonlight glint through the smoky air. A dark-skinned man, whose gray beard curled like a nest in his lap, was fingering long strands of beads and metal pieces. Rachel was drawn to beads and other shiny objects. He walked closer to see the details he would describe to her when he returned. But as he imagined his daughter on his knee listening to him, he heard his wife's voice: "Shame! Lazy dribble from the mouth of a fool."

Suddenly, Catal stopped. Through the fire's flickering red flags, he thought he saw a man he knew. He made his way around, trying to keep the familiar features in sight. A smile of recognition passed between them and his friend jumped up and embraced him heartily. They found a private place nearby where they could share the food from their bags as well as news of their families.

Hrant, with happiness lighting up his broad face, slapped Çatal on the back when he heard of Rachel's betrothal. "Do you like her suitor?" he said, with a curious smirk. When Çatal was slow to answer, he nodded vigorously. "Yes, yes. I understand. I do not lie, my friend. I hated my son-in-law at first. I thought he was lazy, too hairy, and too loud. I told my wife he smelled like a dog that'd rolled in sheep dung."

"You should have refused him."

"No, no. Everything changed with my first grandchild. I do not lie, Çatal, he was delivered by angels. Such beauty. Oh, forgive me. I will bring an evil eye on my house with bragging."

Çatal threw back his head and laughed until tears ran. Hrant had given words to his unspoken feelings. He hoped grandchildren came quickly. "God is merciful," he said.

Hrant yawned, displaying his few teeth, and stood. He suggested they watch for each other at the bazaar so they might make arrangements to ride together on the way home. Çatal agreed eagerly and watched his friend's coltish strut as he walked away winding a bright red scarf around his neck. A moment later Hrant whirled around to shout a Muslim family blessing: *May she sleep on the same pillow to the end of her life.*

It was a beautiful thought, which Çatal repeated to himself as he walked back among the trees to Sütlü. He pulled his soft fleece around his body and listened to Sütlü's rhythmic breathing.

In the morning's papery light, a cloud of dust hung low over the damp earth. The travelers were already scrambling to feed, water, and repack their animals, since once on the trail a hungry horse or a poorly packed donkey would cause trouble for everyone. The men set aside their hunger for these chores, but Çatal, his back against a tree, enjoyed the natural beauty along with the human spectacle. His Sütlü displayed no need for food. She sat with her long legs folded under a warm shaggy coat, placidly watching the frenetic pace. Sütlü, like others of her species, could travel for five to seven days with little or no food and water. Çatal raised his face to the sky, thanked God for their years together and petitioned for another thirty years of her services.

Çatal drank deeply from fresh camel's milk and pulled several strips of dried, smoked lamb from a kilim pouch before retying the bags in front of Sütlü's forward hump. Why would anyone choose a horse over a camel? Then he laughed out loud when he glanced at Sütlü's face. She was thinking the same thing.

After another draught of milk, he rubbed his sleeve across his mouth and reached into his pocket to fill his palm with dried dates. Sütlü's large leathery lips snatched and swallowed them whole. Later, as she felt the need, she would regurgitate the undigested fruit and chew it in cud form.

With one last glance about the camp, the mounted men began to make their way south. Çatal settled comfortably between Sütlü's humps and recounted the items he needed to buy. He would do his best to fulfill the needs of his village, but from past experience he knew nothing at Erzurum was guaranteed—except the Seljuk fortress. There, within the high stone walls, travelers would find a safe haven for themselves, their animals, and their possessions. By the time Çatal arrived in Erzurum, he would sorely need the services they provided.

They found their place in the procession. Moments later Sütlü wagged her head from side to side, snorted and moaned. To Çatal this was her request for a song. He'd been told his voice could strip the bark from the trees, but he reasoned the sound would be carried off by the breeze. Besides, he loved to bellow, something he could never do in the village, and Sütlü's immediate silence confirmed his hunch. It was satisfying to know he had read her mind correctly.

In the afternoon of the third day, the men and animals scaled the narrow Mascit mountain pass where, the year before, an earthquake and subsequent avalanche had sent the ancient trail crumbling to the valley three thousand feet below. A new path had been cut. Nonetheless, Çatal heard a chorus of murmured prayers and speculations float on the breeze. "Mascit still shrugs its shoulders like a man trying on new cloths," someone said, easing his way around stones and earth.

Tall trees lined the pass on one side like guards saluting the bravery of any who scaled their rock fortress. The bronzed trunks held their branches far overhead and made it possible for Çatal to peer deeply into the interior. He imagined the eyes of bear and deer. If only they would show themselves and distract him from the ever steeper slope. Ahead, Çatal saw some men dismount to walk in front of their beasts, but Sütlü was calm and sure footed, even when debris lay across the path. His confidence in Sütlü gave him the freedom to search the forest, which he far preferred to the gorge on the other side.

An unsettling quiet spread among the men and beasts as they moved along in single file. Friendly shouts between riders had stopped altogether and even the bells around the animals' necks seemed muffled. Çatal forced his mind ahead to the bazaar but each crunch and thump of the cart's wheels behind him jolted him back to the mountain and its threat. None too soon, Çatal noted the sun settling among the trees and the gentling slope of the trail. When they reached the forested valley below, the men circled around, drinking from their leather pouches, searching each other's eyes as their fears leached away.

Çatal calculated he and Sütlü had traveled slightly more than ninety-five kilometers. Just a few more twists of the road and he and the other men in the procession would see the windowless rectangle of stone and the intricately carved entrance of the Seljuk caravanserai.

Finally, as they passed through a tree tunnel, he saw the hazy outline of his destination, and with each of Sütlü's footfalls, the details sharpened: massive, gray stone walls surrounded by tents, horses, camels, and people—some in clothing barely distinguishable from the dirt beneath their woolen sandals. All of it was welcome to Çatal. Even Sütlü, without prompting, stretched her long neck forward and lengthened her steps.

7

Grace and Penelope, with shopping bags swinging, were the first to arrive.

"Look, Aunt Nora," Penny gushed. She pulled a pink and white dress with a ruffled skirt from the bag. Sheets of white tissue floated to the floor. "Wait'll you see." She ran up the stairs, taking two at a time.

Grace grinned. "I overdid it. But I kept remembering how insecure I felt entering middle school. I just couldn't say no. She's been badgering me for a month about looking more grown up."

"I remember too," I said. "Dying to look like all the other girls and God forbid you should get separated from your group. Is it just the girls, you think?"

"No, but boys are different. Girls hide behind each other, their clothes, new makeup, or more sophisticated hairstyles. Boys? Defensive. Aggressive."

"How 'bout cocksure of everything."

We heard shoes dropping in Tom's room directly overhead. It seemed natural Penny would choose his room to change. She and Tom were close, enjoyed being cousins and spending hours talking or watching movies together. I kept hoping that Penny's affectionate nature, her openness, and her closeness to her mom, would rub off on my tight-lipped, moody boy.

I led the way into the kitchen to get some lemonade and my eyes fell on a sales flyer for back-to-school clothes. It had triggered a confrontation with Tom before he left for Turkey. I was reading it in the den when he got home from school and asked him to take a look.

"Forget that."

"Hi, Mom. How was your day?" I tried the lightest tone I could.

"There's a no brainer. You were with your rugs, you know, those fuzzy things you can't get enough of."

I stood up and turned to face him. His face was bloody.

"What's this? What happened to you?" I ran into the kitchen for a cloth, ran it under the faucet, and dabbed his forehead. "Was it a fight?"

"Yeah. About stupid clothes. Some jerk said I should model for Victoria's Secret," he said, pushing my hand away.

"That's ridiculous."

"That's your answer? Ridiculous?'"

To keep things from escalating, I offered to take him shopping whenever he wanted.

I shook off the memory and handed Grace a filled glass.

"By the way, a word of warning for you, Val is pretty steamed up over your decision to be in New York the week before Tom goes back to school."

Before I could respond, Penny descended the stairs. She had twisted her long blonde hair and pinned it to the top of her head. That one small adjustment transformed her. She walked slowly, letting us absorb her as a new creature, and when she reached the bottom she swirled, sending the ruffles of her skirt flying.

We clapped.

"Like it?"

"You look lovely. Sophisticated, I believe, would be the correct word," I said, giving Grace a wink.

The front door opened and Val's frown quickly changed my mood. Luckily, Penny was eager to dazzle him with her new look.

"Daddy, what do you think?"

"Who let this movie star in?" he said, leaning over to give Penny a kiss. Then he kissed Grace and I heard him whisper, "I'm not ready for her to be so grown up."

"Well, get used to it." Grace wasn't smiling and Val nodded.

Philip, who'd been standing just inside the door, lifted Penny and gave her a hug and kiss while telling her how beautiful she looked. After he put her down, he welcomed me home and gave me a hug as well.

Val walked to me and stood studying my face. "Welcome home, Nora." His tone was perfect for reading a tombstone epitaph. I turned away and invited everyone into the kitchen for a drink. Earlier I'd set out some lemonade, white and red wines, and a freshly baked flatbread topped with spicy fontina, tomatoes, and freshly chopped basil. Philip cut the flatbread into small wedges. We helped ourselves and walked to the outside deck.

Val stretched back to tighten the band on his braided hair and then sat with Grace on the cushioned glider. Philip chose his favorite rocking chair. It appeared a family ritual had been established. Since my brother's marriage, they'd claimed the same seats at each visit to my home. Penny, on the other hand, was as unpredictable as her age dictated. This time she perched with crossed legs on a barstool. I imagined she was imitating a pose she'd seen in a magazine and I had to stifle a giggle. Grace was struggling with the same impulse.

"Were your client visits successful?" Philip said, wiping his generous lips with a paper napkin.

"They were. I really didn't know what to expect, so I'm relieved. I'd allowed too much time to pass without visiting them," I said.

"You've been lucky in your business. Neglect doesn't usually reap success. You might not be so lucky with Tom." Val's jaw clenched.

"Val, please," Grace said. "We're having a family get together. You and Nora can have a talk another time."

"It's okay," I said. "Maybe you'd think differently, Val, if I told you why I plan to be in New York the week before Tom goes back to school."

I told them about my visit to Deanna Sardis in Paradise, about her struggle with breast cancer and the possibility she'd cancel her special event.

"Her son's capable and there are volunteers in the town who help each year, but the rugs are a financial burden for her right now. I can help with that and I might not need to be there for the entire week," I looked squarely at Val to make sure he got my point. His light green eyes narrowed.

"What's Carlos say?" Philip said.

"Yeah, that's what I want to know." Val's voice leaped out.

"It'll be a family undertaking. We'll work out the plans when I get to Ankara. In fact, he told me he has an idea, an Islamic idea. Isn't that curious?"

"That makes no sense at all." Val was getting a rosy glow on his cheeks and neck. I'd seen it before when he was ready to blow.

"Carlos always makes sense, Val, and I want to hear what he has in mind. We'll decide what's best for our family. Do I tell you and Grace what to do with Penny or how to run your lives?" I glanced at Grace who was looking at Penny. She had slipped off the stool and was standing wide-eyed.

"Nora, Penny and I will help you get dinner on the table," Grace said, getting up from the glider. She placed a hand on each of our backs and not so gently guided us into the kitchen. "Can you set the table, sweetheart?" she said to Penny.

Grace reached into the drawer, where she knew I kept the flatware, and began counting out the needed pieces and handing them to Penny.

"Grace," I said, as soon as Penny's ruffles disappeared into the dining room, "you need to talk to Val and tell him to back off."

"I'll do no such thing. I do plan to tell him to monitor his outbursts when our daughter is in the room, but what he says to you or anyone else is his business."

"Don't tell me you agree with him?"

"It doesn't matter if I agree or don't agree."

"I'm asking. Do you think I'm making a mistake to help Deanna?"

"It sounds like a great kindness, but you and I both know that's not the whole picture."

"You mean Tom and the fact that he's going into middle school. You think I should be home with him? I'm not so sure he'd welcome my help."

"We're not talking right and wrong here. It's for you, Carlos and Tom to figure out."

Penny reentered the kitchen. "I think I did it right. Want to see?"

Grace and I followed her into the dining room. She'd taken a small flower arrangement from a table in the den and placed it in the center of the table. Each utensil had been set in the proper position.

"Beautiful job," I said.

Grace had closed me down and it hurt. It had taken years for me to discuss problems with anybody, and it was Grace who helped me to understand my reluctance was a protective device. Even if she disagreed, Grace could clarify an issue by looking at every option. She'd always helped me to understand the impact of my choices. For a second I wondered if Val had turned her against me. But Grace would never allow that. I followed her back to the deck to finish our drinks and appetizer.

During dinner I mentioned we'd be looking for a house in Turkey. Philip immediately offered to help with the move and any renovation that might be needed. From the time he was old enough to hold a screwdriver Philip had been fascinated with fixing things. He rushed to watch whenever repairs took place in our home, and by the time he was a teen he willingly tried his hand at plumbing, electrical wiring, and woodworking— although not always with perfect results. I caught Val raising his eyebrows at Philip's offer. He was probably biting his tongue with the effort not to mention Philip's missteps and general sloppiness. Val and Philip, despite their differences, were good friends, although secretly I believed Philip's agreeable nature kept the peace. I loved them both...most of the time.

In a quiet space between conversations, I asked Grace to come up to my bedroom to see a Christmas surprise.

"Trying to avoid the rush?" Grace said.

When we reached the bedroom, I closed the door. "You know me better than that. I love the last minute madness. I wanted your opinion about the festival thing. My relationship with Tom is still not where I'd like it to be and I'd really like your help," I said.

"You'll always have my help."

"But I'm asking you what you think, as a psychologist."

"I don't know what you remember about our sessions, but I never gave you my opinion. My job was to help you find your own solution. That's what I'm doing now. Nothing has changed in the way I believe problems are worked out. I involve the parties who will be impacted by the decisions. That's it. Period."

Her smile softened the words, and even if her words were unsatisfying I envied her ability to cut through to what mattered.

"My experience is that life's never that simple," I said.

"It's got nothing to do with how complicated things are. The process doesn't change."

She'd dropped the smile and looked at me wide-eyed. There was frustration behind her eyes, and I felt like a child being told something for the hundredth time.

The next day I stopped by the office to say goodbye to Ed. He assured me he was set for the summer. No surprise there. As I got ready to leave the office, he pulled out a tablet from his desk drawer.

"I thought this might help with the festival," he said.

It was a list of rugs from our inventory he felt would be appropriate for inside the tent. I ran my eyes down the column.

- Six large-pattern Holbein rugs, Çanakkale region
- Three Gördes prayer rugs, floral border, hanging lamp in center field
- Five Caucasus runners, indigo field with red, yellow, light blue overlay
- Two Chinese wool in amber and dark blue, ivory fringe
- Eight square "yatak," sleeping rugs, various colors, patterns
- Six Kurdish rugs, bright colors
- Two Persian silk to hang, 5' x 7' each

"This is perfect. How'd you know what kinds of rugs would sell at this event? You've never been there."

"Well, you always described what types sold. I just used that information to make the list. The only thing I wasn't sure of was the exact number you'd need. Are the two Persians overkill?"

"Not if we want to make their tongues hang out."

It must have taken hours for him to examine the considerable inventory in our warehouse.

"You've nailed it. Great mix here. This'll help me work up an estimate of our total costs too. Thanks, Ed, you've saved Carlos and me a lot of work. I appreciate it. In fact, would you like to go this year?"

"I'd really like that," he said, looking away. I'd never noticed that Ed was an especially emotional man, nor had he ever seemed shy, but he was both at that moment.

I got home mid-afternoon, grabbed a bottle of water from the refrigerator and headed upstairs to my bedroom to finish the packing I'd started with Carlos days ago. In the interim, both Carlos and Tom added items they'd forgotten. I opened the closet to rummage through the suitcases, finally choosing a duffle with wheels. As I dropped it on the bed, the front door chime sounded. I found the Denbys lined up on the doorstep.

"We were out for a walk and remembered you're leaving tomorrow, right?" Jack said, pushing back his baseball cap to rub his matted, gray-streaked russet hair.

"Come on in. You're saving me a trip to your house. I was just starting to look at what I need to take. Want some lemonade?"

"Got any cookies?" Marty said. It was a joke between Tom's best friend and me. Carolyn made cookies several times each week, while I rarely had sweets of any kind in the house. He pulled a Ziploc bag of cookies from his back and held them up.

Marty had inherited his mother's humor and her unflappable nature. It was one of the reasons he was able to weather my son's moods. Any number of times I'd watched him change Tom's perspective with his sly, intuitive remarks. Carolyn often did the same for me.

"Yeah, I just happen to have cookies," I responded, taking the bag.

Carolyn, who knew my cupboards as well as I, gathered four large glasses, while I lifted a pitcher of lemonade from the refrigerator. Jack took over the task of setting out a plate for the cookies. When I next looked at Marty, he had finished one cookie and was reaching for another.

"We've been talking about our visit," Jack said, "and we've worked out an itinerary. There's so much to see, but... What we want to tell you is we think we'll fly straight to Ankara and really do a thorough job of exploring the capital," Carolyn said.

Marty asked if he could have more lemonade, but Carolyn shot him a look that made him withdraw his glass.

"Are you saying you don't plan to travel beyond Ankara?" I said.

"Ankara's the best of everything, isn't it? Atatürk's tomb, the Ethnological Museum, and all that," Jack answered.

"It's a beautiful, modern city, but hardly typical of the rest of Turkey. In many ways, Turkey's more diverse than any country I can think of. Cappadocia, to give you just one example, is unique. When you see those still-lived-in homes that were carved in the lava rock in 1400 BC, you'll think you're on another planet."

Marty's eyes lit up. "Yeah, I saw pictures. It looks like the moon."

"I can't believe you'd fly all the way to Turkey and skip Istanbul, the Aegean and Mediterranean Coasts, the hot springs of Pamukkale, the whirling dervishes in Konya. Why would you *do* that?"

"Okay, it's because of me," Carolyn looked at Marty and then at Jack before she turned back to me. "I'm afraid. Turkey is so close to the war in Iraq; it's dangerous," she said. She felt like a spoiler and the pain showed.

"You're watching too much TV news," I said. "Sure there are problems, but show me a place on the globe with no problems and I'll show you a spot nobody wants to go."

"Don't make light of it. There was a horrible bombing at an outdoor café in Istanbul just last week. And another in Antalya. Isn't that the town on the Mediterranean you recommended?"

"Yes. But the media is only showing you one geographic area. Everywhere else it's business as usual. Do you think for a minute Carlos and I would be thinking of buying a home in Turkey if it wasn't safe?

"I want you to talk to Carlos," I said, checking the cat-face clock on the wall. "Nine hours ahead of us. If he's home, he'll be reading the evening paper just about now." I dialed.

A woman answered. I was so surprised for a moment I didn't recognize Tapis' voice. She explained they'd brought Tom home and decided to have dinner together. I could hear laughter in the background and felt a tinge of jealousy.

"Give everyone my love, Tapis. I'm packing my suitcases now. Be with you soon. Can I speak to Tom or Carlos?"

"Yes, yes, we are eager to have you with us," she said. "Wait a moment."

While I waited for Carlos, I covered the mouthpiece. "Tom's been staying with Carlos' sister and her husband. Now that he's back with Carlos we might get to talk to him." I hadn't intended to sound sarcastic, but I did.

"Can Carlos call you in an hour? We are just sitting to eat," Tapis said.

"Well, I—" The line was disconnected. "Carlos'll call as soon as they finish dinner," I said. My cheeks burned.

Carolyn's eyes reflected the hurt that was surely showing in mine. I might believe that Tom would put me off, but never Carlos. If the phone didn't ring in exactly an hour, I'd call again. Tapis had just handed me another stone for the wall that was growing between us.

The Denbys left with my promise to call on the way to the airport to say goodbye and hopefully to hear they'd changed their minds about an Ankara-only visit to Turkey. I set my watch alarm for one hour and returned to the bedroom to resume packing. But I'd hardly gotten back on track with the sorting when the phone rang. It was Carlos.

"I'm so sorry. Tapis assumed I would prefer hot food to you. I have made it very clear I do not."

"That's good to hear. I miss you all so much. Can't wait to be with you. Is Elena—"

"Is she here? Yes, in the living room with the others. I'm in the bedroom. Noisy bunch. When we learned that Tapis had hung up without telling us you were on the line, Ana made her disapproval very clear. And you know how well she can do that."

"I'd have to use my imagination."

I set aside the dress I'd been holding and walked to the bedroom lounge, wanting to keep his voice in my ear for as long as possible. I missed Elena and made a mental note to remember to call her *Ana*, mother, as Carlos did. She gave me something my brothers never could—a woman's intuitiveness perhaps, but I suspected it was more. Elena occupied a spot I imagined my mother would have filled if she'd lived. There wasn't anything I couldn't discuss with her. And, like Carlos, she demonstrated her love even when we differed, fortunately not very often.

"My sister's changing. It worries us."

I'd never shared my discomfort with Carlos, but I was sure he sensed it. I hoped that spending more time with Tapis during the summers would have drawn us closer, but that hadn't happened.

"Changing? How?"

"Ana says her Christian friends are complaining because she doesn't return their calls."

"Maybe she's spending more time with Muslim women."

"Guess that's possible. Anyway, she loves spending time with Tom." "She needs to get her own friends.

"By the way, Carolyn and Jack stopped by and told me they're getting cold feet. They're imagining terrorists everywhere. They're thinking they'll fly directly to Ankara and restrict themselves to the capital. Wouldn't that be a shame?"

"Yes. They need to be here to see that we are as safe as anyone these days."

"Just what I told them. Call them tomorrow, won't you? I know Marty wants to see the country almost as much as he wants to see Tom."

My thoughts snapped back to Tom and Tapis the instant I hung up. How the heck did Tom get so close to Tapis in such a short time? He didn't make friends easily. There was Marty since kindergarten, then Penny since Val married Grace, and now in a little more than a week he's bosom buddies with Tapis?

8

Dozens of bobbing dark heads were gathered in a clump at the end of the airport corridor, but I knew better than to seek Carlos among them. As much as he enjoyed people, he disliked crowds. Sure enough, I spotted him against the wall. He'd seen me first and was just waiting for our eyes to meet. No sign of Tom. I quickened my steps toward Carlos' open arms. Snug inside his embrace, I kissed the curve of his neck and breathed in his spicy aftershave.

"Were you successful?" he said.

"Very. Wait'll you hear."

"Later. We're not alone." He tossed his head up. I turned around to see Tom, Elena, Tapis and Mehmet.

"Oh, I feel like a celebrity," I said.

"Our celebrity. Welcome to your second home." My mother-in-law was beaming.

Tom stood to the side with his arm around Tapis' shoulder. I knew that vision would be burned into my memory and be the first to reappear when I had a quiet moment.

"I've got a surprise for you back at the apartment," Tom said. He looked really happy. I hoped it was partly because I'd arrived.

"I love surprises, especially from you. Let's go," I said, giving Tapis and Mehmet quick hugs and, I hoped, a sincere smile.

We walked together to the parking garage. Tom held his *Nine's*, his grandmother's, hand while she held a lively conversation with Tapis and Mehmet—something about *kofte*, meatballs. Carlos and I fell behind, unwilling to let go of each other.

"Now that I'm with you I don't know how I could've let you leave without me," I said.

"I felt that before we left."

"You think it was easy for me?"

"Let's just say I'm happier when we're together."

"Me, too," I said. He squeezed my hand, but didn't look convinced.

Tom blocked our way when we got to the apartment door. "Mom, you're gonna know the surprise the minute the door's opened." He pushed the door with a flourish.

"Roasted lamb?" I said, sifting through the aromas that entered the hall. "You made a lamb roast?"

"And more. But the real surprise is I made it myself," Tom said. Tapis jabbed him from behind. "Well, Aunt Tapis helped a little."

"I'm speechless. Just let me freshen up a bit and I'll be right with you. A chef in just ten days, I can't believe it."

At dinner I found myself wishing my brothers could witness my new family enjoying the meal Tom had prepared.

"I like it here more and more," Tom said. He retrieved a piece of meat with his tongue.

Val and Philip should hear that one, too, especially when they start bellyaching about the Middle East.

"Tell me what you like?" I said.

He seemed flustered by my question and took time to look around the table and finally down at his lap where he mumbled "lots of stuff" and finally "I just do, that's all."

"Maybe because it's becoming more familiar and you've made some new friends," Carlos said.

"Yeah." Seconds later he blurted, "Nobody else I know has an American family and a Turkish family." He smiled and looked at Tapis. "Mom, Nine says we've got a pirate in our history."

"Not exactly," Elena said, laughing. "What I said was one of my brothers was a sea captain. You decided to make him a pirate."

"A vivid imagination at work," I said. "And, along those lines, the dinner was great. Those slivers of lemon rind in the sauce: yum. I've never done that, but I will from now on."

"That was my idea," he said, giving Tapis a smug glance to which she responded with raised eyebrows.

I rose to clear away the dinner plates and as I reached across Elena to take hers she touched my arm. "Carlos tells me you will be looking for a house during this trip."

"We could use more space." Turning to Tom, I added, "Have you and Dad talked about this yet?"

"Can we get a swimming pool?"

"A pool? I don't know, Tom, I—" His face fell. "We can talk about it, okay?"

I left them comparing houses to condominiums. My ears stayed tuned until Tapis joined me in the kitchen. "I guess cooking's one thing but cleaning up is still woman's work," I said.

"Yes, it is so in my home. But I rather like the time to myself. Let the men speak of their concerns alone and the women of theirs," she said. Her voice was strident, letting me know once again how she felt about the separate roles for men and women in a Muslim home.

"Thanks for spending time with Tom. It's obvious how much fun he's had. Was Mehmet able to take Tom to his office as he planned?"

"Oh, yes, they are great pals now." She gathered a handful of knives, forks and spoons, looked carefully at each, and set them one by one into the dishwasher's utensil basket. Her movements were precise and graceful—a dance with dishware. "Tom makes us eager for our own children."

"We all look forward to that, Tapis."

We walked back into the dining room where Mehmet was offering Realtors' names, Elena was telling Carlos which neighborhoods might be best, and Carlos was suggesting a less direct approach. "Tomorrow, for starters, I'd just like to drive around a bit."

"I want to be able to walk to your home, so please don't consider anything too far away," she said.

I looked at Carlos.

"Funny you should bring that up, Ana," he said. "Tell her what we're thinking, Nora."

"Oh, okay," I said. "Would you consider making your home with us? It would make us very happy." I shot a quick look at Tapis and Mehmet and then back to Elena.

Her face rippled with emotion and for a moment I thought it might have been better to ask her when we were alone.

Carlos reached for her hand. "Think about it for awhile. It's not a decision you need to make now. What do you think about the idea, Tapis?"

I gripped the edges of my chair. My sister-in-law's face never changed. She nodded to Mehmet, which I translated as her wish for him to respond.

"It is a decision for you to make. Of course, our home is yours also," he said. Tapis sat with her head bowed, hands in her lap. Only her rapid breathing betrayed her feelings.

I got up to get coffee for everyone, and when the mugs were lined up on a tray, I invited everyone into the den where we'd be more comfortable, a condition I knew would take more than softer upholstery for me.

The sound of conversation continued around me but I hid behind sips of coffee, too tired to engage. Several times I glanced at Elena, who hadn't spoken since Carlos asked his question. When I yawned and excused myself, Mehmet rose and said it was time to leave.

He put his arms around Tom. "I will miss your company. And your cooking, of course," he said, winking.

"I hope our house will be close to yours so I can visit," Tom said.

"Distance can't separate us, Tom. We're family," Mehmet said.

"That's true," I said, looking at Tapis. "Let's cook another dinner together soon so Tom won't get rusty." She nodded.

When they left, Carlos and I walked to the kitchen and Tom turned down the hall to his bedroom. Carlos stopped him.

"Hey, Tom, your mom's beat. How about showing her how men can clean up the dishes in half the time women can?"

I watched Tom swagger back to the kitchen. He had a smirk on his face and had puffed out his chest—so much better than a jutting chin.

As I walked to the bedroom, I doubted a hot bath could erase the night's undercurrent. The more I thought about it, the more I marveled at Carlos' approach to inviting Elena to live with us. Was it his basic openness or his courage to face potential problems head on? I decided it didn't matter as long as it got results.

An hour later Carlos sat on the edge of the bed where I was brushing my hair.

"Tom's calling a friend to cancel a date so he can go with us tomorrow." He took the brush from my hand, pulling the bristles from my scalp to the ends, slowly, the way he knew I liked it. But the relaxation lasted only a moment.

"Are you disappointed I chose to stay behind to visit clients? I had the feeling you wanted to say more at the airport earlier," I said.

"It can wait 'til tomorrow."

I turned to look at his face. "I'll sleep better if I know things are good between us."

"I'd rather wait. Let me show you a more enjoyable way to relax." He untied my robe, moved me to my feet and kissed my breasts. Seconds later I'd forgotten how tired I was; I forgot everything but the rising passion.

I woke in the morning to the aroma of freshly brewed coffee. Carlos' side of the bed was empty and cool to the touch. The drapery was pulled aside and the room was bright with sunlight. The colors in our bedroom came to life in the added illumination: deep saffron walls, golden carved oak furnishings, and rust-colored asters blooming on the upholstered chairs and bed comforter.

Thanks to Elena I had a table crowded with pictures of our blended families. A heavily embroidered cloth covered the table, a wedding gift from her. She had created a pattern of designs taken from Turkish rugs, which must have taken hours to research and blueprint long before the threads were worked. It was the kind of gift I imagined my mother would have given me if she'd lived. At my insistence, Elena stitched her name and the date on the cloth to ensure its authenticity as a family heirloom.

I walked to the open window and looked out over the gardens around the building while I slipped into my robe. The landscapers were adding flowers to the ever-changing array of colors, lifting out the fading blooms and replacing them with others. Faded purple and orange flowers were being replaced by pink, white and blue. But not only were the workers changing the colors, they also were reshaping the pattern of the garden. I was transfixed. What had been rectangular patches were now curving waves of alternating colors.

My first visit to Ankara was with Muharrem. He wanted me to meet "a man I highly recommend to be your Turkish contact for antique Oriental rugs." I remembered stepping from the elevator and losing my composure when I looked into Carlos' eyes. They were the color of the sky in autumn, rare in a country dominated by brown and green. In truth, the only other memory of that day was our walk in the garden below, where I began having feelings I'd considered buried forever.

"Nora?"

I jumped at the sound of Carlos' voice. "Come see," I said. "Do you remember our first walk in that garden?"

"I remember learning yellow roses were your favorite."

He gave me a squeeze. We walked down the hall, passing Tom's closed door and continuing to the kitchen where two mugs of steaming coffee waited on the breakfast room table. Carlos had covered it with a bright red cloth thickly satin-stitched with white daisies, green leaves and tiny lily of the valley—another piece of Elena's handiwork. It worked well with the square white porcelain dishes.

"Now," he said, looking at me earnestly. "You asked if I had more to say at the airport and I did. When we left Philadelphia, Tom was disrespectful to you. It wasn't the first time and I know you wanted me to step in."

"It was like you didn't care. He hurts me in so many ways and you say nothing." It was hard to breathe.

"I can't fix what's between you two. What I've seen since we married is that you and Tom share little more than space together. You're not...I'm not sure how to explain it. You're not in tune with each other."

"You mean that business about helping Deanna and Tom entering middle school? It's not going to be a problem. I know Tom," I said.

"That's just the most recent example. From my perspective, neither one of you really knows the other."

I stared while his words, his unbelievable words, sank in. Surely he'd seen the changes in Tom. Yes, occasionally a smart mouth, but I couldn't remember the last time Tom exploded in anger because he didn't get his way. Our home was a far more peaceful place, or as peaceful as one could hope with a twelve year old and his friends. I told Carlos this in a tone I hoped concealed my irritation.

"Peace? You're smarter than that, Nora. He's older, out with his friends. No, it's not peace you want. It's love, a show of affection like what you saw at the airport."

I set the coffee mug down and walked into the living room, stopping suddenly at the threshold. Beneath my feet, the rug's thick pile held the footprints of last night's family gathering. As a child I played a game of identifying our family members by their imprints in the carpet. I sat on the floor and let the tears come. It was one thing to accept your child didn't love you and another to stop wanting it.

"It hurts to say such things to you," he said, sitting next to me. He placed his arm around my shoulders. "You're warm and loving with me, but something gets in the way with Tom. I've seen it over and over again.

"In the last few weeks I've watched how eager he was to spend time with Tapis and Mehmet. They, how do you say it? They got into him immediately. You see the results. When was the last time you took time to do anything with Tom?"

Something rustled and we turned around to see Tom in the doorway.

"What're you doing on the floor?" he said.

I sat up and leaned back against the sofa, unable to speak, not knowing what I could say if words did come.

Carlos patted the floor next to us in answer to Tom's bewildered expression.

"Your mom wants the same close relationship you've developed with Tapis and Mehmet. She wants you to know how that makes her feel."

My heart was pounding in my ears. I looked from Carlos to Tom and back again. The words were like a jackhammer chipping away at a wall inside my head. Now he was handing me the jackhammer.

"Carlos? I can't."

"You can. You know what you want and Tom needs to hear it."

Tom moved to get up. "That's okay, I don't."

Carlos reached out and grasped his arm.

"It's true. I don't understand you, Tom. I've taken care of you, worried about you, put up with your anger. I love you. Then I saw you with your arm around Tapis and I wanted to scream. When did you ever show me that you loved me?"

How could he just sit there looking at me? I instantly regretted letting my guard down. I'd opened myself up to another rejection. I tried to stand, but Carlos restrained me.

"Tom?"

"This is a big, fat waste of time," he said, starting to get up.

The tips of Carlos' ears were a shade of red I'd never seen before.

"Sit down. I'm getting sick of watching the two of you treat each other like, like strangers, sometimes like enemies. Why is that?" he said.

"Because she's never wanted to be around me," he said. His chin was projected so far he had to look down his nose to see me.

I wasn't going to respond to such a preposterous statement. I folded my arms, reciting to myself the times I'd spent with him: dinners and outings with the Denbys, and the time I took him with me to Turkey after Jared's death.

"Maybe I was too busy doing things *for* you I didn't have time to do things *with* you. Should I apologize for that?"

He jumped to his feet. "How 'bout the time you took me to that boarding school because you were too busy opening up your fancy gallery. Uncle Val said I could've stayed with him, but you didn't even ask."

"It was the best boarding school on the East Coast, for God's sake. I wanted you to have the best education. I did it because I was working day and night," I said.

"I hated that place and you didn't care." A vein pulsed on his forehead and his lips began to quiver. Seconds later I watched his back as he walked away. And Carlos let him.

"I did care," I said, when Tom's bedroom door slammed. It was the worst nightmare of my life. I didn't want to think about it, but the scene appeared: The rescue worker climbing into the cave, the waiting and waiting for her to emerge. Finally, all spotlights were on Tom. He was safe, but I learned later he hadn't wanted to be rescued. "I swear to you, as soon as I found out he didn't like the school, I brought him home.

"We're never going to be close. You'll have to accept it just like I have."

"I won't accept it. I don't understand how you can," he said. His whole body sagged. It struck me that for the first time in his life he was confronted by a problem he couldn't fix.

"You said it yourself, Tom is changing and we need patience. Your relationship with him is fine. Maybe in time he'll come around."

"No, Nora, that's not good enough. Tom's capable of great compassion and affection. Why not for you?"

The sadness had gone from his expression and in its place was a look I'd seen only once before, one I hoped never to see again. It was early in our relationship, when we were falling in love. Without any warning the police picked me up and locked me in a prison cell at Izmir Buca Prison. They said it was for selling a fraudulent rug, a rug Carlos sold me. Officially, they said I had "offended Turkishness." I almost died before the American Embassy secured my release, but not before I began to believe Carlos had set me up. I was terribly wrong. A gang of forgers were responsible. But Carlos was horrified I could think such a thing. I almost lost him then because of his intense feelings of loyalty.

"Do you think for one minute I want the distance that's developed between us? Tom's pushed me away for years and I've come to accept it because it hurts too much to keep trying," I said.

Carlos shook his head, left me sitting on the floor, and I heard him go into Tom's room. I went to our bedroom and dressed. Tom's door was still closed when I passed it. Their voices were animated, alternating, discussing something, but I couldn't make out the words. Back in the kitchen I jotted a note: "Went for a walk in the gardens."

The gardeners were still working on the flowerbeds, arms swiveling from flats of flowers to the turned earth. "Very beautiful," I said in Turkish.

One of the men stepped out of the group, removed his cap and walked toward me. Even before he reached me I decided he was the head gardener. His was the only uniform without a smear of brown earth.

"Mrs. Ghazerian, what is your favorite color of flower, please?" He spoke in English, taking me back six years to my first visit to the apartment complex when I met Carlos and his family. I was amazed that day when the elevator attendant welcomed me in English. The staff had been alerted to expect an American and to greet her in her native language. I'd always meant to tell the apartment manager how impressed I was, but never did.

"Yellow," I said.

He turned to one of the men who took a pot of yellow daisies, wiped the surface clean, and handed it to the foreman.

"Like the sunshine, yes? We are grateful you appreciate our work," he said, presenting it with a bow.

"*Teşekkür ederim*, thank you," I said. Turning away, I came face to face with Carlos.

"Can I walk with you? I've had a long talk with Tom and I want to tell you what he said."

"That's a first: Tom sharing his thoughts and feelings. Lucky you."

"Just a lot of angry stuff, pretty much what you've already heard. Listen, there are two things I've learned about you: You like independence and control. You may think you've made every possible effort, but he's still reacting from Jared's abuse and your absorption in your work." He swallowed. "It's not all your fault. You've gone through hell, but you can't give up."

Two couples were approaching from the opposite direction. As they passed I surveyed the flowers, the clouds, and the surrounding buildings.

"What if he never learns to love me? I'm really afraid that's how it's always going to be."

He took the flowerpot from me, placed it on the bench and took my hands. "Promise me you'll keep trying."

I nodded, not because I suddenly knew what to do, but because I wasn't the only one who wanted my son to love me.

The lack of it was eating away at my husband's emotional base: family. He walked back to the apartment, moving from the sunlight into shade. When he disappeared inside, a large white cloud spread its shade over the bench and with it came a soft breeze that raised goose bumps on my forearms. I watched the leaves quiver on the tree branches above and heard the lower branches answer with a low hiss. The flowers leaned lightly in unison to one side and the other before settling with their petals open to the sky, and the air got heavy with their fragrance.

I closed my eyes. For the first time since our marriage, I felt alone. Carlos reminded me I valued independence and that was true, but I didn't want to be alone. I wanted us to be the family Carlos described, the kind I'd had as a child, the kind he had with Elena and Tapis.

I'd been trying since Tom was an infant but he always pushed me away. In more ways than I could count, he'd made it clear he didn't need me for anything. How could he tell Carlos *I* didn't want to be with *him*? And why didn't Carlos stand up for me? I fought with these questions until I understood the answers would solve nothing. Carlos had already told me I couldn't give up. And something more was growing in my thoughts: I was going to lose more than my son if I did.

9

Carlos and Tom were laughing in the kitchen when I returned. Without letting them see me, I went to the bathroom, washed my face with cold water, and combed my hair. When the redness around my eyes faded, I slipped into the kitchen.

"Juice?" Carlos said. "Tom and I were just about to have some."

"No. Okay, maybe just a little." I pointed at the pitcher of juice Carlos was still holding. "Tom, I'm sorry, really sorry. Baderwood's an excellent school, but my timing was too soon after your dad's death. Sending you was a horrible mistake. Your Aunt Grace helped me to see that. Remember she was Baderwood's counselor before she married your Uncle Val? I was scared. I used my business as a refuge, I guess."

Carlos reached over to touch my arm. Tom was staring into his cereal bowl. Now what? Couldn't he say something, anything? "I'm sorry if I made you think I didn't want you around. It's not true; it was never true."

It would have been nice to hear him say he believed me, or he understood, or it was okay. But he didn't and I wanted to shake him. "You don't know what it's like to be alone and responsible for a child," I said.

He lifted his head, giving me the full blare of his steely eyes. "Uncle Val and Uncle Philip wanted me. They told me I could stay with them. But then I would've been too close. Another state was waaaay better."

"That's not fair. Your uncles have their own lives and their business to run. I don't believe in dumping my problems. I don't mean *you* were a problem. It's just that they think they need to take care of me all the time."

"Yeah, you sure took care of me. I sure felt the love." Tom choked and ran from the room.

Carlos stared at the floor. I knew I'd made a mess of things. I wanted to run to my own bedroom, but my feet froze in place. "I've made things worse, haven't I? I wanted him to see that I meant to do the right thing. Help him understand why I sent him to Baderwood. He wasn't the only one who was hurting, you know."

"I'm beginning to see there's a lot I don't know," Carlos said. "But I'm sure about one thing: He's a kid and you're an adult. As hard as it is to accept, you're responsible."

"Oh, God, I can't listen to anymore." I couldn't get out of the room fast enough.

I collapsed on the bed, hearing *You're responsible* again and again. Finally, I turned to face the ceiling and swiped at my face. I'd already accepted the blame. I'd apologized. I'd explained. I took a deep breath and accepted the only option left: Tom needed proof.

Four hours had passed, evidenced by the bedside clock and a dark, wet stain on the bedspread. I circled the bed and considered how to make it impossible for Tom to say I didn't want him around—ever, ever again. And Carlos. What had he said? *I can't fix this. It's your problem.* I felt ready to tell him he was right.

I found him in the living room, pacing. When he saw me, he opened his arms.

"I can see that Tom needs proof that I love him, and I'm going to do my best. It's not too late, is it?"

He couldn't answer, but he tightened his grip.

The apartment's dining area had west-facing windows which gave us a good view of approaching weather fronts. Carlos and

I were watching black clouds gathering and tree branches bending when a flash of lightening and an ear-splitting crack shook the building. Tom came running from his room.

"Wow. That was close. See any fire?" he said, pressing his face to the window.

I caught Carlos' eye and he shrugged. Tom got over his anger almost as quickly as Turkey's storms flared and fizzled.

"Let's get dinner started," Carlos said, "and I'll tell you about an idea I have to help your friend Deanna."

"Huh?" Tom said.

"Oh, that's right, you haven't heard about the Festival of a Thousand and One Nights," I said. I told him about the event and my client Deanna Sardis' illness. "I want to help her but it's the week before you start middle school," I said. "How do you feel about that?"

"What's it got to do with me?" he said. "I can take care of myself, if that's what you're afraid of."

It was the reaction I predicted, the one I told Carlos to expect. "Well," I said, "I know you can handle things without me, but—"

"You're right. I can," he said, pushing out his jaw in the way he knew irritated me. I felt the conversation was going as it always did: ugly and ultimately unresolved, Tom here and me there. But something struck me. Why hadn't it occurred to me to invite Tom and Carlos? I opened my mouth, but Carlos interrupted.

"Fix yourself some cereal, Tom. I've been thinking about this event and Deanna's problem and I want to explain an Islamic tradition that will put a different twist on our involvement," Carlos said.

Did he say "our involvement?" I retreated to the countertop, poured myself a cup of coffee, chose a thick slice of wheat bread, and placed it in the toaster. While I waited for it to pop, Tom and Carlos carried refilled cereal bowls to the table and sat down. With everything else that had happened since I arrived, I'd forgotten about Carlos' mysterious "Islamic idea." Tom, I saw, hadn't lifted his spoon.

"It's called a *hayir*, a charity," Carlos began slowly. "Islam encourages its followers to watch for opportunities to do deeds that will change someone's life for the better. That's what you want to do for Deanna, right? Let's do it as a family," Carlos said.

"Yeah. A hayir. Aunt Tapis told me about that."

Was Tapis going to be part of everything from now on?

"It will take sacrifice," Carlos continued.

"How come you know so much about Islam?" I regretted the edginess but I still felt irritated about Tapis' elevated status with Tom. There were enough problems between me and my son without Tapis trying to play mother.

"But I see where you're going. A hayir. Interesting." I buttered my toast.

"But there's more," he said. "The rugs must be a gift. Our only remuneration is to make the festival successful for her."

I swallowed, calculating $100,000, probably much more, for enough rugs and kilim pillows to fill the tent.

"Yeah," Tom said, "that's really cool. I have some money saved."

"What about school?" I said.

"What about it? Where'd you say this lady lives?"

"Paradise, New York. About four hours north of Philadelphia. You're forgetting something. What about clothes, school supplies, the orientation program you'd miss?" I said.

"I've been to that school already and I don't care about clothes or school supplies. That's your hang-up," he said.

"Not true. I'm the one who said you could handle everything yourself, remember?" My tone was light and Tom rewarded me with a laugh.

The clouds were breaking up, moving off, and making way for a full moon. Thunder still rumbled in the distance, but the storm had passed.

We were clearing up the messy table when Elena called to ask if we'd contacted a Realtor. When I told her we'd decided to begin by surveying neighborhoods, she sounded relieved. She explained she'd spent the morning calling friends and learned of an available home nearby.

"The house is not listed, which may be an advantage to you, if you are interested," she said. "Please don't think I wish to interfere. It must be your decision."

Carlos took the phone when I relayed her message. "Ana, we want your help. It's not interference. Come with us. Tom's coming."

"Oh, well then, of course. I'll be ready and waiting downstairs outside the lobby entrance."

The car filled with Elena's flowery scent. Her thick silver hair was twisted high and held with an ebony ornament. She was suggesting that we drive south to "a very quiet but convenient neighborhood."

"Left or right?" Carlos said when we reached a major crossroad.

"Oh, eh, left," she said, stretching to look down both streets. "Not much farther now," she added, still swiveling her head.

She led us through several more turns, hesitating at each cross street. "Ana, did you bring the address? Carlos can use the map, if you're not sure."

"Nonsense, I've walked to this house dozens of times."

But when we stopped where she expected the house to be, she was silent and looked perplexed. She rummaged in her handbag for a small address book, found the address, and gave it to Carlos. We had strayed several streets from the destination. Moments later we parked in front of a free standing, two-story home. I blinked at the pink-painted masonry.

"Yes, this is it," Elena said, happily. "The Sursoks are waiting to show you the interior."

I looked at Carlos who startled me with a wink. "Ana, you are galloping so far ahead of us, I hardly know what to say."

"Is there a swimming pool?" Tom said.

Carlos upended his palms. The pink masonry rendered me speechless. Tom, though, was out of the car, opening the front gate, and heading for the front door.

As Elena rang the doorbell, I glanced around a stone courtyard that began as a walkway to the front door and continued to wrap around the side of the house. A seven-foot wall draped with bougainvillea provided shade and privacy from the street. Very nice.

The owners greeted Elena as a friend, bowed to us, and welcomed us "in God's name" to their home. They immediately excused themselves and said we should take our time looking at the house. They were going to the market and said if we finished looking before they returned, we must lock the door behind us.

Elena admitted she knew the couple very well. "They are members of my church, but their children live in Izmir and they want to be closer," she said. "Already they have told me they want you to have their house because it is less than one kilometer from my apartment."

"It doesn't have a pool," Tom said, returning from the back of the house.

My reaction to the pink exterior began fading when I saw the polished wood floors and spacious sunlit rooms. Carlos reached for my hand. He looked like he was pleased, too.

"There's room for a swimming pool, I think," Tom said.

We all walked through the dining room to French doors that Tom had left open. Before going outside with the others, I detoured through the kitchen. The equipment appeared to be basic, but mainly I wanted to see if there was room for a small table and four chairs. Better than that, I saw a round table with six chairs set in a bay overlooking the back garden.

Outside, Tom was pacing off the space he thought could be used for a pool. It wouldn't leave room for much else, although when I walked along the back of the house there was a vegetable garden that could be removed to make way for an adequate sitting area, a place to read a book or have a quiet conversation. Given our schedule, raising food wasn't high on my list.

The second floor opened to a wide hall, four bedrooms and one bathroom. Although the bathroom was large, I was disappointed not to find a bedroom with a private bath. Then I silently chided myself remembering that five of my family members shared one small bathroom when I was growing up.

"I know the room I want," Tom shouted. His head poked out into the hall and I walked to see.

"Okay," I said, "but don't you want to look at the others before you decide?"

"This window faces east," he said, gazing out.

Later we dropped Elena and Tom off at the apartment building. Carlos wanted to visit his office and I wanted to have some time alone to talk with him about the house. We went to the office first.

The complex occupied a full city block. There were three warehouses and an office building defining the outer edges. We drove into the center of the compound, a parking area where uniformed men were loading rolls of rugs into a large white van. Ghazerian's Oriental Rugs appeared in crimson Turkish script on the sides, underlined with a flying carpet— professional, but with a whimsical touch.

Carlos rolled down the car window. "Huseyin."

One of the men jogged to him. A right-side chest patch, a miniature of the van's design, identified him as the fleet foreman, a considerable responsibility judging from the dozens of large and small vehicles parked against the buildings.

After a quick nod to me, Huseyin spoke in rapid Turkish. "We are delivering the rugs to the new condominium building."

"Good. How does the sample look? Not just the rugs—the furniture and accessories too."

"Mehlika has done a fine job, I think, but I don't know much about such things."

Huseyin continued to nod in my direction. I nodded back, thinking he wanted to be sure I was included in the conversation. Actually, I was understanding just enough to keep up.

"Thank you, Huseyin. Maybe we'll stop to take a look on the way home," Carlos said. "By the way, you and I will celebrate an anniversary this week. Do you remember?"

"I do. Twenty years today. My family and I are most grateful."

"We're the grateful ones."

Huseyin showed off a set of oversized white teeth beneath his dark mustache before he walked back to his task.

We pulled into an open space. "That man acknowledges every employee's birthday. He's a one-man morale officer for my business."

"Will there be a cake?" I said.

"No, that's Western tradition. Huseyin just thanks Allah for their life and the blessing they are to him."

I laughed. "Wow, wouldn't that disappoint American kids who've been conditioned to expect not just cake but gifts and a party?"

"Exactly what Islam wants to avoid," Carlos said.

Once inside the office I made myself busy looking at photos of Ankara on the walls, while Carlos spoke with his secretary and signed some papers. Ten minutes later he was ready to go.

"I'd like to see those condominiums, if you've got time," he said.

"Yeah, I'd love that. I didn't know you got involved in decorating models," I said.

"This is the first time. I struck a deal with the building's owner because it seemed to be a good way to show what our rugs could do for the residences. So far we've had many inquiries and some sales to new residents, as you see by this delivery."

"What kind of deal?"

"His office now has a beautiful Turkish rug in the large-pattern Holbein style. He loves it."

"Of course he does. And Mehlika?" I said, giving him a sideways glance.

"Ah, Mehlika." He laughed. "She is the daughter of Ana's neighbor, a young girl with excellent taste."

"Ah, Melika?" I said. "Yes, you bet I want to see, especially now."

"A little jealous, are you?"

The condominium was a seven-story, Moorish-styled building with high arched windows and an inner courtyard surrounded by a shaded portico. We took the elevator to the seventh floor and walked along a wide, thickly carpeted hall to room seven hundred thirty-four. My eyes lingered on the door number. It had been inset using a contrasting wood. In fact, the door itself seemed to be constructed with several kinds of wood and looked like a piece of art. I glanced at the door on the other side of the corridor. It too had been put together with a variety of woods but in a different pattern.

I was fascinated but my interest shifted immediately to the young woman who answered our first knock. She looked like a teenager, barely over five feet, with long flowing blonde hair, large brown eyes, and a bit more makeup than Turkish women of any age. She greeted me and then quickly stepped aside so we could look at the room. I walked across the threshold and got a second eye-opener.

Two walls warmed with the color of black coffee, two ivory walls cooled and softened with subtle multicolored fabric hangings. Oversized pieces of ironwood furniture covered in ivory canvas fanned out in a semicircle facing a stone fireplace. The overall effect was bold, yet not overpowering. It took me several minutes to figure out how she'd accomplished this.

"Do you like this living space?" she asked, in excellent English. "I have heard about your gallery from Carlos. He says you have given it a unique style. This is what I want to do. Of course, I have more ideas for those who are not drawn to this décor, but I wanted to make a strong statement and show a fearless approach in creating a special ambience. I would like to know what you think."

Each word she spoke had its own space, until I could almost see them marching in a line from her red lips to my ears. Except for that, which was probably the result of infrequent use, Mehlika's vocabulary and pronounciation were excellent.

"I'm impressed with the boldness and intrigued by the way you've tempered it with the details."

Carlos had walked away, perhaps to free Mehlika to express herself without him in the room.

"Oh, you understand. It is so gratifying." She threw up her hands. "The rooms are large so I have used large pieces of furniture and I wanted them supported by a dramatic floor covering. When I saw this Tibetan Tiger rug, I felt it had the power I was looking for to hold down— No , no, no, to *anchor* the room. This is the correct word, yes?"

"Yes." The tiger's face was presented head-on in the Chinese manner, its charcoal tail curled around a center field of amber. Two narrow borders of geometric patterns, one wider than the other, surrounded the center and they in turn were bordered by a wide band of lotus blossoms and vines. "I like the large black ceramic pots you've placed around the room. The pale grasses in them are a nice contrast to the hard surfaces," I said.

"The pots are Absolute Black Granite, quarried in India," she said. "The polish is awesome, don't you think?"

I nodded. She reminded me of myself, working as a high school student at Sam Bezdikian's Oriental rug gallery. I remember absorbing every detail so I could impress everybody with my knowledge. It was only later I understood the impossibility of mastering the art of Oriental rugs; it was an unattainable goal.   Over the centuries, mystery, myth, and folklore had shrouded their evolution.   "I think this room reflects skill and creativity, Mehlika. You've done an excellent job here."

Carlos joined us in time to hear my praise. "I agree. If you have time tomorrow, please come to my office and we'll discuss some ideas I've been considering."

"I have ideas too," she said. "We can look forward to many more relationships with condominiums and new apartments."

"Of course," Carlos said.

He'd placed his hand in the middle of my back and was adding light pressure. We left Mehlika with a bright blush on her young face and returned to the car.

"Your schools do a really fine job of teaching English."

"I expected you to ask about her blonde hair. She gets it from her Swedish father who was born in Pittsburgh, Pennsylvania. He came to Turkey twenty years ago to do an engineering job with an American company, met and fell in love with a Turkish woman, and never returned to the U.S. When Mehlika was born he spoke to her in English and his wife spoke Turkish. I applaud their decision, don't you? Already it has given her an employment advantage."

"Absolutely. I'm happy Tom's learning Turkish for the same reason."

Shortly after we turned onto the main road, we found a café and stopped for tea and talk. Lunch traffic had dwindled, waiters were setting up tables for the evening crowd, and two young boys were sweeping the colorful, highly polished terrazzo on the outdoor patio. We chose a small, round glass-top table along the outer edge and Carlos ordered mint tea.

"I could be sitting in New York City," I said.

"Do you feel so at home in Ankara?"

Our tea arrived. Poured from high above my glass, it filled the air with its fresh herbal fragrance.

"Yeah, Tom, too. It'll be more so when we have our own house. What did you think of the house we saw?"

We recited the house's features as we remembered them. Except for the pink exterior and lack of a master bath, I agreed the house had everything we needed or the potential for it. My earlier need to look further had vanished.

"Good." He whipped out a piece of paper and a pen from inside his jacket and we began to list the changes we wanted to make.

"I'll call the Sursocks tomorrow to find out if they have a timetable for vacating," Carlos said. "That is, if you're sure."

"Let's talk it over with Ana and Tom first," I said.

That brought a big smile to Carlos' face.

Our cups were empty and I started to rise when Carlos touched my hand. "The deadline for that exclusive showing at Istanbul's Museum of Art is in five days. I must let them know who'll attend."

"The 500 BC silk Chinese? Oh, absolutely, I'd love to see it. And did you say Tom was interested?"

The waiter returned to refill our cups, but Carlos declined and asked for the check.

"Yes, but it was just a casual conversation. I'm not sure he understands what's involved. When we get home, talk to him, if you want him to join us, that is."

I wanted him. I just hoped I wasn't setting myself up for heartbreak again. "I want to spend as much time with him as possible, but, an antique rug? What're the chances he'll be interested?"

Carlos glanced at the check the waiter brought, placed some bills on the table, and we walked through the café to our car.

"You're a saleswoman. Convince him. If nothing else he'll get the message you want to spend time with him."

That warmed me more than the tea.

The shadows of Ankara's high-rise buildings stretched across the boulevard, striping it alternately with waning sunlight. When we turned west, the glare was blinding and Carlos pulled into a parking lot to let the sun move below the horizon.

"Beautiful, isn't it?" he said. But I was thinking of how to make a trip to an art museum enticing to a twelve year old brought up on video game action and raucous soccer games.

Tom wasn't home but he'd left a note he was upstairs with his grandmother.

"This is perfect. Let's go up and discuss the house with both of them together. If the conversation goes the way I hope it will, I'll use it to segue into the exhibit in Istanbul," I said.

"Something up your sleeve?"

"Maybe."

He grabbed my hand.

Normally we walked up the four flights of stairs to Ana's apartment, but Carlos pulled me into the elevator that was open at our floor. He answered my startled expression with a kiss.

"This is going to work," he said. He closed the elevator door and we rode to the top floor.

I wanted to believe him, but past experiences with Tom were rushing at me as fast as the floors were receding below us. His blue eyes could change instantly to cold gray, hurling my memory back to his father's demanding, manipulative tirades. I was never able to stand against him, and unfortunately Tom had witnessed my weakness, learning as a small child to use the same tactics to get his way. Carlos squeezed my hand as we walked the corridor toward Ana's apartment.

My mother-in-law got right to the point when we asked her and Tom how they felt about the house we'd seen. "We have talked of nothing else since you dropped us off. It's your decision, of course, but we think it's perfect," she said, looking at Tom.

Tom brought up the lack of a swimming pool.

"Let's be practical," Carlos said. "A pool requires upkeep. Who will do that when we're in Philadelphia?"

"One of my friends would do it," Tom said.

"Now, that's a creative possibility I hadn't thought of," I said. "You'll use it more than the rest of us so that'd be a nice tradeoff. It's your project to work on."

"No problem."

"I'd agree if the parents would be responsible for oversight," Carlos added.

"Nine, you'll live with us, won't you?" Tom said.

She blinked several times and worked her lips. "I don't know. You are kind to want me with you, but...I must think. I have been on my own for many years. I don't know."

"It's what we all want, Ana," Carlos said. "While we are renovating, would you consider a small, private apartment near or attached to the house? There's enough space, if we eliminate some of the garden area. Perhaps a separate entrance? You would be on your own from September through May." He looked at me, struggling for something more convincing to say. "The Americans call it 'a happy medium.' Something in between, yes?"

Tom raised his arms, calling us all to attention. "If you were living in our house, Nine, you could make sure somebody is watching the pool."

Elena smiled, but her eyes didn't.

10

The decision to buy the Sursoks' home slid to the finish line like a sled on ice—exciting, fun, and somewhat out of control. There was, it seemed, a quick solution to every imagined shortcoming. I knew I was hooked when I began picturing myself cooking in the kitchen, watching Tom swimming in the pool with his friends, sitting at the kitchen table having tea, and making love with Carlos in the quiet of our bedroom. I looked across the table at Tom and Carlos, deep in discussion about who among his Turkish friends would be the best candidate for pool maintenance.

"Do you know these kids," I said to Carlos.

"Some. A few live in this apartment building. I know their parents. The other boys are neighbors of Tapis and Mehmet."

"Invite them over sometime so I can meet them," I said. I got a nod from Tom.

I sipped coffee and watched the two most important people in my world. Physically, they had the same deep blue eyes and dark curly hair, though Tom had inherited Jared's fair Irish skin and tall, lean body, while Carlos was broad and muscular, with skin the color of creamed coffee.

I set my mug down, took a deep breath.

"Tom, Dad's been invited to Istanbul for the showing of a rare Chinese rug. I'd like you to go with us," I said.

"I don't think so."

"That's because you don't know enough about it to be interested," I said. "In fact you don't know much about Oriental rugs, period."

"Don't know and not interested."

"I was just thinking that since you want to be part of the hayir in Paradise, this special showing would make you more knowledgeable, more able to make a positive impact on the outcome of the sales." He looked up and I pressed my point.

"You'd have fun telling people about what you learn, and after the museum showing we could take in the sights. Bet you'd like the Roman cistern. It's a huge underground water storage space that still has water in it. They don't need it for water any more, but the acoustics are fabulous and they hold concerts there."

"I agree with your mother. It'd be fun."

"The underground cistern sounds different," Tom said.

Carlos clapped his hands together. "So, can I tell the event chairwoman there will be three of us?"

"Okay."

A trickle of perspiration ran down my back as Tom left us to call Marty.

Two weeks later, as the sun was setting, we boarded the historic Orient Express overnight train to Istanbul. The cars, gleaming white with blue and red stripes along the sides, filled the platform left and right as far as I could see. A small sinewy man in a cocky black cap scooped up our three pieces of luggage like they were paper bags and stomped down the train's interior corridor ahead of us, while a uniformed porter asked us to follow him to our compartment. We stood outside while our luggage was lifted to an overhead shelf.

When we traded places with the porter—a necessity as much as a courtesy—and Carlos closed the door, Tom said, "My clothes closet is bigger than this."

The train lurched and started moving. People stood on the platform waving. We waved back until we were out of the station, pivoting around each other, taking in the large window, the two facing upholstered seats, and the carpet's blue geometric pattern.

"Not bad. We've got a tiny sink with hot and cold water," Carlos said. "Here's a small refrigerator for the snacks I packed," I added.

"Where's the bathroom?" Tom said, opening a narrow closet door and closing it again.

At that point we picked up a brochure on the sink top. It described the train's features, noting in particular that bathrooms were located at the end of each car, one on the left with a raised Western-style toilet, one on the right with elephant's feet.

"Whoa, elephant's feet?" Tom said. He ran out of the cabin and we stepped out behind him.

"Tom's about to see another difference between East and West," Carlos said. "Let's keep walking to the front of the train. There might not be much to see but I'd prefer it to sitting in that small compartment."

We caught up with Tom at the end of the corridor.

"There's a hole and two round spots on the floor where you're supposed to put your feet. I'm not using that," he said, pointing to the Eastern-style toilet as we passed.

By the time we reached the third car, traffic in the corridor was becoming heavier, but curiosity drove us onward through a dining car to a lounge. We sat and ordered tea and a Turka Coke for Tom. His eyes were jumping from one passenger to another. Most people, like in Ankara, were in Western clothing. But here and there women wore headscarves and long gray coats, and men wore baggy cotton pants and long-sleeved tunics. We watched the intermittent lights, probably small villages, zip by, until Tom yawned. I elbowed Carlos and suggested we head back to our compartment.

It had been transformed in our absence. Bunk beds were made up on one side and a single bed, under the luggage rack, on the other. Lightweight blankets, each distinctly patterned and colored, covered the bunks. We pulled down our luggage and in no time the beds were covered with clothing. I backed into Carlos, he elbowed Tom, and somebody—I couldn't see who—slapped me in the face with a piece of underwear. I started to giggle. Within seconds we were laughing hysterically. Finally, we made trips to the bathroom of our choice: Tom and I took turns with the Western style; Carlos chose the Eastern. When we were settled, Carlos turned off the bedside light, but seconds later a bright light high up on the wall came on.

"Oh, I forgot to tell you. Turks don't like to sleep in the dark," Carlos said, laughing so hard he struggled for breath.

"You're joking," I said.

"Yep," he said. "I must have accidentally turned it on. Just the same, you two need to stay alert to cultural differences."

"That's cool, Dad."

"Don't encourage him," I said.

At Istanbul's Haydarpasa Station on the Asian side of the ancient city, we hailed a taxi and requested a tour rather than heading straight to our hotel on the European side of Istanbul. Carlos asked the driver if he would be willing to spend the day with us. Bright shining eyes responded. We'd shunned the train's dining car and our first stop was an outdoor café where we had a large breakfast, and by early afternoon we were headed across the Bosphorus estuary to Istanbul's European side to see the historic sites, places I'd never explored because Muharrem always hustled me off to the small rural villages to buy rugs.

"I want to go there," Tom said, pointing to a large mosque.

"Really?" I said.

"We've got time and that's the famous Blue Mosque," Carlos said, asking the driver to turn the car in the direction leading to the entrance.

"What time is it?" Tom said, leaning out the open window of the car to look up and down the streets. "Maybe we can see the prayer time. It's awesome."

Carlos began to recite the special features of the mosque's architecture, especially the blue tile covered interior.

"I'm not interested in the tiles, but I'd like to see them praying together like they do at Uncle Mehmet's mosque."

Carlos checked his watch and said the next prayer session was hours away. Tom flopped back into his seat and said we could go if we wanted to but he wasn't interested. I exchanged glances with Carlos who shrugged. The driver turned the car around.

By the time we pulled up at the hotel's entrance, we had just enough time to get ready for the museum's black tie event. Carlos whistled when I unpacked a floor length, red crepe de chin gown, the one I'd worn to my gallery's grand opening.

"How do you expect me to keep my eyes on the Chinese Silk?"

"Whoa," Tom said.

Carlos unzipped a suit bag and handed Tom a tux. I knew they'd rented formal attire in Ankara and I was eager to see how they looked. Tom gave me a shy look and carried his suitcase and the tux into an adjoining bedroom.

In less than an hour Tom made a self-conscious return to our room.

"Whoa, to you, too. You should wear a tux all the time," I said.

"It feels funny," he said, but I noticed he couldn't take his eyes from his image in the mirror.

At eight o'clock a cab dropped us off at the museum. We followed the crowd to the main auditorium, aptly named Treasures of the Silk Road for the array of hanging antique carpets. Only ten tables of ten were arranged in a semicircle around a small curtained stage. A scant one hundred people from all of Turkey? Clearly we were part of a very select group. Before we had time to find seats, Samed Maklu, the museum's curator, walked toward us. He was well over six feet, lean, and elegant. He extended a manicured hand to Carlos, acknowledged me, and motioned to a waiter who sounded a brass gong. The people standing and milling around turned to face us. Had they been waiting for us to arrive?

"Welcome, welcome to your family. How is your mother, Rachel, is it?" the curator said.

"Elena. Rachel is her middle name and she is well, thank you."

"She was involved with children, as I recall. We rarely saw her. I pray she is still blessing the young ones with her kindness and expertise."

"She is very well. You have a good audience tonight," Carlos said.

With that his voice rose to take in the whole room. "Your father's handprint is everywhere in these rooms and corridors. It's sad the acquisitions he struggled to include were not considered significant at the time. Only later was his genius acknowledged. During his administration he filled in the periods in which cultural shifts impacted the arts. By doing so he brought together artisans who might never have been included."

As he spoke, he rotated his body in a semicircle and his voice rose to reach beyond our small family group. After introductions Mr. Maklu escorted us to a table in the center of the semicircle. The chairs and tables were covered in ivory damask. In the center of each table was a black vase of white Calla Lilies. I stole a glance at Tom. He was trying hard to look relaxed, but was failing. I reached for his hand, squeezed, and gave him a smile.

"I'm surprised too," I whispered. Maybe more surprised he didn't yank his hand away. "How are you doing with the Turkish?" He gave me a thumbs up sign.

As dinner progressed, many of the guests came to shake hands with Carlos, and when there was a lull, I asked him if he'd expected the attention.

"Next week is the anniversary of my father's death. He worked closely with a few of these men. Ana and I hear from them on each anniversary. It's how they honor his work to preserve our culture."

"Nice." I leaned toward Tom to pass on what I'd learned.

The house lights dimmed and the room filled with a silence so solid it was like being inside a vault after the door closed. Mr. Maklu walked to the center of a spotlight on the right side of the darkened stage.

"In 1950 rumors of a silk rug, carbon dated to the fifth century before Jesus Christ, trickled out. The world has waited more than fifty-five years for the owners to share its remarkable discovery, and it is a testimony to the respect and reputation of Istanbul's Museum of Art that we are among the privileged few included in its international tour. It will not surprise you to learn that years of secrecy have spawned a story. Listen."

The spotlight closed and opened again on the opposite side where it illuminated a boy about Tom's age seated with a book on his lap. His voice cut clear with an edge of wonder.

"Long ago in a misted valley, all living things were governed by two powerful dragons. Thorn was dark like a moonless sky; Shimmer was the color of honey. Flavorful fruits hung heavy from the trees, nuts sprinkled thick on the forest floor, and fish finned smoothly in deep lakes.

"Peace lay upon the valley, until the day Shimmer flashed red eyes and spewed a stream of orange fire high into the air, flaunting her might in a way she'd never done before. Thorn, along with others from sky and thicket, watched her hold three gray rabbits beneath her craggy claw, all the while smiling at their fear. His patience could no longer hold him and he thundered to her side.

"'Shimmer, enough! Let them go.'

"'How will they know I can protect them if they don't feel my power? You have grown weak, Thorn.'

"He swirled his bulk forward to within inches of her head. 'Weak?'

"Distracted now, Shimmer lifted her claw from the ensnared rabbits and turned her head, one black eye staring, red iris spreading. 'Yes. Look around you, Thorn. What you see is respect and obedience.' She raised her spiked tail to strike.

"'What I see is fear. It must end.

"'Tomorrow,' said Thorn, 'at first light, all living things will gather to watch us battle. If I win, you will enter the ocean and swim until you seek the depths to sleep.'

"Shimmer hissed. She shot her fire into the air without bothering to answer and walked away to her sleeping place in the forest. But, in the night, while she slept, all the living things conspired. Tigers, fox, squirrels, moles, boars, bears and insects joined together. They gouged and scraped a wide, deep trench around her and filled it with water and sea creatures. As a final effort, a blue bird gently lifted a centipede from the forest floor and dropped it next to Shimmer. Then all the living things retreated to the trees to wait, among them the three gray rabbits, peeking beneath the legs of a black wolf.

"The centipede explored its new space. When it reached Shimmer's armored body, it proceeded to climb until Shimmer woke with a start. A brightly feathered starling flew in and gently lifted the centipede to safety while Shimmer thrashed, knocking the earth into the trench until she slipped into the water. Quickly and efficiently eels, crabs, squid and fish lashed her body with roots, vines and weeds. On land the creatures moved to the edge of the moat and watched until the last bubble burst and the water stilled.

"When the sun rose, the three gray rabbits scampered to Thorn to tell him all living things had answered the challenge. And from that day peace returned to the hearts of all who lived in the valley."

The boy closed the book. Mr. Maklu joined him on the stage and shared the blue light.

"Ladies and Gentlemen, Shimmer and Thorn have returned, not only to confirm that evil will always threaten, but also that we live with the hope good will prevail."

The stage curtains opened to reveal the Chinese silk. I was aware that a spotlight had been trained on the rug, but the glow seemed somehow to project outward. We were bathed in its luminescence. Two dragons—one honey colored, the other charcoal—coiled on a dark amber field, facing each other from opposing ends. Green and black vines and yellow chrysanthemums were sprinkled throughout the background, and in one corner, wrapped around a vine, was a small black centipede.

I'd had a picture in my mind of the rug since Carlos first mentioned it, but I wasn't prepared for the real thing. Thousands of hand woven rugs had passed through my life, and I knew each one possessed a special quality if you were willing to look deeply enough. Still, these dragons startled me. I felt they were looking at us, searching for something or someone.

The lights in the room came up and we were invited to look closer. The guests pushed back their chairs, lined up single file, and climbed the steps. We took our places. Except for the soft rustle of moving bodies, no one spoke until everyone had returned from the stage. Even then, voices were hushed. Tom, I noticed, was busy taking in everything and everyone. I was sure he was infected, as we all were, with the magic in the air.

When it was my turn to face the dragons, I was awestruck by the weaver's skill. The colors had been carefully chosen to give each dragon dimension. Their heads thrust forward from their bodies, their eyes even more so. Those red eyes were not passive; they looked back. It might have been frightening, but the effect was one of—it felt like longing, like love.

Tom, arms behind his head, sprawled across the hotel bed after we returned. His bowtie, jacket, and shoes were scattered around the room.

"I wish my grandfather was still around. Nine showed me pictures of him, but she didn't tell me about the rugs and stuff at the museum. I could tell the people really respected him," he said.

"My father would have enjoyed spending time with you. He was passionate about our country and its culture and could have taught you a lot." Carlos put his tux on a hanger and placed it in the suit bag. He did the same with Tom's.

"Yeah. But what's the deal with that rug?" he said. "I get that it's old and everything, but looking at it turned the people into zombies."

I looked at Carlos, but his only reaction was to raise his eyebrows.

"The 'zombies' were just showing their respect. Oriental rugs aren't just floor covering, they're symbols," I said. I'd already decided not to share my own reaction to the Chinese silk, but I didn't think I'd ever forget it.

"That's weird. Symbols of what?" He unbuttoned his shirt and propped himself against the headboard.

I looked again at Carlos. He knew about my special feelings for the rugs, but he didn't look ready to jump in.

"When I was a little girl, our house was full of hand woven Oriental rugs that my parents had received from their parents. I played on them and made up stories about them. So, symbols of family and happy times."

Carlos put his arm around me. "Don't forget those rugs put lamb roasts on our table. Your Nine's too. And, in some parts of Turkey, whole villages work on them. It's been their life for centuries."

"Well, I think they're to walk on."

"We'll probably go to a weaving village when the Denbys visit," Carlos said.

"Yeah, that would be cool. Marty's never seen anything like that in his life."

Tom hadn't either, but I didn't want to dampen his spirit by reminding him. He bounced off the bed.

"There are lots of stories about Oriental rugs just like the one you heard tonight. People like to hear them," I said.

He didn't have to respond. If I knew Tom, he'd be on the Internet looking up every Oriental rug site he could find as soon as we got back to Ankara. He said "good night," and closed the door to his room.

"Let's go down to the hotel's lounge. I'm too excited to sleep," I said.

When he agreed, I called through the door to tell Tom where we were going.

We found a corner table as far away from the television set as possible and ordered mint tea. There was a soccer game in progress and a group of young men were clustered together in loud support for one of the teams. If we'd been in the U.S., beer would have been part of the picture, but we were in Istanbul and I saw orange soda.

"How do you think things are going with Tom?" I said.

My question got lost as a little girl ran past, quickly followed by an older boy. Her tiny legs were pumping furiously although it was obvious she hadn't been walking very long. She squealed happily. Her father appeared and scooped her up and walked off—a family of six altogether.

"I always thought I'd have a large family," Carlos said, staring after them.

"You've never mentioned it."

He turned his head to look at me. "It seemed to me you have enough to deal with."

"You mean with Tom?"

"Well, don't you?"

"I'm doing my best."

He reached across, took my hand and gave it a gentle tug. We left the lobby and walked back to our room. I lay awake replaying Carlos' comment about having a large family. I'd never used birth control and Tom didn't come along until Jared and I'd been married for three years. Pregnancy seemed an anomaly for me. The Chestnut Street Persian Gallery became my baby.

11

At breakfast on our second day back in Ankara, Carlos had a long telephone conversation with a construction company owner, a man Mehlika recommended for the house reconstruction work. She said she'd met him at the condominium and was impressed with his skill and dependability, a priority for us since we'd be out of the country while he and his crew worked. It appeared I wasn't going to need my work clothes after all.

The best news was the exterior could be blasted the day after we signed the deed. We'd be able to see the results before we returned to the States. Construction projects, on the other hand, would take several months after final plans were drawn up, possibly not before mid-August.

"What about the pool? Can't they do that first so we can use it?" Tom said.

"Sorry." Carlos squeezed his shoulder, but Tom's face held onto its frown. When the phone rang, Tom grabbed for it, and walked away talking to Marty.

"Don't bother bringing your bathing suit," he said. "What do you mean, you don't care?" He listened for another moment before handing the phone to me. I reminded him there were other places to swim. He shrugged.

Carolyn was on the line. "We're more excited every day. It's only a week away and we've started packing. Marty just told Tom he can't wait to go swimming in the Aegean. He's been reading the brochures and they say you can see big fish swimming deep in the water."

Poor Tom, he'd wanted to hear Marty's disappointment so he could add it to his own. "Me, too," I said. "Wait'll you see the color of the water. It's the most beautiful shade of turquoise."

Carlos had been successful in calming Carolyn's fears. She said they'd made the decision to fly into Istanbul and then take the overnight train – at our suggestion – to Ankara. It would be fun to hear their reaction to elephant feet toilets. They'd spend a few days with us before we left together for Cappadocia, Antalya on the Mediterranean, the Aegean coastline, Izmir, Ephesus, and Troy. We'd be exhausted by then, and I suggested a couple of days at a thermal spa before dropping them off in Istanbul to catch their return flight.

"Should I go to a Turkish bath?" she said.

"Sure. There's an 800-year-old Roman bath in Antalya, south of here, and we'll be there overnight. Go for it, if you want to get beat up," I said.

"They use hard water?"

I chuckled. "Let's just say once was enough for me."

"Now I'm intrigued."

Jack took his turn, changing the subject to our house plans. I heard Carlos assure him that by the time they arrived most of the plans would be in place. Then he grimaced. "Tools?"

I could almost see Carolyn rolling her eyes. If Jack was advising Carlos about house repairs, I'd have to divulge what I knew. Like the time Jack insisted all it took to replace the water heater was to detach one water line and one electrical connection. The next thing we knew water from their basement door was running the length of our block of houses. Jack was clever as a problem solver, but as soon as a project passed from idea to process, chaos ensued until a professional was called in.

When the conversation ended, Carlos left for work and I cleared away the breakfast dishes, conscious of my own rising excitement. Carlos and I had already been to all of Turkey's unique sites at one time or another, but our visits coincided with business. This was a chance to see these special places through the eyes of first timers.

I was eager, too, for Tom to keep up his friendship with Marty. They'd been together since first grade, and Marty's flexibility and good-natured personality were good for Tom. His new Turkish friends had no track record with our family.

Carlos and I had already divided our responsibilities for their visit. He'd handle the travel plans, including making reservations at hotels. For me, there were menus to prepare, groceries to buy, and sleeping arrangements to figure out. That afternoon when I asked Tom if they could use his bedroom, he raised his voice for the first time in months.

"No way. All my stuff's in my room."

"We've got a two-bedroom apartment. Where would you suggest Marty's parents sleep?"

No answer.

"Let's look at what you'll need and we'll work it out. You can set up a tent in the living room if you like and create a place just for you and Marty. Wouldn't you like that?"

"Since when do you care what I want?" He turned to go.

"Don't be nasty with me, Tom. These are your friends and I'm asking you to share your room. It's a sacrifice, yes, but they'll appreciate it. And I'd appreciate it if you'd give me a break.

"Well, what's it going to be?" I said. He didn't look at me, but his posture projected the old anger. He walked out of the room and seconds later the apartment door slammed.

"Fine," I said to no one, "that means *I* decide what goes into the living room."

I'd purchased three large plastic tubs—one each for Tom and Marty's clothing and one for books, games, and other miscellaneous "necessities."

When I went into the closet to fill Tom's clothing bin, a rug I'd never seen before toppled over my feet. It was wool, approximately three-by-five feet...a prayer rug with the head and shoulder motif.

I carried it out into the room to have a closer look and saw the price tag still attached. Wondering what other surprises I'd find, I glanced up and saw a black arrow on the ceiling. It pointed—I opened the window to confirm—east.   This was more than mere curiosity. Was Tom practicing Islam?

My first impulse was to call Carlos, but what would I say? *Our son has a prayer rug and an arrow on the ceiling.* My second thought chilled. Had Tapis and Mehmet initiated Tom into Islam? Clearing out Tom's bedroom had lost its appeal, and I dropped the plastic tub I was holding and walked to the kitchen.

A quick glance at the wall clock reminded me Carlos would be home soon. I put on the kettle for tea and backed into the counter for support while I waited. When Carlos got home a few minutes later, I was still standing in the same position.

"Did you know Tom is practicing Islam? He has a prayer rug in his room and an arrow pointing to Mecca on the ceiling. Your sister has turned our son into a Muslim."

Carlos took several steps backwards and the silence grew heavy. Finally I asked him what he thought.

"I think you're accusing my sister before you know what you're talking about."

"It's obvious. Why else would he have a prayer rug?"

Carlos shook his head and leaned against the counter. His fists were balled. I'd seen him frustrated from time to time, but never really angry.

"This is ridiculous. You sound like being a Christian means something to you—not something I've ever observed. That's fine with me. Attending repetitious church services week after week has no appeal to me. But if it turns out that Tom is interested in a religious life and it makes him happy, why should you care?"

I was about to answer but he wasn't finished.

"Here's the main thing: I'm offended you think my sister, of all people, would try to influence Tom. You don't know what you're talking about. It wasn't easy for her to convert to Islam. Before she fell in love with Mehmet, she and Ana were very involved in the church." He stopped abruptly. "Where's Tom now?"

"Ana's apartment? I'm not sure. We were getting his room ready for Carolyn and Jack and he became angry and left."

"What did he say?"

"About the rug? He'd already left when I found it in his closet. For some reason he didn't want to give up his room for Carolyn and Jack. I don't know why."

"A simple sleeping arrangement and you turn it into a confrontation about Islam. Let's get some answers." He reached for the wall phone. "I'll see if he's—"

"No, don't. We'll only argue and I'm trying hard to keep our relationship on good terms," I said. I sounded ridiculous and knew it. The whole situation was making me angry. Tom's selfishness. Carlos' attitude. Did I count at all? I used the sleeve of my blouse to wipe my face.

He replaced the phone and pressed his lips together. "Look, I'm curious to know if he's interested in Islam. But, frankly, I'm more interested in why this is making you angry to the point of accusing my sister."

"You're not upset? This doesn't bother you? It's okay with you if our son becomes a Muslim?"

"Tapis is happy."

"But you said she's changed. I don't want my son to change. I mean I want changes that bring him closer to us not move him farther away. That's what I'm working on. Seems like I'm working alone."

We heard the apartment door and saw Tom. He walked toward us.

"Nine said I was wrong to leave you with all the work. I'm sorry. I'll help you put my stuff together," he said. "I think Marty would like your tent idea in the living room. Can we get a tent today?"

"Tent?" Carlos scratched his head and threw his hands up. "I've been gone for a few hours and it's like I've walked back into an alternative universe."

Tom and I explained and as we did my heart's normal beat returned.

"It's okay, Tom, it wasn't that much work. I've put together almost everything I think you'll need, but you should check your room just in case I forgot anything," I said. "But before you do, I want to ask you a question."

Tom waited. Carlos folded his arms across his chest and leaned against the counter. I fingered the napkin holder, suddenly conscious of my heartbeat accelerating again.

"I'm curious," I said. "Are you—"

"I know. I shouldn't have gotten mad and I'm sorry I yelled. Marty's mom and dad can have my room."

I shook my head. "Okay, apology accepted. I understand that your room is your private place. You have your things where you want them and I was messing things up. That's not what I mean. I found a prayer rug in your closet and I noticed the arrow pointing east on your bedroom ceiling. Are you practicing Islam?"

He pulled himself up, out came his chin, and the blue leeched from his eyes. "See, that's what I mean."

"What're you talking about?" I said.

"You. Always asking questions. Poking around in my stuff. I have no rights. You don't care what I think. You think you can make every decision for me. That's wrong. I'm not a baby." His face was red and he was rocking back and forth like he was getting ready to sprint.

"I'm confused. You say you're not a baby. Well, you're not an adult either. Adults talk about things. We make decisions together. We compromise. I don't see you doing that. You keep things to yourself and that makes it hard for everybody."

Carlos held up his hands. "We're just surprised, that's all. You hadn't said anything to us."

"Prayer's private. I don't want to talk about it," he said. His chin receded but there was an edge to his voice, a slight taunt.

"Prayer, yes, but a change of religion is a major thing. It's something your dad and I would want to know about." I glanced quickly at Carlos. Tom followed my eyes. If he saw anything there, he was keener than I.

"Do you want to be a Muslim?" Carlos said.

"Imam Aboud gave me a Qur'an and some prayers to recite. He said Allah would call to me and I would know if I want to be a follower."

I ground my teeth. If I'd asked the question, it would have been an accusation. From Carlos, it was interest. Carlos moved to the table, pulled out the chairs, and asked if I'd make tea. I was glad for the activity, but not too distracted to miss that Carlos had situated himself across from Tom and was smiling. Tom smiled back. Was I included in the relaxation of tension or was I still the outsider, the one who turned everything into confrontation, as Carlos said? The kettle whistled. I poured the hot water over tea leaves in the teapot and by the time I set three mugs on the table, it was ready to pour.

"Tell us how you got interested," Carlos prompted.

Tom said he was spending a Friday afternoon with Tapis and Mehmet when they heard the call to prayer from the mosque near their home. Mehmet asked if he wanted to go to see.

"It was exciting. The men came running from every direction on the street. When they got inside, they formed lines facing east and began saying their prayers together. They stood up and knelt and put their heads to the floor over and over again in unison. Mehmet said I could follow along or just watch, but I wanted to do it. I kept up with them too, but I didn't know the words. That's why I've been practicing, so I'll be ready the next time."

"So you plan to go again?" I said. "And you didn't think we should know?"

"I told you. It's a private thing."

We exchanged glances but there didn't seem to be anything more to say.

Carlos got up. "Thanks for telling us, Tom. If this is important to you, it's important to us. Will you remember that and keep us up to date on your interest?"

"Yeah, okay. Can we get the tent now?"

12

The Bazaar At Erzurum, Asia Minor

Attendants quickly unloaded Sütlü and took her to a stall where she was fed and watered. Çatal was escorted to an upper level to a small but adequate room where he could safely leave his wares and spread his fleece to sleep. But sleep would come later. Çatal wanted to walk among the people, see the booths stacked high with goods, and smell the food, even if the breezes added the sharp sweat of animals and men.

To Çatal's delight, the town was celebrating Sacaea, an ancient Roman festival celebrated between the seasons of planting and harvest. Doors and windows were decorated with greenery—vines stripped from the forest—and Çatal had heard that work, grudges, and quarrels were suspended in favor of dancing and gift giving. These things alone were a pleasant relief from the monotony of village life. But Çatal had heard of other things: carefree sex, lascivious language, and drunkenness. Such outrageous rumors were unimpeded by distance or mountain trails and had spread in whispers even to his remote village between the snowcapped mountains and the Black Sea.

When darkness replaced the sun, hundreds of flickering lights from lamps and candles lit the corridors between the tangles of fabric and hide-covered tents. Blankets heaped with the produce of farmers, carpenters, artists, and metal workers formed an arc around each stall. The voices of the sellers, cawing like ravens, filled the air already saturated with dust and the smoke from flaming braziers.

Çatal's stomach clenched at the smell of cooked meat. He reached inside his tunic for his pouch of coins and chose a skewer of lamb and vegetables sprinkled with cardamom, coriander, and salt. Almost instantly a child's hand shot out and Çatal dropped three coins into its greasy recess.

Flutes and drums started up and Çatal was swept up in the crowd. He pushed forward, holding his skewer aloft, and was just in time to observe—and this he found strangely titillating—a parade of men dressed as women and others in various costumes. Could he clothe himself in something different, something shocking? Could he stare into his neighbors' eyes and not care what they thought? He felt light and detached and, at the same time, strangely connected to those around him.

When the parade passed, he continued among the vendors with meat juices trickling down his face and disappearing into his beard. The music and merriment made him giddy. Lights were brighter, colors more vibrant, smells sharper. Finally, at the outer edge of the raging commerce, he stopped to look out at the black night beyond. He imagined the quiet there. It fascinated him, pulled him like the temptation to step off an edge and soar. But something fluttered lightly against his arm and, imagining the wings of an insect, he slapped it away. Instead, his hand landed on warm brown skin.

Çatal froze, allowing his eyes to prove the vision—first the patch of skin at her hip, then her round belly, then her breasts with wine-colored nipples bulging beneath a diaphanous cloth. He shot to her eyes and felt himself stiffen. Her face was uncovered and her eyes were close set, black and lidded. Golden discs dangled from a band woven through a dark wreath of tightly curled hair that reached to her shoulders. She sought his hand and pulled him into the darkness. He could not see where they walked but her steps were steady and sure. With her free hand, she reached across and touched him. "Just a few coins," she breathed.

She pulled aside the flap of a hide-covered hut and Çatal saw the flicker of a small candle. The captured air within was warm and smelled of herbs and incense. When he turned to look at her, she was kneeling on a fur with arms outstretched to him. She pulled him to her, took his hands and placed them on her breasts, rubbing from one to the other and down across her soft belly. Çatal felt panic well up inside—not fear but need. He unbuttoned the clasp under his tunic and fell on her, finding the place that lay open to him.

Some time later, he woke. He reached to where the candle had burned, sank his finger into the warm puddle, and felt the wax fuse to his skin. He slid his hands into the corners of the fur. The woman was gone. He peered through a slit in the tent and saw the lights of the stalls still stalked by crowds in the distance. Had he been struck with a vision, a visiting spirit? The celebration was, after all, a Roman tradition, decadent in the eyes of Allah. How else could men be duped into dressing like women? He fastened his sash, bowed his head and asked Allah's forgiveness.

He stood for several more minutes wondering if perhaps the woman would return. Finally he pulled the tent flap aside and stepped outside. She was standing several feet to the side, dark except for the glint of firelight on her metal adornments. When she made no move to approach him, he lifted the tent flap and tossed a handful of coins on the fleece. Outside again, he saw her lower her head briefly and smile. Çatal walked dreamlike back among the people.

Later in his room at the caravanserai, he decided there was no other explanation for his behavior. Sacaea had cast a spell on him. "There is no escape when an evil spirit casts its eye," he whispered to the walls. He pulled his fleece across his body, closed his eyes and slept without dreams.

13

The Meander River glistened like molten silver as it braided through the valley. It was our fifth day on the road with the Denbys and we'd settled into our roles. Carlos, the narrator, told us we were entering the fertile Meander Valley, where harvests could be counted on four times each year. This was information any tourist could find in a brochure, but what we got from Carlos were insights into the lives of the people.

"See that village ahead? It's got a unique tradition. You'll have to look sharp to find it," our narrator said.

"I bet I find it first," Tom shouted.

"Maybe." Marty moved closer to the window.

We made it almost to the outer edge of the settlement before Jack said: "Is it the bottles on some of the roofs?"

"Jack's the winner. In this village, when a daughter reaches an eligible age, the father will set a bottle on the roof as a signal that suitors may call."

"Now there's a tradition that has no chance of catching on in the U.S.," Carolyn said.

I was the only one to snicker. The boys, who had set up their own space in the rear of the SUV, hunched down to see the tops of the houses.

"The bottle's taken down and broken when the girl makes her choice," Carlos added.

"Hey, Mom, start saving bottles. I want the girls to come to me." Marty leaned back and folded his arms across his chest.

Carolyn laughed. "Yeah, we'll see. My guess is you'll be hiding in the basement."

If Carlos was our narrator, Jack was his straight man. Whatever the subject, he probed for more detail. Finally Carlos asked if he planned to change his vocation from engineer to Turkish tour guide.

"No, nothing like that, but I'm sadly lacking in knowledge about this part of the world, Islam in particular. I'm curious to know everything I can about life here," Jack said.

"Me, too," Carolyn added.

"I know a lot about Islam. Imam Aboud at my aunt's mosque is real nice and easy to talk to," Tom called from the rear.

"Oh, right. I'd forgotten about Tapis and Mehmet being Muslim. So, have you been in a mosque, Tom, I mean, to see a service?"

Tom's voice took on a storytelling tempo as he explained his first visit, how the imam welcomed him and invited him to ask any questions he might have. After his fifth visit, the imam gave him a Qur'an to read. Five visits? This was new information for me.

Carolyn raised her eyebrows and looked at me like she was examining a specimen in a Petri dish. I turned my head to look out the window. In the rush of preparing the apartment for the Denbys' arrival, topped off by getting ready for the trip, there'd been no time to discuss Tom's interest in Islam with Carlos alone. Maybe it was for the best, since the potential for argument, not only with Tom but perhaps with Carlos as well, made me wish I could avoid it altogether. My role for the trip, I decided, was to listen.

The car slowed. Carlos had spotted a group of people carrying wool to one of the thermal streams that erupted throughout the valley. He pulled the car over on the shoulder and we walked down an embankment to watch. The workers waved to us. They were wearing high boots to protect their feet from the boiling water as they lay down large bags to dam the waters. Within seconds the water was deep enough to empty the large tubs of wool. The women used their booted feet to stomp on the wool. From time to time they disappeared into the steam and we couldn't see them until a breeze cleared the way.

"Won't the wool shrink?" Carolyn asked.

"Yes, but the main purpose is to wash it before spinning. What you're seeing here is the first step in the making of our beautiful rugs," Carlos said. "By the time we finish this trip you'll see the rest of the process—the spinning, dyeing, weaving, final washing, and one of the large distribution centers."

Tom was standing behind me and I turned around. "One more tidbit about Oriental rugs for you," I said.

As we walked back to the car, Carolyn took my arm. "Let's take a walk or something tonight. I want to talk to you."

"Something wrong?"

"Not with me," she said, raising her eyebrows again.

We reached a small hotel in Selçuk by late afternoon. Jack and Carlos unloaded the suitcases and set them on the sidewalk next to Marty and Tom, who were giggling and flexing their muscles. Carolyn and I stayed behind to look at the hedged-in garden flanking the hotel's wide glass doors. An ornate iron bench at the far left end was tucked between tall red hollyhocks.

"That looks inviting but I need to stretch my legs after sitting so long in the van. Are you up for a short walk before dinner?" my neighbor said.

We agreed to meet after settling into our rooms. The men said they were walking too but they'd seen a large boat yard they wanted to explore since we planned to rent a yacht for a couple of days of swimming and relaxing on the Aegean.

Carolyn hooked her arm in mine and we took off at a brisk pace.

"I've been thinking our trip was badly timed because you're preoccupied with house plans," she said.

"Uh, uh. Just the opposite. Your trip couldn't have come at a better time."

"Really? That's a relief. I'm not sure I could handle all the changes you've been facing lately."

"Changes? I feel almost as at home in Turkey as I do in Philadelphia. I've been coming here for years."

"Yeah, I know, but this is the first I've heard of Tom's interest in Islam. Marty's made some comments, but— Look, I know you don't share your thoughts easily, so just tell me if it's none of my business. I'm only asking because it bothers Marty."

"He's sort of dabbling in Islam, curious about it. It was a shock initially but I'm okay with it now."

"Okay? No kidding. I get the willies thinking about what Muslims are doing...and in the name of God too. Jeez, Nora, how can you?"

She stopped so suddenly I pitched forward for several steps until I regained my balance. "I'm not saying it's been easy but Carlos says if faith makes people happy they should pursue it. Elena attends church faithfully, but she never insisted that Carlos do the same unless he wanted to." I felt my face flush.

"Well, there's a lot I don't understand. I'm thinking that's Marty's problem too, and just telling him to be tolerant won't cut it. They've been friends for so long. I don't want that to change," she said.

"Me either."

We reached a small park of cypress and linden trees, crisscrossed with stone pathways and bordered by clusters of small white flowers. In one grassy area, children were playing hide and seek, using the trees and boulders to avoid capture. They stopped to look at us as we passed.

"What's happening with the search for a house?" Carolyn said, waving at the children. "I love their blue school uniforms. Those white lace collars on the girls – so adorable."

"Yeah. It's like we're wearing a sign that says 'Americans,' huh?

"Right now we're talking about locations. We're hoping Elena will live with us—in a guest house or something. She's forgetful sometimes and not as robust as she used to be. Carlos and I think it would be a good idea," I said.

"Really?"

"Well, it's not settled yet. Elena's still thinking about it, but we've decided to build a small guest house anyway. If she doesn't want to it'll be an extra space for visitors. I hope she does. She's a dear. I couldn't ask for a better mother-in-law."

"But all day, every day?"

I laughed. "I've heard all the clichés, but what I've learned from Carlos is disagreements are natural among people and when they love each other they find a solution."

"You believe that?"

"Yeah, I've seen it work in Carlos' family. Besides, Elena is the mother I missed when mine died. I can't imagine having a problem."

"Are you kidding? I didn't want to live with Jack's parents. They're wonderful people, but when they're around it's too much Denby, if you know what I mean."

"I'd never get enough Elena. I really mean that. There's nothing I can't discuss with her and she doesn't take sides," I said.

"What did you mean by 'not as robust' as she used to be?"

"Oh, just little things. She's had some minor dizzy spells that probably happened because she forgot to take her meds. Things like that."

"Well, all I can say is, she sounds like a treasure."

The plane tree boughs rustled overhead, their leaves now black against the dimming sky. We quickened our pace. The sidewalk was uneven with missing pieces of concrete and opportunistic weeds that seemed to grasp our heels. I kept my eyes on the pavement. Carolyn's arm was linked with mine and I gave her a squeeze.

We crossed to the other side of the street for a change of view. The sun had dropped behind the mansions, silhouetting their angled roofs against the remaining light. Four minarets punctured the housetops from behind. Pointing, I told Carolyn she could expect a jarring call to worship at sunrise.

"I'll love that. It'll remind me I'm in another world, different from Philadelphia."

The following day Carlos consulted a road map and checked his watch.

"Would you like to see a Muslim prayer service?" Carlos said. "I know the imam of a small mosque just south of here. Besides being a nice guy he's got a great baritone voice, so he's also the *muezzin,* the one who calls others to prayer. Maybe we can time our visit to hear him perform the call to worship at midday. You might find it interesting, yes?"

"Yeah, you guys need to see this," Tom said, when everyone agreed.

"First, we need some petrol."

We found a café, public rest room, and petrol station shortly after entering the commercial area of the town. Carlos pulled next to a pump where six boys about the same age as Marty and Tom were sitting on a wall.

One boy, taller than the rest, got up and walked up to Tom with a cocky bounce in his step. "Hello, my name is Mesut. What is your name?"

Tom answered and the other boys moved in. They took turns asking each one of us the same questions. It was an on-the-spot English lesson, but as soon as we got beyond exchanging names, the encounter ended as quickly as it started. The boys shrugged, hugged us, said "thank you very much," and walked away.

"*That* was pretty cool," Marty said.

Tom pulled on his shirt. "I could'a done without the hugging."

We ordered food at the café and just as we walked outside to a table, the muezzin's voice sounded. Men and women, including the café workers, poured onto the street, the men drying their hands on their tunics, the women fussing with their headscarves. We bent to finish our lamb kabobs.

"The service won't last long," Carlos said, tipping his bottle of orange drink to get the last swallow. We carried our dishes to the counter where an old woman nodded vigorously and gave us a toothless smile, and then we hustled down an uneven sidewalk, ignoring the tempting shops with their goods set out on tables so intrusively we had to step into the street to get by.

I had to take two steps to keep up with Carolyn's long-legged gait.

The imam, standing with several men at the door to the mosque, saw us approaching and stepped forward to meet us.

Jack leaned into Carlos. "I don't get it. Are Turks always so eager to engage with strangers?"

"In fact they are, as you saw with the children, but in this case the imam knows me," Carlos said. "Yusef, how are you?"

The face I saw leaning over Carlos' shoulder could've decked out FHM's latest cover. With introductions, he moved from one of us to another, holding our hands overly long. It made me uncomfortable. But by the time he completed his courtesies, I decided he'd wanted to make a connection with each of us. His black eyes under black eyebrows were deeply set and surrounded by skin darker by several shades than the rest of his face.

He invited us for tea at his home after the service. "It is just there." He pointed with a long slender finger to a small stucco building topped by an angled red tile roof. Then, he turned and disappeared into the dark interior of the mosque. We stood outside watching the men at the ablution fountain, where ritual washing followed a strict pattern: hands, mouth, nostrils, face, arms to the elbows, head and ears, and feet to the ankle.

We entered the mosque and kept close to the outer wall. Women were clustered on either side of us. Men and boys knelt in the center fields of the prayer rugs. Facing them, the imam led their movements. First, with hands on their shoulders they repeated "Allahu akbar," God is very great. Carolyn elbowed me and pointed to a child desperately following the movements of the man next to him—probably his father. Lagging behind several seconds each time, he knelt, stood, and prostrated himself with his forehead on the floor. His tiny chest fluttered like a bird's each time the movements paused for brief recitations from the Qur'an.

Tom and Marty stared at the proceedings until Yusef sat down with his legs crossed. What followed was a short sermon, although I couldn't hear what he was saying. Marty pulled Tom outside. Within minutes people filed out, followed by Yusef, who joined us and led the way to his home.

While he lit a gas stove in a small alcove and set a kettle of water to boil, we were invited to sit on the carpet, a scratchy kilim of brown and rust. Across the room a curtain was pulled aside just enough to reveal a basin and tub, his bathroom. Since there were no other doors, I assumed we were in his living room by day, bedroom by night. Stacks of old books, three large lamps, and a lapboard with many pencils cradled in a deep groove were the only other accessories in the room. With the exception of the earthy-colored flatweave and a few red book covers, the room had little contrast to the land outside.

As the kettle sounded, Yusef rolled a large round board into the center of the room, invited us to sit around it, and, when we'd found our spots, he spread a loosely-woven orange cloth over the board, overlapping onto our laps—our napkin as well as table covering. He set a bowl of fruit and a knife in the middle of the board and returned to the kitchen. The next time he appeared, he was laughing and carrying a tray of glasses filled with tea.

"At times like this I know why men marry," he said, joining us in the circle.

Carolyn gave me an eyebrow wiggle. We drank our tea, cut and shared the fruit, and told him about the things we'd seen since leaving Ankara.

"You like our beautiful country, yes?"

"Yes. I'm surprised and delighted by how friendly and accepting the people are," Jack said. "I confess, with our country's strained relations with Muslims, I was prepared for a cool reception." He recounted our experience with the children at the petrol stop.

"Their teachers encourage them to speak English at every opportunity because few of them have been exposed to native English speakers," Yusef said.

Jack squirmed in his seat and coughed. "May I take advantage of this time with you to ask something about Islam?"

"Of course. Allah, through his messenger Muhammad, has given us a religion of revelation and reason to share with the world."

"Ah, yes, well— Christians also have one holy book, the Bible, but they're divided into many groups, ah, many ways of interpreting the sacred scriptures. Is that a parallel for Muslims?"

"No, no," he said raising a finger. "The divine origin of the Qur'an is rationally proved in the eyes of all Muslims. Since Muhammad never studied, and had not read the ancient scriptures, he could not have produced such a masterpiece as the Qur'an from his own resources and it was impossible for him to have been the author. The Qur'an is a literary miracle, unique in the religious history of the human race. In the Muslim perspective, the whole Qur'an comes from God. It is the source of all certainty. It provides a perspective on events, and all the faithful who see reality from its point of view feel both personally confirmed and totally secure in their approach."

Jack looked puzzled, opened his mouth, shook his head, and closed it again. Finally, he took a deep breath. "I've heard the Qur'an forbids the killing of innocents." He lifted the last word and paused until Yusef nodded enthusiastically. "So then I don't understand why Muslims all over the world didn't rise up to protest what happened on 9/11."

The light in the room hadn't changed but Yusef's skin darkened. Tom fidgeted. Marty looked embarrassed. Carlos pressed his lips together. Seconds later Yusef raised his hands in the air in what looked like a gesture of supplication and his expression softened. "This is an important question. Its answer will teach you something about Islam which you do not know. But it is not your fault. In many ways, it is our problem.

"I listen to your media. You are told Islam is more violent than other faiths. This is not true. What you think you know about Islam is likely wrong and that is dangerous. It is, as I say, our problem. We are not enough in the public eye in the U.S. We must work to be involved in everything from soup kitchens to government positions."

"But why did 9/11 happen if the Qur'an forbids it, as you say?" Carolyn said. I wasn't surprised to hear her pursue the original question. I respected her persistence.

Yusef raised his arms again and closed his eyes. Was he holding his temper? Asking Allah's help? Trying to distract us? Carlos was chewing his lower lip.

"I put this to you: Isn't terrorism against innocents like violent crime? This occurs throughout the U.S., yes? But this is no indication of Americans' general acceptance of murder or assault. So, the violence of terrorism is not proof that Muslims tolerate it. Indeed, they are often its primary victims. Our faith does not drive this. Politics does," Yusef said.

The room fell silent and Carlos quickly wiped his mouth on the cloth and stood. "If we discuss politics we will be here for a week," Carlos said. "You have been kind to give us your time, my friend."

"Wait, please, you have been patient, very patient. May I—" Jack said.

Yusef nodded. "Of course. It is my pleasure."

Carlos sat back down, although he didn't look very happy.

"Yusef, people have been very kind to us as tourists in Turkey, but I wonder what they think about the war we are fighting against terrorists in Iraq?" Jack said.

Yusef brushed off the front of his tunic and got up. It seemed like a reasonable motion, but there was something about the way he proceeded to pull on his sleeves that raised the hair on my neck.

"First, for over seven years the United States has been occupying the lands of Islam in the holiest places, plundering its riches, dictating to its rulers, humiliating its people, terrorizing its neighbors, and turning its bases in the Arabian Peninsula into a spearhead through which to fight the neighboring Muslim peoples.

"Second, despite the great devastation inflicted on the Iraqi people, and despite the huge number of those killed, the Americans are not content. They come to annihilate what is left of this people and to humiliate their Muslim neighbors." He pushed the lap cloth aside roughly and got up. "Yes, we are courteous to you because you are guests in our country and our culture demands it, but what I tell you is the truth.

"Your government's actions are a clear declaration of war on Allah, his messenger, and Muslims."

To say we were eager to leave didn't describe what happened next. With frozen faces, we shook hands and thanked him. No one spoke until we were inside the car.

"I'm so sorry. He said my question was important and I thought it was a unique opportunity." Jack's voice drifted off. "It was like talking to two different people. He was completely oblivious to how he contradicted himself."

"Don't worry about it. My conversations with him have always been nonpolitical, so I had no idea he held such a viewpoint. He's a really nice guy," Carlos said.

"You can say that after what we just heard?" I said.

"I can and I do. I gave up trying to understand organized religions long ago," Carlos said. "They all teach kindness and commit unimaginable cruelty, show mercy and yet seek revenge. Frankly, it disgusts me."

The car, which seemed spacious earlier, was tight with tension and unanswered questions. Even the boys had moved to opposite sides of the back seat and were fixed on the passing views. I wondered how Tom felt about Islam now. What's more, Carlos' neutrality was untenable as far as I was concerned.

I was successful in my business because I faced problems quickly and efficiently, but I couldn't say anything and the effort was making my head throb. I rummaged in my handbag for aspirin, tossed two tablets into my palm and swallowed them with bottled water. Everyone, it seemed, had retreated to private thoughts.

"Could we make a stop at a drugstore?" Carolyn said. "This dry air is doing a job on my contacts."

"Sure." Carlos turned the car around. "I think there's one on the next street."

He turned down a cross street and pulled up next to a sign: *eczane*. "Do you need a translator?"

"I can handle it," she said. "I already know that says 'drugstore,' right?"

She trotted off with Jack and Marty close behind. When the car door slammed shut, Carlos gave me a smile.

"Seems to me your friend Yusef has been brain washed," I said.

"What?" He dropped the smile.

"He answered Jack's question like he was reading from a script. It sounded rehearsed or something. At least that's how it sounded to me," I said.

"If that's what you think, Yusef's comments about American Muslims needing to be more exposed applies to you as well."

"What do you mean by that?"

"I mean, you don't know what you're talking about. You've had no real interaction with Muslims, yet you judge their motives."

"Yeah, Mom, you hate Islam and you don't even know why. That's prejudice," Tom said. He propelled himself from the back seat and faced me, his chin two inches closer than the rest of his features.

"Hey, hey, take it easy, Tom," Carlos said.

"I don't hate anybody, but you have to admit the terrorists *are* Muslims. And remember, Muharrem's a Muslim and he's been my friend since before you were born."

The car doors opened. Carolyn, holding onto a small bag, slid into her seat behind me. "What's the topic? You all look like you were really into it."

Tom retreated to the rear.

"We were just sharing our opinions about Islam. What do you think after talking to Yusef?" Carlos said.

Jack cleared his throat. "In a nutshell, I'm confused. If there's only one interpretation of the Qur'an, there are lots of Muslims breaking their holy law. As horrible as that is, Christians are the same. The Crusades and the Inquisition are lousy examples of 'Love your neighbor as yourself,' you know. That's what I hoped to get at, but..."

"Exactly. And I was hoping to learn more about women's rights," Carolyn said, "but we got sidetracked with terrorism. "Carlos, how's your sister managing the transition from Christian to Muslim?"

"Aunt Tapis says Muslim women are considered treasures by their husbands." Tom's voice shot from the back like a cannonball to my head.

"Tapis is happy and Mehmet's a great guy. No problem," Carlos said.

"That's good. But I still wonder why the women were mashed against the outer wall, separated from the men at the prayer service? I wanted to ask Yusef about that," Carolyn said.

Carlos chuckled. "Simple answer. It's a matter of decorum...eh, you know, bending over with a man perhaps behind you," Carlos said.

"Oh, that makes sense. Also makes a case for trousers," she said.

Thank you, Carolyn. The throb in my head, first at my temples, was creeping to the back of my neck, and my shoulders had begun to ache. I didn't hate Muslims.

We entered a populated area and Carlos announced our next stop: a tour of a large distribution center where rugs from outlying villages were prepared for outlets all over the world. Inside, rugs were divided into large rooms according to size and type. After expressing an interest in a pile rug for her living room, Carolyn was escorted by a tall, handsome Turk to one of many corridors spiraling off from the main lobby. She cast a smug smile over her shoulder at Jack as she walked away. Jack decided not to follow and I turned away to hide my smirk.

"What's new in kilim production?" I said to the center's owner, Ogun Guler.

A smile spread across his face. Without a word he conveyed his message: Just wait until you see what we have. You will be amazed.

Past experience with Ogun told me I wouldn't be disappointed. He raised his arm and beckoned another salesman, equally impeccable and good-looking. Maybe it was a requirement for the job.

"He speaks excellent English. This is best for your guests, yes?" Ogun said.

We followed the young salesman down the hall. "Perhaps the strongest trend is away from the prominent slits in older flatweaves. Today the use of warp sharing and interlocking wefts has eliminated the slits completely."

Carlos was listening intently, Jack's brow was accordion pleated, and the boys were holding an impromptu race on a runner that covered the length of the hallway. We turned into a room with waist-high piles of assorted kilim. A polished dark wood bench with colorful, multi-pattered, kilim-covered pillows, lined the outer walls. Our guide stopped and swept his arm from side to side.

"Because of increased demand, soumak is the dominant weave here. It's an ancient technique which originated in the Caucasian city of Shemakha and has been found with mummified human remains in China's Zinjiang Province. Very sturdy. They run the fibers over two warps from right to left, with the rows running in contrary directions. Then—"

"May we walk around and look at the rugs? Ask questions?" I said.

"Most certainly," he said with a bow. He retreated to the doorway.

Carlos gave me a smile. Jack looked like a prisoner set free. The boys had disappeared.

"You know what would be fun?" I said after we'd walked between several piles of kilim. "Let's go to the silk worm processing area. The boys would like that."

We caught up with Tom and Marty in the lobby, sitting in high-backed chairs. I hooked a finger and told them we were going to see the silk worms. Their eyes lit up and they bounced our way. What is it about boys and worms?

Small oblong cocoons were bobbing in warm water until the threads floated away and were picked up and spun onto spools. Then the threads were picked up again, pulled into long strands to dry, and spun again onto large cones. The entire process was automated from cocoons to cones. The next process was the dyeing but we chose instead to see the looms.

A recording was activated by our passage through the door. "Only young girls, sitting in four-hour shifts, are chosen for this weaving. Fifteen hundred threads to the inch are normal for these rugs which are prized for their beauty and durability."

Tom and Marty were engrossed, or maybe it was the girls. They might have hoped for some reaction, but the girls were focused on their tasks. Working without a pattern, the girls' small fingers flowed across the loom rhythmically. They sat on their bare heels with skirts gathered up in their laps. Each wore a different colored headscarf, wrapped identically around their heads, an indication they were from the same village.

The rugs they worked on were in different stages of completion, but enough of the pattern showed to indicate the head-and-shoulder center fields of prayer rugs.

"A broken silk thread is disastrous," the voice warned. No wonder the girls needed a break after four hours.

Carolyn was beaming when we met her back in the lobby. She wanted Jack to see a rug and we tagged along.

"I love this, Jack. It's light and airy and the colors are perfect for the living room furniture."

"How much is it?"

"Muammer says it comes from a village along the Aegean coast near Izmir. These—"

"Muammer?"

"These round things around the border are called medallions. Aren't they interesting? He's the young man who showed it to me. Are you listening at all?"

"Did you hear me ask how much it is?"

I picked up the ticket under the rug's ivory fringe. "Translating the Turkish lira into dollars, it's about $8,000."

I'd never seen Jack's neck bend the way it did at that moment and Carolyn's eyes bulged slightly before she walked away looking defeated. Carlos, I noted, had left the room. The boys were hiding from each other behind the carpet piles. I walked between the stacks with Jack, transcribing more sales tickets, while trying to get him to focus on the rugs themselves.

"I'm not saying you shouldn't compare prices, Jack, but Marty's grandchildren will be able to enjoy this rug."

Ogun and Carlos came back with matching smiles. "So, you like the Milas, yes?" the owner said.

Jack, arms folded over his chest, made a sound, but stopped when Ogun held out his hand. "Because of my friendship of many years with Nora and Carlos, may I offer you this rug for 4,000 American dollars and complimentary shipping to your home?"

Two days later, Carolyn was still smiling. We were soaking up the sun on the deck of a rented yacht. Two sublime days of feeling the soft ocean swells, watching the tethered sailboats bob along the shore, and sampling our captain's creativity with grilled seafood had lulled the adults into a state of nirvana. Our twelve year olds, on the other hand, were immune to anything resembling peace. They spent the days swimming and diving into the clear turquoise water under the watchful eyes of the captain's teenaged son. Or they played chess. That is until Marty suddenly threw over the board.

"Give it a rest, will ya?" he shouted. He grabbed his towel, walked into the cabin and descended the stairs to the bedrooms.

Our eyes followed Carlos as he walked over to Tom.

"He's just mad because I beat him again," Tom said, putting the chess pieces into a pouch.

Later after a dinner of bread, hummus, tomatoes, olives and grilled *hamsi*, a mild white fish, Tom and Marty excused themselves to take up a favorite spot on the roof of the boat's cabin, where they could search the sky for constellations.

"It's a relief to see them together," Carolyn said. "Did you hear the tiff this afternoon?"

When I said I hadn't, Carolyn told me Marty became angry because Tom said Christians were out of date, that Muhammad came to continue and refine the work Jesus started.

"Marty said he quotes verses in answer to everything. Nora, it sounds to me like he's doing more than dabbling. He's memorizing the Qur'an."

Carlos' forehead looked plowed. He took a sip of wine and sighed. "I'm sorry he made Marty angry, but it's typical Tom. When he gets interested in something, he dives in head first. He'll come to his own conclusions when he's ready. Still, he needs to know how he's affecting others. I'll talk to him."

I nodded. Better him than me.

14

The morning after our return to Ankara, I propped myself on one elbow and watched Carlos' chest rise and fall in the slow rhythm of sound sleep. Dark curls cascaded over his forehead and ear. His eyes shifted under light brown eyelids and his mouth jerked several times before it came to rest with lips slightly parted. I wondered what he was dreaming about. I'd watched the hands of the bedside clock tick off the hours.

Careful not to wake him, I pulled aside the sheet at twenty minutes past six. Elena would be dressed and ready to begin her routine of prayer and scripture reading. I wanted to talk to her about Tom.

I picked through clothes piled on the chairs, tossed from suitcases after our arrival, and chose a sweater and slacks by feel rather than sight. I tiptoed my way around upended suitcases to the bathroom. My body ached from the tension that had been growing since we'd said goodbye to the Denbys in Istanbul. As he said he would, Carlos told Tom to soft pedal his Islamic rhetoric. He made it clear we understood his interest, but annoying our friends wasn't acceptable. Tom at first denied there was a problem but promised to be more sensitive. I was grateful for that, but somehow his promise didn't set my mind at rest.

Elena answered my first soft tap on the door of her apartment.

"Nora, my goodness. I thought all of you would sleep until noon. Come in. Have some tea with me."

As always my mother-in-law looked fresh from a salon, her hair upswept and fastened with a tortoise shell comb. Her satin slippers skimmed across the pale yellow Chinese rug that had taken my breath away the first time I saw it. As distracted as I was, I still admired the artistry of the blue dragons that stretched from border to border. Carlos said it had "lived" with his family for generations, something I understood completely.

I followed Elena to the kitchen like a wind-up doll, and when she stopped I was startled.

"Something wrong, darling?"

"Yes, I'm worried about Tom. I need your advice."

I poured out everything: finding the prayer rug in Tom's room, his arguments with Marty, accusing me of prejudice.

"Carlos doesn't understand why this upsets me. I think it will add to the distance between us just when I'm working so hard to find ways to be closer to him. You must have gone through this with Tapis. How did you manage when she said she planned to convert to Islam?"

I followed her graceful motion as she placed her teacup on the oval glass-topped coffee table in front of us. The blue spiked heads of both dragons on the rug below peered through with bulging red eyes, seeming to wait for her answer as eagerly as I.

"With much difficulty, Nora. She loved the small Christian church we used to attend together. She knew how much I would miss her company so it wasn't easy for her either. But that wasn't the only part that troubled me. As a Christian I believe what Jesus said to his disciples: 'I am the road, also the truth, also the life. No one gets to the Father apart from me.' I feared for her eternal soul."

"But, Ana, I don't sense any strain whatsoever between you and Tapis. How do you manage that?"

"I sought help."

"Where?"

"The pastor of my church: Pastor Ajemian. As you might imagine, mine was a story he'd heard many times before, serving Christians here in a Muslim majority. He urged me to do two things: first, to give the situation to God and to trust the outcome. Second, to judge the lives and not the words."

I drained my cup, rattling the saucer awkwardly when I set it down. "Judge the lives? Not the words? I don't understand."

"Nora, I don't know how much religious background you have. You have never spoken about your faith, and, although I know he calls himself Christian, Carlos has no patience for the church. In our talks together he says he believes, as I do, that Jesus stepped into history to show us how to love God and each other. If we accomplish this in our lives, then our faith has served us well and saved us from the world's evil ways. I came to understand that God is at work in Tapis as she embraces her new faith. Only her words have changed. Do you see?"

"But Tapis is a grown woman. Tom's a child."

"Yes, but he is maturing." She hesitated while a look of amazement took over her expression. "It just occurred to me. Scripture has something to say about the twelfth year. When Jesus was twelve, he wandered away from his parents. They were sick with worry until, finally, they found him in a synagogue, a temple, asking questions, learning, and teaching. God set Jesus in motion, engaged him for his great purpose, when he was twelve. Maybe God is reaching for Tom."

Carlos was still sleeping when I got back to our apartment. The bedcovers were as I'd left them. So too was the chaos of clothes and the not-quite-emptied luggage. In the time between leaving and returning I was the one who'd changed. My spirit was easier about Tom, and after talking to Elena I believed I had a better handle on why Carlos wasn't threatened by our son's growing Muslim faith.

I stood still, watching him sleep. He came into my life when I had lost the connection to my family. Parents were gone and brothers were smothering me with their caring, until I turned away and threw myself into work. It occupied me but fell short of making me happy. Carlos did that. And even if our family hadn't reached the unity we hoped for, we provided something we each needed: someone to share life with. His words of five years ago echoed: *I'll work with you or fight with you – whatever it takes for us to be a family. The only guarantee I can give you is my love.*

I took off my clothes and slid under the sheet, pressing my back into his chest, letting the warmth of his body spread through me. He responded as he always did. Waking slowly from sleep, he wrapped his arms around me, pulled me closer until every part of his body was in contact with mine. He groaned with pleasure, pushing my hair aside, kissing my neck, breathing me in. The rhythm we'd developed in five years of loving took hold. His hands stroked my breasts. I turned to face him and his eyes opened, narrow sapphire rings surrounding a dark center. There was no mistaking the love reflected in his face. I kissed him again and again while he ran his hands over my back and cupped my buttocks, pressing me closer. I felt his eagerness and it fueled my own. Without a word between us, he lifted me over him lightly, and I settled into pleasure. Moments later, with the room's details taking shape in the pale morning light, we lay sated in each other's arms.

I rolled to my back.

"Welcome home to you too," he said.

"I needed...the only way I can explain it... When we make love it's like we're one, and—"

"Not just when we make love. What's wrong?" He sat up and turned to me.

"While you were sleeping, I went to see Ana to find out how she dealt with Tapis' adoption of Islam. I should have gone to her sooner. I'm not afraid anymore, Carlos. I'm not going to make an issue of this with Tom so there's no reason for it to come between us."

"I never thought it would. Why would you think that?"

"Because while you were comfortable about Tom's interest in Islam, I wasn't. And it's not because I'm prejudiced. You know I don't hate Muslims."

"Yes and Tom knows it too. He looks for ways to involve you emotionally. Unfortunately, he does it hurtfully. My heart tells me he won't feel that need as you get closer.

"Ana was the perfect one to help you, yes?"

I nodded. "She told me to trust God and, in a way, to trust Tom to handle his own feelings. If I deny him the chance to explore his search for God, I'll damage my relationship with him. In fact, she said her connection with Tapis is stronger than ever since she became a Muslim."

He rubbed his face and ran his fingers through his hair. "I didn't give it much thought at the time, but I knew Ana struggled over what it would mean, and what she says about how everything worked out is true. We enjoy each other's holidays and rituals; the differences don't matter to any of us. It's in God's hands.

"Ana, Tapis, and I decided we wouldn't let the differences get in the way of our love for each other." He pursed his lips and blew out his breath. Then he looked at me.

"You've sensed that, I know you have."

"Definitely, and I trust Ana....completely."

He pulled me to his chest and kissed my head. The warmth of his lips seeped through my hair. "Ana may be on to something more. Tom could be offering you an opportunity to share a special time in his development as a man. Do you think you can think of it in that way rather than something that separates you from each other?"

Trust God? I'd had a lot more experience trusting myself. But, Ana could be trusted. I knew that. I pulled his face to my chest and allowed his curls to slide between my fingers. They gave way to the pressure before they snapped back to hug his head.

"I promise you I won't snap back to my old ways, and I'll make sure he understands we both support him."

He nodded. "Good. One more thing, don't ever doubt my love for you and Tom." He got up and kissed the end of my nose on his way to the bathroom.

I walked to the dresser and saw my face in the mirror—a little dopey at first, but becoming sober as I affirmed that my husband's love was not for me alone. It was for family.

Carlos and I were having a second cup of coffee when Tom, looking puffy eyed, joined us.

"What's for breakfast?" He flicked on the television as he passed it on the counter.

"Eggs and peace," I said, watching his face.

"Turn that up, Tom. Something has happened," Carlos said, hopping off his seat and walking to the TV.

The announcer was showing people and vehicles crumpled in the street. Emergency vehicles were pouring on to the scene from all directions. The camera focused in on a hysterical man carrying a small child. A leg was on the ground at his feet.

"This just moments ago on Istanbul's major business thoroughfare. An explosion in front of this business, followed ten minutes later by an even bigger explosion, just as people rushed in to help. Police believe terrorists are responsible but they will not confirm this until an investigation is completed," the commentator said.

"Carolyn's nightmare, come true," I said. "Horrible. Thank God, they're home safely by now. What good does this kind of attack on innocent people accomplish?"

The news report turned to another subject and Carlos turned the TV off. "They'll see this on the news in Philadelphia for sure. It's about five there now; let's call them."

I picked up the wall phone and pushed their number. Jack answered and I put him on speaker. "Did you have a good flight home?"

"Everything was smooth but we're wacked out with the time change."

I heard Carolyn's 'hello from the city of brotherly love' in the background.

"Put the news on. There's been a double bombing in Istanbul this morning," Carlos said.

There was silence until a male voice droned from their television.

"You missed the shotgun, as they say." Carlos screwed up his face.

"You mean we 'dodged a bullet,' don't you?" Carolyn said. "Thank God, but how very, very sad this is. When's it all going to end?"

We shared our mutual worries in a way that wouldn't have been possible before their trip to Turkey. They were as ambivalent as I was when it came to the Muslim people. What was happening all over the world was in total counterpoint with the kind, generous actions we'd both experienced. When we finished, Tom walked off with the phone to talk to Marty.

I was clearing away breakfast dishes when Tom returned, rubbing his tummy.

"Some eggs?"

He nodded, and I grabbed two eggs, cracked them into a bowl, and whipped them.

Carlos asked Tom if he thought Marty enjoyed the tour of Turkey.

"Yeah. He told me he liked swimming in deep water better than any old pool. But we're still getting a pool, right?"

"Maybe we'll have it by next summer. It depends on the construction company. Turkey's not like the States. Pools aren't so common," Carlos said.

"The law of supply and demand. I learned about that at school." His nose was in the air.

I put a glass of passion fruit juice in front of him. "Sorry, there's no more orange until I do some grocery shopping."

He nodded and drained it. "I like this stuff too, but passion fruit's a stupid name."

"Tell me, Tom," Carlos said. "Speaking of supply and demand, is Marty still your best friend or have you got a favorite Turkish buddy?"

Tom ran his finger around the lip of the glass and sucked his finger before he answered.

"Marty's still Marty. No surprises. Kind of boring, but I still like him. Marty doesn't have a clue about some stuff though—stuff I like talking about with my Turkish friends."

They'd moved from the counter to the table and I joined them, setting toast and scrambled eggs in front of Tom.

"Marty didn't like hearing about Islam, did he?" I said.

"He said I was different from him."

"Are you?" Carlos said, snatching a forkful of eggs.

"I've always been smarter than him. Hey, get your own; I'm hungry."

"Even if that's true, you won't have many friends if you think you're better than they are. Everybody deserves respect," Carlos said.

"Do you think Marty said you were different because of your new interest in Islam?" I said.

Tom spun his spoon like a propeller on the table. "It's private. I deserve respect, too, right?"

Carlos carried his dishes to the sink. "Right. And so do we. We want to know what you like about Islam."

Tom's face flushed. He grabbed the bottom of his chair seat and pushed it behind him. "The Muslims are.... I like they way they do stuff together. Well, not the bombing. They're crazy people." He walked out of the kitchen and pounded up the stairs to his room.

Carlos sat down again, tilting his chair back on its rear legs. "That was helpful."

"Are you being sarcastic?"

"Have you ever known me to use sarcasm? I believe Tom has given this topic a lot of thought. In some way Islam meets a need for him." he said. "We just learned he's not ready to talk about it yet."

The conversation hadn't gone exactly as I'd hoped. At least Carlos let him know we wanted to share his interests. It was typical of Tom to be defensive, but he'd think about what was said.

I carried his breakfast dishes to the sink, poured myself another cup of coffee, and offered some to Carlos.

"Okay for now. In the meantime, there's the festival. I know he thinks I don't enjoy doing things with him, but he's going to change his mind."

Late in the afternoon, Muharrem called to arrange our schedule for the following week. He asked if we'd seen the report on Istanbul and I told him we'd just spoken to our friends who were back in Philadelphia.

"This makes people hate Islam. My heart is heavy because of this."

"Most people know these atrocities are the work of extremists, Muharrem," I said.

"I do not agree," he said and changed the subject.

While we traveled with the Denbys, Muharrem said he'd been actively researching contacts for the rugs I needed—a few for the festival and replacements for my general inventory. He was more than an agent for me, more than the one who gave me access to Turkish rug dealers, he carried my current inventory in his head. He seemed instinctively to know when I would be open to something new and exactly where to take me. He embraced Deanna Sardis' festival with his usual enthusiasm and efficiency.

"We won't need too many days, will we?" I said. "I have so much to accomplish before we leave for New York. Did I tell you Tom is willing to help Carlos and me in a small way with the rug sales at the festival?"

"No. He's interested in the rugs?"

"He's trying to learn so he can be helpful."

"Will he come with us to Torbal and Usa Dagh?"

Take Tom on a buying trip? I hadn't thought of that. "That's an interesting idea, my friend, and a good one. I'll see what Carlos thinks, but I feel confident he'll like the idea."

Our conversation ended with an agreement that he'd pick me—hopefully, us—up in a couple of days and conclude our work in three. The more I imagined Tom with us, the more I liked the idea.

"What do *I* think? A couple of things. First of all, it's more important to find out what Tom thinks about traveling around in search of rugs. And second, have you considered the additional pressure you might be placing on him to perform at the festival? You say you know your son, but it's my observation that he may interpret such a trip as your rising expectations of him."

My temples started to throb. "I'll be sure to tell him my reason for wanting him with Muharrem and me."

"And that is?"

Only the upturned edges of Carlos' mouth saved me from a defensive response. "Okay, I'll ask Tom if he'd like to go with us just to see how the negotiations work, maybe even see some of the actual rug production like the preparation of the dyes and the weaving. I won't say anything about how it will help him with sales at the festival. It'll just be for fun. How's that sound?"

The festival couldn't come soon enough for me. I needed something to replace Islam in my thoughts.

15

Heavy rains pelted the car most of the morning, and Muharrem was bent over the steering wheel as though being closer to the windshield would help. He steered cautiously around the ruts and holes newly carved by swirling runoff. When he announced we were nearing Torbal, I knew it wasn't because he could see it through the gray wall of water surrounding the car, but because he'd been watching the odometer since the last recognizable landmark.

I was sitting sideways on the back seat behind Muharrem and Tom, steering through my own muddy questions. How was it that Tom, my taciturn Tom, was holding a non-stop conversation with him? It began with how Muharrem got started in the business and continued with questions about what elements to watch for in the upcoming negotiations. I could have answered all of it if he'd asked.

Muharrem's reaction to Tom, on the other hand, was just as I expected. He came from a large family, no kids of his own, but nieces and nephews aplenty. When Tom agreed to come with us to Torbal and Usa Dagh, I knew Muharrem would enjoy his company. I listened, until my mind wandered to my first unnerving visit to Torbal's Mayor Nerman Ysilada, the area's flamboyant rug distributor.

Outwardly charming, Ysilada was a formidable negotiator who changed tactics unexpectedly and shattered my balance. I remembered his sudden outburst after my first offer, the rise of red on his neck and face, the flip of his arm when he lifted his sash, tossed it over his shoulder, and turned his back on me. I thought I'd offended him, but when I glanced at Muharrem and saw the semblance of a smile, I resisted the urge to respond, composed myself and waited. I remembered the sweat running down my back. Moments later Ysilada turned back to me and lowered his price. By the end of the negotiation, I had acquired a fine collection of rugs at a very fair price. He didn't try to intimidate me again, but I promised myself I'd never drop my guard with him.

Though Torbal attracted rug dealers from many areas, it offered little more than tranquility and abundant wildflowers to its residents, so when Muharrem told me to prepare myself for change, I was skeptical. Most small villages expanded their population baby by baby. Muharrem said Mayor Ysilada decided to change that and used his considerable financial resources to stimulate business and raise the standard of living for the townspeople.

As we approached the turnoff, the sun threw a rainbow over the town, a patch of blue sky burst through the clouds, and the rain stopped. The transformation I saw was nothing short of miraculous. I took it as a good omen as far as Tom was concerned. Up to this point his exposure had been limited to Ankara, a large modern city with tourist destinations, hardly reality for most Turks. Any villages he'd seen were no more than a few stone or cinder block homes and scatterings of sheep and goats. Torbal would show him a middle level of Turkish life.

Torbal's commercial center was stretched out on both sides of a newly paved street with a center divider dotted with benches and saplings. Already men were crossing the street, wiping down the tables and chairs to continue their never-ending games of dominoes.

"What's that thing those guys are holding?" Tom shouted, head out the window.

I remembered asking the same thing on my first trip to rural Turkey. Each village had its tea and coffee shop and *nargile*, water pipe. The fragrance of apple tobacco reached the open window. I explained and couldn't help adding: "Water or not, it's still damaging to the lungs."

Up ahead I saw the long, low, windowless building that was the mayor's showroom and once again I admired the large copper and silver shield, his family crest, on the massive carved door. We parked the car and as we approached the door it opened and the mayor stepped out to greet us. His wife and three sons, holding the soccer balls I'd given them on an earlier visit, stood just inside the door. Clearly, Muharrem told him I was bringing my son.

Custom dictated that we have tea together before beginning work, but the boys asked Tom if he'd like to go to the park to kick the ball. Tom hesitated and looked at me.

"Mayor Ysilada, your boys are very kind, but my son is interested in learning about the rugs."

"I see, of course," the mayor said.

"Ah, thanks, but—" Tom said, embarrassed by the boys' dejected faces.

"Very well," Ysilada said, waving his boys off. He looked back at Tom with a half-hearted smile. "You are a serious boy, yes?"

"Are your sons interested in your business, mayor?" I asked.

He seemed not to hear me and we were led into the side room where we'd had tea on former visits. It was customary to discuss anything other than the business at hand during teatime, but this time the mayor focused his attention on my son, and there was nothing I could do about it.

"I am most interested in why you prefer to learn rather than play," he said.

Tom straightened himself and laced his fingers in his lap. "I'm involved in a hayir."

The mayor set down his glass of tea. He opened his mouth to speak but changed his mind, taking his time to look at each of us. There was no way to know where this was going. And as I glanced at Tom and Muharrem, it appeared I was the only uncomfortable one.

I moved to the edge of my chair and placed my glass on the table to my side. "I have a client in New York who is ill with cancer," I began. I stumbled and hesitated, not certain of the appropriateness of sharing the story with the mayor, but his facial expression kept me talking. I told him of Deanna's plight and our plans to help with the festival.

"You are Christian, are you not?" he said when I finished.

"Well, yes, and, like you, I know the importance of charity," I said. This discussion was moving farther and farther from my comfort zone. If I should inadvertently offend, our negotiations would be ended—perhaps forever.

"*I* am a Muslim." The penetrating voice was Tom's.

Ysilada smiled, rose from his seat, put his arm around Tom and led him into the salesroom. They exchanged a few words but I couldn't hear them. I looked at Muharrem and shrugged. His nod seemed to convey that all was well.

We'd passed through the main display area when Ysilada turned away from Tom. "Nora, let me show you the latest work of our local weavers." We were back on track and I sighed with relief.

At the end of the hall we entered a room with carpets piled waist high along the outer edges. Ysilada invited us to sit on one of the benches between the rugs, while he walked from pile to pile. Finally he lifted a rug and spread it before us.

"We have a new weaver, the wife of our town's grocer. She is from a small town in the Kuba district and an excellent stylist."

The rug was approximately nine by ten feet with a central medallion of blue and red. Flowers and repeating bands of asymmetrical clouds surrounded the center, no ordinary rendering. He moved to the next stack, flipping an all-over pattern of rosettes and single flowers on a dark brown field with several borders of alternating dark and light bands. The dimensional effect was startling, like stepping down into the center of the rug.

"These rugs are heavier than most because she uses more wool and one hundred and fifteen knots per square inch," he said, moving to the next pile and swirling off the top rug as he'd done before. There was pride in his exaggerated arm movements, and his chest had puffed up. I fully expected swollen prices to follow. But when he finished and I asked how much, I was surprised. He said he would sell ten of her rugs for nine hundred American dollars each. When I countered with six hundred each, he accepted with only slight hesitation and delivered a huge smile to Tom.

"Did she do this one with the horse?" Tom said. He had moved to the next stack of rugs, more Kuba-style.

The mayor moved to Tom's side and placed his arm around his shoulders. Was Ysilada so fond of children?

"Yes. This is her work. Are you interested in horses, Tom, or in the rug?"

Tom looked at me. I gave him a weak smile. Ysilada was driving this conversation and I had no idea where it was going. Tom seemed calm and took his time answering. He walked around the rug, tapped each individual pattern, flipped to the underside, and let the ivory fringe trail between his fingers. Still he didn't answer.

Winged creatures were exercising in my stomach. I looked at Muharrem. If his face was any indication, he was loving every minute. Ysilada's body began to convulse in chuckles as he watched Tom go back to the stack we'd just left. He repeated the walk, tap, flip, and fringe split.

"Yes, I'm interested in this rug. How much is it?" My son's face was granite and he held the mayor's narrowed eyes when he spoke. I fought to keep a straight face. Where did he learn this?

"Twelve hundred American dollars would be a bargain for this unusual piece," Ysilada said, matching Tom's poker face.

"The rug beneath this has a horse just like this one, the colors and the size of this rug are just like the ones you said were nine hundred dollars each. I think you should sell it for six hundred."

The mayor further narrowed his eyes and turned down the edges of his mouth. Then he laughed. "Agreed, but next time, don't tell me what you've noticed. Just make your offer," Ysilada said. "Now, dear boy, can you pay for this rug?" The question was for Tom, but the mayor looked at me.

"Yes, I save some of my allowance every week in my own bank account, right, Mom?" Tom said with his chin leading his words. He fixed me with a hard stare—I had no idea what that meant.

Finally, Ysilada grabbed his ample sides and delivered a belly-shaking guffaw and Muharrem joined him. Only then did Tom allow himself a smile.

Three hours later, with a successful negotiation behind us, we were approaching a small hotel where we planned to have a meal and spend the night. The sky was ablaze with a saffron sunset, colors unreal, like the experience in Torbal.

"You got some nice rugs today, Mom," Tom said. He exchanged waves with the desk clerk.

"Yeah. You got one too and at a great price."

"I think he let me have it for fun, like he was playing."

Muharrem stopped in his tracks, turned, and placed his big hands on Tom's shoulders. Tom's neck bent back to see his face. "He was enjoying himself, but he was not playing; it was a test. You are almost a man, Tom. It is the time when a Muslim father tests his son's character. You passed the test better than most. I have known the mayor's sons for many years and they are fine boys, but they do not have your maturity and determination. Maybe you would like to be my partner some day, eh?"

Tom turned his head toward me. "I think the mayor put you in a tough spot, Tom, and you handled it very well. Did you have fun?" I said.

"Yeah. The mayor's a cool dude."

I wanted to say more—how proud I was of his quick thinking, his confidence, his fearlessness, his careful observation. But I remembered Carlos' warning about raising expectations. Should I ask Muharrem to be less effusive with his praise? No. Tom saved his worst reactions for me. Praise and encouragement from others was probably okay.

In light of his encounter with Ysilada, what harm could there be in speculating about Tom's contribution at the festival? He might mingle with people as a greeter, or point out the features in the different types of rugs to passersby, or help Ed with the point-of-sale work.

We reached our rooms and agreed to meet for dinner in an hour.

The hotel's dining room was tucked in a basement room but gave no impression of being an afterthought. White damask covered the dozen or so tables and a massive breakfront displayed copper bowls, a rainbow of china dishes, and a steaming samovar. The walls were native sandstone. We were shown to a table with a waiter in black shirt and pants standing by. Ringlets of light brown hair framed his face and just the faintest beginnings of a mustache followed the curve of his upper lip. I guessed he was no more than sixteen. He plucked a red pencil from above his ear and asked for our drink order—in English.

"I'm learning Turkish," Tom said.

"Do they teach my language in your school?"

Tom's face fell. "Can I have Turka Coke?"

When the waiter left, Muharrem asked Tom where he was learning the language.

"Just talking to my friends. My aunt and uncle made me speak Turkish when we ate together. But I'm going to get some books so I can learn faster."

"I'd like it if you practiced with me," Muharrem said.

I settled back and enjoyed listening to my agent slip into his "uncle" mode. He was patient and Tom didn't mind having his mistakes corrected. Another shining moment.

Muharrem went to his room after dinner to email his wife, and I asked Tom if he'd like to sit in the hotel lobby to talk about the rugs. He agreed with an eagerness that sent a shot of adrenaline through me. We found two upholstered chairs in a quiet corner.

"Am I reading you right, Tom? You really got into it today," I began.

"Yeah. At first I was bored, but it was fun when the mayor asked me to bid. I liked it. Do you think Muharrem was right about the mayor testing me?"

"That's how it looked to me. You handled the negotiation well, but the best part is that you didn't back down. That's always been a part of your character, and today I got a glimpse of how well that trait will serve you no matter what you decide to do with your life."

He was looking at me with blue, not gray, eyes. His color of contentment. He was happy and that was good enough for me.

The next morning Muharrem and Tom were waiting for me in the lobby, their suitcases at their sides and grins on their faces.

"Hey, we're going to work, not to Disneyland."

"Muharrem says the kids at Usa Dagh usually run inside when strangers visit their village, but he thinks they'll come out because of me."

"It'll be interesting to see what they do." We walked down the hotel steps to our waiting car. "But if they don't, it's because they're shy. They don't often have foreign visitors," I said.

"The kids at the petrol station came right up and asked Marty and me questions, remember?"

"Yeah, I know, but there's a difference between rural and city kids."

"Maybe they're scared."

I buckled my seat belt before I answered. "Then let's be extra friendly." I wasn't being completely honest. Villagers as a rule were conservative; they didn't want their children influenced by foreigners. Old traditions were tightly held, particularly religious ones affecting the roles for women.

A short time later I pulled a headscarf from my purse, slipped it over my head and wrapped the ends together behind my neck. Once, because I was bareheaded, I offended an elderly woman in a rural village. I wasn't going to make that mistake again regardless of Turkish law, which said they weren't required.

"There it is," Muharrem said, slowing the car to hold down the dust. It had rained briefly overnight, leaving puddles around the hotel and along the sides of the road. But the clouds had cleared and the desert sun, along with a hot breeze, had removed any trace of moisture from the ground and the air. Usa Dagh, set in a narrow cleavage between high, rolling hills, enjoyed a constant breeze, a natural sucking of air through the canyons. I'd been there on days when the sun was merciless, finding villagers clustered under the trees in relative comfort, loose cotton tunics flapping. It was such a day.

Once we left the main road, only the faint imprint of wheels suggested the way to the village, just one of the clues to Usa Dagh's isolation. Muharrem chose his own path through the high grass, finally stopping under the shady canopy of an Aleppo pine near the stone building we knew to be the weaving house. We walked around the building into the center clearing where five large pots steamed over fires, the only indication of human activity.

A man, as wide as he was tall, appeared at the door. Muharrem quickly walked to him and kissed him on both cheeks. They stood talking for several minutes before Muharrem turned and extended his arm to us with an encouraging flip of his hand. A closer look revealed deeply scarred skin under a blue-black beard that had been chopped haphazardly from ear to ear to clear his neck from his broad shoulders.

"*Merhaba*, hello," Tom said, waving and extending his hand. I jumped at the sound of his chipper voice, only to see the man break into a laugh and take Tom's hand.

My reception was cooler but not unexpected. A woman, especially a businesswoman, was an anomaly. Our commerce would proceed with caution and reluctance, and Muharrem would carry the conversation with whispered asides to me. Tom was wide-eyed, his body rigid with expectation.

We were invited into an adjoining room where twelve women sat at looms, some twelve to fifteen feet across, others no more than a yard. Rugs were piled around the outer perimeter of the room, waiting for a final wash in the nearby stream. The room slowly filled with others. At one point I glanced outside, amazed to see the number of people tending the vats and fires. I wondered where they'd gone while we underwent the scrutiny of the scar-faced man.

"Let's go outside for a few moments," Muharrem said, when our guide bowed and left the room. "There have been many changes here since our last visit."

We circled the well-tamped ground around the fires while Muharrem explained that our guide was Hanim Samasti, a master dyer who married the daughter of Usa Dagh's mayor. His reputation throughout the weaving communities was legend, until he broke tradition and moved to Usa Dagh, the village of his new wife, instead of bringing her to his home.

"There must have been a good reason for that," I said.

"Oh, yes, a bloody dispute with another family in his village. His entire family moved here with him. I wasn't told the details of the dispute, but it must have been serious to cause such a move. There will be bad blood between the two villages, perhaps forever."

The mayor, Muharrem explained, immediately ousted Usa Dagh's dyer and installed his daughter's husband. There was no outcry; everyone accepted his superior skill and since then their rugs have gained huge successes in the rug distribution center.

"Hanim tells me you will not steal his village rugs as you have done in the past. I am sorry to use this word, but you must know his feelings. He is a proud and passionate man," Muharrem said.

There was more than pride and passion at work in this village. I wanted more time to discuss the situation with Muharrem, but there were too many ears close to us, and English was understood, if not spoken, by more people than I might know.

While we waited for Hanim to return, I searched my memory for what I knew about dyers. For one thing, they were second in value only to the designer because of the impact on the rug's ultimate appearance and sturdiness. Usa Dagh was committed to reproducing in the traditional way and that narrowed their selection of available dyers. Most weaving communities were making use of the cheaper and equally good synthetics. Usa Dagh appeared to be targeting an elite market of traditionalists, and I had no doubt the mayor saw a political and financial advantage to placing his new son-in-law in a position of importance.

Several people carrying long poles approached one of the vats, and we drew closer to watch them pull out the yarn. It was bright blue and I saw several heads shake. One of the men called for Hanim and an argument ensued. Muharrem bent to explain to Tom and me.

"Hanim says he is not pleased. He wants a muted blue and they are arguing about what to add to tone it down."

Seconds later a woman ran from the building, carrying a sack of some kind of plant material. Hanim thrust his hand into the sack, brought out a few leaves and stems and rubbed them between his palms, studying them in various angles of light. Then he took the sack and emptied a small amount into the vat while another man stirred. Hanim repeated this no less than five times before he grunted, handed the sack to the woman, and walked back into the building. At the doorway he turned and shouted something about time to the men with the poles.

I tugged on Muharrem's jacket. "Are we dealing with Hanim today or the mayor?"

Muharrem frowned. "I have already asked this question but received no answer. I am not sure how to proceed."

This had never happened before, but I wasn't going to let village politics get in the way of my work. Either they were in business to sell their rugs or they weren't. I walked to the building.

16

Hanim looked at me briefly when I entered the room and then went back to what he was doing. Energy surged through my body while I waited for him to acknowledge me. When he didn't, I walked back to Muharrem. It would work against me with these men to show anger.

"I want to talk directly to the mayor. If you think that's a bad idea, let's leave."

His green eyes flashed. "To the contrary, courtesy demands we take our leave of the mayor," he said. He stifled a chuckle, and leaned toward Tom. "This is going to be very interesting," I overheard him say.

We found Mayor Mesut Emiroglu in a small sitting room near the back of the building. I explained that we were leaving and wanted to thank him for his hospitality. Since no hospitality had been offered, I hoped my comment pricked.

He fidgeted and pulled on his sash while he swept the floor with his eyes. "Yes, I am sorry not to greet you when you arrived. I was having tea with my wife and daughter."

"Congratulations on your daughter's marriage, Mayor Emiroglu. We have met Hanim and seen his work—an extremely talented dyer and very focused on his work today," I said. "I imagine the familial pride you must feel these days when you deal with those of us who wish to buy your rugs."

He nodded. I waited.

"Yes, yes. Must you leave now? I am free. It would be my pleasure to show you what we have."

I looked at my son and then asked Muharrem if we had time before our next appointment. "Perhaps we have a few minutes to spare before we reach... Iquilur," he said with just the right amount of hesitancy. Iquilur's rug production was well known, a fierce competitor in the area, and quite possibly Hanim's former home.

We were whisked to the showroom where we *stole* a large number of outstanding rugs, perfect specimens for the festival.

For the next day and a half, as we drove toward Ankara, Tom, Muharrem and I discussed the people we'd met, the new rugs we'd added to my inventory, and the upcoming festival. There was a celebratory tone to every word, a feeling of shared success, of accomplishment, of fun, and of plans for the future. For me, something more seemed to be happening. Between the conversations, the glances, and the body language, there was a connection to Tom I'd never felt before. At one point, I warned myself how quickly things could change. But I shut down the thought. Not this time.

We passed through a small mountain village to look for a place to have some lunch and saw a small parade of young men. Muharrem parked the car and we walked to where others were lining the street to watch. Three men were playing wooden flutes, two kept the beat on drums, and another tapped a tambourine with the heel of his hand. Behind the musicians six men balanced trays of large bundles on their heads. The tray was wrapped in pink cellophane and tied with ribbon,

"It's Dowry Day," Muharrem said. "They will walk along every street in the village collecting gifts for the newly wed couple."

People joined the parade as the group passed. They clapped their hands to the music and sang.

"We can go with them, if you like. It is accepted," Muharrem said.

"Yeah, come on." Tom was already falling in line.

"Where?" I asked, but it didn't matter; we were already caught up in the festivity.

After about fifteen minutes we turned a corner where several hundred people were milling around. Three flatbed trucks stacked with furniture, bundles of fabric, and boxes of all sizes bound with rope were parked nearby. The music stopped, the crowd froze, and all eyes turned to the doorway of a two-story stone house with a red tile roof. A burst of cheering shattered the air when a young couple appeared in the doorway. Six large dogs ran between Tom and me, shaking the ground with their weight, and startling me with their deep throated barking. I jumped to the side and collided with an elderly woman. Fortunately the man next to her kept her from falling.

I apologized. Their smiles assured me she was not hurt. She said something but I couldn't hear over the noise.

"What do we do next?" Tom said, like he considered himself a guest.

"The bride's mother, with the help of friends and family, will provide drinks and food for everyone," Muharrem said. "They will drive the couple and their gifts to their new home, help them get set up, then leave them and come back here to celebrate well into the night. We would be welcome if you want to stay."

"Well…" Muharrem looked neutral, a practiced look, meant not to influence me, but Tom was radiating yeses and pleases. "How can we show our good wishes to the bride and groom?"

"Nothing is necessary. The Qur'an instructs that no one must be excluded from a wedding, not the poor, and not the stranger. They will be happy you offer them an opportunity to fulfill Allah's wishes."

I nodded and we walked toward the house. A man with a flower in his lapel greeted us at the door. Muharrem pressed close to him to introduce Tom and me. "He says his name is Masut, his wife is Fatimah, and he is honored. We must go to the kitchen and have a drink."

At each step someone shouted a welcome, until I feared we had taken the place of the bride and groom as the featured guests. Out of the corner of my eye I saw Tom being led off by young boys. He was laughing.

I caught quick glimpses of the expansive kitchen: a huge shiny stovetop with an open grill, double oven and microwave. The walls were tiled from floor to ceiling with large ten-inch squares of peach, yellow and green, reminiscent of the range of colors in van Gogh's Sunflowers. A double tier of white lace curtains flapped in the large open window. A computer, surrounded by eye-level shelves stacked with papers, was on a corner desk. The screen saver glowed with happy faces; I recognized the daughter and her parents among them. A large glass of something pink was handed to me before the mass of people flowed by and scooped me up with them.

We moved out of the kitchen in a solid mass, which made me giggle and think of the Keystone Cops in a jerky old movie. I took a sip of my drink—maybe pomegranate juice, mildly sweet and cold—during a brief stopover in the living room. Muharrem motioned to the front door and I began to weave my way around the exuberant guests to get to him.

At the door I had the sensation of being blasted from a cannon, floating in open space, feeling a cool breeze on my face.

"I'm so glad we came. That was fun, but we'd better find Tom and get going," I said.

The crowd had thinned, or perhaps just spread out, but I didn't see any of the young people among them. That is, not until we walked to the back of the house. Tom was sitting on a glider with two boys on each side, all of them talking at the same time, looking like old friends. I hesitated to interrupt, but Tom saw me. He got up and waved. The boys slapped him on the back and waved as he walked to us.

"Mom, you gotta learn to make that cake," he said as we walked to our car.

"I didn't have any."

"It was flakey and had sweet, gooey stuff inside."

"Baklava," Muharrem said, rolling his eyes. "How did I miss that?"

I suddenly realized I was still holding the glass of juice.

"I'll take it back," Tom said.

I tilted it to get the last swallow and handed it to him. "Thanks, but don't get tempted to stay. They looked like they wanted to keep you." It was rare to see Tom blush.

It was nearly midnight when we reached Ankara's suburbs. The streets were vacant and halos of light formed a precision border as we sped past. When we stepped out of Muharrem's car at the door to our apartment building, the deep bong of a clock sounded, twelve vibrating strokes. We said goodnight to Muharrem and I promised to be in touch from Philadelphia.

Carlos' voice rang out from the lighted kitchen when we opened the door. "Finally. This place has been so empty without the two of you," he said. He wrapped his arms around both of us and planted a loud kiss on each of our heads. "Was it a good trip?" He was looking at Tom for an answer.

"It was terrific, wasn't it, Mom?" He yawned and stretched his arms high.

"The best time I've had in a long time and you had a lot to do with it."

Carlos' eyes shifted back and forth between us. He took a deep breath and let it out slowly while he nodded. "Let's go out for breakfast in the morning and you can tell me all about it."

The next day we asked Elena to join us, and the four of us walked to a small café near the apartment complex. A busload of tourists was being ushered onto the outdoor patio. Their guide's voice rose above the din to say they needed to reassemble at the bus in an hour when they would proceed to Ataturk's tomb. I was relieved we found seating inside the café.

Tom needed no prompting to launch into a litany of our experiences in Torbal and Usa Dagh. He said the highlight for him had been the wedding and the boys he'd met.

"I got their email addresses so we can keep in touch," he said.

"Did you enjoy learning about the rugs?" Carlos said.

"Yeah. Did Mom tell you how I negotiated all by myself with the mayor of Torbal?"

"The mayor?" Elena said.

Tom recounted the experience, embellishing everything with details: the mayor's sons, the showroom, the new weaver and her work, how he examined the rug, and finally every word of the negotiation. When he used a deeper voice for the mayor, I had to press my lips together to contain myself.

"Well, you crammed a lot of learning into a very short time," Carlos said.

"You can't imagine how proud I was of him. I think the mayor would have adopted him on the spot," I said.

"No way I'd live in that village. I like Ankara."

We dug into a large bowl of yogurt and fruit. Elena drizzled honey over hers and handed the small pitcher to me, while Tom and Carlos helped themselves to a variety of breads heaped on a platter kept warm on a heated tile. The whine of Turkish music filled the background with an occasional burst of tourist laughter.

When the table was cleared and our coffee cups refilled, Carlos announced he had a surprise for everyone.

"Nora, Val called yesterday. He thought you'd be home or he said he would have waited until today," he said.

"I'll call as soon as we get back to the apartment."

"No need. He wanted to know how we'd feel about a visit— Philip, too. Of course, I told them it would be great."

I nodded enthusiastically, but I was thinking of the list of things that had to be accomplished before we headed back to Philadelphia to prepare for the festival.

"I told them about the house," Carlos said. "He said you'd mentioned it but he seemed surprised when I said we'd already signed the papers."

I knew exactly what was going through my brothers' heads. A house meant roots and they wanted our roots entwined with theirs in Philadelphia, not halfway around the world. Next step for them would be a condo in Ankara to be near us for the summer. They'd already begun to cut back on their electrical engineering business as a preparatory move toward retirement. It seemed to me the caretaker role they assumed with me when our parents died was still operating despite my marriage to Carlos. To them I'd always be "baby sister."

"The timing is good, I think. They can check out the electrical system in the house for us," I said.

"Is Penny coming?" Tom said.

"No, Tom. I asked that too, but she has two more weeks of tennis camp and then her grandmother is taking her shopping for new school clothes."

"That's stupid. Coming here is way more interesting than tennis, and shopping is a waste of time."

"Don't be so judgmental. In case you haven't noticed yet, girls don't think like boys," I said.

"Hey, what about the festival? Will they come? They'd like it. And they'd like to see me working, too," Tom said.

"They would. We can tell them all about it next week."

By the time we left the café, the sun was directly overhead, its heat bearing down with vengeance. The plane trees along the sidewalk provided shade, but when they didn't, we quickened our pace to the next protected spot.

In Philadelphia the children and many of the adults would be dressed in as little as possible: shorts, halter-tops, and sandals. But on Turkey's streets shorts were rarely seen, bare bellies never. Instead, light cotton clothing that hung loose from the body was preferred for men, women, and children. It seemed sensible given the intensity of the sun.

Elena took my arm, slowed her pace until Carlos and Tom were well ahead of us. "I want to thank you for inviting me to have my own living quarters at your home. I'm thinking about it, but I have heard that such arrangements do not always work out well, I mean, sometimes problems arise between people when they live together."

I squeezed her hand. "Yes, it can happen. I love Carlos with all my heart and there are times when he irritates me."

She laughed. "Yes, but different generations? In the Middle East it is common, but this is not so in the United States, yes?"

"I think it depends on the people involved," I said.

"Yes, of course. I guess I wanted you to know I am aware of this. You know you can talk to me about anything."

Another squeeze.

"Now, dear one, how can I help you? May I offer you my two empty bedrooms—one for Val and Grace and one for Philip? It would be wonderful to have voices other than my own in my apartment."

"Well, now that you bring it up, would you make Paella Valenciana for us one night while they are here?" I'd fallen in love with this savory mixture of seafood and spices the first time Carlos' mother made it for me. She said it was one of many dishes she learned to make as a child growing up in Northern Spain. As with all good cooks, her culinary accomplishments began to include Turkish dishes when her family moved and she met and married Carlos' Armenian father in Istanbul.

"Of course. It will be my pleasure. But what about the rooms?"

"It's generous of you. I'd like to talk to Carlos first, okay?"

She nodded.

"Say, do you know how to make baklava?"

"What kind?"

"There's more than one?"

"Oh, yes. Nuts, fruits, and combinations of both."

I told her to choose and added one more reason to hope she'd share our home. The only threat she might pose was to my waistline.

17

Val and Philip arrived in Ankara planting kisses on my face and calling me their baby sister. Grace stood aside. After six years with Val, she was accustomed to Lebanese effusiveness. The fact that they looked tired made no difference, although as we drove through the city Val swiveled in his seat to catch the sights, while Philip, whose swarthy skin glistened with perspiration, had leaned back and closed his eyes.

"I hope you will make my home yours," Elena said, when she greeted us at the door to her apartment. "Do whatever makes you comfortable."

Philip took her hand and kissed it. "In that case, I need a short nap." She walked him down the hallway to the bedrooms and he took his leave with thanks.

Before we separated, Val made an announcement. "No one's going to cook. I'll take us to dinner and maybe we can drive by your new house on the way. How's that?"

Elena graciously accepted, although I knew she'd prepared a light supper for us. Grace rolled her eyes.

Before they married, I'd warned her about Val's need to control everything, and over the years I watched her cast out all the line he wanted, while she kept her finger on the reel. She called it her "catch and release" strategy: *Catch only when necessary and release as often as possible.*

Would I ever manage that?

The sun still cast its glow at the horizon when we parked in front of the Sursock house. We stepped into the front courtyard and choked on air heavy with the smell of plaster, paint and dust. Carlos slipped inside and turned on the outside lights. For a second I thought we'd stepped into a black and white movie. Everything was coated with a fine gray dust.

"That can't be good for the plants. They'll starve for sun and die," Val said.

While they filed into the living room, I uncoiled the garden hose and turned on the water. The transformation was immediate. Even in the diminished light, water droplets on the red and white bougainvillea sparkled. The flagstone slabs displayed their blue and gray striations and the grass changed from gray to green. I rewound the hose, dried my shoes on the straw mat at the entrance, and walked toward the voices inside.

As I passed the stairs, Tom shouted: "Come see my bedroom." Philip, at the back of the group, heard him and turned around. The others were fully engaged in discussing the kitchen.

"I'd rather talk to Tom than see the kitchen." He winked at me and took the steps two at a time despite his bulk. I thought he looked more like my father every day, while Val and I shared lighter skin and hair and tended to be lean.

The kitchen had been scraped clean of all features and seemed double its original size. Grace said she could picture our breakfast table and chairs under the window.

"Hopefully we'll be able to eat outside most of the time," I said.

Tom and Philip joined us, but when I moved to follow the group out onto the patio Philip took my arm and held me back.

"Nora, Tom said his window—"

"Faces east," I finished.

"Is he interested in Islam?"

"It's no big deal. He's investigating and Carlos and I have decided it's a healthy thing. Elena says Carlos did the same when he was about Tom's age." I walked into the backyard.

We were three days into their visit, sated with Elena's Paella, and sitting on her apartment's spacious balcony when Val asked Tom if he still considered Philadelphia his home. My breath caught.

"I like it here, but Philadelphia's home," Tom said.

"Have you made friends?" Grace asked.

"Yeah."

Elena called him from the kitchen. Grace gave him a high five as he passed and asked me about the festival in Paradise.

"Sounds like another new adventure for our baby sister," Val said.

"I hope you can all attend. It's going to be really great," I said, practicing my ability to ignore the sting.

Elena joined us with Tom on her heels carrying a tray of steaming mugs. Coffee vapors followed their wake. He lowered the tray slowly to the coffee table.

"Yeah, you gotta be there. I'm going to be working in the tent."

"Doing?" Val asked.

For the next few minutes, while we sipped our coffees, Tom explained the hayir.

"And all the money for the rugs will be for Deanna," Tom said. He was beaming.

"All that work and no income?" Val said, turning his head like an owl. He set his mug down.

Carlos got up. He leaned on the balcony's railing still holding his mug. "We will gain the pleasure of helping someone through a crisis."

Val sipped his coffee.

"Mom, I've been thinking about telling Hoja stories to the kids. There's gonna be kids, right?"

"Sure, but remember, Deanna has hired several storytellers to entertain," I said, watching Tom's face fall. "I'm not saying you can't. It's a new idea, and it's Deanna's show."

"I haven't been there, but Tom may have something, Nora," Grace said. "Something special for the children might free up the parents to shop for rugs. Are they children's stories, Tom?"

Philip, his face crinkly with pleasure, explained that when he was in elementary school in New York, family friends in Lebanon sent comic books that featured Hoja stories. "Kids like them because they're silly but adults can find irony and serious truths in the humor. Hoja is the Charlie Brown of the Middle East."

While we listened to Philip, Tom left and came back carrying a tall stool and a turban. "Allow me," he said, bowing from the waist and sitting down on the stool. He shoved the turban forward on his head until it came to rest just above his eyes. His chest swelled with a deep breath.

"Ladies and Gentlemen, Nasreddin Hoja was a roly-poly, turbaned man, mounted on a donkey. He was wise and foolish, a trickster and the butt of tricks. He was devout, but had many human failings. He was happy, but had his share of troubles. He was sweet-tempered, but he could be grumpy too. Listen, and I'll tell you one of his stories."

He hopped down from the stool and acted like he was riding a donkey.

"Hoja had journeyed long on his donkey to reach the town where he'd been invited to dinner. Stiffly, he dismounted and knocked on the front door. When it was opened, he saw that the feast was already in progress. But before he could introduce himself, his host, looking at his travel-stained clothes, told him curtly that beggars were not welcome, and shut the door in the startled Hoja's face.

"Hoja went to the saddlebag on his donkey and changed into his finest attire: a magnificent silk robe trimmed with fur, and a huge silk turban. Then he returned to the front door and knocked again.

"This time, his host welcomed him warmly with many courtesies and conducted him to the main table. Servants placed dishes of delicacies before him. Hoja poured a bowl of soup into one pocket of his robe. To the astonishment of the other guests, he tucked pieces of roasted meat into the folds of his turban. Then, before his horrified host, he pushed the fur facing of his robe into a plate of rice, murmuring 'eat, fur, eat.'

"'What's the meaning of this?' demanded the host.

"'My dear sir,' replied Hoja, 'I am feeding my clothes. To judge by your treatment of me a half an hour ago, it is clearly my clothes and not myself, which are the objects of your hospitality.'"

Tom bowed. Elena shouted "bravo" and led our applause.

"Do you know others?" I said.

He glared at me.

"The voices were fantastic. Where'd you learn to do that?" Philip said.

"I liked the way you acted out what Hoja was doing," Grace said.

He shrugged.

"What do you think, Carlos?" I said.

"The kids will love it. But let's not— What do you say? Put a wagon in front of a horse?"

"Sort of, but we get the idea," I said.

We were clearing the lunch dishes on the afternoon of their departure when Grace asked me to go for a walk. She said she wanted to stretch her legs before the long flight. We took the elevator down to the lobby and walked out into the gardens, resplendent in purple delphinium, orange poppies, and white iris.

"I've been dying to tell you what a difference I see in Tom," she said.

I pulled her down on one of the benches. "Do you really? I've been feeling the same thing, but I don't trust my judgment when it comes to Tom."

Up ahead one of the gardeners turned on a sprinkling system and we heard a shush-shush sound beneath the plants. In several places the walkway darkened. The air around us cooled noticeably. Grace drew my attention to the stems and leaves lifting as they soaked up the moisture.

"Last time I was in this garden Carlos told me he was troubled by the lack of relationship between Tom and me."

She kept her eyes on the pavement.

"It frightened me, Grace. I've tried for years to warm up to Tom and vice versa. Nothing worked. I've accepted that's the way it's going to be. After all, someday Tom will go off to lead his own life and, well, I can live with that."

"But Carlos wants more?" she said.

"Yeah. And he says I'm responsible." I bit my lip. "I don't think Carlos is being fair."

"When kids are involved, adults must be responsible, Nora."

"It would be nice if someone gave me credit for the things I've done for my son."

Grace started to say something, but I cut her off.

"I've given him the opportunity to go with Muharrem and me to learn about the rugs since he's interested in this hayir thing. He really got into it and now I think he's excited about helping at the festival."

"I'd say he's very invested. Did he surprise you with the Hoja idea?" she said.

I nodded.

"Actually, when you think about it, it's quintessential Tom," she said.

"Taking everything to the extreme?"

"Taking your idea and making it his own."

I nodded again. I'd played to his ego and set his creativity in motion.

"I'm really proud of him, Grace, and he knows it. Working on a project together is already improving our relationship."

She put her arm around my shoulders and hugged me. "I'm rooting for both of you."

At the airport, Val pulled me aside. "What's this nonsense about Tom becoming a Muslim? Don't you have any control over your kid?"

"Not that it's any of your business, but Carlos and I are aware of his interest."

"What are you going to do about it?" he said, grasping my arm.

I pulled away from him. "We don't feel the need to control Tom, like you'd like to control everyone around you. When are you going to learn it doesn't work? All it does is drives people away."

I reached down and picked up the last piece of luggage and followed Carlos and Grace to the porter who was loading everything on a cart. My face was burning.

We had less than a week before our own departure and a long list of ends to tie up before then. Tom left shortly after breakfast to visit his friends, Carlos went upstairs to see his mother, and I placed a call to Ed at the gallery.

"Soon as I get your latest purchases, I can ship the rugs to Deanna," he said.

"You still want to go?"

"Are you kidding?"

Sounds came from the living room right after I hung up the phone. Carlos was back, sooner than I expected. He was fidgety, rubbing his hands across the back of the sofa, changing the position of a small ceramic dish.

"Carlos?"

"I think the reality of moving with us is uncovering issues Ana didn't anticipate," he said.

I walked over, took his hand, and pulled him down next to me on the sofa. Our hands together always seemed a perfect fit, my fingers woven into his, feeling the throb of his heart where the pressure was firmest, his skin, not exactly soft, but smooth and supple like tanned leather.

"I know, but I told her not to worry about interfering in our lives," I said.

"What?"

"Mother-in-law problems. She said it can sometimes cause difficulty when generations live together."

His jaw flexed. He shifted to look straight at me and moved his hands to his sides like stabilizers. "You still don't get our culture, do you? You may have difficulty opening yourself up to your brothers' love, but that has never been a problem in my family and I want to keep it that way."

My stomach quivered.

"I know you understand what I'm saying, Nora."

"Of course I do. Look, I love Elena with all my heart. I assured her it would be wonderful to have her with us. Did she say otherwise?"

"That never came up. She's having an emotional struggle with her belongings—things that hold memories of my father, of happy times together when Tapis and I were children."

I turned away. My stomach released but so had my tears. "I think you're very quick to judge me. It's not fair. Sometimes I react to Val, but it's because he's never accepted my work."

"In my view, it's not your work but the effect it's had on Tom. And I agree with him on this."

"You can say that after the effort I'm making now?"

"We'll see. It's not over yet."

Tom went to his room right after dinner to play a new video game. Carlos loaded the dishwasher while I scrubbed a pot we used too often to wait for. When Carlos grabbed a dishtowel to dry it, I took his hand. "I'll do it. You've been eyeing that newspaper all evening. Go on up and I'll bring coffee and join you in a few minutes."

He smiled, kissed me on the back of my neck, and gathered up the Sunday Zaman, the Turkish newspaper he relished. I felt the warm print of his lips as I dried the pot.

Our bedroom was over-furnished. It struck me each time I entered. While I regretted how little the bold geometric patterns of our Northern Caucasus rug showed, our evening ritual of reading together in matching lounge chairs took precedence. Carlos was slouched in one of them. The newspaper formed a semicircle on the floor around him, a thatch of dark curls showed above the sheet he was holding. I set the coffee mugs on the table between us and picked up Sotheby's latest catalog of Fine Oriental and European Carpets.

"The Chinese Silk is on the move," he said.

"Still on exhibition?"

"Sold. The latest owner has a large gallery here in Ankara. The article says 'Galeri Dagi's owner Lale Ozturk says, with the acquisition of The Chinese Silk, she believes she adds not only beauty but also blessing to her gallery.'"

"I thought it wasn't for sale."

"Listen to this: 'I have no doubt of the rug's power,' Ozturk says. 'While The Chinese Silk was exhibited at the Museum they received a research grant they have wanted for many years, a grant which will lift the Museum to world class.'"

"Ankara? Do you know her?"

"Very well. We were kids together."

"Why'd they sell it?" I said.

"For the right price, everything's for sale. Anyway, Lale owns it now. The article says she can't wait to see what miracle comes next."

"Miracle, eh?"

He turned the page and slipped his arm around my waist, pulling me down into the space next to him. "I could be persuaded to perform a miracle of my own, if you're in the mood."

"For the right price?"

He pulled me to the bed. "Some things of value have nothing to do with money. Any Oriental rug broker worth her salt knows that."

18

The Bazaar In Erzurum, Asia Minor

In the morning Çatal walked among the merchants again. Everything was transformed, purposeful, brought to its senses in the sunlight. He breathed in the clear cold air and he, too, felt filled with energy and purpose. Yesterday the festival had overwhelmed him with unfamiliar sights, sounds and behavior, but it was time to attend to his journey's purpose. He began a determined walk along the stalls to compare the quality and prices of the items he needed.

Try as he might, Çatal could not keep to his purpose, once stopping to stare at a man who towered over him wearing a white-feather-topped headpiece and a chain belt hanging with knives and spiked balls. Turning a corner, another man with skin the color of ebony and sharp protruding cheek bones swiveled his head from side to side as though someone were pursuing him. Suddenly he blocked Çatal's way and fixed him with a look that sent a cold blast of fear through his body. He quickly slipped between two tents to wait for the man to pass. Better to disappear than to challenge a mercenary who sought pleasure through fear and stealing. When Çatal could no longer see him, he joined the shoppers again.

The bazaar's goods dazzled him. He stepped closer to a long pole stretched between the trees to see some woven shawls.

Çatal lifted one and was amazed to see the shadow of movement behind it, so fine were the threads. Like a rainbow, the shawls were pale shades of gold, red, blue, and purple. Perhaps one in the color of the sky would sweeten his wife's mood, bring back the smile she had lost over the years.

But while he considered the shawls, a knotted pile rug on another pole suddenly billowed in the wind and snapped as if to call him. The rug, the length and width of two men, was lightweight and skillfully woven. Silk, he judged. Two dragons—one black, the other the color of honey—circled each other with sharp talons outstretched on an amber field. Chrysanthemums sprouted from black and green vines and, in one corner, a small black centipede clutched a vine. Something stirred in Çatal and he reached to touch it.

A short, dry cough startled him and he turned to find the shop's owner at his side. On his face was an expression of satisfaction, the look of a man who knew his goods had sold themselves. But Çatal turned his face and walked away. Undeterred, the vendor's voice extolled the rug's virtues: "finest Chinese silk...excavated from an ancient tomb...a mystery woven in its fibers." He would return later, Çatal thought. But several steps away, he spun around with the sure knowledge the rug would be his because the vines and leaves were the color of his daughter's eyes.

"I wonder, what will the authorities say about a rug stolen from an ancient tomb?" Çatal said, raising his hand to attract a uniformed security guard.

The shopkeeper tripped over a tent pole to reach and pull down Çatal's arm. "Not true, I swear."

Çatal shook his head and took several steps toward the main path. "I'm not a fool, merchant. You have proof?"

"Feel this silk. Softer than a woman's breast, is it not?" the shopkeeper said, holding up a corner of the rug. "You are a man of principles. I want you to have it. Fifty silver denarii. A fair price."

"No price is worth losing a hand or dying in prison."

The shopkeeper blinked his eyes. His chest, puffed up moments ago, sank. "Twenty five silver denarii; my final offer. You cannot refuse."

Çatal walked away, this time with determination.

"No," he said, trotting after Çatal. "Please. Fifteen silver denarii." Minutes later Çatal rolled the rug, tossed it over one shoulder and walked away toward the fortress. Later, in his small enclosure, he draped his arm over the rug's silky nap, sure he'd found the perfect gift. But also sure the words he'd spoken to the merchant had not been his.

For the next two days, Çatal bargained for household goods, using his family's brightly colored kilim as trade. He bartered for braziers, wooden bowls, spices, and some sturdy tent poles of a wood stronger than those he could make from the trees around his village. Such poles would be prized when the men moved their sheep and goats to distant pastures. His last purchase, before retiring to the caravanserai to sleep, was a gossamer sky-blue shawl for his wife.

As Çatal walked through the caravanserai's inner courtyard, he heard a familiar wail. It was Sütlü. She was wagging her head from side to side in a way he recognized as distress. Anger welled up in his chest imagining she had been tethered since their arrival while he enjoyed the enticements of Sacea and the bazaar. He searched for an attendant. Had she been fed and watered? Had she been exercised? He ran his hands over her fur, between her humps, and finally her rump. When he pulled his hand away, it was sticky with a dark wet substance. He rushed to a torch on the wall to look closer—blood.

Çatal called out, but when no one responded, he began to circle the courtyard to find the attendants' quarters. He found more than a dozen men inside, huddled tightly together. He unleashed his rage at them—his camel was wounded and untreated. The fortress was a protection against such happenings and he demanded an explanation. He was met with expressions of fear but no reasons for their failure to fulfill the contract he had made with them.

Çatal was about to grab one of the men, to shake him until he received his due, when there was a sound behind him. It was a uniformed man, who identified himself as their commander. Orders were shouted and immediately the men scrambled to give Çatal a chair. Another offered him wine. Another was sent to care for Sütlü's wound. And when the commander finally snatched the chair next to Çatal and sat, he began to explain quietly, cautiously, never taking his eyes from the door.

A band of wild men, warriors, he said, had entered and taken over the caravanserai shortly before nightfall. They herded his men into their quarters and bolted the door, while demanding services for their horses and themselves. Only after they threatened to kill every camel and horse in the fortress and every attendant, did the commander order his men to do so. The warriors had left not more than an hour ago, leaving all of them shaken.

Çatal could smell the fear in the room and pitied them. They had no choice, he assured them. His cup was filled twice more while they talked, and when Çatal rose to leave, the commander left with him to inspect Sütlü's dressed wound. A patch of fur had been shaved away and the wound—cleaned and sprinkled with a white powder—had stopped bleeding. She had folded her legs into her sleeping position and her neck was stretched out on fresh straw. Her eyes were heavy. Çatal sat next to her until he was sure she would sleep and he saw that an attendant was nearby. Only then did he go to his room on the upper floor.

In the morning he found Sütlü bright and eager. A scab was already forming over her gash. Somehow she knew they were leaving and she pawed the ground with impatience. Çatal took her rein and together they circled the fortress to look for his friend. He climbed to the top of a large boulder and surveyed the crowd, much larger it seemed than when he'd arrived. Finally he gave up hope of Hrant's companionship and began to load Sütlü for the return trip. He rolled the rug tightly and secured it to Sütlü's rump. The last item was his wife's shawl, but as he wadded it to fit into a bag, he decided instead to slide it across his chest between his tunic and woolen vest. He reasoned it would add no weight but would shield him from the fierce wind, always stronger on the return trip through the mountain passes.

Çatal guided Sütlü toward the northernmost trail leading out of Erzurum before he mounted her and once more searched the crowd for his friend. But the man behind him shouted and the press of animals forced him to quicken his pace and join the procession of horses, camels, and donkeys.

Up ahead Çatal heard shouting and saw people running away from the caravanserai, and when he passed the courtyard opening, he saw a large group of dark, sharp cheeked men circling each other. Long curved daggers and swords rattled against their leather-clad legs. Their mounts were unlike any Çatal had ever seen: big-headed horses with stiff, standup manes. The horses snorted wildly and the men's voices had the rhythm of an unfamiliar language. Çatal saw the frightened faces of the attendants. They scattered and hugged the inner walls to get out of their way. Where had these dark men come from? How had they reentered the caravanserai without being seen? Was this more of Sacea's evil spirit? Suddenly the riders burst through the Seljuk gate with an ear splitting scream, heading north.

19

It was getting harder and harder to leave at summer's end. Tom had become especially close to three boys his own age. He asked if they could come for a farewell lunch and I welcomed the chance to meet them. The boys shared the same light green eyes, close-cropped black hair, and T-shirts featuring some wild-haired electric guitarist.

"Why can't you go to school here?" one of them asked.

They dove eagerly into yogurt, tomatoes, olives, cheese and bread—Tom's requested menu.

"We are already studying science on a higher level," he said, carefully swallowing before speaking. "And, we study English from the elementary grades." He shoved his brimmed cap sideways until it stopped at a rakish angle against his protruding ear.

I was standing well away from the table but his comments were aimed at me.

Tom answered. "I've already thought about this. I want to go to Georgetown University or William and Mary College for political science, and I don't think my high school credits would transfer from Turkey, will they, Mom?"

"I don't really know," I said.

As they left to "give Tom a soccer game to remember," they lined up to shake my hand and thank me for lunch.

We'd arranged to visit with Elena that evening to say goodbye. She surprised us with a walnut-filled baklava and coffee and we talked about the house, the upcoming festival, and Tom's new school. Our departure early the next morning hung in the room like stale air. Nobody was willing to open that window of sadness.

"We're counting on you to keep an eye on the house construction," Carlos said.

"Especially the swimming pool."

"I will do better, Tom. I will go for a swim and tell you all about it."

A little laughter helped.

If asked, I'd say Philadelphia was still my home. Buying a house in Ankara wasn't going to change that. Carolyn called the day after our arrival to invite us to a barbeque at their house. Carlos and Jack, each holding a bottle of beer, launched into details of construction on the house. Tom and Marty disappeared into the Denby's enclosed porch, otherwise known as Marty's pack rat nest. Carolyn and I found a quiet spot.

"Are you coming to the festival?" I said.

"Can't. Marty decided to give football a try and they'll be practicing. Sorry," she said.

"How did Tom handle leaving his Muslim buddies?"

"Three had lunch at the apartment before we left. Nice kids. I don't know if those interests will fade now that we're back or continue, but I don't see how they can. Besides we're only four days till the festival and there's so much to do."

As we walked home, Tom said he would have tried out for the team if he'd been home. "They're not a very good team and Marty's not going to help much."

"That's nasty, Tom. Marty's your friend. Be happy for him. I think you're jealous," I said. He increased his speed and walked ahead of us.

I shook my head and looked at Carlos.

"I wish Tom felt better about himself," he said.

"I was thinking just the opposite." Tom seemed to think he was the best at everything.

I spoke daily to Deanna and shuttled back and forth from the gallery, making sure everything was ready. I found notes under the door from customers and a couple neighboring shop owners saying they'd see us in Paradise. Tom spent hours in his bedroom, but assured me he was getting ready to do his part for the hayir. I shrugged off my curiosity and started packing what we'd need.

We'd just left the turnpike and stopped to pay the toll when Carlos pulled off to the side and asked to see the map.

"How far is it from here to the turnoff?" Carlos said.

"Maybe seven miles. Don't worry, I know the way," I said.

He pulled back onto the road and within minutes we saw a freshly posted road sign: "Paradise, founded in 1827. Population 95,000. Home of the Festival of a Thousand and One Nights."

"Wow, looks like the publicity committee's been busy," I said. "Deanna said the town doubles. The mayor's donating shuttles to help with the parking. Good idea, huh?"

Carlos slowed to a crawl as we entered Paradise's quaint commercial area. Jewel-toned banners hung from every streetlight. Men in overalls clamored around a platform being constructed in the town's center square, and near the main entrance a billboard announced several upcoming musical performances and belly-dancing presentations.

Centuries-old oak trees shaded the sweep of velvet lawn surrounding Deanna's home. I guessed the house had a history and a brass marker over the front door confirmed it: Johann Bauer, 1829. Deanna was waiting on a wrap-around porch supported by white Iconic columns.

"Welcome to Tall Oaks," she said, recovering her breath. I'd held mine as I watched her descend the four steps to the driveway. There was no handrail. Two teenaged boys appeared from nowhere and reached for our suitcases. As they disappeared into the house through a wood paneled door with beveled glass inserts, I introduced Carlos and Tom.

"It's a pleasure to meet someone who can turn a whole town upside down," Carlos said, taking her hand and planting a kiss. I'd never seen him do that before.

"Oh, my, no. It's taken on a life of its own. I've had very little to do with it," she said. "You can pull around back. There's a spot for you to park. I've been offered hard cash for it, but decided to save it for you." She slid her eyes sideways at him, but Carlos, still unaccustomed to certain types of American humor, didn't get it.

"Don't doubt that for a minute," I said. "I can't believe the preparations this year. Bigger and better doesn't even begin to describe it." I gave her a gentle hug. Her hazel eyes seemed to look at me from watery depths, but despite her difficulty with the steps, she seemed less frail. As I walked across the porch behind her, my mind wandered back to the hard-nosed businesswoman I'd once dealt with.

I'd been brokering for five years the first time I drove to Paradise to meet the owner of the Sardis Gallery. My research indicated that Deanna had just taken over her uncle's gallery after a brief career with a Boston-based travel agency—hardly a solid background for an Oriental rug dealer. Wrong. I later learned Deanna's expertise was in guiding groups through the Middle East. She had a working knowledge of the languages, the cultures, and the textiles. I never approached her again without making sure I was thoroughly prepared with the latest information possible. Thereafter, we were like diplomats: mouths in one place, eyes and ears in another. But that was then.

"How are you feeling?" I said.

"I'm excited, and it seems to have improved my appetite. I've gained eight pounds since you were here. Energy's back where it used to be. Can't even begin to tell you how timely that is. Every day I learn about some new activity springing up. The advertising is great. Tomorrow, Friday, there will be a full-page spread in the newspaper. Would you believe The White Swan Bed and Breakfast is hosting a group from Japan? And, Tom, just wait till you see your tent."

I waited for Tom to react, but a painting of a nude woman inside the entrance had distracted him.

She led the way through a large, flower-filled entrance hall, sweet with the fragrance of roses and jasmine. A long sweep of mellow wood flooring ended with a curving staircase to the second floor. We climbed the stairs and I deliberately felt for seams in the banister. I suspected there wasn't one and I was right—an amazing achievement with a solid piece of wood. A chandelier with hundreds of tiny hanging crystals sparkled overhead and illuminated the upstairs hall, but my eyes dropped automatically to the rug on the landing. It had a central rose and gold fluted medallion, surrounded by a dark blue field, bordered in pale blue clouds on a rose background—a North Persian wool, I guessed.

"This one's for you and Carlos," Deanna said with a sweep of her hand toward a bedroom. "And, Tom, you're at the end of the hall. You'll like it. It used to be Brad's room and we've kept all his 'guy stuff,' as he always called it."

I had to have a look. The "stuff" turned out to be models of jet airplanes and wall posters of air races around the world.

"There was a time Brad wanted to be a Blue Angel," she said.

"He changed his mind, yes? It looks very dangerous to me."

"Oh, no, Carlos. Brad doesn't change his mind once he makes it up. Unfortunately, he has glaucoma. It's controlled with medication. That stopped his dream but not his determination. He became an aeronautical engineer instead. He said if he couldn't soar in the sky, he'd support from the ground. That's what he does nine to five. On Fridays and Saturdays he helps at the gallery, something I regret, but…

"Well, Tom, how do you like the room?"

He gave her an approving smile and said thanks, slipped in, and closed the door behind him. "You can use the bathroom across the hall," she projected through the barrier. He opened the door and said thanks again. "Uh, did you say something about a tent before?"

She threw her head back and laughed. "That's what I said. Get settled and we'll drive to the park so I can show you."

That seemed to satisfy him and he withdrew.

"Nora, your rugs arrived yesterday and they're gorgeous. They should be in place, but please feel free to rearrange them as you like.

"By the way, my friend Heidi Rose owns The Vintage, a bed and breakfast at the end of our road. She will be delighted to host your family when they arrive. I'm sure she can add your gallery manager—Ed Gallo, right?"

"Thank you, Deanna," I said. Earlier we'd discussed securing hotel rooms for them. This was better. We'd be nearby and, knowing my brothers, they'd make a new friend.

Our room had a bay window that faced the front of the house. From the second floor I looked through a curtain of fluttering oak leaves to the town's central bell tower. At that moment it rang three times.

Behind me Carlos was opening and closing drawers. He'd already hung his shirts, trousers and jackets in the large wardrobe.

"Everything's falling into place, don't you think? And Tom...I think he's fitting in nicely."

He walked to the window and took me in his arms. I wondered if I'd always have the same reaction to his embrace. It was more than affection; it carried a message of acceptance and comfort. It told me I belonged to him and, for the moment, I felt assured of his love.

"Do you see, Nora, what a difference it makes when you reach out to him?"

I nodded with my cheek against his chest, feeling the warmth, hearing the rhythm of his heart. I was looking forward to the events of the next few days. For so many different reasons it made my head spin.

The tent rose from Temple Park like a palace in a once-upon-a-time story. I counted twelve peaks topped by jewel-toned flags and, along the path to the tent's main entrance, banners of the same colors flapped on high poles with golden balls on the ends. I was not prepared for the tent's cavernous size.

"Did I send enough rugs? This is gigantic, so much bigger than I imagined."

"You won't think so when the people start pouring in. Look, the rugs you sent couldn't be better," Deanna said, tracing a wide arc with her arm.

At the threshold was a traditional Mashad, easily 90 knots per inch. Nothing less could produce the intricate pattern of scrolling green vines with rust and brown leaves sprouting in every direction, densely filling every space in the center field. The borders were a dark contrast to the honey-colored center. Alternating narrow and wide strips of pale flowers on black and black rosettes on gold completed the outer edges.

I bent to stroke the nap with my palm and remembered the specific negotiation with a tall, imperious Arab whose sharp features matched his tongue. Several times he addressed Muharrem and avoided eye contact with me. It was the first time I had to ask Muharrem to leave to show my authority and force the Arab to deal with me. When I later apologized to Muharrem, he assured me it was the only thing I could have done.

"Autumn wool, right?" Deanna said. "I couldn't resist touching it myself."

I nodded, acknowledging again how versed she was in every aspect of the Oriental rug business. In the Mashad area of Iran, the sheep are sheared twice each season, producing softer wool in the fall. It might have been slightly less durable, but made up for it in the velvet-like texture. I made a mental note to pass along that information to Tom.

Every rug I looked at invoked a memory. They were an album of photos in my mind, of people and places, of acceptance and rejection, but primarily of learning. Pieces of my life.

We walked to the far end of the tent and stopped at the stage.

"How do you like the lanterns?" Deanna said.

"Clever. They look like real flames."

"Those lanterns were just one of the early hurdles I had with the fire department. I wanted the authenticity of torches, but they wouldn't allow it. They didn't care that the tent is treated with fire retardant. These look pretty good, though, don't you think?"

The stage, tables with lanterns, and a corner bar were spread along the three outer edges. Small halogen lights, set strategically overhead on metal poles, spotlighted each rug, drawing out the colors. For a few seconds I felt the same reaction when switching on the lights in my gallery. I knew it was impossible but the fibers seemed to respond to the light, to vibrate, as if they were calling attention to their beauty.

Deanna had walked on. I traced her steps around the large kilim pillows stacked on each rug for sitting or reclining. Tom was trying one out.

"What do you think, Carlos?" I said.

His grin was his answer.

"Good, now come and see the surprise I have for you, my entrepreneurial young man."

Tom jerked to attention and we followed her outside and around to the rear. There, a white tent, with its own colorful banner flying on top, was being fitted inside with artificial turf. A long table, a stack of child-sized plastic chairs, and a bar stool waited for placement.

"I hear you tell your best stories perched on a stool," Deanna said.

"Yeah. Thanks," Tom said.

"Some of the parents and neighborhood kids want to help the children make turbans, but I told them I wanted to ask you first," she said.

"I don't know. What do you think, Mom?"

Tom asking my opinion—that was a first. "Well, if the children are occupied, you can give your voice a rest," I said.

He shrugged.

"Excellent. I'll call Mrs. Fenster to give her the go-ahead with the turbans. She's very clever with crafts, the kind of person who can make something from nothing," Deanna said. She pulled her cell phone from a pocket and dialed.

The day before the event we were out of bed before the sun. Carlos was leaving for the train station to retrieve Philip, Val, Grace, Penny and Mrs. Bonseur. I stayed behind to have a second cup of coffee with Deanna. Through the open window, I heard the car's wheels crunch on the gravel and then quiet settled over the house. I imagined Deanna alone with her worries in a house that held memories of her husband, long passed, and the running feet of her boy, the future Blue Angel. No doubt her gallery business filled the gap. I knew the feeling. I took a long sip of dark, rich coffee, and stared into the liquid, wondering what Tom would be like as a man.

"The lull before the storm," Deanna whispered. "Nice, huh?"

"Wonderful."

"It won't last long. I guarantee once the festival is underway Paradise will feel like a runaway train. I'm sure glad you're here, Nora."

"Tom's ecstatic about the Story Tent. Thank you for that," I said.

She placed her hand on her chest. "I've had a feeling about Tom since you called to tell me about his idea. Young people like Tom deserve all the encouragement and positive reinforcement we can give them. Brad was just like him at that age."

"I'll be happy if he turns out like Brad. He's been a difficult boy." I hid inside the coffee cup, waiting for the chill I normally felt when opening up about Tom. It didn't come.

"Head strong?"

"You could say that."

The curtains were suddenly sucked out the open window. Voices filled the foyer and Carlos called out.

"We're in the kitchen," Deanna said.

They paraded in, all five of them, plus Ed Gallo.

"We met on the train," Ed said, when I told him I was surprised to see him so early. They'd had a good time together, more a gathering of old friends than a meeting of strangers, though that's what they were. The festival had brought us together for a common purpose and, by the time they asked questions and we gave answers, we were an organized unit, ready for the work of the day. They left to drop their bags off at The Vintage, promising to be back within the hour.

At the park, Ed was eager to meet Brad and set up a cashiering point. As we walked, he pulled me aside.

"Nora, I just want to thank you for the opportunity to be here. I'm proud to work for a gallery that is willing to make this kind of generous sacrifice for another gallery owner. I wanted you to know it means a lot to me."

"We're doing it together."

He looked on the verge of tears and I thought it best to quicken our pace and join up with the others.

Philip and Val were saying they hoped they'd be given some responsibility, but had no idea what might be needed. Deanna gave them the name of the equipment rental company's foreman. Penny, Grace and her mom wanted to shop and asked where the shops were. They were happy to hear the festival area was within a few blocks of Paradise's center square boutiques. But when Penny saw Tom working with other young people and a few adults in the Story Tent, she changed her mind and stayed with her cousin.

We went our separate ways. Deanna and I decided to do a 'walk through.' More than a timetable, we actually imagined ourselves to be visitors—to see what they'd see, to hear what they'd hear, to smell what they'd smell. It was what every event planner must do. We were more than satisfied with the results.

Townspeople were stationed at all entrances to the park. They gave out brochures that contained a detailed map of the area, a schedule of events, and suggested places to eat and stay. I caught my breath when I saw a framed box with a headline: "Special for Children. Thomas Reardon Ghazerian, The Hoja Storyteller." Below that was an invitation to listen to a story and make a Hoja turban. The picture showed a short fat man on a donkey wearing a feathered turban on his head.

A voice rang out: "Is this the Philadelphia rug broker we've been hearing about?"

Deanna and I turned to watch the approach of an imposing young man with a dazzling smile.

"Frank, hi. Yes, this is Nora Ghazerian. Nora, our Festival Chairman Frank Denegawa."

My hand disappeared into his as he loomed over us. He was the Hollywood screen image of an American Indian: chiseled cheekbones, tanned skin, and athletic build.

"Great job with this, Frank," she said, holding up the brochure. "Have you met Nora's son Tom yet? He's in the Story Tent now."

"No, but I sure want to. Was it his idea, about the Hoja stories, I mean?" He directed his question at me.

"Completely his," I said.

"Gotta meet this kid. See you later." He bounded off with a quick wave.

"That's a bundle of raw energy," I said to Deanna.

"Isn't he though? Still single, and every young gal in town is in hot pursuit."

"What's his story? He's American Indian, right?"

"Oneida. His family's been in this area for generations, fought with the colonists during the Revolutionary War. He owns a very successful insurance agency just down that street." She motioned with her hand.

We continued our 'walk through' and then Deanna left to
return to the house to rest. I decided to walk to the Story Tent
to show Tom the brochure.

I found him already looking at a copy. "Mr. Denegawa just
gave it to me. It's cool. So was he. He's the chairman of the
whole festival, did you know that?" he said, his eyes lingering
on the printed framed box.

"I just met him too. You ready?"

"Yeah, but I'm not making turbans."

"I am," Penny said.

"Figures."

Penny slapped him on the arm.

A boy about Tom's age stuck his head in the tent. "Hey,
towelhead."

"Shut your mouth," Tom said, lunging toward the boy.

"Let's have none of that, Michael," Mrs. Fenster said. The
boy backed out.

"What's that all about?" I said.

"Nothing. I can handle him," he said.

Penny stepped to Tom's side. "We can handle him, Tom. I
know his type. Bullies are all noise."

"I don't need a girl to help me," he said. He brushed past her
and walked over to the table where Mrs. Fenster was showing
three little girls the fabrics they could use to make turbans
when the festival started.

Penny's lower lip was quivering. I leaned over to her. "Tom
knows you'd do anything for him, Penny. You're more than his
cousin; you're his friend. I think he's nervous. He'll apologize
later, you'll see."

She nodded. "I guess," she said, and walked over to watch
Mrs. Fenster. Tom smiled at her and her face lit up.

Later outside I found Val and Philip driving a small go-cart
stacked with trashcans. "There'll be food vendors all over the
park," Val said. "It's our job to put the cans on these green
spots. See?" He held up a map. "When we finish this, we have

to put some smaller ones in the tent. There'll be a sign that says 'No food inside,' but you know how that goes."

I guess it was part of their training as engineers to concern themselves with the smallest details. In their hands even the placement of trashcans was going to be handled with precision.

Beyond Philip I saw Brad snapping his head from side to side. "See you later," I said to my brothers and started walking toward him. When he saw me, he turned my way. "I think I'll take a few minutes to check on Mom. She's supposed to be resting at home, but I don't trust her."

"Looks to me like everything's in place, don't you think?" he said.

"It's fabulous. Can't wait for tomorrow."

At nine sharp the next morning, the festival kicked off with the high school band escorting the storytellers to Temple Park. Deanna, assuring us she was well rested, insisted on going with us. We piled into the car, which had to stop at each intersection to let people cross the street. We were ready to do our part, whatever in our individual minds that might be. In actuality, Tom and Ed were the only ones with real assignments. Tom wanted to work with the rugs, but wasn't sure he could now that he had his own responsibilities. Either way, Tom was involved. I had accomplished that much.

"So many police. Have you had security problems?" Carlos said.

"No, but since 9/11 they believe it's what they need to do. I think it makes people jumpy, but I can't convince the police."

"Their presence is important," Val said. "One of the officers told me there's been a graffiti campaign going on for the last week—all aimed against Muslims, too ugly to repeat. As soon as it shows up, they send out a clean-up crew."

"That's horrible. It's never happened before. Maybe it's outsiders. This town's always been so gung ho about the festival," Deanna said.

"Don't be naive. There's a war going on. Of course, there's going to be an emotional response to anything that smacks of the Middle East," Val said. "I'm glad the police are here in force."

The park filled with people and the roar of voices swelled in counterpoint with the band. We shouted our plans to each other: Carlos and I were going to check out the rest of the park. Val and Philip wanted to join the "action," wherever they could find it. Penelope pleaded with Grace and her grandmother to get to the tent early. She pointed to the brochure, which indicated the mayor would introduce the storytellers at ten and she wanted to be "up front, not in the corner at the back of the tent." They agreed and I said we'd join them later.

Tom's tent was open for turban-making from ten in the morning until four in the afternoon, with pauses for Hoja stories. He was scheduled to tell a Hoja story at eleven and the same story again at three. He wanted to stay around the Story Tent and we told him we'd be back to hear his first story. There was so much going on and Carlos whispered he'd had enough of the crowd. We went directly to the main tent and joined Grace, her mother and Penny.

I saw Ed with Brad at the cashiers' table and gave him a wave. We'd hardly seen Ed since he arrived. He shunned all the social and sight-seeing activities to make certain the rugs were priced correctly and insisted I should "circulate." He assured me I would be needed only at the close of the festival when the sales activity intensified. I didn't press him further.

We found our group directly in front of the stage. "I hope you like looking up the storytellers' noses," Grace said, when we joined them.

"At least we won't miss what they say. It's noisy in here," I said.

But the noise dropped to a murmur when the mayor walked to the front of the stage. He had tiny slits for nostrils, escaping nose hair, and the voice of an orator—good thing, since his belly distanced him from the microphone. The storytellers were lined up behind him, a costumed variety of eccentric-looking men. Two wore turbans, one sported a fez, three looked like they had been coifed by a mad stylist, and the last head shone like a mosque dome—one storyteller for each night of the festival. If their appearance was an indication of their stories, I expected to be dazzled.

The mayor declared the official beginning of the weeklong festival and welcomed the crowd. When the cheering and clapping ended, he announced the program. Each storyteller would introduce himself and give a provocative sentence or two about his story. I saw people taking notes, most likely choosing the nights they'd attend. I glanced at my watch and nudged Carlos. "Let's get over to Tom's tent." We slipped out, under their noses, so to speak.

There were seven fidgety children about five or six years old sitting in front of Tom with their turbans at various angles on their heads. If he saw us enter the tent, he gave no indication. He was showing the children a large poster of Hoja—where he got it was a mystery to me—and telling them to pretend that he was Hoja.

"You're not fat."

"You're not even old like him."

Carlos put a restraining hand on my arm when he felt me squirm.

"I've got a magic lamp here," Tom said, pulling a small silver oil lamp from inside a voluminous purple coat Mrs. Fenster had made for him. "When I rub this lamp, the spirit of Hoja will enter my body."

He rubbed, and when the next few words came out of Tom in a totally different voice, their eyes were transfixed. He had

them. He told a story I'd never heard before about the day Hoja
stopped to take a nap under a tree with strong branches and
tiny brown nuts hanging over his head. He asked God why He
made the big strong tree hold tiny nuts when large, heavy
pumpkins were held together on the ground with skinny vines.
But when a tiny nut fell on his head, he acknowledged that
God knew best.

I couldn't tell if the children were laughing at the story or at
Tom's voice and actions, but there was no question they'd
liked it.

As the children left the tent, Tom whipped the turban from
his head and wound the coat around his body, waddling oddly
with the bulk.

"What did you think? It was my first one and I'll probably
get better each time," he said. His chin was jutting ever so
slightly.

"You were terrific. Those kids loved it," I said.

"They'll be standing in line before three o'clock," Carlos
said, ruffling Tom's hair.

Mrs. Fenster called to him and we left. Just outside the Story
Tent it struck me that Tom could be anything he put his mind
to.

20

Seconds later Tom came barreling out of the tent behind us. "See you later," he said.

We waved at his back and turned to explore another part of the park.

A touch on my shoulder stopped me.

"Did I miss him?" It was Philip, gasping for breath and drawing his stocky brown fingers through his hair. "Did you hear Tom? I tried to get here earlier, but Penny wanted us to have our pictures taken with the camel and the line was endless."

"Camel?" I said, craning my neck to see.

He pointed to a beehive of children. "Can you believe it?"

"Where'd they get a camel?"

"He'll be on again at three, Philip. Don't miss it; he was amazing," Carlos said.

He nodded and set the alarm on his watch to three o'clock. "There," he said. "Just in case I get distracted." He started to move off, but stopped suddenly and lifted his head.

"I smell kabob," he said. "Say, why don't I bring some back to the house for dinner?"

We'd had no lunch and I was hungry. "That's a great idea, but I'd better check with Deanna to see if she's up to having people in the house. I'll call you later this afternoon. And if it's okay with her, we'll pick you up when you've got the kabobs."

We opened and closed the front door quietly, expecting that Deanna would be resting in her room, but she shouted from the kitchen.

"I have fresh lemonade. Come have some with me, and take those worried looks off your faces. I'm fine," she said.

I took the same seat I'd had earlier; Carlos sat across from me, shifting his chair so he could see both of us.

Deanna's kitchen was a natural gathering place of comfortable furnishings and muted colors: pale blue walls, ivory wainscoting, and lime-colored tile floor. The breeze from the window lifted my hair, a massage with floating fingers.

"It's great having all of you here," Deanna said, dreamily. "Feels like family. Brad's all I've had since my husband died, and I don't believe you know Brad lost his wife last year."

"God, no. Jenny?"

"They'd only been married four years. Just started the paperwork to adopt a baby from China. Watching him try to cope nearly broke my heart."

"What happened?" Carlos said.

I caught my breath. "A baby, oh, Deanna."

"He got the call at work." She swallowed several times before continuing with a constricted voice. "Jenny had invited a girlfriend to lunch and when she didn't answer the door, she looked in the window and saw Jenny on the kitchen floor. She'd fallen off a ladder…broke her neck."

She inhaled roughly. "We've been keeping brave faces for each other, but it's a farce. Anyway, things started getting better when he decided to throw himself into the gallery. Too busy to think, is my guess."

"It takes time." Carlos said.

"Just in time actually. Latest word is the adoption contract is being rewritten for Brad as a single parent and I'll be a guardian as well. It's what he wants and I think it'll be good for both of us. Children bring us hope for the future. We can use a dose of that."

She cupped her face in her hands. I thought she was going to break down, but it was just a gesture, a cleansing movement. "Brad needs this—me, too, for that matter."

I didn't know what to say. After a few seconds, I got up and refilled our glasses. "We'll help in any way we can," I said.

"Having family and friends around and doing something you enjoy—best medicine in the world," Deanna said.

"Yeah. I haven't always found a good balance between work and family, but I'm improving."

I locked eyes with Carlos.

That night we set up a buffet with the lamb kabobs and a large Greek salad, courtesy of Philip. After filling our plates, we wandered out to the side porch, some to sit on the chairs while Tom and Penny chose the stairs. The air was warm and the sprinkling system had just shut down. Almost immediately robins flew from the tree branches, stationing themselves at intervals. Like choreographed dancers, they ran several steps, stopped, cocked their heads from side to side and pecked at the grass. The lucky ones pulled up worms. I picked out the robin that was me, the one who got the worm every time. After seeing the preparations for the festival fall into place, it was hard not to project ultimate success.

The doorbell rang and Tom put down his plate to answer it. When he came back he said there were policemen at the door. Carlos accompanied Deanna, and the rest of us remained on the porch with ears trained to the alternating voices at the front door.

Several minutes later the door closed and Deanna returned. "Well, that's a sign of the times, I suppose," she said. "They wanted verification from me that I knew you. I apologize for our police department."

I looked at my brothers' and Carlos' Mediterranean faces and understood.

"No problem, Deanna," Philip said. "They may be suspicious of our looks, but they love our food. These kabobs are excellent. They happen to be my specialty so I know."

Sweet Philip, always finding the positive side of everything. Val, on the other hand, rolled his eyes. It was rare that he allowed Philip in the kitchen, and to make up for it, I requested kabob whenever we were invited to dinner at their house just to let Val know he wasn't the only cook.

"Did you hear about Tom's smashing success in the Hoja Story Tent?" Philip said, changing the subject. "I heard the three o'clock performance and Mrs. Fenster said it was even better than the eleven o'clock. We have a star in our midst," he said.

Tom stood and took a bow.

"Hey, look at the time," Grace said. "Now that our Hoja storyteller has put us in the story mood, we should get over to the big tent. Eight o'clock, right?"

We wrapped up the food, tossed the dishes in the sink and left the house in two cars. The sun had slipped below the horizon; in its place was a rosy glow. People streamed along the pavements from all directions. We found a parking spot and stepped out into temperatures decidedly cooler than during dinner. There were people everywhere, but there was a difference. I almost wanted to call it reverence. The tent, glowing saffron from the lamps inside, was absorbing people soundlessly. We found an Egyptian pile rug large enough to hold us and settled down in the hush to wait for the program to begin. Tom and Penny shared a kilim pillow.

Heads turned in unison with the "ting" of a finger cymbal. A single dancer was making her way down the center aisle, hips rolling, flashes of light from coins and bangles picking up the lanterns' flames. The sharp tinny beats multiplied and accelerated with each undulating forward movement, and when she reached the stage, she stopped, raised her arms and, with an ululation, called to the storyteller.

He ran to the stage, jumped up and turned to face the audience. Bigger than life and completely mesmerizing, he pierced the audience with his black eyes. I couldn't look away. The dancer had vanished. He raised his fabric-draped arms and began, cleaving the silence with a ripping "Tsssss! Prepare your mind, prepare your heart, but guard your soul. The Princess Scheherazade comes with demons and jinns, gold and sparkling jewels. We will travel the wild ocean, where sultans and sailors journey to lost lands, and to dark underground caves where a serpent with the face of a woman turns men to ash with her glance...

"But first, give ear to the beginning. There was a sultan named Shahriyar, who loved his people and reigned over them with justice and mercy, with one exception. His wife betrayed him and when he learned of it, he slew her. In his disillusion, he ordered his wazir to bring him a maiden every day. He married her, spent the night with her, and in the morning ordered the wazir to have her head chopped off. That is, until he met Sheherazade..."

His voice rumbled from the depths of his chest, at once thunderous, then barely a whisper. Light shimmered around his figure and then gradually his words became a backdrop to the pictures in my head.

"An impoverished fisherman waded into the ocean and cast his net in an arc over the clear blue water. It sunk to the bottom and settled over a clay pot, which the fisherman hauled to shore. Disappointed that his children would be hungry for another day, he fell to his knees, grabbed a rock, and using his entire body's weight, crushed the pot.

"A mist surrounded him on every side and when it cleared a giant jinni with arms folded across his chest thundered his thanks and offered the fisherman three wishes. 'I have one wish only, O Great One—fish to feed my family,' he said. As the last syllable left the fisherman's lips, the jinni vanished, leaving the poor man doubting the giant had heard his wish.

"But the following day the fisherman's net contained four fish unlike any he had seen before—one red, one white, one blue, and one yellow. Believing such astonishing fish should belong to the King, he walked to the palace and presented them. The King was pleased and gave the fisherman 400 dinars. The next day the fisherman's haul was equally astonishing and the King gave him 400 gold pieces. Finally, the King demanded to see the place where the fisherman found such fantastic fish.

"The old man, reluctant to divulge his lode, led the King over a mountain and across a great desert, hoping the King would grow weary. But the King was undaunted, and when finally they approached the fishing spot, the fisherman was shocked to see a palace built of stone and plated with iron. The palace gate was open, but the fisherman shook with fear and tried one more time to discourage the King by telling him an evil spirit had taken residence. Still the King was determined to know the secret of the fish and proceeded boldly inside.

"There, on a couch in the middle of the palace sat a young man. He wore a silken robe studded with pearls and an Egyptian gold crown embedded with gems. The King saluted him courteously and made his request to know the secret of the fish. The youth opened his mouth to speak but shook so hard with sobs the words would not come. When the King asked what was wrong, the young man pulled aside his robe and displayed the lower half of his body. It was stone from his navel to his feet!

"The King took pity on the lad and asked what he might do to help. It was then the youth told him the fish were a warning. 'How is that?' said the King."

Suddenly the tent lights went up and the storyteller was gone. I seriously thought I'd been under a spell. My muscles ached from being frozen in place, and when Carlos touched my hand I jumped.

"Now you know why Sultan Shahriyar couldn't bring himself to kill Scheherazade," he said.

I leaned over to Tom. "That was something, wasn't it?"

"He gave me some new ideas I can use," he said.

"I'll bet he could get some good pointers from you, Hoja."

He looked away, but not before I caught him trying to hide a smile.

We got up, ready to go. Tom asked if he could stay for a while. He wanted to find the boy who was helping Mrs. Fenster in the Story Tent.

"Stay away from him," I said.

"Not him. Another guy I met."

I gave him an hour, hoping Carlos would walk around the grounds with me. Mystery and magic still hung in the air, and I wanted to savor it as long as I could. He agreed and took my hand. The rest of the family had already wandered away with a wave and a promise to call in the morning.

A chill breeze played around us and the leaves and evergreen needles hissed overhead. The park lights cast stripes across the pavement, ebbing as we passed. My hand was curled in his, warm and safe, while my head spun with vivid scenes of cruel jinns, beheaded wives, deranged apes, kings and princes, pleasures and poisons. The storyteller's skill, it seemed to me, was to present each character and each action with just enough detail to capture but never enough to satisfy. At the very moment we felt the approach of a conclusion, he launched us into another dilemma, then left us hanging. Missing the next night was out of the question.

I lifted the collar of my jacket against the wind and rapidly dropping temperature. "Leave it to the Orient—the stories, the images. I never tire of it. Maybe the rugs have done something to my head." I snickered.

"Definitely prejudiced, but I like that about you," Carlos said, giving me a squeeze.

We quickened our pace around the perimeter of the park, about a mile square, before turning back toward the tent to meet Tom. Oddly, the saffron glow seemed brighter as we reached the path to the tent's major opening. Orange and red blared from inside. Someone screamed, "Fire."

We ran to the front opening and looked inside. Flames were exploding behind the stage and reaching to the tent top. People were running to the two smaller exits at the sides of the stage. Several men dashed in with small fire extinguishers. Carlos started in behind them. I tried to stop him, but he was already out of hearing range. People were running up the path, some calling out names.

Tom. Where was Tom? I ran back into the tent to find Carlos, but a policeman appeared from nowhere and stopped me, pushed me back to the gathering crowd and told all of us to back away. "Fire trucks are on the way," he said.

"My son may be in there," I shouted. "My husband's in there." I grabbed his jacket but he shook loose.

"We're clearing everybody out. Get back, now. You're in the way."

Flames that were concentrated at the back end now licked across the top of the tent. Smoke boiled toward the entrance and out onto the grounds. Shouting and screaming came from all directions and authoritative voices barked back. Like a solid trembling mass, we backed away down the path, away from the heat.

Carlos had to come through that opening. Tom had to be with him. The rugs. Oh, God, the rugs. I dialed Carlos' cell but there was no answer and I wouldn't have been able to hear over the sirens and shouting anyway. I stood watching with the others.

"I heard some kids knocked over a lamp," a man behind me said.

21

People were swarming around the perimeter of the taped-off area. I was caught between the police and others like me who'd last seen their families inside the tent. The woman next to me tried to pick up her frantic toddler, who'd been reduced to a circle of blonde curls with a hysterical disembodied voice. I tried to give the mother room to bend but couldn't. Voices pressed in, rose in high-pitched panic, and over them were the sirens of approaching emergency vehicles.

My face was within inches of a pock-faced officer whose preoccupation with planting his bulk against us was suddenly more than I could bear. I wedged my shoulder into him, pushed through, and ran. No one stopped me; the police were intent on containment. I stumbled around to the back, unable to keep my eyes from the fire.

Flames were climbing the sides, swallowing the tent like an emerging underground beast. The fire engines had parked and men and women in yellow slickers dragged water hoses toward the tent. Water blasted from several directions into the tent's center but the flames lashed under and over the watery arches. As I stood frozen, the interior poles collapsed and the tent imploded, sending an expanding black cloud high overhead, hiding one horror but unleashing another. I sent my prayers bolting through the remaining heavenly vault before they could be stopped, and when I lowered my eyes, I found that my own space had disappeared. I careened forward, choking and

tearing, unable to see my feet and desperate for a breath of
air.

Several emergency vehicles parked at the back of the tent
area were barely visible. One of them began backing away
and started up its siren. I searched the area for Tom and
Carlos, but saw only firemen and policemen. An angry
voice came up behind me.

"How'd you get in the restricted area?" He took my arm
and pulled me.

"I'm looking for my family. Who's in that ambulance
that just left?"

The steady whoop-whoop of another ambulance sounded
and I saw it backing up toward the street. White-jacketed
people assembled to lift bodies onto stretchers. I yanked
free.

"Hey, hey, I can't let you get in the way, lady." He
grabbed me again.

"Who's in charge here? I want to see somebody now," I
said.

"If you don't get back, I'll show you a jail cell."

"Please, isn't there somebody who can tell me if my son
or my husband is in those ambulances?" I choked, this time
it wasn't from the smoke.

He took my arm again and swung me around, pushing me
back behind the tape that now surrounded the tent. I paced
back and forth, watching the firemen. I circled the still
smoking tent. It looked like pictures I'd seen of the
Hindenburg, when it caught fire, plunged to the ground,
and lay crumpled and smoldering. Anyone inside would
have been caught by the imploding tent or smothered by
the smoke. I clung to the idea that everyone had time to get
out before the fire spread. But if that were the case, where
were Carlos and Tom?

All my efforts to catch the attention of someone in charge
failed. I could see groups of firemen and police standing
around, but they couldn't hear me when I called out. I

decided to widen my circle and hopefully find Carlos. Tom
would be with him. Brad had to be nearby, but the crowd
was thick around the tent area and I couldn't see. I decided
to be systematic and force my way through the crowd in
ever-widening circles until I found a familiar face. At least
it was something to do.

By the time I'd wound around to the front of the tent a
second time, I found Val, Grace, Penny, and Mrs. Bonseur.
Philip, who was standing to the side, saw me first.

"Nora, thank God you're all right. We've been frantic,
looking for all of you," he said. With loud sobs and tears
running down his cheeks, he held me in a bear hug until
Grace cut in and asked about Carlos and Tom.

"I can't get Carlos on the phone and the police won't tell
us anything," I said. Grace had wrapped her arms around
me, and Penny grasped my waist. "We were almost back to
The Vintage when we heard the sirens," Grace said.

"Carlos went into— I couldn't stop him. They won't tell
me anything. Somebody said some boys knocked over a
lamp and started the fire," I said, mopping my face with my
palm.

"That makes no sense. The lamps were electrical." It was
Val's dogmatic voice, but it was welcome this time. Unlike
Philip, Val was calm, his voice decisive, just like he was
when I got word Tom was missing from the boarding
school's campground. He drove me there. He was my rock
as they searched for Tom. That was the Val I loved. I
reached out to hug him.

"Right. I'd forgotten that," I said. "How'd a fire break
out then? They told me the tent's fire proof. Last time I saw
Tom he was going to meet some boy he'd met."

"It's so hard to just stand here," Grace said. "Why don't
we fan out in different directions and meet back here in an
hour. The firemen are beginning to haul their hoses in.
There's still lots of smoke, but I don't see any flames, do
you?"

"I'll stay here with Penny," Mrs. Bonseur said.

"I'm going to check the Hoja Story Tent. Call me if... Call me," I said, moving away.

When we got back to Mrs. Bonseur, our stories were equally bleak: no Carlos and no Tom, anywhere. But Mrs. Bonseur had news. She said one of the park officials told her they were gathering information and, until they were sure, nothing would be broadcast. He said lots of people were taken to the hospital for smoke inhalation, and he said park workers took children home to keep them safe. In any event, we were encouraged to go back to Deanna's to wait for a call. Nothing was making sense. Carlos had a cell phone. Why hadn't he called?

At Tall Oaks, I checked the first floor for Deanna. A cold chill surged through my veins when I couldn't find her. Somehow it seemed wrong to shout in the silence of the large house. The others went into the living room and I went to check the porch. I thought she'd be there if she'd heard about the fire. The porch was empty. I climbed the stairs and walked to Deanna's bedroom. I smelled sulfur, turned the door handle, and pushed the door aside. Deanna was on her knees at a prie dieu before an altar bright with candles.

"Deanna," I said softly, not to startle her. She jumped and clutched her chest anyway. "Oh, Nora, Come in.

"This is my little sanctuary," she said, waving me to a bay window with the same view Carlos and I shared in our room. "I came up here as soon as my neighbor called about the fire."

Two loveseats, upholstered in an overlapping leaf design and accented with small Bargello-stitched pillows, faced each other. Deanna dropped heavily onto one.

"Let me tell my family I found you. I'll be right back." I went to the top of the stairs and called down. "Deanna's fine, just resting. I'll stay with her for a bit."

As I started up the stairs, Philip grabbed my arm. "Eh, do you mind if I see if Heidi Rose is okay? I won't be long."

I nodded. Back in the room, Deanna hadn't moved from the loveseat. I sat opposite her.

"I was just thinking how quickly things change," she said. "One minute we were watching our plans unfold successfully, then... "

I swallowed. "I don't know where Carlos and Tom are. Maybe at the hospital, but— They promised to call as soon as they know anything."

"Ah." She sank back. Her face drained of color; her body, from face to torso, seemed to collapse. "No word from Brad either. It's not like him."

I reached over and took her hands in mine. I looked through the window and saw the candles and my face reflected.

"You pray?" Deanna said.

"Only when I need something and can't get it for myself." The logic of that had always eluded me. Maybe it was a throwback to my childhood. "After my father died, though, I saw my mother crossing her chest with her arms, asking God to take her away. And she lit candles."

She came over and sat beside me, taking my shoulders in her hands.

"We have to be patient. Imagine the hundreds of people involved. I know our people. They're efficient and caring and doing the best they can. We'll hear soon."

"I couldn't find Carlos or Tom. He ran in the tent to see if he could help, and the last time I saw Tom he was going to look for a friend." I stood, finally overcome with holding back. "Why hasn't Brad called? He has to know something."

She reached for her phone. We chose to stare at separate designs on the rug at our feet while we waited for a connection.

"Brad's not answering. He must be busy."

I saw her shoulders slump and curve forward to accept her head which slipped slowly into the forming depression.

The collapse of her spirit was almost palpable and I felt ashamed to have added to her distress.

But moments later she raised her head. "Come on, let's go downstairs. I'm sure we'll hear from Brad soon."

In the middle of the stairway, my cell phone rang. I reached into my bag but it caught on something and shot out of my hand. Val, standing at the bottom of the stairs, grabbed and tossed it to me.

"Carlos, thank God. Where are you? Are you all right? We've been frantic. Why did you wait so long to call? Is Tom with you?"

His voice was raspy. He was at the hospital, waiting for a policeman to drive him to us.

"Is Tom— " He was gone. I put the phone back in my purse and told everyone what he'd said.

We sat. Philip returned and gave me a weak smile which I took to mean Heidi Rose was all right. The clock in the hall clunked, the spring rewound, and the tubular chimes sounded twice—a half hour, waiting. When the sharper sound of the doorbell intruded, a uniformed policeman, hat under his arm, came walking in the door with Carlos. I buried my head in his chest and breathed in the smoky fabric.

After a few moments I moved aside while Grace and Penny and my brothers took their turns.

"Dr. Moynihan said he shouldn't talk too much," the officer said. "His throat was seared by the heat and— "

But Carlos stopped his recitation. "I couldn't find Tom and no one had information that helped. I didn't want to call you before I checked the hospital for him. He's not there, at least he's not on the admittance record." His head dropped and tears marked his shirt.

I could feel his body quivering. I led him to a chair and stood next to him, holding his hand.

"Someone told me kids were taken to private homes until their parents could come for them," I said. "But how do we know where they are?" I directed my question at the officer, who looked away.

"You should be getting word about that soon, ma'am."

"Soon. I'm sick to death of that word. I've been hearing it all night. Who's in charge of gathering that information?" I said.

His eyes moved to Deanna.

"Hello, Gil. What about Brad? Have you seen him? He hasn't called," she said.

The front door was still ajar and I heard another car. Doors slammed and we turned to see two more officers ascend the porch steps. Deanna greeted them by name and invited them inside. We all moved back into the living room, lowering ourselves tenuously onto the seats like crows on a high wire.

"What is it, Russ?" Deanna said.

"The firemen couldn't begin to clear a way into the tent until the heat dissipated. We— "

The phone rang. Philip answered and said the call was for Officer Gilmore. We watched his face as he listened. He wasn't getting good news. His jaw clenched, his head dropped. Suddenly I didn't want to hear anything he had to say. I let go of Carlos' hand and grabbed my face, unable to stop an explosion of wails. Through the sounds I heard him say they'd found Ed.

"Mrs. Ghazerian, I'm so sorry. He was badly burned and died on the way to the hospital." Did I have the names of his family?

My hands were frozen across my mouth. Carlos told him he believed Ed was a bachelor and had no family as far as he knew. "Nora?"

"No one," I choked. He never mentioned anyone to me. My gallery clients were the closest to friends he had. That was all I really knew about Ed. And now he was gone. I pulled at the front of my damp blouse.

"I'm going to make coffee," Philip said. He walked with his shoes scuffing the floor. Grace and Val each took Penny's hands and followed him.

I leaned into Carlos and his arms held me close. The officer paced.

The hall clock chimes rang again. I tried but lost count of the hour. I was listening to words inside my head: No news is good news. Over and over and over.

We sat in the living room, spread around the room, listening to each other make small talk while thinking of other things. Carlos made room for me next to him on the chair. I breathed in his aftershave to cancel the smoke.

There was a tentative knocking on the door and Val went to answer. It was Frank, the festival chairman, looking ten years older than the young buck I'd met in the park. Black smudges marked his gray pinstripe suit; his red tie hung like a viscose thread around his neck. He hesitated on the hardwood floor because he said he'd been walking through ashes and was afraid to mark the rug. We urged him to take his shoes off and sit down, but he shook his head. "I wanted to bring you the news as soon as I heard it."

22

"First of all, Brad and Tom are safe," Frank said. "They were both transferred to the hospital a short time ago."

"Hospital?" Deanna and I spoke almost in unison, after our collective sigh of relief.

"Yes, but they'll be okay. It's taken time to unravel what happened to them," Frank said.

He explained that festival officials started looking for Brad as soon as the fire broke out but he was nowhere in sight. "It didn't make sense, because you know as well as I he'd be wherever he was needed.

"We expected the worst when we started combing through the ashes, but he wasn't there either. I wanted to call you so many times, Deanna, but what could I say? Then about a half hour ago I got a call from a man who told me he'd picked up someone carrying a boy. He took them to the 24-hour clinic on Seymour Street and that's when Brad asked him to call me."

"Is the boy my son?" I said.

"Yes, Nora. He has minor burns on his hands and he's on oxygen because of smoke inhalation. Not bad. Just a precaution. The doctor at the clinic says he'll be fine. Brad saved his life. Brad was in the tent, in the thick of it, when he tripped over your boy's body. He got knocked out or something. They're still figuring things out. By the time Brad got out of the tent he was disoriented and wandered into the street."

"And Brad? Is he hurt?" Deanna said.

"Some burns as well, I'm sorry to say."

Let's go," I said, grabbing my purse on the table.

"No, please, Nora. Dr. Moynihan has asked if you'd wait until tomorrow. I just wanted you to know they're okay. Get some rest and go to the hospital in the morning. You'll see for yourself. The— "

"I'm not waiting until morning. They can't keep me from seeing my son for myself." I walked to the door but Frank grabbed my arm.

"The last thing I did before leaving was to look in on them. They were asleep."

"I don't care if the whole hospital's asleep. Are you going to drive me, or do I— "

"I'll take you. One more thing...six bodies were found in the ashes, two of them young boys."

"Oh, God," Deanna said. "Who?"

Frank recited the names, each one landing like a blow to Deanna. She collapsed on the sofa, where Philip wrapped her convulsing body in his arms. My purse slid to the floor and I clutched the door frame. No one moved. Finally, Penny closed her eyes and slipped sideways against Val.

"We should go," he whispered.

Deanna agreed she hadn't the strength to go to the hospital and I promised to look in on Brad. I walked back to Carlos and kissed him on the forehead. He never opened his eyes. We separated outside, agreeing to meet at the hospital at ten o'clock—Frank's suggestion.

Just as Frank had said, Brad and Tom were asleep. After Frank assured the floor nurse I only wanted to look, she agreed to let me in. Tom's head was bandaged on one side and both hands as well, but he was sleeping peacefully, partially on his side with his pillow supporting his head and arm.

"We'll be replacing those bandages for much smaller ones in the morning. Next time you see him, he'll be fine."

"I had to see him," I said as Frank drove me back to Tall Oaks.

"I know."

Philip and Heidi Rose were filling a plate with buttered toast and had coffee ready when Carlos and I reached the kitchen the next morning. His voice still carried a hint of huskiness. Moments later Val and his family appeared at the side door almost simultaneously with Deanna's entrance from the hall. She had waited for our return from the hospital before going to bed, but hers were not the only puffy eyes in the room. No one seemed to have anything to say beyond murmured amenities until Deanna set her mug down and cleared her throat.

"Have I told you how much it means to have all of you here?" She put her hands on either side of her head and groaned. "I couldn't stand being here alone. It's great to know Brad and Tom are safe, but there are so many who can't say the same. I'm so sorry about Ed. He'll be hard to replace."

"Impossible," I said. Why did I know so little about Ed? He impressed me as a quiet, efficient worker who enjoyed serving my customers. Only when I noticed his reaction to helping at the festival did I see another side of him—a generous, caring man. He would have been here with all of us, wanting to help us deal with our concerns for Tom and Brad. "Let me get my purse. I'll meet you at the front door."

As I turned I saw Philip hug Heidi Rose. She gave me a shy glance and when Philip joined us he turned and blew her a kiss.

Tom started to cry when he saw us. I gave him a quick peck on the cheek along with everybody else. Only Carlos' hand in mine kept me from embarrassing him with more kisses.

"You're going to be fine," Carlos said, touching his shoulder and bending awkwardly because I wouldn't let go of his hand. "How's your throat feel?"

"A little sore. Brad found me. I wouldn't be here if he hadn't found me. Is he here? Is he okay?"

"You both have burns. According to Dr. Moynihan, Brad's are second degree," I said. "That long robe Mrs. Fenster made for you protected your arms and legs. Brad wasn't so lucky. But he'll be fine, too. Deanna's with him." Carlos told him that Ed had been caught in the tent and didn't make it.

"Ed, gee, nice guy. That's awful," Tom said. He quickly glanced at me and I nodded.

The hospital room door opened and Frank stepped inside. His bright smile was made more so by his tawny skin. He set a basket on the side table. "Some munchies for you, nothing too scratchy. The kids I work with can't go more than fifteen minutes between snacks so I figured you'd be hungry.

"Were you able to tell the officers anything about the fire, Tom? They said you were in the tent when it started."

Tom stared at his hands while he spoke. He said Mrs. Fenster asked him and four other boys to help clean the Hoja Story Tent so it would be ready for the next day. It only took a few minutes so they moved on to the main tent to lend a hand. Tom and another boy arranged the kilim pillows, while the others picked up programs. That's all he could remember.

"They're not done with the investigation, but one of the possibilities is a short in one of the heat lamps. Those heat lamps were my idea," Frank said. "Our late summer weather can jump into fall really fast. I didn't want people to be cold, so I had the lamps on standby. I gave the order for them to be turned on. I guess I'll regret that for the rest of my life."

Carlos reached over and squeezed Frank's shoulder. "No one will blame you for wanting to make people comfortable," he said.

"Even if there was an electrical short, shouldn't the fireproof tent have contained the fire? The tent exploded; I saw it," I said.

"Fire *retardant* tent. We're checking the company's maintenance records. We want to know when the tent was treated last. We're also looking into other accelerants in the tent that could have pushed the temperatures beyond the tent's resistance," he said.

"Like...the rugs," I said. My throat closed around the words.

Frank's nod was slow to come. He turned to go and then, reluctantly, turned back.

"I almost forgot. The coroner wanted me to ask you how Ed's body should be handled. I hate bringing this up, but..."

Carlos answered. "I'll call him within the hour with the name of a funeral parlor in Philadelphia where Ed can be taken."

"Ah, thanks," he said. He left, promising to stop by again soon.

A nurse slipped in while the door was open, saying it was time to exchange 'those large bandages for smaller ones.' We kissed him in turn and began to leave the room. "Tom, I'm going to find out when you can leave the hospital and I'll let you know. The sooner the better, right?" He nodded.

Paradise mourned. Temple Park was cordoned off, but every day people stood around its perimeter to stare at the charred heap. Black ribbons marked the homes where loved ones had been lost. Along with Deanna, we visited each home to share their sorrow, and found others there doing the same.

Tall Oaks had no black ribbon, yet townspeople came because they knew Deanna would be devastated by what had happened. The kitchen filled with white boxes tied with twine and large platters wrapped in clear plastic. The refrigerator door resisted closing. Women were in the kitchen; men roamed the garden. They knew our names, knew about Ed, knew how we mourned for the failed festival.

"Coffee, Nora?" someone said as I walked through the kitchen early the next day.

I glanced at the woman who spoke, shook my head, and attempted a smile. Several others stopped what they were doing to look at me. The breakfast smells made my stomach jump, and I quickened my step to the back door and walked to the far end of the porch, a private spot hidden by thick shrubbery.

My heart ached for Deanna. Each day, her eyes sunk deeper, yet she said she appreciated the outpouring of kindnesses, didn't need anything, and held her head high. Only the tense muscles in her neck and shoulders gave her away. I pitied Frank, who wished he'd never ordered the heat lamps. And I recited my own litany of hurt: Ed was gone. Tom had another bad memory. How many nightmares could a twelve-year-old boy stand?

A pattern had taken hold at Tall Oaks. Val's family spent the greater part of every day with us. Heidi Rose came a little later after she finished her work at The Vintage. She took charge in the kitchen and Deanna knew her well enough to let her. Philip insisted on helping and planted himself firmly until Heidi Rose gave way. By the second day, they moved together like trapeze artists: She released him to perform a task and he returned ready for her next move. Philip, we knew, found his own comfort in nurturing others. Now Heidi Rose knew it too. He went seamlessly from one task to another. Only his face, normally the window of his feelings, was expressionless. I knew my brother was keeping a lock on his emotions. It was unnatural for him and I was glad he'd found someone to help him release the hurt.

As for myself, finding a quiet spot had done nothing for me except magnify the pain. I went back inside to join the others and get lost in the bustle of people trying to help. Maybe that was the best way after all.

On the third day after the fire, I opened my eyes to a pale line of light seeping through the edges of the shuttered window in our bedroom. The hands on the bedside clock divided the face in half and the house was quiet, not unexpected after the excitement of bringing Tom home the day before. He would sleep late, as would the rest of the family. I turned toward Carlos and found his blue eyes trained on me.

"Let's go for a walk before the house fills with people," he said. "I want to talk to you about a couple of things."

Why not? Every muscle in my body ached, not from exertion but from exhaustion. No matter how many positions I tried, I couldn't find the right spot in the bed. We dressed and tiptoed through the house and out the kitchen door.

"I know you don't want to think about Ed's remains, so I have a suggestion." I stopped walking. "You said he had no relatives so it's up to us. I've already looked into a burial plot at Washington Memorial Park and, if you agree, we could invite a small gathering of your customers and neighboring business friends to pay their respects at the park."

"That would be perfect," I said, taking his hand and stepping over a raised slab of concrete. "Thanks. I'm sure the funeral parlor can wait a few days until we're ready."

I fingered the leaves of a hanging maple tree and admired its scarlet color and symmetrical veins—nature's trustworthy pattern, imposing its cycles in the midst of human chaos.

"Can we talk about that? Tom begins classes on Monday. Don't you think we should go home?" he said.

I wasn't ready for that. How could he think our duties were finished in Paradise? We should go back to Philadelphia and pick up our lives like nothing happened?

We reached the end of the street where the smell of burned leaves clung to morning humidity. A thin line of smoke climbed from an ashy pile, hanging in the air along with Carlos' question.

"But Brad's being released today. Deanna will need us." Not a direct answer and only partly true. "Tom will want to see him and he's not the only one who wants to show gratitude for what he did."

Carlos admitted I was right. "They're bringing him home this morning, right? Can we be on our way early afternoon?"

"It feels rushed to me."

"It's important, I think," he said. "Get back to our routines." He'd stepped in front of me.

"Get back on the horse?"

"Yes."

"Dead horse."

We walked the rest of the way in silence until we came to the edge of Deanna's rear lawn. The tree shadows stretched long across the freshly-cut grass. Twelve bulging black plastic bags lined up against a wooden trash bin: grass cuttings and the residue of generous gifts of food and flowers.

"Dead horse? Is that what you're calling your life's work these days?"

There was a time when the gallery and my brokering business flowed through me like the blood in my veins, nourishing my heart and mind with excitement and contentment. Was it just weeks ago when I rekindled those feelings at the VanBommes? I didn't feel it now. I suspected loosing Ed was part of it, but only a part.

Carlos squeezed my hand as we turned back toward the house, climbed the back porch steps and entered the kitchen where coffee, toast, and pitchers of juice filled the counter top—neighborhood caregivers at work. We smiled our thanks but declined. Once inside our bedroom, Carlos pulled our suitcases from the closet. I piled the pillows against the headboard and leaned back.

"If you're worried about the gallery, I'll help you to reorganize and hire someone to fill Ed's place—whatever you decide."

I didn't answer. He walked from the closet to his open luggage, back and forth over the rug's pattern of pale chrysanthemums. My eyes followed his steps, but my thoughts had dropped like a body on a scaffold. His eyes avoided mine until he stopped abruptly and said he was going to tell Tom we were leaving.

"Wait." I stood, felt my legs quiver and sat down again. "I think Tom still needs a few days to unravel his feelings."

Carlos frowned. "That's ridiculous. He told me he wants to go home. He says his fingers are a little stiff, but he can hold a pencil and he doesn't want to get behind at school." The frown slowly receded. "That's not it, is it? What are you keeping from me?"

"I know the fire wasn't my fault, but I wonder if Tom will remember the festival as another bad experience I got him into."

"Where do these ideas come from? Why do you think always of what a bad mother you are? Stay right there." He walked down the hall and I heard him calling Tom's name. A cold chill ran up my back.

Tom followed him into the room, kicked off his shoes, and hopped up on the bottom of the bed.

"Your mom and I were just talking about the festival and we want to know how you feel about what happened."

"You mean the fire?"

"Not just the fire, the whole experience," Carlos said. I hugged my knees.

"I feel really sad. I mean Ed and all those other people...it's horrible. But before the fire, it was great. Don't you think it was great?" He looked at me.

"You did all you could to help at the festival—learning all those stories and taking leadership in your own storytelling tent. I'm so sorry you got hurt and that everything turned out so horribly, but..." I couldn't go on.

"I think your mom wants you to know we're very proud of you."

After he left, Carlos sat next to me. "Convinced?"

I nodded and put my head on his shoulder. Convinced? The irony was Paradise had turned into Hell.

23

Val and the rest of the family were already in the kitchen when Deanna came down to breakfast. We explained our decision to leave. She insisted we could stay as long as we liked, that our presence was fortifying, but in the end it was Grace who put a positive spin on our departure.

"We've been through a tragedy—personal and collective. But I'm thinking about how your spirit was bouncing back before the festival. That should tell you a lot about your power to heal. Besides, a new baby is counting on you," she said.

Deanna's whole demeanor changed with the mention of the baby. She stiffened and said she felt overwhelmed just thinking about taking on the responsibility with Brad. But as she ticked off things like remodeling one of the rooms for a nursery and hiring a nanny so she could spend a few hours each day at her gallery, her expression disclaimed her words.

"Actually, last night," she said, "a school friend of Brad's, a talented watercolor artist, asked if I could use him at the gallery. His paintings don't sustain him yet and he could help out just until Brad got on his feet. I'm thinking I'll take him up on his offer and give him a wall at Tall Oaks for his canvasses."

There was a tap and Frank suddenly appeared at the kitchen window.

"Hey, you're all together. Great. Thought you'd like to know the police commissioner's investigation is finished. They know how the fire started and they know who started it."

Heidi Rose poured him a cup of coffee, offered cream and sugar, but he waved them off, giving her a nod and a smile.

"Tom, you remember the kid who called you a 'towelhead'?"

"Yeah. A royal pain."

"Michael Banihan. He's been stirring up anti-Muslim sentiments for weeks now: graffiti on the Mediterranian grocery's storefront, a rock thrown through a window at the Hanifah's home, signs calling anyone attending the festival a traitor or anti-American. That's why the commissioner beefed up security, and when Mrs. Fenster mentioned the episode in the Hoja Story Tent, he put the police on Michael's tail. They've got a sheet this long on that kid." He spread his arms. "Oh, and that crack on your head, Tom? He confessed to hitting you before he poured gasoline on the rugs and set them on fire."

Tom's mouth gaped.

"Oh, my God," Deanna said. "How old's Michael?"

"Seventeen, just misses being tried as an adult. Still he's going to do time. Six people are dead because of him, and it could have been much worse." He tipped his coffee cup. "Lots to do, but I wanted you to know. Looks like I just caught you. Leaving?"

"After Brad gets home," Carlos said.

Heidi Rose refilled our mugs with fresh coffee.

"We're sorry we can't stay for the funerals." I wanted to say more but couldn't.

"They'll understand," Deanna said, "We all understand."

Brad arrived and except for bandaged arms, he looked well and very happy to be home.

"I heard about Ed. I'm so sorry. Can't tell you how many times he mentioned how happy he was to be helping. I got the feeling he had no family, that right?"

"As far as we know," I said.

"Well, he loved being part of ours and said so."

Someone called Brad a "hero" and the noise level rose. But Brad wanted no part of that and settled for handshakes until the awkward maneuvering around the bandages turned comical. It felt good to laugh.

Shortly afterward I walked up the steps to help Carlos with the luggage, and I saw Philip wrap his arm around Heidi Rose's shoulders. The expression on his face was the one my father had when looking at my mother, the one he called "the keeper of his heart and soul."

Carlos gave his full attention to the road as we drove to Philadelphia, Tom slept in the back seat with his hands folded over his chest, and I tilted the car seat. I didn't wake up until our garage door rattled open. Carlos pulled me to him.

"Admit it," he said, it's good to be home." He kissed my head.

It took several trips before we'd emptied the car and I realized how tired I was. Tom lifted his suitcase and grimaced, but when I protested, he said: "The nurse told me I should use my fingers or they'll get stiff. I'll be careful."

Carlos and I dropped our luggage in the bedroom and went back down to the kitchen to make tea. I heard Tom talking on the phone as we passed his room—Marty, I guessed. After filling the mugs, I grabbed them and Carlos carried the pot to the outside deck. In the dark, it seemed to float free of the house. I felt my way to a lounge. Without vision, night sounds filled the void: whispering trees, an owl's who-who-whooo, an unidentifiable crick-crick, and underneath all of it, the distant drone of air conditioners and expressway traffic, sounds that kept no hours in our inner city neighborhood.

"Nora?"

"Hmmm?" I rolled the warm mug across my forehead.

"Are you worried about handling the gallery by yourself?"

When I didn't answer he let out an exasperated breath. "Talk to me, will you?"

It was rare for him to be testy. I weighed the dangers of pleading exhaustion against digging into feelings I hadn't identified myself.

He probed again, softer this time. "Are you worried about running the gallery yourself?"

"No, of course not. I've done it before. It's more than that. Too many memories or something, I don't know," I said.

"You don't think you're responsible for Ed's death, do you?"

I dropped the mug on the table without looking. It teetered on the edge and fell to the deck. I let it roll. "He wouldn't have been there except for me."

Carlos reached for the mug and set it next to his on the table between us. I felt his eyes seek me in the dark.

"I know I'm not to blame for what happened," I said. "I'll miss Ed, of course, but...right now, I can't deal with anything."

Carlos got up and gathered up the mugs in one hand, the teapot in the other. "Maybe you'll feel better when you get some sleep." He gave me a kiss and urged me to follow him soon.

I sat on the deck until I couldn't hold my head up. A light breeze was blowing. It rustled the trees overhead and made me shiver. I knew the cold I felt was more than temperature. Deanna would get on with her life: her gallery, her son, and a baby to love. For as long as I could remember, my rugs were my shelter. Tom's anger still simmered under the surface. Jared's cruelty, my obliviousness, and now the festival's frightening fire—what possible reason did he have to trust me?

I woke to sounds in the kitchen—Carlos making breakfast. I stepped out of my sleep shirt and into the shower. Usually refreshing, the water's spray released a surprise of tears.

Sleep had come easily but my head ached. I lathered up and let a final blast of cold water run over my face. Swollen eyes would raise Carlos' concern and I'd given him enough grief in the past few days.

"Want to go to the gallery?" He studied my face.

"Might as well. What about Tom?" I said, filling a bowl with dry cereal.

"Not an issue. He's already at Marty's house."

I poured milk over the flakes and dug in. They tasted better than I remembered. I added more to the remaining milk in the bowl, poured myself a cup of coffee, and dropped a piece of bread in the toaster. "You don't have to go. I can handle it."

"I want to go with you. You still look tired to me."

"I've slept. I'm eating—more than usual, I might add. I just want to get this over with. Maybe once I'm there...I don't know. I can't be tired but that's how I feel."

"Hey, Chicken Little, you sound like the sky is falling. It isn't."

Ed burned to death, six others too. Brad and Tom were injured and my rug inventory was devastated. If the sky wasn't falling, there was a threatening front coming through.

24

The following day I stepped into the gallery while Carlos removed the sign on the door: "Gone to the Festival of a Thousand and One Nights, Paradise, New York. Saturday, August 23 through Friday, August 29. Join us." Reading it now had a whole new meaning.

"I'll go tell your neighbors you're reopening," he said, stepping back onto the sidewalk.

With a flick of the switch, the gallery lights washed over the rugs. I walked to one of the alcoves and waited for the vibration of colors, the rush I always felt. Nothing. I ran my hand over the nap of a late nineteenth century Bakhtiari tree-of-life design, a lustrous Persian. Nothing. Nothing but nap.

Carlos came looking for me when he returned. "I told them about Ed and that we'd be in touch as soon as arrangements for burial were made."

"Thanks. They needed to know." I pivoted in place, taking in the whole room, and swallowing the lump in my throat. "I was thinking we should shift some of the small kilims to the front."

I tugged on a stack while Carlos pulled and when we'd created enough space, we gathered the pieces I wanted and began to create a new display. One action created another and after the third pile I leaned back and rubbed my shoulders.

"I should work on the ledger," I said.

"Go ahead; I'll keep going here."

The sun poured through the window and over the desk. It looked like a warm spot, but I knew better. I sat in the chair and reached for the red book. Ed's tidy, perfectly balanced columns...

The fine-point black pen we used exclusively for the ledger wasn't in its usual place. I reached into the drawer and shifted some papers. One was a newspaper clipping, an obituary page. I ran my eyes from picture to picture, reading the names until I recognized Gallo.

Rosetta Coselli Gallo, born June 21, 1934, in Hammonton, New Jersey, ended her long battle with breast cancer on February 3, 1989. Preceded in death by her husband Angelo Vincente Gallo and survived by her son Edward and daughter Dolores D'Angelo.

Stapled beneath was another article about a tragic auto accident on New Jersey's White Horse Pike. I skimmed the article: *Dolores D'Angelo...killed instantaneously...buried her mother just the day before.*

I walked into the gallery and handed the articles to Carlos.

"Nineteen eighty-nine is when Ed came to work for the Gordons who owned this gallery before I bought it. I kept him on because he knew their customers and I needed someone.

"This makes sense of a lot of things, doesn't it?" I stared at the clippings which Carlos had clutched in both hands.

"I'll see if there's any remaining family in Hammonton," he said, walking to the phone.

Twelve boys I'd never seen before filled the entrance hall, dropped their backpacks against the wall, and took off their shoes. They shook hands with me as Tom called out their names.

"I'm the club president," one boy said. He shook the ends of my fingers gingerly.

"Club?"

He nodded. I told them I'd bring something for them to drink and Tom led the way to his bedroom.

A few minutes later I climbed the steps with a tray of juice and stood for a moment outside the door to listen. They were talking about food, about favorite dishes their mothers would make. I knocked and the door was opened quickly.

"All this talk about food must be making you hungry. Do you want some snacks?" Heads shook. "What are you planning, a banquet?"

"Eid al-Fitr, the breaking of the Ramadan fast," Tom said. "Thanks for the juice, Mom."

It felt like a dismissal and the hair on my neck prickled. "I'd be more than happy to contribute and meet your families too. Tom's dad and I would enjoy that." Their faces were blank and I saw Tom exchange glances with the boy who said he was the club's president.

"Well, let me know when you're ready to finalize plans." I closed the door behind me and went looking for Carlos.

I found him pulling weeds in the yard. "Something's cooking."

"Good, I'm going to have a huge appetite after this." He rubbed his chin and cheek and creating a half-moon dirt smear."

"Did you know Tom joined a club for Muslim kids? They're up in his room right now planning a dinner and I got a feeling their parents will be part of it but we won't," I said. My hands had landed on my hips. I lowered them.

"That doesn't sound right. You sure?"

"I know what I heard. Ask him about it at dinner and you'll see I'm right."

"Maybe he'll tell us of his own accord."

We got through dinner with no mention of Tom's meeting and I was tired of waiting. "I enjoyed meeting your friends this afternoon. Such good manners."

"I understand you're planning Eid al-Fitr together," Carlos said.

"Yeah, a guy in my math class invited me. It's only for Muslims," he said, with a quick peek in my direction before he excused himself.

"Just a sec. Are your dad and I invited?"

"You don't invite me to everything you go to," he said. His chin made its pugnacious appearance. "It's like a holy meal. They said it's an honor for me to be included."

"Have we ever excluded you from a family activity?" Carlos said.

"Maybe they'll make an exception. I can ask," Tom said.

"I don't want our family to be an exception. This hurts, Tom," I said.

"Yes, it does," Carlos said. "We are your family. You need to give this some serious thought."

He went to his room.

"I was right," I said. "Right about not being included. Right about knowing this interest of his is going to drive him farther and farther from our family."

Philip called the following day to invite us to have dinner at his apartment. In itself the invitation was natural enough. My brothers, unlike me, had never broken the Lebanese tradition of family togetherness. Weekly dinners together and daily phone calls were routine. Carlos reveled in the closeness, never failing to add his wish that Elena, Tapis and Mehmet could be with us.

This gathering included Heidi Rose. Since our return from Paradise, her name had been popping up in one way or another in conversations with my shy brother. I was aware he'd made a number of trips back to Paradise, providing news on his return not only about the town's recovery but about Deanna and Brad, all of which we appreciated. Still our curiosity was growing. And when Philip greeted me at the door with Heidi Rose at his side, his beaming face said everything.

Grace and Penny rose to hug me when we got to the living room. Val handed me a glass of wine, planted a kiss on my cheek, and winked. Good mood, for a change.

"Who's tending The Vintage?" I said to Heidi Rose before finding a seat between Grace and Penny on the couch.

"There is no one to tend. It's been that way since the fire," she said. "But I don't mind. It's given me some badly needed leisure time." Her eyes locked onto Philip's.

There was an awkward silence.

"For God's sake, Philip, are you two an item, or what?" Val said.

The room filled with nervous laughter. Heidi Rose flushed. Philip coughed and ran his finger around his shirt collar. "That's why I invited all of you to dinner. We are, eh… We've decided to, eh—"

"What he's trying to say is that we enjoy each other's company," Heidi Rose said. There was a slight German accent I hadn't noticed before. She gave Philip a shy glance that seemed to melt over my brother like warm syrup.

"Does she have to say it for you? Philip, you're in love," said Val from the far end. He banged the coffee table with his fist to make his point. Grace grabbed her wineglass to keep it from spilling and gave Val a sharp glance.

Philip took Heidi Rose's hand. "Yes, we're in love. It surprised both of us." Then he turned to Val and his eyes hardened. "Before you ask when we're getting married, we're not, at least not for awhile." Val looked offended.

I shimmied forward, got up, and put my arms around my beaming brother. "I'm so happy for both of you. This is wonderful news."

"I worried that, you know, it's too soon after everything that's happened," Philip said.

"I think it's great. Haven't we spent enough time mourning?" Carlos said.

"I can wear my tux again at the wedding, can't I?" Tom said.

"Then I'll need a new dress, right, Mom?" Penny added.

"We can wait a bit before making that decision, I think," Grace said. Her answer served for me as well.

We toasted Philip and Heidi Rose, who blushed again and disappeared into the kitchen to bring dinner to the table. Lamb kebabs, of course, and, Heidi Rose announced a German Zwiebel Torte, onions wrapped in a flakey crust.

"Hope you like it," she said.

We did. It had melt-in-your-mouth texture and a sweet onion flavor that was both flavorful and mellow—traits that could have been used to describe Heidi Rose. She seemed the perfect companion for Philip. We learned she'd lost her entire family to tragedy: a car accident on the way home from a picnic. At the last moment, Heidi Rose declined to join them because she wasn't feeling well. She was twenty-five at the time.

"Everywhere I looked there were painful memories, so I sold our home and moved to Paradise because I learned there were many German immigrants there. It was to start a new life, but I was frightened and hoped to find something familiar."

"I think you're very brave, Aunt Heidi Rose," Penny said.

"Oh, 'Aunt Heidi Rose,' that's music to my ears."

"Will you teach me to make it?" Tom said, pointing to the torte.

"Oh, and much more, if you like, Tom."

As we drove home, Tom launched into a description of the meal he'd prepared for me in Turkey.

"I could be an international chef. I already know some Turkish recipes and now I'll get some German ones."

"Your Nine gave me a number of her favorite recipes. Why don't I copy them for you and you can take a look? Isn't it about time for another surprise dinner? You can't afford to let your skills get rusty," I said.

"Yeah. I'd like to show Aunt Tapis I can do it by myself. And, ah— "

"Don't worry, I'll help if you need it," I said.

"No, I wanted to tell you I told the Muslim Boys Club I wasn't going."

Carlos slipped his hand from the steering wheel to my side. I grabbed it and squeezed.

At home the light on the phone's answering machine was blinking. It was Deanna, who said we could call her until eleven o'clock. I hesitated momentarily, noticing it was ten forty-five, but then I pushed the speed dial.

When I started the conversation by asking her how she was, she laughed. "I was afraid you'd think it was bad news. It isn't. I've got two news items—both of them wonderful."

She said she'd been to the oncologist earlier in the day for a report on her latest tests. Her cancer was in remission. She would be taking medication but no more radiation, no more chemotherapy either, and the doctor didn't need to see her for six months. She sounded delirious.

"I put you on the speaker phone, Deanna, so Carlos can hear. That's wonderful news. What's the second item?"

"The baby's coming in three weeks. Three weeks. Can you believe it? I'm so excited. Hope I'll be ready."

"Of course you'll be ready. And, if you're not, the baby won't care. All a baby needs is love and you and Brad have plenty of that to go around."

When she asked about our family, I gave her Philip's news. She'd known for weeks and had begun to wonder why we hadn't said anything.

I laughed. "Philip's private and thoughtful. A great listener. Val, on the other hand, speaks his mind, even if you don't want to hear it. But he's level headed and fun too."

"You seem to be a little of both, am I right?"

"Depends on the subject matter," I said.

"Speaking of Heidi Rose, did you know she's a psychiatric nurse and has a degree in nutrition?"

"I didn't but it explains why she's so good at managing The Vintage, doesn't it?"

Deanna laughed and when she caught her breath she added: "It also explains why she was at my door the day after I was diagnosed with cancer. She came with all kinds of information about what I should expect from my treatment and what kinds of foods would support my body. She's an exceptional woman and very loving. Philip's a lucky guy."

We wrapped up our conversation.

"Hmmm," I said, "soon we'll have a psychologist and a psychiatric nurse in the family. Is somebody trying to tell us something?"

Business was slow at the gallery, not unusual for summertime in muggy Philadelphia. People closed their houses and headed for the beaches on the Jersey coast. I welcomed the time to work physically, especially with Carlos. One afternoon we drove to my warehouse and brought back an 1890 Senneh gallery carpet from Northwest Persia to hang in the alcove, choosing it for the red palmette border and dark blue *herati*, lozenge-shaped forms with floral figures at the corners, in the center field.

Carlos stood looking at it and announced that it needed a blue flood light to bring out its colors. "I think it'll draw attention to the rug's beauty and away from the minor moth damage along the right edge. What do you think?" he said.

I felt the prodding in his voice. Usually I was the one giving instructions, forcing my will on the gallery's exhibits and marketing direction, and unwilling to yield to suggestions from anyone. This time I felt nothing but glad that he was making the decisions.

"Carlos," I said, folding my arms across my chest. Without intention, his name seemed to land like a heavy sack. "I want to tell you something about the gallery." His sapphire eyes sparked as they always did when I brought up a subject he knew was important to me. "I'm thinking of selling my business—all of it."

"What? Everything? All of a sudden you want to sell the gallery? I can't believe it."

"It's not really that sudden. I thought maybe I was just tired and then I didn't know what to blame. I honestly thought my feelings for the business would return. They haven't," I said, unable to separate the surprise from the disbelief on his face.

"Have you thought this through? It's been your whole life," he said, stepping aside as if he needed to see me from a different perspective.

The last time he asked if I'd thought something through, I was offended, so sure of myself, so determined that I always knew what was best for me. This time his comment washed over me as confirmation.

"Maybe *too much* of my life. How might things have been if I'd treated my business like a business and not like a life?" I said.

"Are you asking me?"

I shook my head. "Not really. I know I can't redo my life."

He pursed his lips, ready to speak, but I stopped him. "I don't want to be around the rugs anymore, but how can that be?" I said.

"Am I allowed to respond now?" he said, waiting with a twinkle in his eyes for my nod. "If you're asking how I feel about it, I can honestly say it doesn't matter to me if you work or don't work. Do whatever makes you happy.

"Have you made mistakes? Sure. You're not perfect but I like sharing your imperfect life." His laughter helped.

"I needed to hear that. It's the same for me," I said, leaning into his chest while his arms closed around me.

"I believe that's all we need to know for now," he said.

Carlos left me in the office while he went to arrange some new runners in the showroom. I pulled out the ledger to balance the accounts. It still hurt to see Ed's neat entries on the page and sometimes it made me cry. The funeral service and Ed's burial turned out to be an amazing experience. Our research didn't uncover any relatives, but listening to the stories told by shopkeepers and customers, introduced me to an Ed I never knew. I was ashamed. That was never, never going to happen again. I closed the ledger. "Gone but not forgotten, Ed, I promise," I whispered.

About an hour later Carlos had finished and joined me in the office. He sat on the only other chair in the room.

"Bad news in the ledger?"

"No. Everything's in order"

"I've got another thought," he said.

I closed the ledger, slipped it into its spot on the bookshelf above the desk.

"The next time we're with Grace and your brothers let's tell them what you're thinking. They may have some thoughts that'll help you decide what to do, yes?"

I nodded. Actually, I'd been thinking about sharing my change of attitude with Grace. Unlike Val, she could be objective about my career. In fact both brothers would probably stand and cheer if I mentioned selling the gallery. That would make me mad. When I told Carlos, he shrugged, but not before he smirked.

The next day the phone interrupted our breakfast. It was Tapis. I was used to her brusque "hello," followed immediately by a request to speak to her brother. This time, though, she sounded panicked and I frowned as I handed the phone to Carlos.

He alternately shook his head and nodded. Something was wrong. After a time, he lowered the phone to his chest and pressed the off button. "She's worried about Ana."

I sat down.

"Tapis received a call from Ana's apartment manager to say he found her wandering around on the third floor. Ana was crying, upset because she couldn't find her apartment."

"Third floor? Who does she know there?" I said.

"I'm not aware of anybody. Tapis wants me to go home. She's making an appointment with Ana's doctor and she wants me to be there."

"Isn't she on medication for blood pressure?" I said. Carlos nodded. "Maybe it's reacting with something else she's taking, or maybe he's changed her medication. It could be that.

"Whatever it is, you've got to go. Tom and I will be fine," I said. "When you get back, I'll have the gallery problem sorted out and settled." My attempts to lighten the moment failed. He pulled me to his lap and cradled me in his arms.

"You're right, she's on several medications, and I don't remember any discussion about interaction. This happens often, doesn't it?"

"Unfortunately, yes."

"Besides, we were with her not long ago and she was fine. This is something that's come on suddenly and will be quickly fixed. I'm not worried. I'll go."

"My brothers will help me, if I need anything."

"It's good to hear you say that. You've grown closer to them, haven't you?"

"Because of you." I wrapped my arms around his neck, pulled him closer, and kissed him.

"I need something before I leave," he said, taking my hand and leading me to the stairs. When we reached the bedroom, he reached under my shirt and my knees buckled. We hadn't made love since before we left for Paradise and all I could think of was how much I wanted him. I was quivering before his skin met mine and when he entered me, the pleasure was so intense I shuddered from head to toe, kept the rhythm, and clung to him until he cried out.

We showered together, fingers slippery with suds, still hungry for the thrill of intimate touch, massaging each other's pleasure zones again and again. Carlos slid his hands around, cupped my buttocks and lifted me. We made love again under the cascading water, my arms around his neck. Afterwards we fell across the bed, reluctant to let go.

25

On The Trail, Asia Minor

Çatal stopped breathing and clutched his animal's rope until his fingers hurt. He hid his fear like the other men, but beneath his outer shell his body had petrified. His eyes widened in fear and watered in the cold air but he dared not blink. A spiked ball could be swung, a dagger could be drawn, or a horse could ram his precious Sütlü and trample her beneath bony hooves—all in the instant of a blink. Each man in the procession had frozen in the same way, each hoping to be invisible until the danger was over.

When the last horse galloped past with stringy white froth hanging from its mouth, a collective sigh rose from the travelers like a prayer of thanksgiving: Allahhhhhh. But suddenly the last rider turned in his saddle, lifted his crossbow, and fired an arrow that hissed inches from Çatal's head. He fell forward and wrapped his arms around Sütlü's hump.

No head turned; all eyes were focused ahead. Then a foot nudged the side of a horse, a rein loosened, a chorus of soft signals sounded around Çatal, and the animals shifted forward. Soon the clatter of goods, the scrape of wooden wheels, and the clop of hooves started up again and Çatal was left with his questions: Who were those frightful men? Back in the caravanserai's courtyard, they had circled like a coiled snake, and when they shot forth from the gate people ran to protect themselves. Where had they come from? Where were they going? Were there more like them?

Çatal reached behind for his goatskin but instead his shaking hand rested on the silk rug. Instantly, his other hand dropped the rein. One hand grabbed the ivory fringe while the other closed around the amber field and he pulled the edge across his lap. It glowed in the sun and sent a warm surge from his hands to his head, across his chest, then down his legs. Like trying to recall a dream, thoughts of the fearsome men faded and Rachel's face appeared behind his closed eyelids. He saw his hut on the other side the mountains, smoke rising from the cooking fires, tea brewing in a kettle, and fruit set out for cutting. He pictured his daughter's lips red with the juice of cherries, her fingers stained by walnut shells as she picked nut meats.

What seemed like only moments later, he released the rug and opened his eyes. His fear was gone, replaced by the comfort of the men around him and the progress they were making. On the trail up ahead Çatal saw that the caravan had splintered. Men were dismounting and securing their animals. He raised his face to the sun and saw that it was directly overhead. Perhaps Sütlü's gentle rocking had lulled him to sleep. How else could he account for the quick passage of time?

Çatal tied Sütlü to a large tree with low hanging clusters of green leaves. He slid down her side and removed the heavy wooden poles from her sides. Before he left to join the others, she was tearing branches with her sharp teeth and winding her long tongue around the leaves. She grunted and Çatal walked away smiling at what he considered her thanks.

Someone called his name. It was his friend Hrant, waving, inviting him to sit by a fire already spreading within a circle of black rocks. Hrant explained

apologetically that in his eagerness to leave Erzurum he
was pressed into the first grouping, and though he'd wanted
to turn back to search for Çatal, he couldn't. That said,
Hrant hung his head and stared into the fire. Çatal was
about to place his hand on his friend's arm to assure him he
was not offended, but he noted the other men had adopted
the same posture.

By this time there should be loud laughing, even bawdy
banter—the sounds of men relieved of the saddle. Food
would be passed around and after a time they'd settle back,
watch the fire's embers, and tell each other about their
experiences at the bazaar. Although nothing could induce
him to speak of the small candle-lit tent beyond the stalls,
he secretly hoped others might. A shiver, traveling on the
waves of memory, passed through his body.

This night the men's thoughts were turned inward and
Çatal, though disappointed, understood. Fear had sealed
their lips; no one wanted to admit how he'd trembled. But
Çatal's desire to know nagged. As he wrapped up the
remainder of his food, he asked Hrant to walk with him.

They walked to an area where some men chose to cluster
their animals and goods for the night. Later in the evening
the men would form a circle around them to sleep, but it
was still early and the area, except for an occasional snort
or grunt, was quiet. Çatal, with his voice barely above a
whisper, asked Hrant what he knew of the dark men.

His friend's eyes showed white and he shook his head
from side to side. Çatal waited, increasingly concerned he
had broken some unspoken rule or trespassed on a religious
tenet. Hrant, Çatal knew, lived in a village no larger than
his and in an area equally remote. But then Hrant
whispered, "Gazies, warriors for the faith." He told me that
small bands of Muslim outlaws, like the Gazies, coming
from the North and East, were pillaging and killing in the
countryside. "They hear that Muslim armies are defeating
the Romans and that Rome is weakening. Soon the

Byzantine Empire will be no more. I fear for your family, Çatal, for all Christians." He placed a hairy hand over his mouth and his shoulders began to shake.

Haltingly, he told Çatal about a family of Christian Armenians, friends he came to know near his home. For years they had enjoyed times together during holidays—Muslim and Christian. It had been so joyful to know that their faiths were bound together by many shared values: respect, hospitality, charity, and love of family.

Then one day he and the father and grandfather of this family had gone together to sell sheep at a larger settlement, a town where men of wealth would pay them well. When they returned after two days, his friend's family was not there to greet him. They searched for hours with growing fear, seeing signs of turmoil—plants trampled by the feet of many horses, household goods scattered and broken, and smears of still-wet blood. They followed the trail of blood to a pond where, in the deepest center, they found his wife, six children, aunts and uncles floating like ghosts beneath the water, bound with wooden crosses around their necks.

Çatal asked forgiveness for opening his friend's wound. Why had he given in to his curiosity when other men instinctively knew better? This time, his thirst for knowledge had caused pain. His heart ached as he walked back to Sütlü to sleep. Sleep? He would not sleep. He had hurt his friend and filled his own head with fearful scenes. Çatal stared at the ground, knelt next to his camel and spread his fleece. He breathed in his camel's musky scent and pressed his back into her soft fur. Sütlü shifted like a mother accommodating her calf and as she did the rug fell sideways. Çatal clutched the rug's nap and pulled it to his chest. Heat radiated through his fleece vest, his cotton tunic, the wadded shawl, and finally to his skin. His heart slowed. He drifted away, first on the air, then cradled in a bed of fragrant grass. Beyond him he heard Rachel's soft laughter, saw her stroking the petals of a wildflower. In the far distance there were snowy mountains, blue-green rivers, and flowers, tall and flamboyant. Paradise.

Çatal woke to the gritty shuffle of sandaled feet. He squinted in the morning light, finally focusing on a massive, moon-faced man reaching for his rug. Çatal bolted upright. The man took several steps backward, tucked the loosened end of purple fabric into his turban's folds, and apologized. Çatal stood, raising the rug with him. He recognized this man, remembered seeing him in the crowd near the caravanserai, seated elegantly on a festooned stallion with four ebony servants on foot alongside a covered, horse-drawn cart.

Çatal shrank inside his shabby tunic and, through the corners of his eyes, glimpsed the royal color and intricate embroidery on the nobleman's coat. He maintained his silence and hoped the man would move on, bored by a dull, uninteresting peasant. But still the man stood looking at his rug. After a moment he looked up at Çatal and smiled—a warm, friendly smile. Çatal struggled with an urge to return it, but there was a glint in the man's eyes that stopped him. Çatal had seen such a glint before in the golden eyes of a wolf.

"Salaam alakum, peace be upon you,*"* the stranger said.

Çatal matched the man's greeting, his bowed head, and his arm pressed to his chest, still fighting the fear-laced caution welling up in his chest. He chided himself. The man's intonation, though different from his own, was no reason to miss an opportunity to meet a stranger. Weren't these the very things Çatal wanted to teach his daughter and the other children in his remote village? He returned the smile.

"Only one rug? You are not a trader, eh?" the man continued, since Çatal had not yet completely found his tongue. "You bought this in Erzurum, perhaps for its colors or for the dragons?" His head bobbed up and down with enthusiasm.

"I found it pleasing, yes," Çatal said. He began to roll the rug. With each twist, the rug gathered in his arms, yet instead of increasing weight, it seemed no more than air. He tossed it over his shoulder.

"It is a gift for my betrothed daughter," Çatal said, beginning to feel his comfort return with the hope of interesting conversation.

"Ahhh, I can think of no better gift," the man said. He rubbed his hands over his sides and Çatal noticed the sparkle of gems on his fingers. "Every day a rug will feel the happy feet of your daughter and her husband. Perhaps later the rug will learn the footsteps of your many grandchildren. I know this joy. I have many daughters of my own.

"Please, since it is for your daughter's dowry, let me trade your rug for something better. I am returning home with rugs from many excellent weavers. I know just the one for you," he said, reaching for the ivory silk fringe below Çatal's shoulder.

From nowhere the smell of rotting meat suddenly filled the air. Çatal blinked at the open mouth of a honey-colored dragon in the trader's place. Before it vanished, its face was the face of the nobleman. Çatal spun around, fanned the air, turned his free shoulder toward the trader, and planted his feet firmly. His heart was pounding.

"Thank you, no," Çatal stammered. "This rug is perfect for my daughter. Allah's hand led me to it in the bazaar." Çatal quickened his pace to Sütlü.

"Please," the trader said, rushing to keep up. "Yes, yes, I understand, but you lack knowledge. This rug..."

The trader's voice broke and Çatal turned around, curious now to hear what the moon face would say about his rug. What he saw was sweat percolating on the broad face.

"I have the knowledge of rugs from many places—places you have never seen," he said, mopping his face with a madder-dyed cloth. "I can tell you stories which you can share with your daughter. May I see?" The trader extended his hand again to the rug which, after studying the man's face, Çatal allowed to drop at his feet.

For a long moment, they stared at each other—the trader catching his breath, Çatal still considering the trader's intent. Then the trader lowered his bulk to the ground. Çatal sat opposite him and, with a flip of his hand, unrolled the rug between them.

"I have heard a story," the man began. While he spoke he flipped over a corner of the rug and drew his fingernail over the knots, creating a drumroll sound.

Camp activity swirled around them: rattling metals, thudding hooves, animal grunts. But Çatal listened enraptured while the trader spun a tale he said he'd heard from a Chinese weaver.

"Many years ago, during the Sung dynasty, Buddhist monks prepared for an invasion by Tibetan Tanguts by sealing more than 10,000 items of value in the Caves of the Thousand Buddas, near Dunhuang, a station on the Silk Road in northwestern Gansu. One of those items was a silk rug made for Princess Jin of the Han dynasty between 206 BC and 221 AD.

"Her father, the emperor, had searched far and wide for a virtuous young woman to weave the rug, and the chosen weaver was so thrilled she promised the emperor every silk thread would pass through her fingers with prayers and blessings for Princess Jin.

"When the young peasant girl presented the completed rug, the princess was enchanted with the majestic honey and charcoal dragons stretching fringe to fringe. She begged her father to allow the girl to live in the palace as her special friend.

"No one knows what happened to Princess Jin's rug, but legend has it the blessing remains in its silk threads."

The trader searched Çatal's face until he became uncomfortable. Was this *his* rug? If he should ask such a question, what might the consequences be? He recalled the words spoken by the merchant in Erzurum: *finest Chinese silk, excavated from an ancient cave, a mystery woven in its fibers.* A chill surged through his veins and delivered an answer: He would not ask. There was no need to know. If the rug carried a blessing for his daughter, it was Allah's wish.

"A fine tale. I will tell my daughter. Good night," Çatal said, hoping his tone would tell the trader he knew a good story when he heard it.

But the trader lingered nearby as Çatal fastened the rug to Sütlü's haunches, mounted, coaxed her to her feet, and nudged her toward the line of travelers. He pretended not to hear the man's desperate "wait, wait" fading behind him.

26

Later, as Carlos loaded the dishwasher with our lunch plates, I called Val to tell him about Elena and that Carlos had booked himself on the next flight to Turkey. When he asked to speak to Carlos, I left to wash my face in the adjoining bathroom. I overheard pieces of the conversation: promises to keep in touch and that he'd be back in "a week at the most."

On my way back to the kitchen, I heard the front door open and the familiar "thunk" of Tom's heavy backpack hitting the floor.

"We're in the kitchen, Tom," I said.

Carlos told Tom about the call from Tapis. My stomach twisted as I watched Tom's expression go from expectant to worried.

"It's getting late in Ankara, but we were waiting for you so we could talk to your Nine together," I said, dialing the number.

She was relieved to know Carlos would soon be with her. When it was my turn I mentioned the effect of medication as the possible culprit.

"I hope so, my darling, but it's frightening. When I learn about my actions, when I cannot remember—ach, well, we'll see."

I passed the phone to Tom. Carlos took my hand.

"I wish I didn't have school... Nothing hurts you, does it?... Yeah, I know... Yeah, I'll study hard... Here's my dad." His face was wet.

By the time the conversation ended, her voice had brightened. I said it was because Carlos would soon be with her but he shook his head and put his hands on Tom's shoulders.

"Do you realize how much maturity you've developed in the last few months?" he said.

Tom was fingering his shirt collar and the corners of his mouth were curled.

"You let Nine know how important she is to you and that's beautiful—encouraging and healing," I said.

"When are you leaving, Dad?"

"Tomorrow. The morning flight out of La Guardia. I'll be gone before you get up in the morning."

"I'll write Nine a note right away so you can take it with you," he said, recouping his backpack and taking the stairs two at a time to his room.

The bedside alarm rang at five. I eased quietly from the bed, walked to the window, and pulled aside the drape to take in a favorite sight: the tightly packed city silhouetted against a brightening sky. Not this morning. A curtain of gray rain and fog hid everything. Below me at the street level, a truck moved slowly with heavy mist swirling in its headlights.

I heard a rustling behind me and turned to blow Carlos a morning kiss. Minutes later, while he snapped the lock on his suitcase, I tiptoed to the kitchen to make coffee, set out some breakfast items for Tom and jot a quick note about calling him at the Denbys later in the day.

I dropped Carlos at the airport and watched him disappear into the crowd, then started to make plans to fill the time while he was away. First, as Carlos suggested, I'd discuss my feelings about the gallery with my family to get their reaction.

And if I determined to close that part of my life, he suggested a preliminary talk with a lawyer for the legalities involved.

Tom was going to Marty's directly from school. Jack was taking them to a Friday night basketball game at the nearby high school and, since it ended late, Tom would spend the night with them. I'd been invited for their traditional Saturday morning breakfast: a waffle fix-the-toppings-yourself extravaganza. I called Val as soon as I got home.

"Two calls in two days? Is this my independent sister or an imposter?" Val said.

"Don't start. There's something I want to discuss."

"Now I'm sure you're an imposter. My sister doesn't ask for anybody's ideas; she always knows what's best."

"Val, you've just provided the perfect example of why I don't ask your opinion. You never listen because your own opinions are more important to you than anyone else's," I said. "You know what? Forget it. You're absolutely right. I don't need to discuss anything with you." I slammed the phone into its base and folded myself into the nearest chair. Moments later the phone rang. It was Grace.

"Nora, for reasons I don't understand, Val reacts to you in ways he never does with others. Please come over. I promise you, if I can't figure out why he's so snippy with you, I'll drag him by the ears to one of my psychiatrist friends. Please come."

"I'm on my way, but have a gag ready just in case."

"By the way, it's great that Carlos is going to be with his mother, but did it surprise you that Tapis asked? She seems competent to me. Maybe she thinks the man of the family needs to be the one to make decisions for his mother?" Grace said.

"Maybe. I hadn't thought of that, but knowing how close knit they are, it's the right thing to do."

When I arrived at Val's, Penny met me at the door with a smile. "Where's Tom? Papa says I should go to my room. I guess you're going to yell at each other."

I hugged her. "No, sweetheart, no yelling, I promise. Tom's with Marty. I have an important decision to make and your mom and papa can help me."

"You know what's not fair?"

"What?"

"I'm supposed to ask grown ups when I have decisions to make, but I can't help them."

Her chin pushed forward, so like Tom's it made me chuckle.

"I'll tell you something, Penny. There are things I'd talk to you about before anybody else."

"Like what?"

"Well, I think your hair always looks so pretty and I've been thinking of changing my hair style. Let's talk about it soon, okay?" I said.

"Anytime." She bounced up the stairs.

"Penny?"

She twirled like a ballerina on the step. She did that a lot lately.

"I'm thinking about selling my gallery," I said. She stopped, turned around, and sobered.

"What will you do if you're not working?" she said. She came down two steps where our eyes were on the same level. I had a sudden vision of her as a grown woman, a lovely grown woman.

"I suppose I'll cross that bridge when I come to it."

"I can think of a zillion things we can do together. I'll make a list for you," she said, continuing her dash upstairs and leaving me warm all over.

Philip stepped into the hall. "Thought I heard voices out here. Sorry to hear about Elena. I'm sure she'll be okay."

"Me, too, Philip," I said, stepping into the hall where I heard voices. "Ahh, the whole family council is present. Give me a minute to call Tom and I'll be right in."

Carolyn answered and told me Marty and Tom were getting their homework done so they could eat dinner and get to the high school gym for the opening basketball hoopla.

"Well, don't call him because there's no news about Elena or anything. Just tell him I called to tell him to have fun and I'll see him in the morning for the waffle extravaganza. About nine?"

"You're on."

I joined the racket in the kitchen, where Val was pouring wine. He handed me a glass and folded his hand over mine. "I'm sorry. I think sometimes my mouth belongs to somebody else, somebody who gets me in trouble with the people I love."

"I love you, too. And you're not the only one with that problem."

"Well, what's the big powwow about?"

We carried our wineglasses into the living room. Grace set a tray on the coffee table—nuts, tiny crackers sprinkled with poppy seeds, and fresh strawberries dipped in dark chocolate. They looked inviting but my stomach disagreed. Instead, I got right to the point. Val and Philip were shocked speechless—a first for Val.

"Why do you want to make such a drastic change?" Grace said, plucking a strawberry from the tray and walking to the sofa where Val had left a space for her.

"It's not as sudden as you might think. Ever since Paradise, I've felt my interest in the gallery sinking. I don't want to do it any more," I said.

"Is there something else you want to do?" Philip asked.

"No, at least I can't think of anything right now. Maybe later..."

Val topped off our wineglasses. He returned to the sofa and sank into the cushion. For a man whose usual position was the edge of his seat, composure made him look awkward.

"Carlos suggested talking it out, that maybe I'm overreacting to what happened in Paradise or-"

Philip interrupted. "I just can't believe you'd give it up after so many years of your life. For God's sake, Nora, it *was* your life."

Grace said: "Me too. There's a why in there somewhere. Do you know what it is?"

Val opened and shut his mouth. Thank you, God.

"Look, Carlos and I have been at the gallery every day since our return from Paradise and it just feels different. I've lost interest," I said. "I don't even want to be around them."

"It would be a drastic move—even a risky one," Val said, his voice low and measured.

"Risky? Isn't it okay just to know I want to make a change?"

"Not really," Grace said. "If you want the change to be a good one, you need to get to the reasons behind it. When you say you 'don't even want to be around them' I'm suspicious. Suppose you sell it and then discover you'd made a mistake. You couldn't just take it back."

"That's why I'm here. I don't know what to make of this. I think my feelings about the rugs in the past were almost visceral. They reminded me of our home and family before Mama and Papa died—a kind of security blanket, maybe." I looked at each of them in turn, waiting to see the understanding I hoped for, waiting for them to finally know me.

"And now you have Carlos?" Philip said.

"Maybe. He's opened my eyes to how closed I've been with Tom, with you. But what's that got to do with how I feel about the business? Each time I go to the gallery confirms I'm done with the rugs."

"Don't want to be around them, or don't feel the *need* to be around them? There's a big difference," Grace said.

Before I could answer, Val said: "How do you think you can avoid them? Oriental rugs are Carlos' livelihood, the business that supports his mother and you."

Grace changed the subject to Elena and defused what felt like yet another sharp jab from Val. She reminded me of their concern to know any new information that might result from Elena's appointment with the doctor.

"Elena reminds me of our mother," Val said. "Don't laugh, but there's something unique about the love a woman gives."

He put his arm around Grace and she took hold of his hand. "It makes me happy that you have Heidi Rose now, Philip."

Then he looked at me. At first it seemed natural enough since he was talking about our mother. But suddenly I wondered if somehow he had looked to me to fill the gap our mother left. I lowered my head to examine my hands and remembered Philip telling me that Val had a breakdown a year after her death, a fact I had to be reminded of.

"It's true, I'm a lucky guy," Philip said. Heidi Rose is a warm, giving woman, like Elena. From the moment I met Carlos' mother she made me feel important, like she already considered me part of her family. That was very much like our mother, don't you think?"

"Positively." I saw pictures in my mind of my mother-in-law's attentive face, her loving words, her total acceptance of Tom and me. "I should get home, but I promise to call as soon as I have any information. Thanks for listening to my concerns about the gallery. I've got a lot of thinking to do and your comments helped."

After Val closed the door, I sat for several minutes in the silence of the car's interior. Had they really helped? I listened again to their questions and knew my answers were not going to come like a bullhorn announcement. They were going to come like whispers from my heart.

27

Carlos called on Monday with the results of Elena's visit to the doctor. Tom was sitting next to me at the kitchen table, twirling a pencil in and out of his fingers like a baton. I hesitated for only a second before pressing the speaker button.

"Tom and I are both here. What's the news?"

"Hello, Tom. The doctor has scheduled some tests for her early next week—blood work and a CT. We won't know the results until the middle of the week," he said. His tone reflected impatience and I registered the fact there was no way he'd be home in a week.

"Do you know what he's looking for?" I said, glancing at Tom. He'd tilted his chair back and closed his eyes.

"That's what I want to know," he whispered.

Carlos coughed and said nothing until I suspected he didn't want to share his worries.

"I know, it's best not to borrow trouble, right? We'll wait until you have the report," I said.

"How's school?"

Tom's one-syllable answers brought their conversation to a quick end. He got up and left the room, saying he had homework to do.

"I talked to my brothers about the gallery."

"And?"

"Nothing definite, but they urged me not to do anything until I know why I want to sell my business."

"And?"

"It's hard to disagree when five people I respect say the same thing."

"Five?"

"I told Carolyn and Jack at breakfast a couple of days ago," I said.

"Aren't you full of surprises? So, do you disagree with what they're saying?"

"No. I think it's the only thing that makes sense. I'm going to call Sam. See if he knows someone who could take over in the gallery. If I still feel the same way after I've been away from it for awhile, I'll have my answer."

"Hmmm. How long is long enough, do you think?"

"Good question. A month, maybe."

Three days later, standing behind the copper-toned Central Persian Mahal in my gallery window, I watched a man approach. When he stopped on the brick herringbone sidewalk and examined the building's façade from the classical cornice supporting the roof's edge to the polished brass railing and beveled glass door, I knew it was Orhan Dumanli, the man Sam Bezdikian recommended.

An ephemeral smile played along thin lips before he placed a well-buffed black shoe on the first marble step and noticed me at the window. The smile receded as he nodded. I opened the door.

"Mr. Dumanli. Welcome to the Chestnut Street Persian Gallery. I'm Nora Ghazerian." He clasped my hand with mild pressure and I felt soft, smooth skin.

A perfect set of gleaming teeth presented along with green eyes. He was tall and thin with an aquiline nose, probably in his sixties. His voice complemented his face with just the right balance of geniality and intelligence, something I already knew from the first few seconds of observation. Even if he hadn't come with Sam and Esther's recommendation, I'd have been impressed. He had the bearing of a formidable negotiator, one, I'd wager, unused to failure.

He wanted to know the history of the gallery, nearest competition, other stores occupying space on Chestnut Street. Nothing about me. Perhaps Sam covered that base. His next questions had the precision of a surgeon's knife. What was my percentage of markup? What was my philosophy behind how I determined pricing? Was it my practice to divulge the source of my rugs to clients?

Clearly, he was probing my integrity. Sam's word wasn't enough for him. I respected that. It was a peek into his own integrity, which I had every intention of verifying. Sam's word was valuable but I wanted my own evidence. I answered Orhan in detail and enjoyed the peculiar, but effective, way he had of looking at me until he was satisfied with my answer. At that point he nodded his head and moved on. He walked from stack to stack, making comments, sharing tidbits of his knowledge. After a lengthy, somewhat pompous discourse on a Persian tree-of-life design, he was getting under my skin. I had to remind myself he came with Sam's recommendation.

We moved into the office where he requested an overview of my major clients at the gallery.

"Did Sam tell you I broker rugs for galleries along the East Coast?"

"How many?"

"There are currently twelve. The market is huge but I limit my clientele to those who've dealt with me exclusively for at least ten years. The bond is strong and will be difficult to break."

"For you or for them?"

"Don't know; it's untested territory." I added "impertinent" to the profile I was logging in my head.

Several times throughout the day, we were interrupted by customers. He stood close enough to monitor the interaction, and afterwards questioned me about my responses. He challenged me once when he thought I'd missed an opportunity to advance a sale.

"I believe the rugs sell themselves and my job is to provide service," I said.

"Interesting, Mrs. Ghazerian, but I disagree, respectfully. Loyalty results from knowing more, not only about the rugs, but also about the client's status. Do you see this difference in philosophy as a problem?"

I studied his face. "Not at all, just a different path to the same goal." Just how did one assess a client's status at the first meeting?

At closing time I shelved the bookkeeping materials and shook his doughy hand. We agreed to meet the following day and walked to our respective cars in the rear alley.

"Mrs. Ghazerian?" I turned back reluctantly. "Do you have confidence that I can manage your gallery?"

I had no doubt about his abilities, but— "Well, yes, but you said it was important to know my clients and obviously that will take time. Tomorrow we can—"

"What I want to propose is this: Sam has told me you wish some time away from your work, and I am willing— able, I might add—to manage your gallery. As for your clients, I believe I can learn much from a review of your files. You keep a history of purchases, correct?"

"Of course. There are extensive notes." I looked at the brick wall to escape his face.

"Why don't I begin tomorrow? If I have questions, I'll call you."

My mind spun like a dog chasing its tail, objections just beyond reach, until I reminded myself that Sam had never steered me wrong. "Fine," I said, but I was thinking 'sink or swim.' How much damage could he do in a month?

He bowed from the waist. I handed him the keys, fought the image of the metal burning into his open palm like a brand, and walked as fast as I could to my car.

"I'll call you each evening at eight-o'clock to report," he said. He buttoned his suit jacket and used both hands to assure the proper alignment, a movement so like Ed's I was glad my tears fell after I closed the car door.

"I just left Orhan in charge," I said to Sam as I drove home. "Talk about confidence—I almost felt my instructions were superfluous. How thoroughly did you brief him?"

"Good, my darling girl. Hardly at all except for the reason you needed him. He knows the business and, just between you and me, I think he's sorry he retired. In my opinion, you are doing each other a service."

"Oh, God, Sam, I'm a mess—missing Carlos, worrying about Elena, trying to decide what to do about the gallery. It's just hard to leave it to someone I hardly know," I said, taking the turnoff to my neighborhood. I could have added Tom to my list of concerns, but decided they worried enough about my family.

"You just take care of yourself. You've done the right thing. How can you decide the importance of the gallery in your life if you don't get away from it for awhile?

"One more thing about Orhan: If you decide you want to get out of the business, I'll bet he'd be interested. Gold jingles in his pockets," Sam said.

"I don't know, Sam. Val and Philip convinced me it's a big step so I'm going to take my time."

"Okay, keep in touch, my darling. We'll be anxious to hear a report on Elena. We haven't seen her since your wedding, but she made an indelible impression on Esther and me. I'll talk to Orhan often too. Try not to worry."

Tom, home from school, was in the kitchen when I emerged from the basement garage. A jar of peanut butter was out on the counter, along with two jars of jam, the butter dish, and two sticky-looking spoons and knives.

"I was hungry."

"Just don't spoil your dinner." I rummaged in the freezer for inspiration, deciding finally on a chicken breast.

"Can I go to school in Ankara? My Turkish is good enough and I want to be with Nine. She doesn't have anybody with her in her apartment, and-"

"Whoa. You're making it sound like she's an invalid or something. For all we know, she's got a virus that'll be over soon," I said. "Stop worrying. We'll have more information next time your dad calls."

He dropped his unfinished snack and left the room. I wasn't happy waiting either and now Tom had seeded new thoughts. What would we do if she were seriously ill? Would Carlos be content to leave the day-to-day care to Tapis? She couldn't handle one visit to the doctor without him, how could she shoulder all of Elena's care? Now I *was* Chicken Little.

As I passed the den, the phone rang. It was Grace.

"Want some company later this afternoon? Penny and I thought we'd come over. It's her idea actually. What did you say to her about hair? She's on a mission—tearing pictures out of magazines every chance she gets. She says she wants to show you some hairdos that will suit you."

I laughed. "Oh, that'd be a godsend. I told her I'm looking for a new style, and you two are just what I need to help me get my mind away from Elena and the gallery."

"When you see some of these hair suggestions, I guarantee you'll be distracted."

An hour later the door chime sounded. Penny, twitching with anticipation, was holding a shoebox tied with a blue ribbon. Behind her, Grace shrugged, an indication this was going to be her daughter's show. We walked into the kitchen and Penny dropped the box onto the counter.

"What have you got for my makeover?" I said.

"You don't need a makeover, Aunt Nora, just a new hairstyle. That's why I'm glad I'm not a boy. They all look

the same. So boring," she said, emptying the contents of
the shoebox on the kitchen counter.

"Who understands boys, period? Speaking of that, where's
Tom?" Grace said.

"Doing his homework, I hope. Have some cheese and
crackers while I get a comb and some clips from my
bedroom," I said.

I stopped to knock at Tom's bedroom door to tell him
Penny and Aunt Grace were downstairs. He flew out of his
room and took the stairs two at a time, but by the time I'd
gathered what I needed he was on his way back to his room.

"That was a quick visit."

"Stupid girl stuff," he said, closing his door.

The kitchen counter was covered with magazine pictures.

"Lots of blondes here. Are you suggesting a new hair
color?"

Penny looked at me like it was the first time. "Your skin
tone would clash."

"I'm in the hands of an expert," I said.

Grace laughed but stopped when she saw Penny's hurt
expression.

"You know, Mom, my friends and I are serious about
these things: hair, makeup, and clothes. Decisions have to be
made and we help each other. The important thing is to
develop your own style."

"Sorry, I didn't mean you don't know what you're talking
about," Grace said.

"It's okay. My friends and I understand we're at an age of
transformation and our parents are not ready for it."

I winked at Grace when Penny's back was turned to me.

"Now, Aunt Nora, tell me the message you want to give
the world," Penny said. She was deadly serious.

My cell phone was ringing inside my purse on a chair in
the entrance hall. It was Elena.

"Please forgive me, Nora, but I have been to your
apartment several times this morning and I wanted to talk to

Carlos. Where have you gone so early in the morning? You didn't mention anything to me," she said.

She didn't sound anxious, just mildly curious. Still, Carlos was staying with her so what was she doing at- I glanced at the clock and saw that it was eleven o'clock in the evening in Ankara.

"Oh, here he is, Nora. How silly of me. I look forward to seeing you at dinner tonight," she said.

Carlos said he'd call me back in a few moments. I walked into the kitchen shaking my head and replacing the phone in my purse. Penny had cleared the counter and was holding a magazine picture in each hand. I quickly explained the call from Elena, just finishing as the phone rang again.

Carlos sounded desperate. His mother had been confused all day and he'd encouraged her to go to bed early. He hadn't heard her leave her room and was concerned that if he went to sleep, she might leave the apartment.

"It's painful to see her distress when she becomes aware that something is wrong."

Carlos said he'd called the doctor, only to be told nothing could be done until the results of the tests were in.

It was the logical response, but in the period between not knowing and knowing, we were left to imagine the worst. Carlos did too—I heard it in his voice. I saw it on Grace and Penny's faces, and when I turned around, Tom looked miserable.

After Grace and Penny left, I went to the den. Tom followed. He sat next to me and reached for my hand.

28

The moment was surreal. In a room where nothing had moved, everything had changed. I felt Tom's blood pulsing where our fingers pressed together. All those times I'd reached for him and was rebuffed paraded through my memory. Twelve years.

"You think Nine's gonna die, don't you?" he said.

"No, I don't think that. We have to wait for the test results."

"I like having a grandmother. It's not fair that she's sick."

"I know. She thinks you're pretty special too. The best thing we can do for her is let her know we love her."

There was so much I wanted to say, but talking this way and hearing Tom express his feelings was making my heart race. I wanted to tell him I understood completely how he felt. Elena had filled the place my mother held before she died. To lose her would be to lose my mother a second time.

But what if he didn't want to hear how I felt? Was he too young to see beyond his own need? He'd matured since Carlos came into our lives and I'd seen glimmers of a generous, empathetic young man. But those expressions had been toward others, not me. Still, he was holding my hand.

"I know how you feel about wanting to be with Nine now. Let's think of some ways we can let her know she's in our thoughts even if we're not with her," I said, turning to look at him.

"She likes getting letters. She says they're better than email because she likes to see my handwriting. She told me she can tell a lot by looking at someone's handwriting. She said mine is good and I don't make mistakes. I'm going to write her right now, okay? If I put it in the mailbox tonight…

"Here's a better idea—I'm going to write in Turkish. She'll be really surprised, won't she?"

"She'd love it. Tomorrow you can call and tell her it's coming."

He let go of my hand and ran to his room. I could still feel the pressure of his skin against mine.

The waiting was over several days later. Elena had a fast growing tumor in her brain. Carlos, sobbing on the phone, had called from the doctor's office while his mother chatted with the doctor in another room. He repeated the medical terms exactly as the doctor had recited them. I knew he didn't completely understand. I didn't either. We understood the implications clearly enough and they were serious.

"Just talk to me until I can leave this room with some control. I wish you were here. I feel like a child," he said.

"We're all children at times like this. But, Carlos, listen. Medical advances are made every day. Will she need surgery?"

"Yes, very soon. I must calm myself. Just talking to you helps. You know, she has been so confused, but after the doctor gave her the results, she became calm and rational. She was the one asking questions, not me. My tongue was glued to the roof of my mouth. I'm so ashamed."

"Ashamed because you love your mother? No, my love. You'll be her strong support. Call me later. Tom and I send you our love."

I had taken the call upstairs and now sat on the end of my bed with my mind spinning. Turkey's medical care was good as far as my limited experience could tell, and the family had the resources to provide for all her needs. But was the care as advanced as in the States? Did Carlos know? I decided this would be my way to help. There were calls I could make before Tom got home from school. If I could just find something encouraging to tell him.

My first call was to Carolyn. She'd been a nurse at the University of Pennsylvania's hospital until Marty was born. She took the news with her usual composure. I'd never known Carolyn to make snap judgments or face problems with anything but rational examination. Perhaps nurses learn these skills while dealing with distraught patients and emergencies.

"I'm so sorry," she said. "There was no evidence of that when we saw her this summer. It's good that Carlos is there.

"The University's hospital is where I'd want my family to be. Their reputation is well deserved. What's more, they routinely care for people from all over the world. She'd get leading edge care, the latest and best of everything."

I grabbed a pencil and paper to jot down the contacts she gave me in the oncology unit. As she spoke, I grew cold as images from my own confinement at the Pennsylvania hospital flashed across my memory. The corridors, the overhead lighting, the nurses' uniforms, the ringing phones at the nurses' station—I could see them all, just as it was when I returned from Izmir Buca Prison. The prison's damp walls, the roaches, and the guard with the white streak in her black hair passed in review until my lunch twisted in my stomach.

"Carolyn, I feel sick. I'll call you back."

I hung onto the edges of the toilet as wave after wave of nausea rippled through my body. It had been years and I thought the memories of those dreadful days of terror were gone. It was bad enough to be forcefully removed from the airplane at the airport and thrown in a cell for three weeks without explanation, but when an American Embassy representative finally came to tell me I was being held for fraud, I nearly lost my mind. It got worse after my release to the hospital in Philadelphia and my brothers told me they believed Carlos had betrayed me. I hadn't thought of these things for years. I didn't want to think of them ever again.

The front door slammed. Tom was home.

"Mom," he called.

I opened the bathroom door and said I'd be down in a moment, quickly washed my face, and looked at myself in the mirror until I could configure something that wouldn't frighten Tom into thinking the worst about Elena. Yet he had to be told the bad news and that, I knew, would hurt both of us. It wouldn't do to raise his hopes about bringing Elena to the States. I'd have to find a way to discuss that with Carlos alone.

Tom was in the refrigerator up to his waist in search of something to eat. At the mention his dad had called, he closed the door and his eyes. The last thought I had before giving Tom the news was of Carlos asking me to talk to him until he regained control of his emotions. Would Tom look to me for help?

"Nine has a cancerous tumor in her brain," I said.

He took several quick breaths and then stood straight and stiff. It was more than I could stand. I reached for him, shaking with my own sobs. For a second I wondered if he'd pull away, but his arms wound around my waist and I had the answer to my question. He showed me bravery; I told him how our family support would give us strength.

Tom went to his room to do his homework and I went to mine, closed the door, and called Carolyn. In the time that had elapsed, she'd retrieved the name of a health counselor in the oncology department who would be able to answer my questions and make recommendations.

I made the call immediately and ran into the usual gauntlet of gatekeepers until the doctor was on the line. I grabbed a pencil and paper and took notes. He provided statistics regarding recovery under specific treatments, and, although an assessment needed to be made based on her scan and blood work, he could say with certainty that the University had equipment surpassing, if not all, most of what was available in the Middle East.

During dinner I told Tom what I'd learned, organizing the information in my head as I did.

"I knew our hospitals would be better here. Let's call dad now and tell him," Tom said.

"Finish your milk. It's midnight in Ankara, and after the kind of day they've had, I hope they're both sound asleep."

Tom thundered down the stairs the next morning and handed me the phone.

"I already figured it out—it's five in Ankara. You didn't call without me, did you? You promised to tell me everything, remember?" His chin shot out.

"No, I haven't called. I was waiting for you," I said. I managed a smile but it was half-hearted at best. During the night I'd begun to wonder if my research might appear too controlling. "Before we tell Dad what we hope will happen, let's find out what his thoughts are. Maybe Elena won't want to travel or maybe— "

"No, Mom, tell her it's better here. We have a room for her and I'll help," he said.

I dialed Elena's apartment but there was no answer. Thinking they might be with Tapis, I tried her. After a few amenities, she put Carlos on the line and I put the speaker on.

"We seem to be going in circles here, trying to agree on the best treatment plan," Carlos said, "but there are so many unanswered questions, I'm frustrated. No one we know has experience with brain cancer and until Ana is scheduled for surgery, the assistant in the doctor's office says she cannot give us information."

"I see. Would it help if I told you some of the things I have found out?"

"What things?"

"I called Carolyn for a contact at the University of Pennsylvania. You remember she worked there until Marty was born. The oncology department counselor gave me general information, specifically regarding international patients," I said.

Carlos listened to my accounting and surprised me by remembering the outstanding treatment I'd had. It seemed no one had forgotten those days.

"It hadn't occurred to me that Philadelphia might be an alternative option for her treatment. I'll get back to you. I miss you."

"Me too, but Tom and I are supporting each other the best we can until you come home," I said, hoping Carlos would catch the gratitude in my voice.

"Is he there?"

"Yes, and listening to every word," I said.

"Dad, we really want Nine to come here. We have the best doctors and everything."

"It has to be her decision. Don't forget she's lived most of her life here. But I'll tell her what you said and it will mean a lot to her to know you love her and want to take care of her.

"And, Tom?"

"What," Tom said, his voice flat, impatient he had to wait for others to make decisions.

"I know I can count on you to keep your mother's spirits up along with your own. I can concentrate completely on Nine because you have everything under control in Philadelphia, yes?"

Moments later Tom left for school with a look of contentment on his face. His father's praise, I knew, was replaying in his head. My head, on the other hand, ticked off the mundane household chores I planned to do to pass the time. None of it happened. By noon I'd run out of energy. I climbed the stairs to my room and stretched across the bed. Within minutes I fell asleep.

When heavy footsteps sounded outside my door, I turned to look at the bedside clock—three thirty. I'd slept two and a half hours, in the middle of the day, something I hadn't done since I was pregnant with Tom.

"Tom, that you?" I called, walking to the door. Tom's back was receding down the hall. He stopped and turned around.

"Can I go to Marty's? We're working on a history project together."

"Oh, sure. Be home by six for dinner, okay?"

Seconds later the door slammed and silence settled in. I still felt groggy, like I could sleep again. Instead I went to the bathroom, splashed my face with cold water and changed into a sweatshirt, pants, and bedroom slippers. Perhaps a layer of outside comfort would spread to my insides. I plodded to the kitchen to pull a container of homemade chicken soup from the refrigerator.

I was having an after-dinner coffee when I heard my cell phone ringing. I had to go to the table in the hall to retrieve my purse and by the time I reached it the caller had hung up. I was surprised to see the call was from Tapis—almost dawn in Ankara? I called back immediately, thinking the worst.

Without saying "hello" she began screaming at me. I struggled to make out her words and when I did my blood ran cold. She was furious I should suggest that Elena come to the States for treatment. She was the daughter; it was her duty and honor to care for her mother.

"Please, Tapis, it is only a suggestion. Of course, I want what is best for all concerned. How does your mother feel about it?"

"She deserves the best care from people who love her," she said, ignoring my question. "You are too busy with your work to care for your son, why would I let you care for my mother?"

My mouth opened and shut again. I was speechless, and then the line went dead.

29

There was no safe place for my anger. Tapis obviously had lost her reason. Even if she'd stayed on the line, nothing good would've come from arguing with her. No good would come from telling Carlos either—it would set off a firestorm, and Tom didn't need to know how much his aunt disliked me. I gathered up my purse and went to bed, though sleep, I knew, would be a long time coming.

I stared at the ceiling fan wheeling overhead. Maybe Tapis would tell Carlos her feelings, but if she didn't... No, I couldn't. My insides screamed at the injustice, but I was not going to cause any kind of rift. Elena was fighting for her life and that was the only fight that mattered. Tom had held my hand and hugged me. I could stand up against my sister-in-law's indictment.

Orhan was expecting me at the gallery. He'd had a puzzling call from Max Taibi and, rather than discuss it on the phone, I told him I'd stop by. Actually, I was glad to get out of the house. Elena's health aside, it didn't escape me that I was spending a disproportionate time at home. I'd never been so tired. The emotional ups and downs were taking their toll. The crisp morning air was invigorating and traffic was light. The forecast was predicting heavy autumn rain by late afternoon.

I forced myself to notice the changing leaves—red, yellow, peach, and rust—against that special shade of crisp blue sky,

October's gift before the perennial gray winter tarp fell over the northeastern coast. A downpour would loosen their hold on the branches and turn the leaves into sodden brown mush along the curbs. I told myself that beautiful colors and Tom were my hedge against the bad times.

Orhan, watching for me through the office window, stood in the doorway as I parked. He locked the door behind me and inquired about Elena before getting to the reason for my visit.

"It's kind of you to ask. We've been gathering information and looking at the best ways to help her," I said. "It amazes me how complicated things can get, but we'll sort it out.

"Now, tell me about Max."

"I wasn't sure how to proceed. He seemed irritated when I told him you were not available. Is he more than a long-time customer?"

"Max? Actually, we've been friends since I was a teenager, just getting my toes into the nap, so to speak. What does he want?"

"I'm not sure but he wanted to know who I was and said something about being 'out of the loop'."

"Maybe I should've called my customers to introduce you and tell them I was taking a leave of absence, but..."

"It's not like you've abandoned them. The gallery's functioning and I'm willing to answer his questions. After I talk to him I'll call you, but I assume you don't want me to encourage him to call you at home."

"No, I don't. You can tell him I need some time to take care of my family. He's a very good customer. You'll enjoy doing business with him."

I felt obliged to walk through the gallery before I left. As I expected, everything was as it should be. My rugs were beautiful, the gallery had a distinctive elegance, and I revisited my pride. Nevertheless, there was a difference. My preoccupation with it was gone, and when I waved goodbye to Orhan and walked to my car, it was with a feeling the ghosts had kept their prickly fingers to themselves.

Before I reached home, Orhan called to tell me he'd already spoken to Max and it had gone well. He'd explained my family situation and Max sent his best wishes and offers to help in any way. Dear Max. Then Orhan continued with a litany of the rugs Max felt he needed.

"I assured him we would fill his requests immediately. Your warehouse inventory includes everything he needs and I'll set up the delivery later today," he said in his clipped, efficient voice.

"You've already been to the warehouse?"

"Of course. I went after closing on the first day. For me, it wasn't enough to see the rug list in the office. I had to see them for myself, get a sense of their uniqueness, of their power. I know you understand what I'm saying."

"I do. See if Tony is available to take the rugs to New Hope. He's a capable young man who has my complete confidence."

"Why not your senior workman? Since Max is a long-standing customer and friend, he deserves the best," he countered.

"Fine," I said. In the space of so few days, Orhan's knowledge of my rugs had quickly expanded to my personnel. Bully for him. I knew that Tony aspired to advance himself, a trait I admired and wanted to encourage. Except for that knowledge, I'd have chosen the worker with greater seniority too. Mr. Shiny Shoes was a long way from knowing everything.

I jumped at the sound of Tom's voice, surprised I hadn't heard him come in the front door.

"Any news?" He scavenged for his after-school snack.

I handed him a peach and waved my hand toward the soap at the sink. The phone rang and he reached for it with lathered hands. I intercepted him and heard Carlos' voice. He was shouting.

"Take the phone, Tapis. You had no right. Mehmet would agree. This is unforgivable." His words blared in a steady stream, giving me no opening to tell him that Tom was with me. Another voice, sharp and angry as well, was interrupting in the background. Tapis.

One look at Tom's face and I understood something else: This was not a conversation he should hear. I hung up. In the time it would take to realize I was no longer on the line, I could explain...what?

"Tom, I want you to trust me. Your dad's going to call back, but I need some private time. I'll come up to your room as soon as I finish."

"No, you promised to tell me everything about Nine. You promised." He looked so desperate I gave in.

"Okay, your aunt called me last night. She was upset and said some things... People say awful things when their emotions are raw. Your dad will— "

"Is Nine gonna come here to get well?"

"I told you that's something she has to decide. Maybe that's what they're arguing about. Maybe your aunt doesn't want her to come here. Your dad will get it worked out, Tom.

"Marty's been asking about you. Why don't you surprise him?"

He gave me a look that went from concern to pique, and then he went to his room.

I made myself a cup of tea while I waited for Carlos to call back and when he didn't, I picked up the newspaper to pass the time. The warm tea did little to soothe. On one hand, I was relieved to know Carlos was aware of Tapis' attitude. Relieved, too, that I wasn't the one who told him.

The newspaper wasn't what I needed. I began washing and chopping vegetables for an Asian stir fry. Tossed along with some spices and leftover chicken, it was a meal that required little of my brain, and little was all I had. I imagined Carlos, already distraught, arguing with his sister, and the idea was so contrary to their usual solidarity it hurt. What's more, it was the last thing Elena would imagine in her family and the worst thing for her to face in her illness. I could only hope she wasn't aware of what was happening. I put my trust in Carlos and Tapis to work things out and chopped harder.

An hour later Carlos still hadn't called and Tom came stomping back into the kitchen, asking if he could help with dinner.

"That would be nice. Your dad hasn't called back."

"Yeah, I know." He had a self-satisfied look on his face. It made me curious but not enough to probe and possibly ignite another challenge.

I filled our plates with Japanese Udon noodles and spooned on the stir fry mixture: green and red peppers, crunchy water chestnuts, and shrimp. We made small talk, avoiding the topic most on our minds. When we walked to the sink with our soiled plates, he asked if he could go to see Marty.

"But call me if dad calls back, okay?"

I gave my word and dried my hands. The mail lay unopened on the counter, but as I reached for the topmost envelope the phone rang. I doubted it could be Carlos; it was the small hours of the morning in Ankara.

"I ask you to forgive me, please," Tapis said. "I would not believe Carlos to tell me the truth about you because he loves you, but Tom I believe. He says you love Ana as much as we do and— "

"He says? Tom called you?"

"Yes. I remember how you leave your son alone and you love your work more than your home. Tom tells me no more. He says you are a good mother, and if Ana says she will go to Philadelphia, I will be sad but I trust you."

Tom's self-satisfied expression took on meaning, and a lump rose in my throat.

"Yes, of course I forgive you. Our world has turned upside down. I don't blame you for protecting your mother. Believe me, Tapis, she is my mother too, a sacred companion since the moment I met her. Ana is my example of how a mother's love can influence her children. I have made many mistakes with my son, but I have always loved him."

"Yes, I believe this and I am happy for this truth."

"If Ana decides to come to Philadelphia, why don't you come with her?"

"Really? Oh, thank you, thank you."

A gloomy fog hid the street below my bedroom window the next day. Ghostly streaks from car headlights were the only indication that traffic persisted despite the weather. At least the drivers were going somewhere, unlike Tom and me—stuck in a holding pattern dictated by doctors, attached to cables and wires for information.

As I cleared the breakfast dishes and Tom shouted his goodbye, I realized I envied him. The school halls would be vibrant with young voices and the classes would offer challenge and distraction. Carolyn came to my rescue. She invited me to the Museum of Art to see a new exhibit of Chihuly glass. I jumped at the chance, invited her for coffee and a biscuit to pass the time until the exhibit opened at ten thirty. I dashed upstairs to dress.

Twenty minutes later we were no more than five minutes into conversation and coffee when my cell phone rang. The voice was Carlos, albeit garbled and frantic. He was giving me a telephone number but it wasn't clear. I dialed his cell phone. No answer. Likewise, no one picked up the phone at Elena's apartment or in our apartment. I hesitated momentarily before dialing Tapis' cell phone.

"We are at the hospital with Ana. Carlos is here. Just a moment," she said.

I threw my purse on the table and sat on the bar stool, supporting myself on my elbows. Carolyn went to the sink and began washing the mugs we'd used.

"Nora." It was Carlos. His voice was a mixture of relief and desperation. "I have lost my cell phone somewhere, I don't know. I wanted to tell you we have brought Ana to the hospital."

"What happened?"

Elena, he said, had collapsed in the apartment. Her breathing was labored, she was thrashing about, and he called the doctor who called for an ambulance. He began to sob uncontrollably and couldn't go on. Tapis continued for him.

"We have just come from her room. She is attached to…it's horrible. You must come, and Tom. She is asking for you. Carlos wants-

"She is dying. The doctor says the tumor is pressing on…I don't know. Her organs are failing. She wants to see Tom, to see you. You can come, yes?" she said.

"Yes, yes. I'll let you know our arrival time. Don't leave her. I'll take a taxi from the airport to the hospital." The phone bounced before landing in its cradle and felt myself slipping off the stool.

"Nora, what?"

I felt Carolyn's arm around my waist. We walked to the den while I tried to tell her how Elena's condition had suddenly deteriorated, but I couldn't keep my thoughts together. I heard my voice and Carolyn's response one moment and felt myself slipping into unconsciousness the next. By the time I felt the support of the sofa's cushions around me, all I could do was take the hand Carolyn offered and hold on.

"I'm all right," I said, trying to sit up. "Really, I am. I don't know what happened. Tapis says Elena is dying. It's shock, right?"

Carolyn, unflappable Carolyn, was taking my pulse. She was searching my face—no, more like examining my face. Her normally placid gray eyes penetrated beyond skin.

"Probably. But I think you need to tell your doctor about this," she said. Her words flowed evenly but the tone left no question that "need" meant must.

"Don't be silly. Besides I don't have a doctor."

She frowned. I knew that Marty had a yearly physical and dental appointment, which was probably so for Jack and her as well.

"Look at it this way. You're going to Turkey, right? Wouldn't you like to be sure there's no problem before you go—for Tom's sake, for Carlos and Elena?" She didn't wait for an answer. "I'll bet Dr. Burroughs, our family doctor, would squeeze you in today." She reached for the phone with one hand and into her purse with the other. Out came an accordion card holder.

I walked to the bathroom to splash my face while she called. Her voice pierced the closed door as I dried off. "Dr. Burroughs says he'll see you in half an hour. How's that?"

30

The doctor's office was empty, including the usual corps of receptionists, but before we sat down, he came barreling through the door.

"Come on back. Everybody's taking lunch break, so let's have a look at you." He led the way while Carolyn's hasty introduction faded behind us. I managed to shrug my shoulders before the door closed on her thumbs up sign.

He ushered me into a small room with the usual examination table, wall cabinets, sink, rolling stool, and chair, and instructed me to undress while he held up a wrinkled blue fabric. He called it a "gown." A wall poster of animal faces with cigarettes dangling from their lips caught my eye. The message: "You look just as stupid."

"Ties in the back," he said, closing the door.

I liked his brusque manner. It meant I'd be out of there quickly, and the sooner I got home, the better. There was no choice about the bad news Tom had to hear and our imminent flight to Turkey. Tom deserved a strong mother at his side, one who wouldn't crumble in the face of sadness, one who had confidence in his ability to cope. I reminded myself how he'd surprised me with his capabilities during the festival and his resilience afterwards. I'd let him down so many times in the past, but this time I'd show him he could count on me. Elena was asking for us. Carlos needed us to be with him. My thoughts flashed to the hospital room awaiting us in Ankara and my stomach fluttered. Fortunately, Dr. "Brusque" entered and whisked away my thoughts.

He set the stethoscope in the middle of my chest. "This might be a little cold," he said. "Cough, please. Swallow." His fingers followed the movement down my neck. Then he fastened a blood pressure cuff on my arm, squeezing, watching the gauge, listening. "Hmm, hmm," came from the depths of his throat. His eyes—black and unreadable when open—were so tightly closed that deep lines radiated around their perimeter.

"A little anxious, are we? Relax, Mrs. Ghazerian. Lie back, please. Carolyn tells me you have an illness in the family and will be traveling to Turkey?" He didn't wait for my answer before probing my abdomen with his fingers under the blue wrinkles. "Lately you've been fatigued? Some nausea?"

"Ouch."

"Sorry." He hesitated only a second before he continued poking.

"When was your last menstrual period?"

"Ah, I'm not sure. I've had a lot of stress—"

"Yes, yes, of course. I understand. Not unusual. I'll be back in a moment. Get dressed."

When he returned, it was with a smile. "You seem in perfect health to me. I find nothing wrong, but I have a suspicion." He handed me a pregnancy test. "This will confirm what I'm thinking, if you'd be so kind."

"What? You're kidding."

He directed me to the bathroom, ignoring the fact that my lips were working another question. I shoved the door closed with my foot, followed the instructions, and when the plus sign appeared I sat on the toilet seat to grasp the unthinkable: I was going to have a baby. Did I *want* a baby? Another life in mine? I hardly believed my own answer: Yes, yes, yes. Carlos was going to have his own child, Elena another grandchild, a brother or sister for Tom.

Dr. Burroughs was waiting outside the door, still smiling. "In my work I see a preponderance of sick and sad faces. Your expression has brightened my day, even my tomorrow. Want to know if it's a boy or girl?"

"Why would I want to know that?"

"Well, you've been out of the baby business for twelve years, knowing the gender would help you to prepare."

"I think I can get my act together in nine months."

"Make that six and a half months."

I placed my hands on my abdomen. "A baby's been developing in me for two and a half months?"

"Do you use a birth control of some sort?"

I shook my head.

"I'd really like you to think about having an amniocentesis test. Not just to determine gender, but since it's been twelve years, you're at higher risk for certain problems. The test would put your mind at ease or give you an early warning."

"Oh, I didn't know that," I said.

He pulled out a chair for me and described the test. There were risks but they were minimal. I would know in two to four weeks. "Completely up to you. You're going to Turkey tonight?"

I nodded.

"Well, think about it and call me when you get back. If you want the test, I'll make arrangements for you. Better yet, I encourage you to see a gynecologist soon. They can set the test up for you."

He walked me to the end of the hall, halting under the exit sign. He shook my hand. "Whatever you decide let me know the outcome. I'd like to know."

I walked into the waiting room, trying without success to reconfigure my face. Surely I looked as dopey as I felt.

"I take it you're perfectly well," Carolyn said, standing and handing me my jacket.

"I'm pregnant," I said. The words felt like marbles in my mouth.

"My God. That's— That's incredible. I'm totally shocked, aren't you?"

"Beyond belief. What's more I'm two and a half months pregnant. I'm stunned, but I know Carlos will love it. Elena too."

There was no doubt about that. This child, not yet fully formed, had the power to bring happiness, even as we prepared ourselves to say goodbye.

"What about you?" she said, suddenly serious.

Her question struck me as odd, but it quickly made sense. The excitement I felt when Tom was born was short lived. That scarlet face, contorted in anger. That demanding cry. Never a moment to myself. It wore me down until I began to find any excuse to escape. It was a relief when Jared took over his care and I was free to concentrate on my business. I'd been paying dearly for that ever since.

"Yes, really, I am. It's my second chance and I'm not going to blow it," I said.

Carolyn drove the back streets on the way home. Red lights turned green as we approached. No trolley, no bus impeded our progress. Who waved a magic wand? This never happened in center city, particularly at noon. In a few more hours, the cars of workers would be parked on both sides of the street and traffic would back up. A few city blocks might take thirty minutes or more to navigate.

"Are you going to tell Carlos right away?"

I'd lost all sense of Carolyn sitting next to me, even where I was at that moment. My mind was creating a fantasy around our family of four—in the kitchen, on the deck, at my brothers' homes. Carlos and I were a family, but this....

She was parking in front of our house—another jolt because I'd lost all sense of distance only that we were moving and nothing was getting in our way. Since hearing the doctor's words, I'd thought of little more than the joy my words would bring to Carlos, but Carolyn's question provoked another.

When would I tell Tom? So much had happened since he left
for school. He didn't know about Elena's sudden decline. He
didn't know we were going to Turkey as soon as we could. My
mind was galloping and the hurdles were coming into view.

I invited Carolyn in, telling her I needed her calm head to
help me sort out the morass that was quickly piling up. We
walked to the kitchen and I grabbed a pencil and paper to make
a list.

"Do you want to see a gynecologist before you leave?"
Carolyn said.

Bless her first-things-first thoughts. I shook my head—no
time to wait for an appointment. My condition wasn't an
emergency and chances of being squeezed in as I'd been with
Dr. Burroughs weren't likely with a specialist.

"Okay, so the gatekeeper for what has to happen is the
airline reservation, right?" I said, feeling like I was already
getting a handle on the situation. I picked up the phone and
spent several minutes with our travel agent. Travel was quickly
arranged for the evening flight, as I'd hoped. We were entitled
to bonuses like reduced ticket cost for family emergencies and
I chose seats in first class for added comfort. When I hung up
the phone, Carolyn had made tea and a call to the school as
soon as she heard when we were leaving.

"The principal sends her best wishes. She assured me they'd
give Tom every support he might need when he returns.
Furthermore, she offered to take him out of class and bring him
home within the hour."

"Thanks. That's perfect," I said, picking up my mug. I
motioned for us to sit in the den to wait for Tom to get home.

The activity had calmed me. "I'm not going to tell Carlos
about the baby until I'm with him. I don't want to miss his
expression when he hears," I said. Carolyn nodded. "And
Tom?" she said.

"Well, he's being taken out of school so he'll know we're
leaving town and he'll be upset. I've been trying to be more
open with him. We're closer than we've ever been because I'm

including him in my plans and telling him my thoughts and feelings. I'll admit Carlos had to push me, but it's become easier and easier. Still, I dread telling him about Elena."

She nodded again.

"I'm going to tell him about Elena as soon as he gets home. Then I'm going to tell him about the baby and we'll tell Carlos together when we get to the hospital."

She touched my arm. "You seem so sure Tom's going to welcome your news."

Her question caught me off guard, again. I *was* sure. "Maybe it's overconfidence but I don't think so. There've been so many signs lately. We're in a different place." I soaked up the feeling. "And Tom loves kids. You should have seen him in the Story Tent, Carolyn. He'll love being a big brother." Mentioning the festival brought a moment of sadness, but I let it go.

Another nod. She carried our mugs into the kitchen. On the way to the front door she made arrangements to drive us to the airport, then gave me a hug and left me standing on the front steps.

A hail of dried leaves swirled in the air, landed and scratched on the cement paving until they were trapped and created eddies in the corners at the base of the steps. I stared as the force of the wind crushed the swirling leaves, their last worldly effort before joining the earth to start the cycle of rebirth. I caught my breath. What if my happy news disrupted the natural flow of grief for Carlos? Since learning of the new life blossoming inside my body, it had nearly taken over my thoughts. What if there was some mourning ritual in the Middle East that I was unaware of?

A car pulled up along the curb. Mrs. Dellapola, the principal, shouted her good wishes through the car window as Tom got out. He shrugged out of the backpack and let it fall to the floor just inside the door. His face was stoic, already preparing himself for bad news.

"Get a snack and I'll bring you up to date," I said.

"Tell me now."

"Okay." I put my arm around his shoulders and we walked to the den. He'd gone to school wondering where Elena would receive treatment and heal. Now, he had to be told we must face her death. My chest ached.

"Your dad called a little while ago. Nine is in the hospital and she wants to see us," I said. He chewed his lower lip.

"That means she's going to die, doesn't it?" He blinked but it didn't stop the tears.

I nodded. "We have seats on the overnight flight to Ankara tonight."

He babbled something and for a moment he balled his fists. I moved to put my arms around him, but he got up and walked to the kitchen. I followed, watching him sit at the table and finger the salt and pepper shakers.

"There's something else to tell you," I said, sitting across from him.

He shook his head and started to cry. "Don't tell me any more. I don't want to hear anything else."

"Don't you want to know you're going to have a brother or sister?"

His eyes widened; his mouth opened and he stood without moving the chair back. It banged to the floor.

"Aren't you too old? I mean, I'd love to have a… I'm sorry. You're not old, but…Does Dad know?"

"I thought we could tell him together when we get to Ankara."

He sobered again, remembering the reason for our trip.

"This will make Nine happy too, won't it?"

I nodded and welcomed his arms around my waist. He was crying again. So was I, but nothing could overcome the lightness of my heart.

Tom went to his room to begin packing. Seconds later he came pounding down the steps. "Hey! Is it a brother or a sister?"

"Won't know that for a few more weeks."

He made a U-turn.

"I have to call your uncles," I called after him. "Can I bring you a snack when I'm finished?"

"No, not hungry," he shouted.

Grace answered and listened while I repeated the news about Elena. Val took the phone next, expressing his sadness. Elena was leaving a mark on everyone in my family. I wanted to lift his spirits with my news, but Carlos had to come first. Carlos. He'd given me so much, and now a child.

31

On The Mountain Pass, Asia Minor

At the foothills of the Mascit, Çatal and the men milled around. They agreed the air carried the smell of rain but the sky was clear and it was only midmorning. A voice was shouting and the men turned to see a rider thrashing his horse. With a yank of the horse's halter, he came to a stop, sending a spray of earth outward.

"They, the Gazies, they're coming," he struggled to find his breath. "I saw them from that peak. This way, they're coming this way." He pointed to a high rise, one they'd traveled earlier.

"We have no choice then. I say we take the high mountain road now," someone shouted and turned his horse so all could hear. Voices rose to agree, but one voice suggested they scatter and hide in the woods.

"Fool! We make enough clamor for a blind man to find us," said another.

"We can be through the worst of it well before dark," said a smooth-faced youth.

"And if not, what then, boy? I have witnessed the anger in this mountain. I say we wait here. How do you know they mean us harm?" The rider's voice was strong and commanding, probably a leader of men.

"You think you can buy your life with what you have in that cart of yours," another voice said from well in the back. There were sounds of agreement.

"You misunderstand, friends. You saw how this mountain still shudders when we last passed through. Have you forgotten? It was a warning." He searched their faces for agreement, but he was disappointed.

"We're well ahead of the rain and I'm not willing to see what they will do or sit watching for clouds that may very well change direction." The speaker did not wait for consensus and turned his camel onto the trail. Others followed.

"I'm for putting the worst behind me as quickly as possible," said another. He spurred his donkey ahead and moved in behind the leading young man. After the first switchback, someone started a song. It was not familiar to Çatal but he liked the sound of it.

"The mountain's a woman, everyone knows...Shining snow for her hair, flowers for her toes....." Deep bass voices blended with higher baritone and the mood quickly lightened. Soon Çatal had learned the tune and the words and added his voice to the others. Here was something new he could share with the village children.

The valley below disappeared with the first steep traverse, ending the men's efforts to scan for the warriors. Çatal turned his attention to the statuesque trees ahead, but he glanced regularly at the strong sun and blue sky above for assurance. He noted he wasn't the only one, and when they made the next turn, the change in the air made him wary. A short time later the strength of the wind bent them forward on their beasts.

There was a shout. Çatal lifted his head and saw several arms pointing to the crest. The sight sent icy spikes through his body. Angry black clouds were muscling their way over the top, gobbling the sun like it was an egg set before their starving mouths. The clouds suddenly burst, blasting all with sheets of rain and hail.

Loud warning cries were coming from the line ahead and seconds later Çatal saw a wooden cart plunge over the edge.

Then another figure tumbled into oblivion. Horrified, his eyes fastened on a bright red scarf, twisting end over end, descending in the murky haze.

Sütlü balked and took several steps backward. Çatal slid to her side, grabbed her harness, and buried his face in her fur. For a moment he felt secure in the tight space between the wall of earth and Sütlü's body, but something groaned behind him. The earth bulged, pushed him forward onto the trail, while at the same moment a horrific pain shot through his legs. A boulder, set free by cascading mud, had pinned Çatal from thighs to ankles. The last thing he heard before he lost consciousness was Sütlü's high-pitched wail.

He was far from his village, leaning against his camel's hump with his eyes closed. His heart was pounding in his ears, making it hard to hear the high-pitched wail through the raving wind. A child? In this desolate place? He turned his camel even as he argued with himself. If he failed to find shelter from the approaching black boil of clouds, he would be lost. Once more he listened and nudged his camel toward the sound, but the camel hesitated. Çatal steadied himself between the camel's humps while he judged the distance to a rocky promontory he'd spotted a few hundred feet to the east. Satisfied he still had a few moments before the storm struck, he strained to hear again. A child? How could it be? A precious child.

The wail reached him again. There, below him, with its neck stretched along the barren earth, was a baby camel, a lump of matted fur, wailing with each exhaled breath—the baby's cry.

Çatal scooped it up. It folded like a well-worn rug over his arm. He pulled his camel's rope toward the rocky outcropping just as the wind and rain exploded around him. Without prompting, his camel tucked its legs and dropped to the ground and Çatal, with the baby pulled to his chest, nestled into his camel's deep fur. He probed the limp body curled in his lap and felt her protruding ribs and weak heartbeat.

Çatal shifted slowly and thrust his hand into the goat skin he had filled with camel's milk for his journey. Careful not to spill a precious drop, he coated his finger with its fatty richness and rubbed it across the baby's leathery lips. No reaction. On his third dipping, he lifted the baby's lip and allowed the milk to run across her emerging teeth. She trembled. She had the will to live, he thought.

The sky brightened. The storm, like a chariot of destruction, was moving on. He noted its direction and hoped it would falter before reaching the village where he planned to buy vegetables. Reluctantly he acknowledged the baby camel most likely belonged to its residents, but once there, he learned each camel was accounted for. Moreover, they warned him the baby's white fur carried an evil spirit which the mother rightly rejected at birth, and they strongly advised Çatal to return it to the spot where he found it to let the spirits carry out their will.

But by the time the trading was over and Çatal loaded the vegetables onto his camel, he knew in his heart that he would raise the baby himself. He decided to call her Sütlü because she was the color of tea with milk. No one needed to know how much she meant to him.

Çatal jolted awake. The storm raged on with blinding rain, lightning and thunder. He no long felt pain; his legs were numb. Suddenly, at his side, Sütlü's legs buckled and she slid slowly sideways. She turned her head to him as her legs slipped over the trail's edge. With eyes bulging in terror, she slipped by Çatal's face and disappeared into the tarry abyss.

The camel behind him tried to turn around but lost her footing and took the driver tumbling with her over the edge. Up ahead a large boulder crashed onto the trail, carving a trough through which earth and ever larger rocks cascaded. Once more, Çatal heard the earth groan and crack. He clutched his chest as a boulder that blocked out the sky pressed him to the dirt and snapped his ribs one by one. He closed his fist around the baby ring, forced Rachel's face to his mind and then, with sparks exploding across his eyelids, imagined her first-born child cradled in the silk rug.

32

At Ankara's airport a queue of yellow and black taxis, vibrating like yellow jackets, lined the curb. Moments later we were weaving in and out of traffic at a speed well past the limit. The driver shouted over his shoulder that we shouldn't worry. He was a racing car driver on the weekends, he said in Turkish, and the police would not fault him for taking a family to the hospital.

The hospital's white walls rose like glaciers in the narrow hall, and the air smelled of food. Here and there stainless steel carts on wheels held trays and pitchers. We walked to the reception area to request Elena's room number and were directed to an elevator where we punched the eighth floor. When the door inched open, I saw Carlos in the hallway ahead. He looked haggard but he brightened when he spotted us.

A small alcove with chairs was nearby and Carlos, with arms around us, pulled us in. His face was blotchy, his eyes swollen. Words tumbled from him like the sudden release of water from a dam: disbelief that her tumor should assert itself so quickly, anxiety that she might be in pain, and then relief that we were with him.

I translated a palliative care sign over her door and told Carlos my understanding of the term. "Their job is to keep her free from pain. Every effort will be made for her comfort so we can have as much quality time with her as possible."

"Yes, that's what they say, but it's the end...the end of our time with Ana and I can't stand it. I'm not ready for it," he said.

Tom was staring at the door where he knew his grandmother lay inside. When Carlos noticed, he changed his demeanor. A mask formed over his face, a deep breath followed by a look of resignation. He took Tom's hands and, in whispered words, began to prepare him to see her.

"She's been waiting for you, but she's very tired and her speech is slow. Her special spirit is there still, you'll see.

"Do you want to go by yourself? We can go with you if you like," he said.

"Mom?" Tom said. I read his eagerness to share the news we were holding for this moment. I nodded.

"Dad, we have something great to tell you...and Nine."

Carlos searched his face and then mine. I smiled but couldn't stop the tears that were flooding my eyes.

"I'm going to have a baby sister or a brother," Tom said, in an overly loud voice.

Carlos' mouth dropped. He reached behind for a chair, but before he sat, Tapis walked into the hallway and rushed to greet us.

With a face still reflecting disbelief, he told Tapis that I was pregnant. She reached out to hug me and whisper her joy in my ear. We shared Carlos' handkerchief since neither Tapis nor I, scraping the depths of our purses, could find tissues.

I told them how I'd been worrying about the appropriateness of joy at such a time. But the words were no sooner out of my mouth than Carlos and his sister simultaneously blurted the same thought: how happy Elena would be to know about the baby.

"Let's check with the nurse before we tell her," Carlos suggested.

Moments later the nurse disappeared into Elena's room and when she reappeared, it was to wave us in.

In contrast to the blank white of the rest of the hospital, Elena's room was petal pink. She smiled at us from under a floral comforter. I leaned to kiss her forehead and take her hand. It was soft and cool, cooler than usual.

"I wanted much more time to get to know you." Her sapphire eyes were as intense as ever, taking me in like an embrace, just as they did the first time I met her.

"I can't bear to lose you, Ana," I said. Carlos slipped his arm around my waist. I held back my tears only because I didn't want to miss a word.

"It's God's plan to fulfill our purpose and move along. I assure you I regret nothing. My happiness is to know you are safe in each other's keeping."

Tom was pulling on Carlos' sleeve. "Tell her."

"Ana, we are having a child."

It was wondrous to watch her face light up, her eyes widen. "Ahhh," escaped from her lips and she looked from one to the other, lingering longest on Tom, then back to Carlos. "Do you remember when Tapis was born? You developed a frown that lasted a month." She laughed softly and closed her eyes and seemed to drift. Her lips continued to move but no sound came. We were about to leave the room when she grabbed Carlos' sleeve and her eyes opened again. "Tell Tom how you lost your frown, my dearest."

"I remember, Ana. It was the first time she smiled at me. At that moment she became my sister...*my* sister. The idea that she was my blood, my bones, my family, hit me with such force that I've never forgotten the moment, never forgot the deep meaning. It forged my identity in a new way. I was no longer a single unit, the center of the family. I shared love and guardianship for a tiny, helpless being," he said.

The nurse opened the door. Without words we got the message that we should leave. But again Elena reached with her hand, this time for Tom.

"There is something...I want to say to Tom...alone."

The nurse shrugged and we followed her out of the room.

The longest five minutes passed while we waited for Tom to emerge. When he did, he wasn't the same boy who'd entered.

He was leaning forward, lunging with the upper part of his body, while his legs lagged behind awkwardly. His chest pumped with short breaths. I rushed to him and pulled his head to my chest. Carlos came just behind to envelop both of us.

"Nine wants to tell you something," he choked.

When Tom had gained control of himself, I motioned to the nurse who monitored Elena's room. "I feel like we're tiring her, but she wants to see us again."

"Her wishes are the only ones that count. I'll be right outside if you need me," she said, with a perfect balance of professionalism and empathy. I doubted that training could provide such perfection for the circumstance—perhaps experience, though she looked to be no more than twenty.

Elena, her head facing the door, watched us approach. One slender finger lifted.

"Tú eres un tesoro. Tú eres una bendición," she whispered in her native Spanish.

Carlos drew back and placed his hand over his mouth. "I remember, Ana. 'You are a treasure. You are a blessing.' The words you said over Tapis and me each night."

Elena nodded. "My children...Tom...now...another."

The smile froze. Stillness spread through her body and we knew she was gone.

I missed my brothers. Carlos' many friends included me in their concern and sorrow for our loss, but it wasn't the same. They didn't know I'd lost my mother a second time. They didn't know how she'd renewed my security with her love for me, with her examples of how to love others without reservation. When they said they'd never forget her, I wondered if her lessons had had enough time to change me forever. But then I looked long and hard at her son and knew I was safe from my old self. My brothers knew. The baby growing in my womb would know.

A few days later people spilled onto the church courtyard and a carillon pierced the air, an anomaly in a place accustomed to the call of the muezzim. It was a large, mixed-age group of people dressed in western and eastern garb. Pastor Ajemian stood by our side as people greeted us on a small patio encircled by a white oleander hedge. To our side a group of young children clustered around several female guardians, and when Carlos saw me looking at them, he told me they were orphans. Ana, he said, had been on their board of directors and was an active fundraiser.

"I had no idea, but I can't say I'm surprised," I said. Tom, who'd overheard, left us to join them. "Our boy likes kids. Remember how he threw himself into the Hoja stories?" Tom's success with the children, along with remembering other happy times at the festival, were helping to lessen the hurt we'd all suffered. I hoped the same was true for Deanna and Brad—all of Paradise's residents for that matter.

Carlos, nodding his agreement, ruffled Tom's hair when he returned.

"Next summer I'm going to work at the orphanage," he said. His voice was determined. "That lady said they're going to change the name of the orphanage to the Elena R. Ghazerian Home for Children. Nine would like that, wouldn't she?"

"She'd probably be embarrassed, but she will love seeing you there with the children," Carlos said, swiping his cheeks.

Messages were piled up on the kitchen phone when we returned to Philadelphia shortly before noon. Jack and Carolyn wanted to welcome us home; Philip and Heidi Rose said they'd chosen a wedding date; Val, Grace and Penny wanted to invite us to dinner "as soon as you're settled," they said. It felt like they'd conspired to keep us from dwelling on the past by throwing us into the future.

"I'd love to have them all here together, but—" I kicked off my shoes.

"After you've rested," Carlos said, rubbing his face. Purple seemed just under the skin around his eyes. "We can do a BYOF, yes?"

I was getting better at translating his skewed colloquialisms. "We call it a potluck," I said.

Carlos walked to the den and I saw him stretch out on the sofa. The phone jingled.

"We have a beautiful baby girl." Deanna shouted. Her voice quivered with excitement. She said they'd received a call from the adoption agency, telling them of a baby girl just brought to a Chinese orphanage. Since all of their paperwork had been cleared, they were invited to pick up the child at the earliest convenience. We were the first to hear their news, she said.

"We're so happy for you."

She continued. "We made arrangements right away. I think we were afraid if we delayed something might happen. Nora, she is so precious, happy, and bright."

"We'll come to see as soon as we can, but we're just back from Ankara. Carlos' mother died."

"Oh. And here I am bubbling all over when you've—I'm sorry."

"It's been very hard on all of us, but it's great to have your good news."

I heard the front door. Tom was home. Carlos jumped up to meet him and I waved them in. "Hold on a sec. I want to tell Tom and Carlos your news."

"Ask them to come too," Carlos said.

I gave him a "thumbs up" and relayed the invitation. "Please come. We can't wait to see the baby. I'll call as soon as I get hold of everybody. We can bring you up to date on our news when you get here."

"What's going on?"

"I'll be in touch soon, I promise." As much as I wanted to tell her about my pregnancy, my brothers had to come first.

Tom, who'd been listening to the conversation, said something about a "population explosion," while he yanked open the refrigerator door for his after-school gorge.

The following day a storm on the Atlantic coast was moving inland with high winds and rain. Carlos and I rushed through the house to be sure the windows, usually open for fresh air, were shut. It bothered both of us to breathe air conditioning all summer, and with autumn's crisp breezes, the windows were opened wide. While Carlos checked the office next to our bedroom, I stood at the window by our bed watching the red maple leaves snap free of the branches and spiral to the pavement. In the morning I'd be able to see more than I wanted of the traffic and rushing crowds through the thinned out trees.

Below, a large rug store truck moved between the cars. I hadn't given my gallery a thought in all the time we'd been gone. Orhan, informed we'd be away, hadn't called and since we returned...well, other things filled my time.

Carlos checked the view. "Somebody's getting a rug delivery, yes? You haven't said anything lately about your gallery," he said.

Had I married a telepath? "Surprises me too."

"The month is almost up, yes? Can Orhan stay on if you're still not sure what you want to do?"

"He said as much. To be honest, there're times I miss having something to do and others when I'm glad to be doing nothing. I just don't know if the gallery is the cure."

I leaned back, my head on his chest. As always his arms curled around my waist. When warm breath filtered through my hair, I closed my eyes.

"Bored? I've got some thoughts about that," he said, turning me around and giving me a look I couldn't identify until he undid the button on my blouse.

33

I didn't want to admit it, but it felt good to linger in bed. The gynecologist Carlos and I saw within days of getting home had recommended taking it easy, and even though the amniocentesis test was a simple procedure, I was nervous and glad Carlos was with me. I stretched and ran my hands over the cool silky sheets before I forced my legs over the side of the bed.

I had no plans for the day, but that changed when I slipped into my bathrobe. It was shockingly snug. I wasn't ready to shop for maternity clothes, but perhaps it was time to tell Orhan I was pregnant before he guessed it himself. I picked up the phone and found him eager for a visit. In fact, he said he had an idea he wanted to discuss.

I stood looking for something to wear, a task that was getting harder every day. Finally I chose a white blouse, a black jumper without a waist, low-heeled black pumps and some pearls—professional but boring.

Carlos was sitting with the newspaper at the kitchen table. An empty cereal bowl, a small plate of unfinished toast, and a drained cup were spread out around him. He peeked over the top of the newssheet and whistled.

"I'm a woman on a mission to a beautiful downtown rug gallery," I said. He didn't need to know I'd had trouble zipping my jumper.

Orhan opened the office door as I parked in the alley. "You're just in time to walk through the inventory with me.

"The kilim are selling better than ever, and I've had walk-in and telephone requests for pillows. You see, we have none on the floor. I've already checked with the warehouse, and I'm doubtful your supply will hold through the holidays. Your business increases in December, doesn't it?" he said.

He was wearing a cinnamon leather suit jacket, brown pants, and an open-neck checkered shirt. The palette was soft and warm, and even his green eyes had taken on warm amber highlights. Something had shifted; it wasn't just his clothing.

Distracted by my thoughts, I'd lost track of his question and my face flushed in the silence.

"What do you wish to do?" He was mildly amused by my lapse.

"Ah, I guess Muharrem could ship some but it would take a couple of weeks."

He pumped his head several times and I understood he expected I would make the call as soon as I could. But when we returned to the office, he leveled a more direct question at me.

"Do you need me to stay on for another month? I realize your recent loss was unexpected and—"

"There's a new complication—one of the reasons I wanted to see you today. I'm expecting a baby."

He smacked his thigh and offered his congratulations. "So, you need me to stay, right?" I hadn't known him that long, but his exuberance seemed out of character. It felt like he was congratulating himself as well as me.

"Can you? I need the time—everything is more complicated."

"My pleasure. And would you have any objection to a pre-holiday event? As I've said, I would want more kilim—rugs, pillows, bags—and I'd want to bring a greater variety of rugs from the warehouse. I must say, your gallery's sparse display is elegant, but an abundance of color and pattern will add excitement for the event."

He went on and on. It was almost as if he'd expected my pregnancy and was prepared for my request. I realized what had shifted was his sense of ownership. The man who stood before me now had a full grasp of my business. He was directing the music and the tune had the sharp "kaching" of the cash register. He wanted his leadership to show on the books.

"You'll need an assistant for a big sale. I hadn't planned on that."

He seemed offended, took a step back, and then collected himself. "Of course, it was only a thought. There's no need to change anything, if that's your wish." His disappointment couldn't have been clearer if it had been tooled on his leather jacket.

"Let me think about it for a couple of days." We shook hands and I left.

I felt shivery on the way home. The car windows were closed against the brisk air so I couldn't blame the feeling on temperature.

The unmistakable fragrance of lentil soup propelled me up the basement stairs where Carlos was stirring the pot. I slipped out of my pumps and carefully set a white bakery box on the counter, a dessert I'd bought on a whim. Tom occasionally dropped a comment about the brownies, cookies, and ice cream popsicles he enjoyed at the Denbys.

"I was beginning to wonder." He kissed me quickly and then checked the contents of the box. "Hmmm, coconut cake. We must have coffee too, yes? All this time at the gallery?"

"I'll make it," I said, reaching for the coffee canister. "I told you I was going to see Orhan. Now, there's a man who's full of surprises, but later, we don't have time to talk about him now. Is the soup ready?"

Normally Tom responded quickly to Carlos' voice, but it took an octave lower and a decibel louder to bring Tom from his room. He apologized, saying he was on the phone, weighing the pros and cons of trying out for the school's soccer team with Marty.

"Couldn't that wait? You'll probably see him after dinner. Or haven't you finished your homework?" I said.

He shrugged and bent over his bowl. Moments later we
loaded the dishwasher and cut the cake. I wrapped the
remainder in foil and suggested he take it to the Denbys.

"I could tell Mrs. Denby you made it, but she wouldn't
believe me," he teased. I threw a dish towel at him as he
scooped up the foil package and ran for the door.

It was too chilly and damp to sit outside. Instead, Carlos
picked up a serving of cake and I carried two mugs of coffee
into the den.

"You said Orhan surprised you today."

I told him Orhan agreed to a month's extension in light of
my pregnancy, and then mentioned the proposed sale.

"He wants to hold a pre-holiday sale which led to a remark
about insufficient inventory."

"Yes?"

"You don't think that's more than an interim manager should
take on?" I said.

"It takes some aggression to be successful, you know that.
Why do you think he's overstepping?"

I didn't know why. Was I jealous because he was doing
what I used to do? Was he showing me up, maybe trying to
tell me I couldn't handle the gallery any more? True, my
energy wasn't what it was, but I expected that to return
soon enough.

"Let me add something new to the mix," he said. He set
down his mug and folded his arms across his chest. The
movement raised the hair on my neck. "I felt sure another
month wouldn't be a problem for Orhan, so let me tell you
about something Mehlika introduced to me when I called the
office today.

"She wants to learn more about the business—the finance
and the management. She wondered if you would be willing to
have her as an apprentice."

"You mean during the summer while we're in Ankara?"

"More. She'd be willing to come to Philadelphia. What do
you think?"

My mouth had sagged open and I clamped it shut. I got up
and opened the French doors to exchange the air I thought had
become stuffy. The trees were bending in the wind and large
clouds skulked across the sky like pirate ships outlined in silver
by the setting sun. I imagined myself in a black hat, captain of
the ship, hands on hips, dagger between my teeth, ready to
defend it from hostile takeovers.

"Total surprise doesn't begin to describe it, Carlos. All I've
been trying to figure out is whether or not I want to sell my
gallery, but new ideas keep confusing the issues."

"Well, think about it. Once she's trained, you'd call the shots
and be only as busy as you want to be."

Carlos wasn't looking for a decision. He said he merely
wanted me to have as many options as possible. I couldn't
deny feeling some excitement. Mehlika? I liked her eagerness
and ambition, so like my own at her age. Suddenly, I imagined
the influence she might have on Tom, a link between
Philadelphia and Ankara for him, another bond with the life
Carlos and I had forged together.

It took three weeks to arrive at a dinner date everyone
could agree on. I stayed in bed in the mornings while
Carlos saw Tom off to school. My energy level rose and
my appetite grew. My mouth watered thinking about the
special dishes each family was bringing. At four in the
afternoon, Carlos and I had two hours until they arrived
and I was already hungry, something happening more
frequently of late. We set three extensions into our dining
room table to accommodate a buffet for the number of
dishes expected, and while I gathered and placed the plates
and flatware at one corner, Carlos ran out to buy yellow
roses.

By the time I finished with the buffet table, I heard noise at
the basement door. Flowers burst into the room.

"I took every yellow rose they had, but it wasn't enough.
This is a celebration, yes?"

We worked together to fill three vases: one for my mother's Chippendale table in the entrance, one for the buffet table, and another for the den.

"Maybe yellow and white will be my new favorite. They're beautiful," I said.

"You're more beautiful every day. How is that possible?"

"I'm six pounds heavier." His smile got bigger.

At six the door bell rang. A radiant Deanna and proud Brad posed on the doorstep. One look at the baby's almond-shaped black eyes and high pink cheeks and I could see why. Deanna threw her head back and dark red curls flew across her face.

"Oh, those beautiful curls are back," I said, touching the side of her face.

One by one family and friends filed in. Tom took their coats, helped by Marty and Penny when they arrived, and instead of going upstairs, they stayed. Tom, with exaggerated care, took the baby and set her on a blanket Brad provided. The three of them formed a circle around her and never moved until dinner was ready. She was, as Deanna had described, a happy child, who stretched her neck to see the new faces watching her every move.

"Her name is Ono. Watch," Brad said. "She already responds to it."

Sure enough, her little head snapped around at her father's voice.

"Make way, Oprah," I said.

We left the circle of admirers and joined Philip and Heidi Rose who were talking about a wedding between Christmas and New Year's Eve. Val had already agreed to be his best man, and Heidi Rose, despite her years in the States, confessed ignorance of American wedding traditions. She wanted Deanna, Grace and me to be her best women. Nobody knew if it had ever been done, but we were willing and to heck with tradition.

Carlos and I locked eyes several times during the evening, which I interpreted as both of us straining against the urge to share our news. Finally, when we were sitting together in the living room, some of us still balancing dessert dishes on our laps, Carlos stood. Carolyn, who'd kept my secret from Jack and Marty, leaned over and whispered.

"Just in the nick of time. I'm about to bust."

My anticipation had been growing too, and I shifted positions so I could see everyone's face when Carlos announced my pregnancy. But the look on his face was anything but joyful. He began speaking about his mother.

"I always knew how important family and friends were to my mother, but her death raised my understanding to a new level. Thank you all for holding us up and helping us through."

That wasn't what I expected. Even the baby's expression changed when she found no one looking at her. Carlos was shaking his head and seemed close to tears. Then out of the corner of my eye, Tom came from nowhere to stand next to his dad.

"And, guess what? There's gonna be somebody new in our family," he said, pointing at me.

Val was first to find his tongue. "What? Nora?"

The room exploded into exclamations when I nodded. Everybody was on their feet congratulating us—the scene I'd expected, the sharing we wanted, the projection into the future we needed.

In the hubbub, I hadn't noticed Carlos move to the other side of the room and pull an oblong box from behind a table along the wall. He asked everyone to sit because he had something else he wanted to say. I braced myself for another surprise. For someone who insisted on openness, he'd been keeping some things to himself.

"Tom, will you open it?" he said.

Without hesitation Tom opened a flap at one end and, with some difficulty, pulled the contents out. The Chinese Silk unfurled, snapping the ivory fringe at our feet. Our guests hardly knew the full extent of what it meant to us but their appreciation of its beauty was instantaneous.

"This silk rug has traveled all over the world since it was excavated in 1950, Carlos said. "It's more than twenty-five hundred years old. It was lost in a storm, they think, on the Silk Road somewhere between the Black Sea and Erzurum. Nora, Tom and I saw it first in Istanbul at the Museum of Art, where my father served for most of his working life. The myth that follows this rug tells of a struggle between good and evil and the victory of good won by small, unified efforts."

"And it carries a blessing, a nimit, wherever it goes, right, Dad?" Tom was standing over the rug now.

"It's yours, Tom. Your Nine wanted you to know you were her blessing. You gave her the love of a grandson she never thought she'd have. The rug was meant for you."

Tom's eyes fastened on the rug for several seconds before his shoulders shook with sobs. Penny, true to her nature, jumped up and put her arms around him. It was not like Tom to show his feelings like that and absolutely amazing to see him accept Penny's comfort. When he regained his composure he ran to his room, shouting about having a copy of the myth. He read it while Penny, using a pink lacquered nail, traced the rug's features: the dragons, Shimmer and Thorn; the twisting vines; and the tiny centipede hidden among the green leaves.

Carlos' comments about his mother filled me with contentment. Because of her, my life had taken a turn for the best. Word by word, hurt by hurt, joy by joy, my life was reshaping around that roomful of people and the child inside me. Like the fingers of the weavers who choose one color over another to produce the long-remembered patterns, I knew I finally had it right, knew how my business, my family and my friends fit together.

Later in the evening after everyone left, the three of us sat in the den watching the last lick of flames among red embers in the fireplace. We spread The Chinese Silk at the hearth where the amber of the centerfield glowed and the flickering shadows gave dimension and movement to the dragons. Tom was lying next to the rug, stroking its silky nap.

I nestled my head into Carlos' chest. "You surprised me more than once tonight. Last I heard, that woman you grew up with—Lale, was it?—owned this rug. She sold it to you?"

"She *gave* it to me."

"Gave?"

"Yes, a gift to my family. Lale was a small child when she was brought to the orphanage. Her entire family died in an earthquake in 1959. My mother became her surrogate parent."

When she was old enough to leave, Carlos said, Elena found work for her in a small Oriental rug gallery. "She lived with us until she could support herself." He said Lale had a flair for business and ten years later when the gallery's owners died, she took over. Her success with the gallery was sensational. "She never lost contact with my mother, though, and when Lale heard about her illness, she sent the rug to me in the hope it would restore her health. She believed in the blessing of The Chinese Silk."

"Come on, just because the Museum of Art received a huge grant after acquiring The Chinese Silk, doesn't mean anything. It was a coincidence," I said.

"Believe what you want, but you'll never convince Lale. A few weeks after she purchased the rug, an elderly woman, her mother's best friend, walked into her gallery bringing photographs and stories. The woman didn't know Lale had survived until she read about her in a newspaper article about the gallery. To Lale, this was a gift of her family's history, something she never dreamed of having."

"What a beautiful story. I agree, it's magical no matter how it came to be."

The logs fell together in the fireplace, sending sparks and ash in every direction. Carlos grabbed the poker and stood in front of the fire until the logs settled. Tom pulled The Chinese Silk to a safer spot.

"Since we're having a night of surprises, I have a couple of my own," I said. "I don't want to sell the gallery to Orhan. If he's willing to accept Mehlika as a trainee and assistant while I—I mean, *we*—adjust to the baby, I'd like to invite her to Philadelphia as soon as it's convenient for her."

"Can I get trained too? I already know lots of stuff about the rugs," Tom said.

"What's to learn? They're just floor covering," I said, looking at the ceiling.

"I don't think that anymore. They tell stories and this one carries a blessing, right?"

"That's what they say. I hope it will always remind you that you were a blessing to your Nine, and you're a blessing to your mom and me.

"You said two surprises."

"So I did. While you were out buying flowers, the gynecologist called. Our baby is a girl, a perfect little girl."

Tom sat up. "Cool. I'm gonna share this rug with her. Hey, what'll we call her?"

"I was thinking we might call her by Ana's middle name," I said, looking at Carlos.

He put his hands on my face and whispered, "Rachel."

About the Author

Fran Marian is a former journalist and public relations director. The Rug Broker, her first novel, was sparked by travel in Turkey, a fascination with Oriental rugs and the fun of throwing problems at a strong woman. Fran lives in Tucson, Arizona. She and her husband John have two sons and five grandchildren.

Other Books By Fran Marian
The Rug Broker

Nora Reardon and her Turkish agent, Muharrem El Habashy, travel Turkey's rock-strewn rural roads to purchase rugs. Not just any rugs. Her eyes are searching for colors leeched from desert beetles, patterns that flow onto the loom from ancient memories to calloused fingers, fibers washed in the streams and dried in the sun – the kind of Oriental rugs preferred by her discriminating East Coast clients.

Nora is driven by a passion for the rugs and a need to be independent of her conservative, Lebanese brothers who, since her husband's death, insist her place is in Philadelphia with her five-year-old son, Skipper. That's not what Nora wants.

She struggles with her business and a desperate desire to bond with her son. When she meets Carlos Ghazerian, an Ankara-based broker of antique Oriental rugs, he guides Nora to financial success, until she is thrown into a Turkish prison and her son spirals into a suicidal depression.

Reader Reviews of
The Rug Broker

"Enjoyed the book thoroughly. The words flowed fluidly and the story grasps your imagination. For a first book, its characterizations are believable and interesting. I felt the book was right up there with The Kite Runner (also a first book). It was fascinating to learn about Turkey and how Oriental rugs are made and the dealings involved. It showed the author had done her homework very well. An easy and excellent read."
Evelyn Gross - Warminster, PA

"The Rug Broker by Fran Marian concerns a young Lebanese-American widow's attempts to rebuild her and her son's life in Philadelphia after the Sept. 11, 2001, terror attacks. Throw in a short course on the Oriental rug trade, and you've got yourself an interesting summer read."
J.C. Martin - The Arizona Daily Star

"It's a page-turner. Description, dialogue, character development and writing style are brilliant. Action is advanced to an intriguing level. Couldn't put it down; waiting for her second book to come around."
William Killian, Actor - SAG, AFTRA, AEA

"The story drew me in and caught my interest and compelled me to keep going."
Mike Mahoney - United Methodist Pastor, retired

"I really enjoyed it. Having done a little rug shopping in Istanbul, it was fun to relieve the place. Could really picture it all with the great descriptions. I liked the psychological sub-plot too."
Charlotte Cordes - Tucson, AZ

"The book was wonderful. It really resonated with me, as I have experienced many of the same things Nora did in the story. Nine years ago, my husband passed away suddenly and I had two boys and a business to run. Your story reinforces the hope and positive attitude I have. I look forward to her next book."
Jan O'Brien - Tucson, AZ

"It captured me and I just wanted to keep reading. The descriptions of light, scenery, etc., are poetic."
Diana Edeline - Willcox, AZ